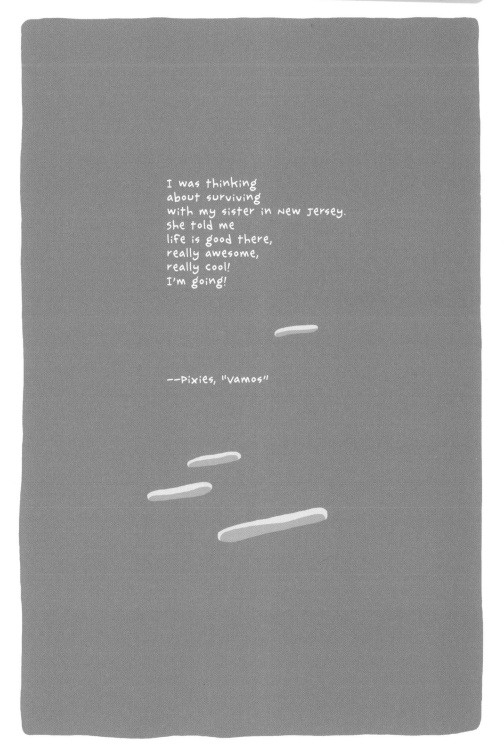

I was thinking
about surviving
with my sister in New Jersey.
She told me
life is good there,
really awesome,
really cool!
I'm going!

--Pixies, "Vamos"

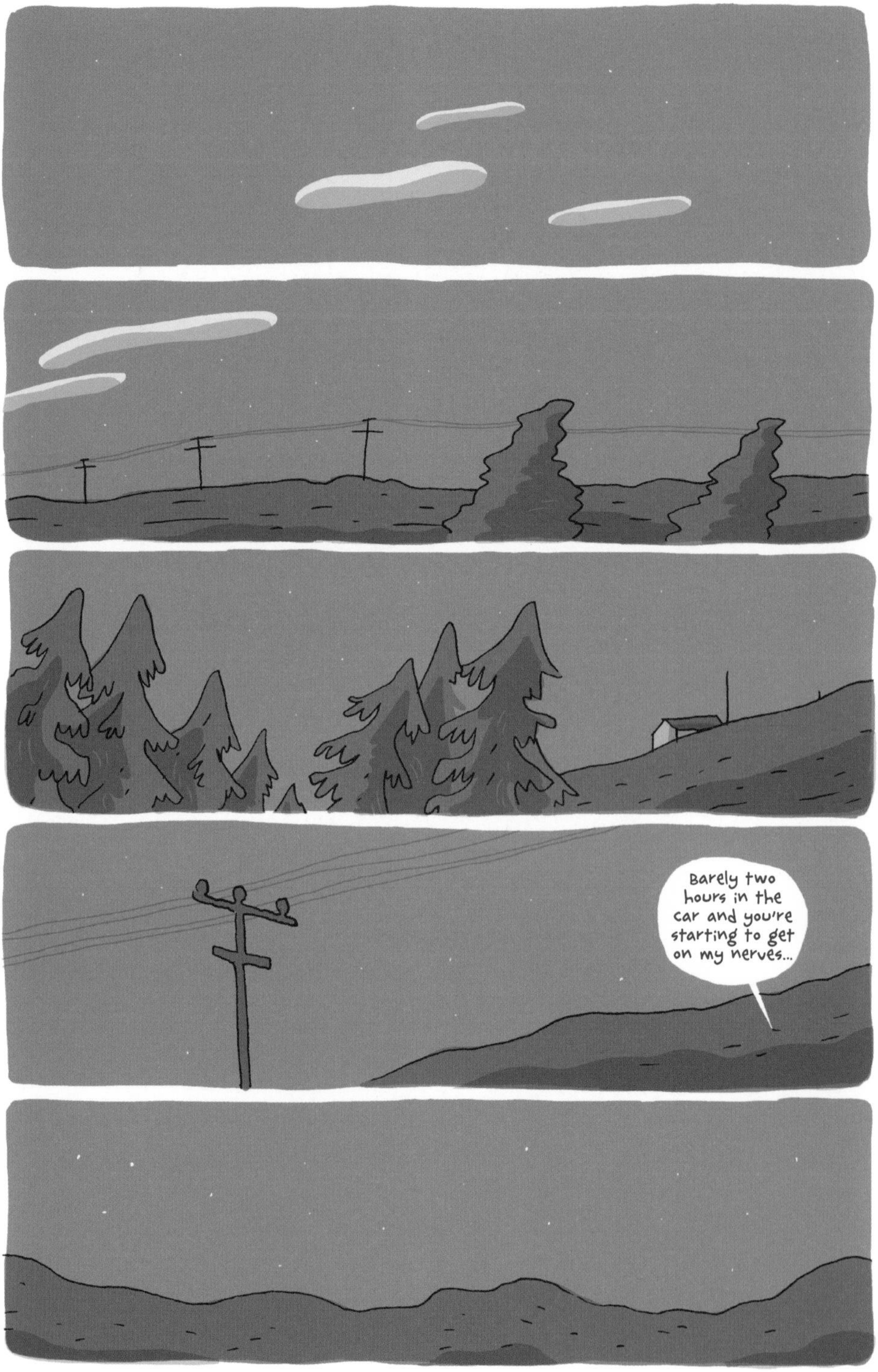
Barely two hours in the car and you're starting to get on my nerves...

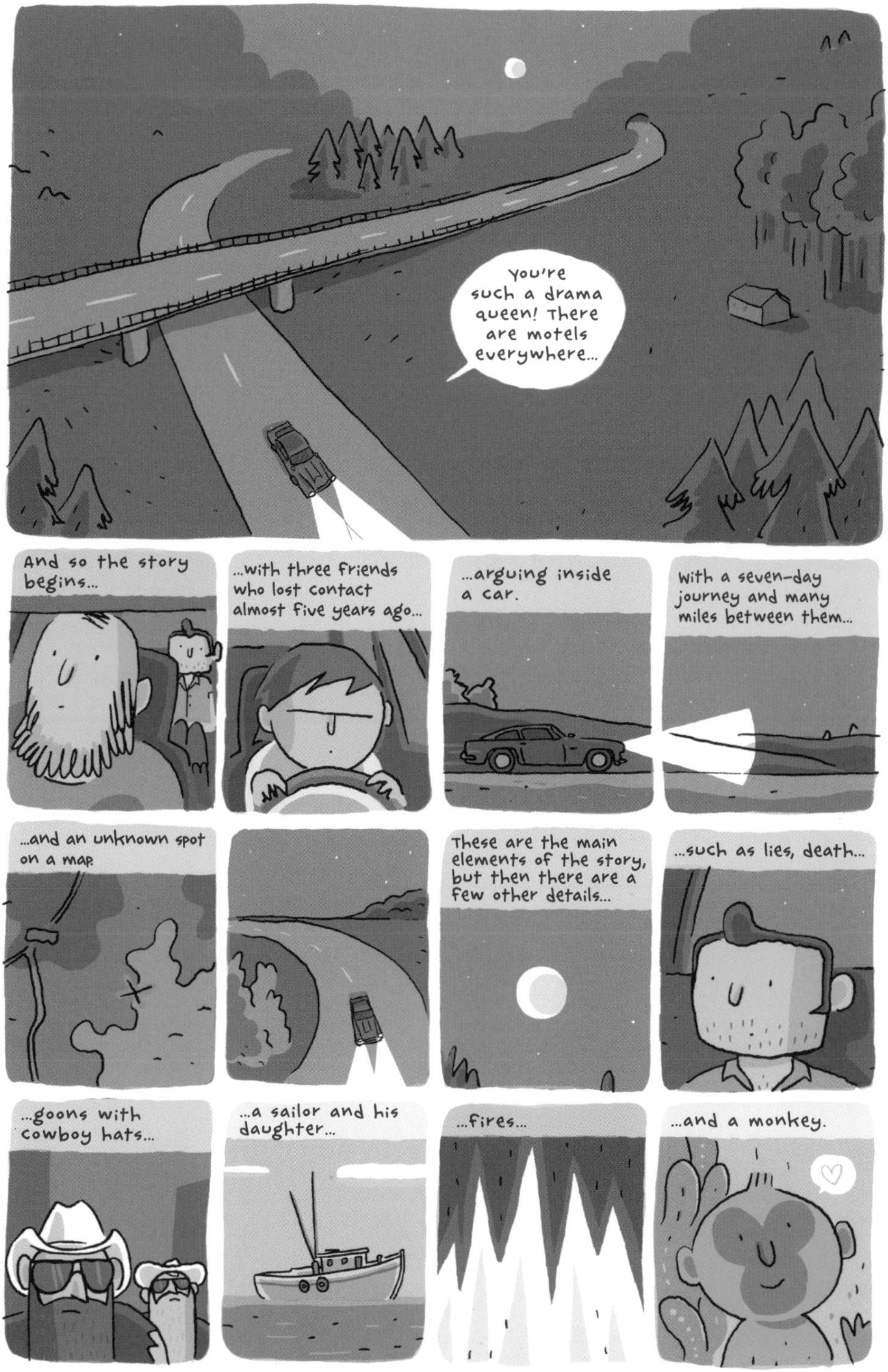
You're such a drama queen! There are motels everywhere...
And so the story begins...
...with three friends who lost contact almost five years ago...
...arguing inside a car.
With a seven-day journey and many miles between them...
...and an unknown spot on a map.
These are the main elements of the story, but then there are a few other details...
...such as lies, death...
...goons with cowboy hats...
...a sailor and his daughter...
...fires...
...and a monkey.

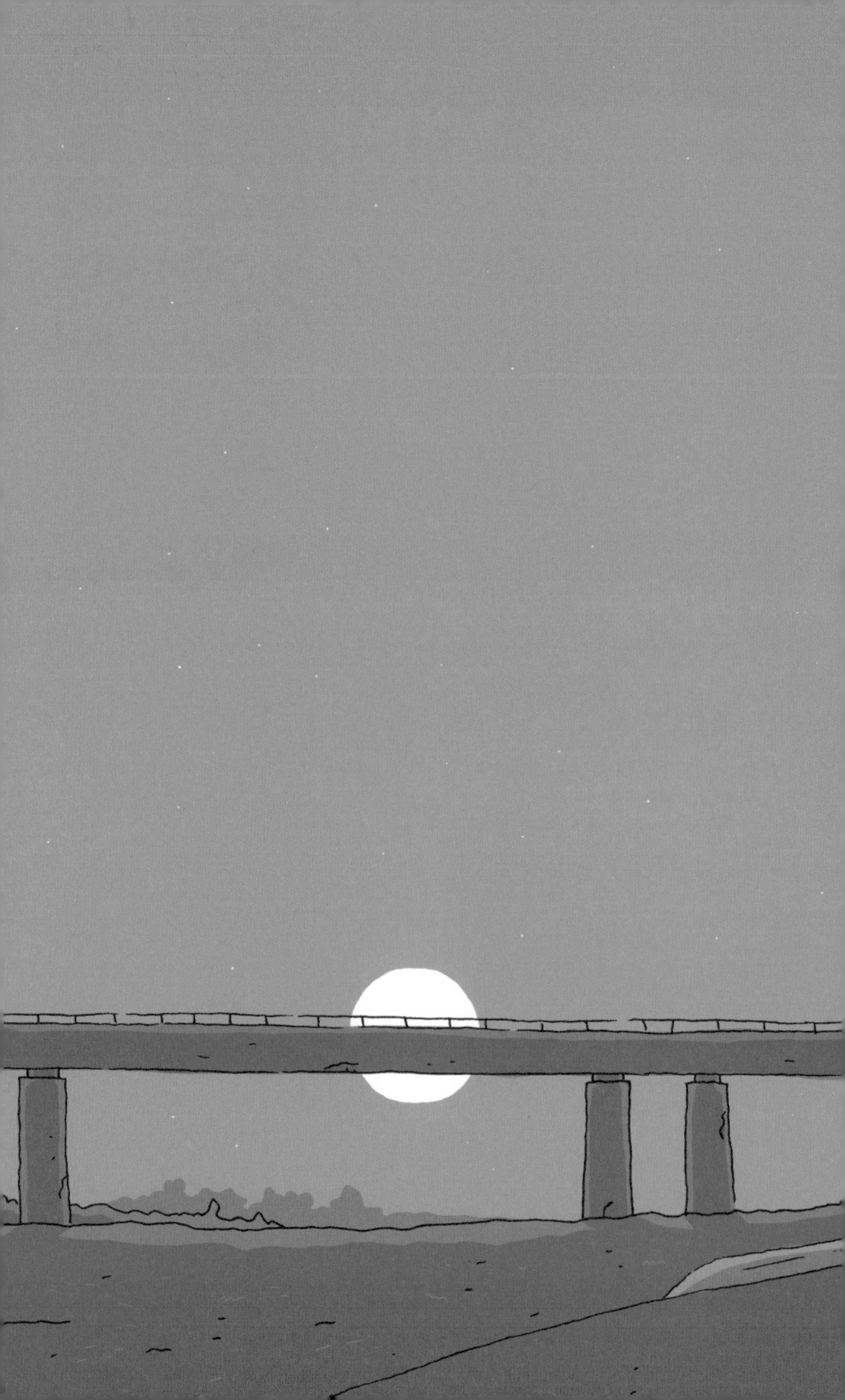

ASHES

a comic by
álvaro ortiz

translation by
eva ibarzabal

Published by agreement with Astiberri Ediciones.

English-language translation © 2023 Top Shelf Productions.

Published by Top Shelf Productions, an imprint of IDW Publishing, a division of Idea and Design works, LLC. Offices: Top Shelf Productions, c/o Idea & Design works, LLC, 2355 Northside Drive, Suite 140, San Diego, CA 92108. Top Shelf Productions®, the Top Shelf logo, Idea and Design works®, and the IDW logo are registered trademarks of Idea and Design works, LLC. All Rights Reserved. With the exception of small excerpts of artwork used for review purposes, none of the contents of this publication may be reprinted without the permission of IDW Publishing. IDW Publishing does not read or accept unsolicited submissions of ideas, stories, or artwork.

Translation by Eva Ibarzabal.

Adapted by Leigh Walton.

Lettered by Krystal Beisick.

Cover illustration and design by Álvaro Ortiz.

Layout by Manuel Bartual.

Editor-in-chief: Chris Staros.

ISBN 978-1-60309-517-4   27 26 25 24 23   1 2 3 4 5

Visit our online catalog at www.topshelfcomix.com.

Printed in Korea.

okay, so, the story begins on a Wednesday...

CAFÉ PALACE

...but let me go back to the previous Thursday.

Because there are a few interesting things to tell before the characters--

--sorry, before we-- get into the car.

What the hell do you mean you're not coming?

What?

Like I said in my email...

...everything is awful... I have a job...

A job?

You?

Ha!

(Thursday)

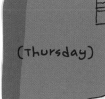

Very funny...

yeah, I'm hilarious.

I just don't understand why you're insisting...

...on making the trip right now...

B-b-but...

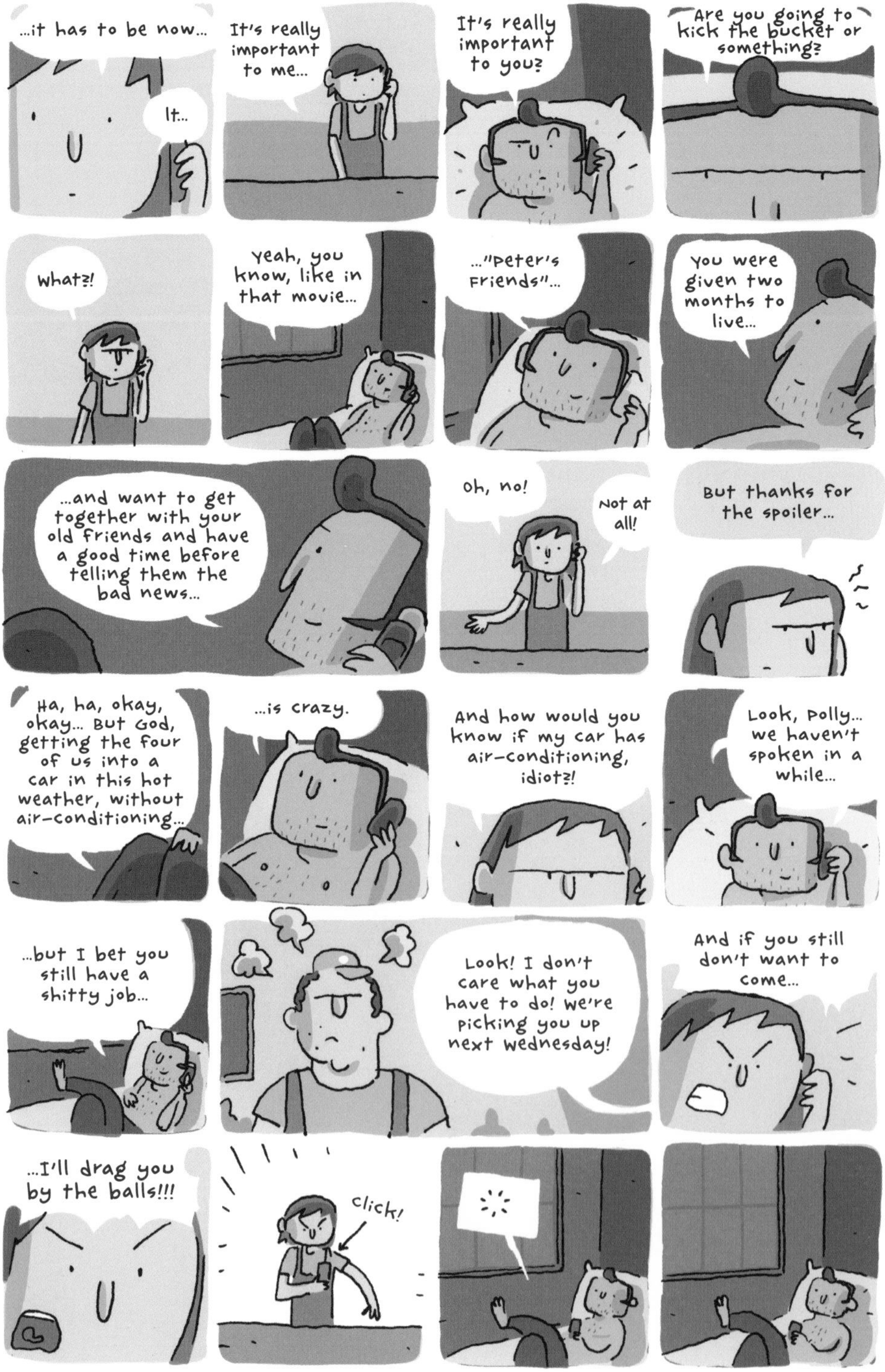
...it has to be now...
It...
It's really important to me...
It's really important to you?
Are you going to kick the bucket or something?
What?!
Yeah, you know, like in that movie...
..."Peter's Friends"...
You were given two months to live...
...and want to get together with your old friends and have a good time before telling them the bad news...
Oh, no!
Not at all!
But thanks for the spoiler...
Ha, ha, okay, okay... But God, getting the four of us into a car in this hot weather, without air-conditioning...
...is crazy.
And how would you know if my car has air-conditioning, idiot?!
Look, Polly... we haven't spoken in a while...
...but I bet you still have a shitty job...
Look! I don't care what you have to do! We're picking you up next Wednesday!
And if you still don't want to come...
...I'll drag you by the balls!!!
Click!

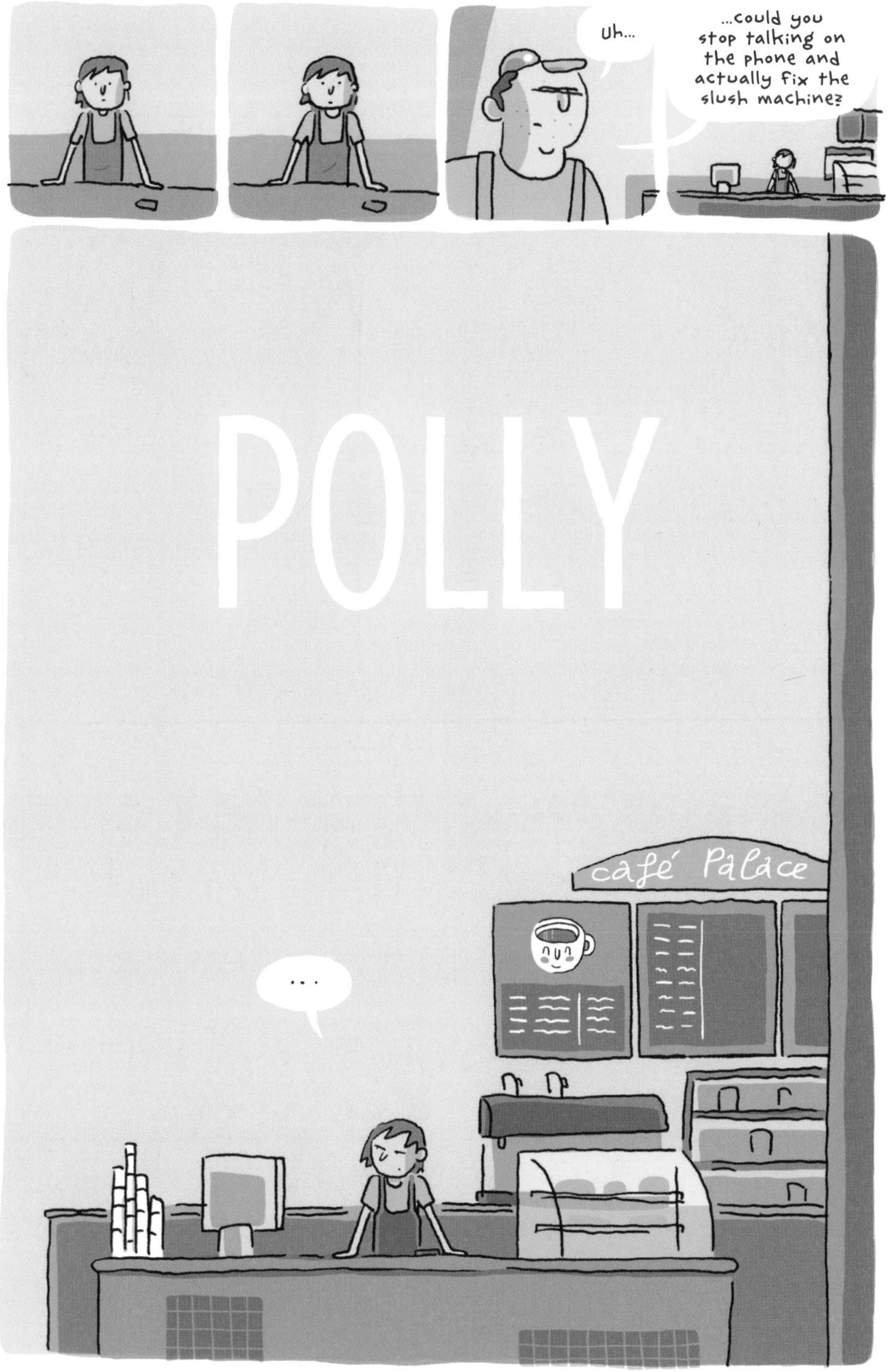
Uh...
...could you stop talking on the phone and actually fix the slush machine?
POLLY
café Palace
...

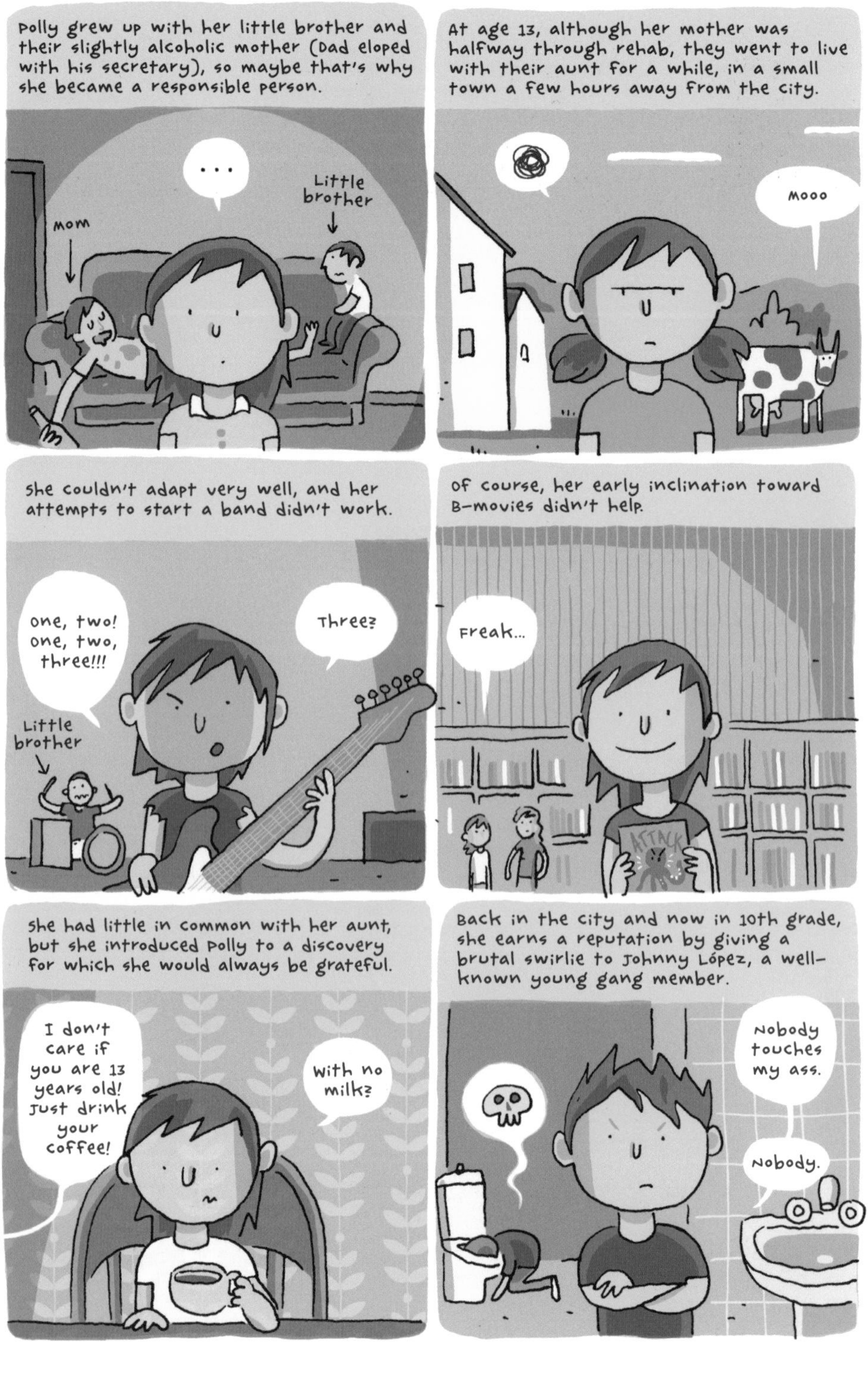

Polly grew up with her little brother and their slightly alcoholic mother (Dad eloped with his secretary), so maybe that's why she became a responsible person.
...
Little brother
Mom
At age 13, although her mother was halfway through rehab, they went to live with their aunt for a while, in a small town a few hours away from the city.
Mooo
She couldn't adapt very well, and her attempts to start a band didn't work.
One, two! One, two, three!!!
Three?
Little brother
Of course, her early inclination toward B-movies didn't help.
Freak...
ATTACK
She had little in common with her aunt, but she introduced Polly to a discovery for which she would always be grateful.
I don't care if you are 13 years old! Just drink your coffee!
With no milk?
Back in the city and now in 10th grade, she earns a reputation by giving a brutal swirlie to Johnny López, a well-known young gang member.
Nobody touches my ass.
Nobody.

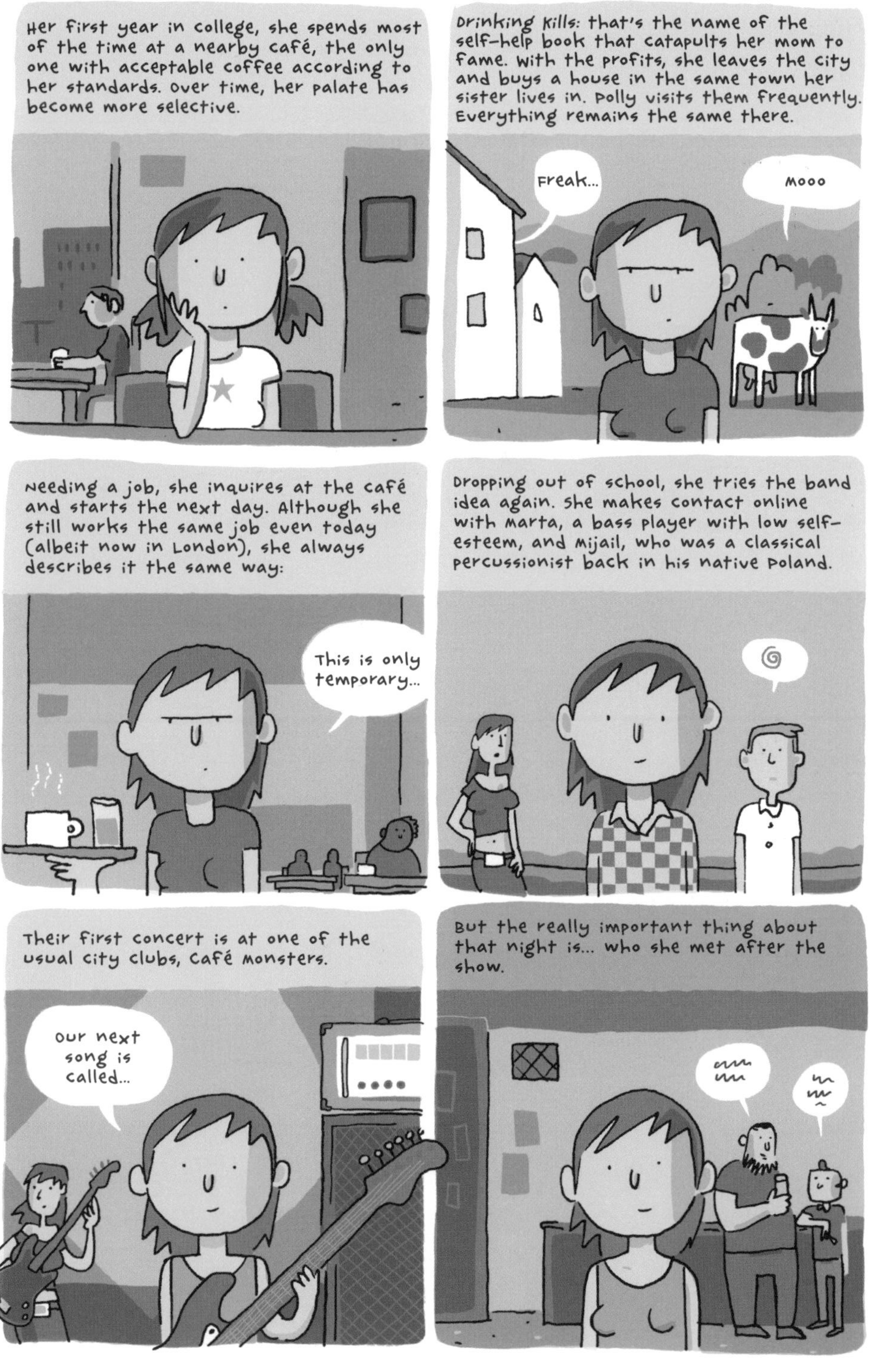
Her first year in college, she spends most of the time at a nearby café, the only one with acceptable coffee according to her standards. Over time, her palate has become more selective.
Drinking Kills: that's the name of the self-help book that catapults her mom to fame. With the profits, she leaves the city and buys a house in the same town her sister lives in. Polly visits them frequently. Everything remains the same there.
Freak...
Mooo
Needing a job, she inquires at the café and starts the next day. Although she still works the same job even today (albeit now in London), she always describes it the same way:
This is only temporary...
Dropping out of school, she tries the band idea again. She makes contact online with Marta, a bass player with low self-esteem, and Mijail, who was a classical percussionist back in his native Poland.
Their first concert is at one of the usual city clubs, Café Monsters.
Our next song is called...
But the really important thing about that night is... who she met after the show.

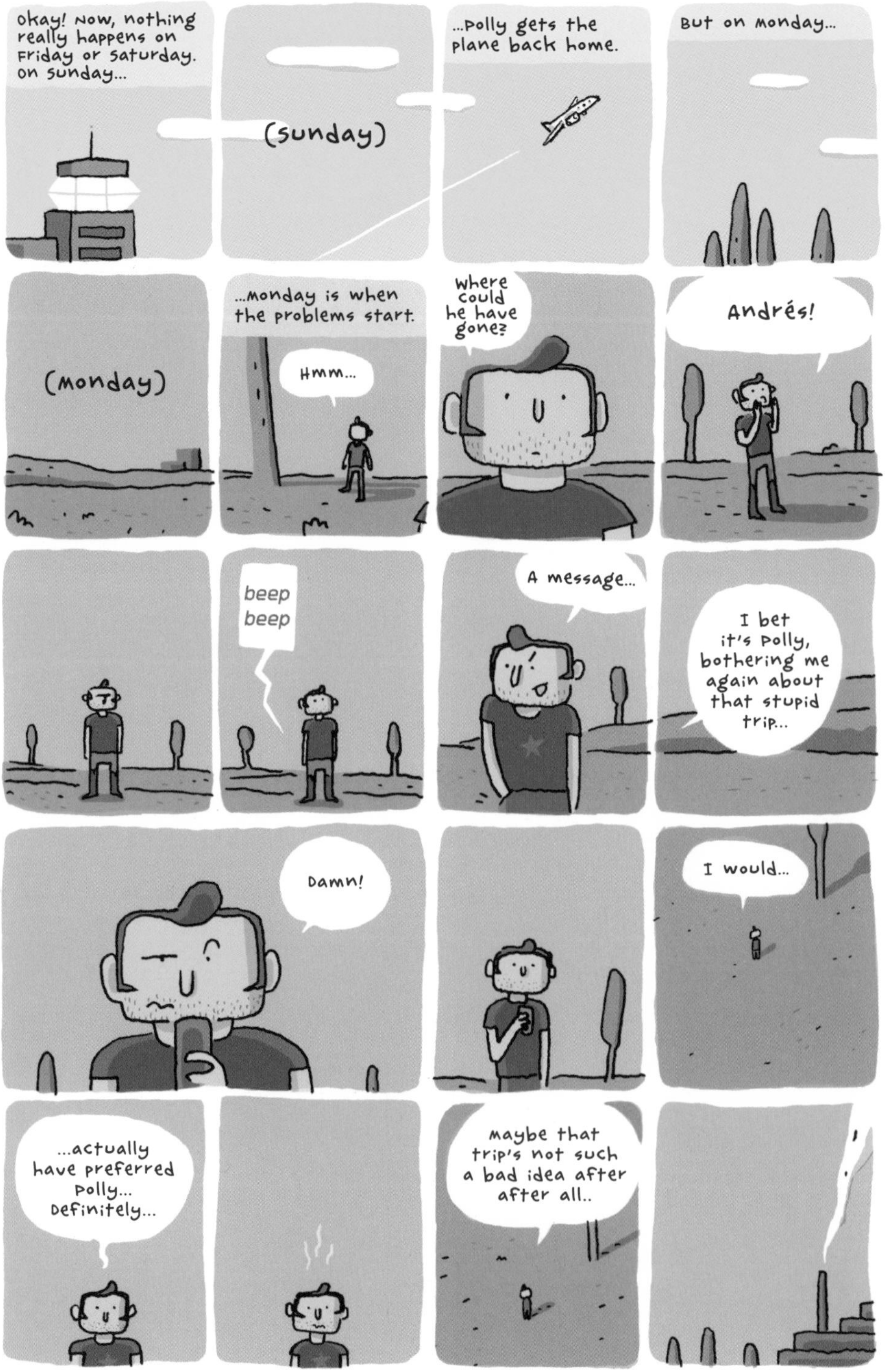
Okay! Now, nothing really happens on Friday or Saturday. On Sunday...
(Sunday)
...Polly gets the plane back home.
But on Monday...
(Monday)
...Monday is when the problems start.
Hmm...
Where could he have gone?
Andrés!
beep beep
A message...
I bet it's Polly, bothering me again about that stupid trip...
Damn!
I would...
...actually have preferred Polly... Definitely...
Maybe that trip's not such a bad idea after after all..

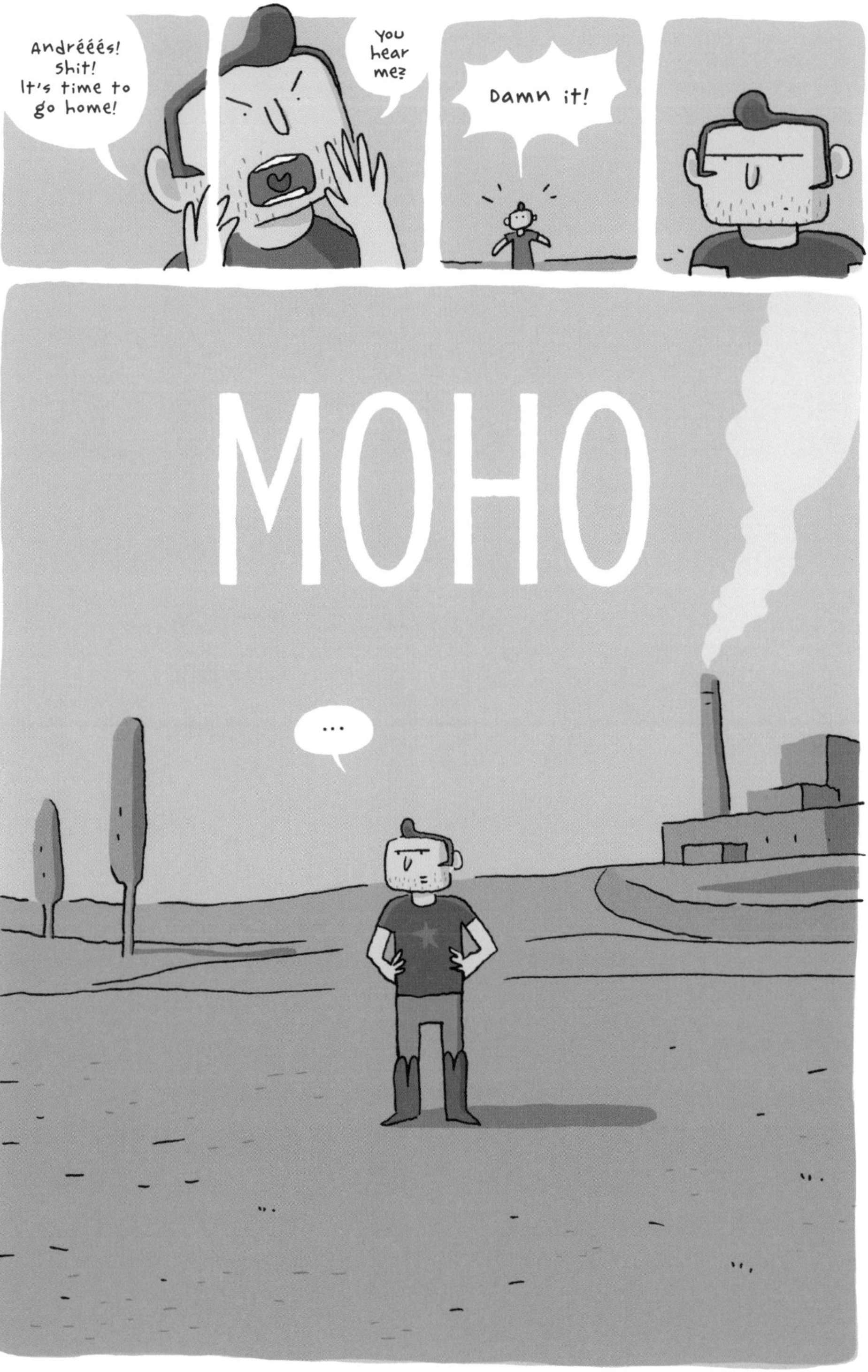
Andréééés! shit! It's time to go home!
You hear me?
Damn it!
MOHO
...

Moho was always an expert at attracting problems. Since he was a kid.

Problems that grew along with him.

> Does anybody know why all the class windows are broken?

At the age of 12, and after repeated threats by his parents, Moho is sent to a godforsaken boarding school.

> Look, a new girl's arrived...

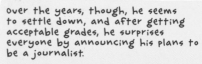

It's not long before before Moho becomes a little capo, controlling all the drugs and alcohol within the school. But by the end of his second year, he gets kicked out for threatening a teacher.

Over the years, though, he seems to settle down, and after getting acceptable grades, he surprises everyone by announcing his plans to be a journalist.

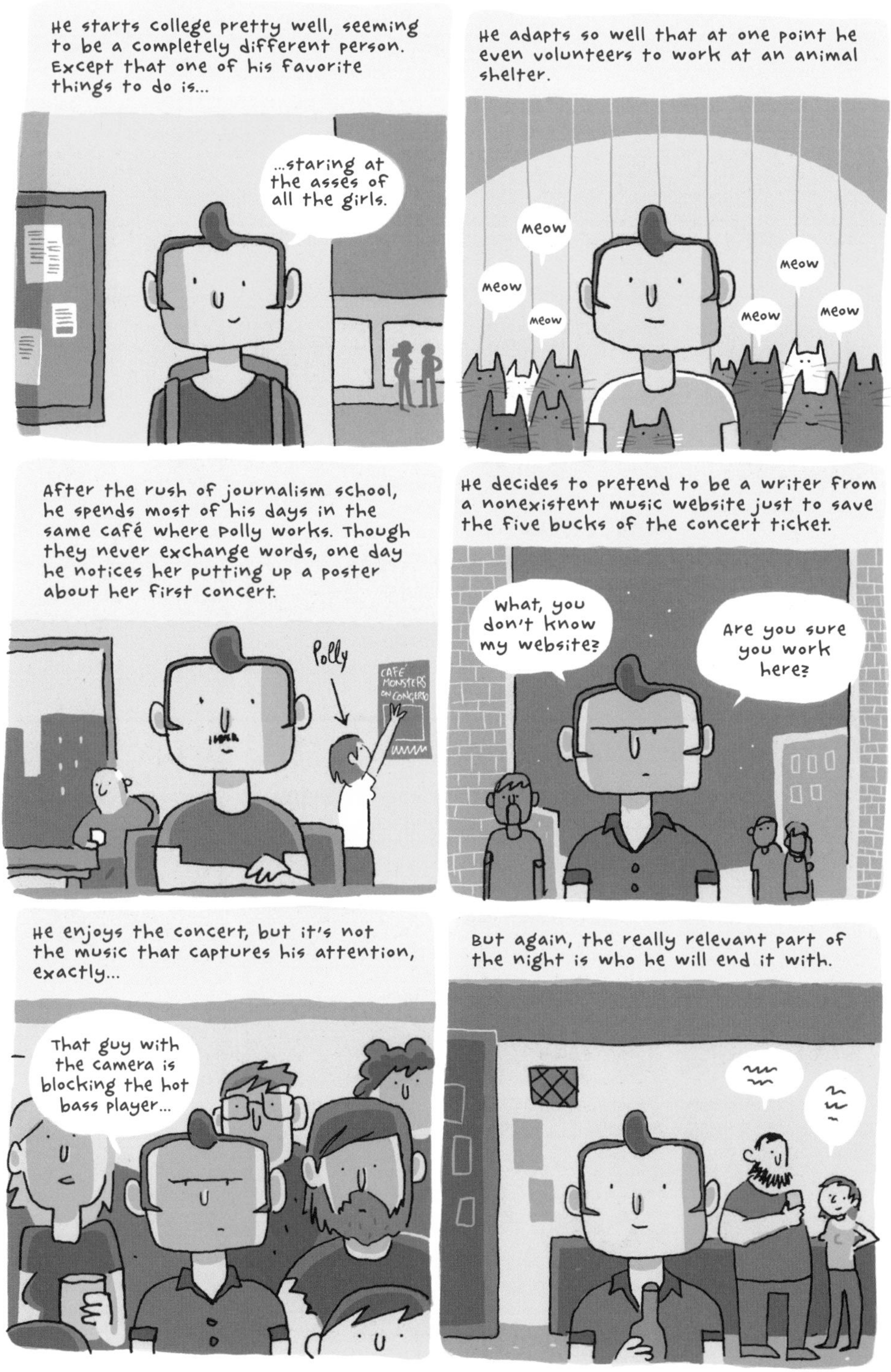
He starts college pretty well, seeming to be a completely different person. Except that one of his favorite things to do is...
...staring at the asses of all the girls.
He adapts so well that at one point he even volunteers to work at an animal shelter.
meow
meow
meow
meow
meow
meow
After the rush of journalism school, he spends most of his days in the same café where Polly works. Though they never exchange words, one day he notices her putting up a poster about her first concert.
Polly
CAFÉ MONSTERS ON CONCERT
He decides to pretend to be a writer from a nonexistent music website just to save the five bucks of the concert ticket.
What, you don't know my website?
Are you sure you work here?
He enjoys the concert, but it's not the music that captures his attention, exactly...
That guy with the camera is blocking the hot bass player...
But again, the really relevant part of the night is who he will end it with.

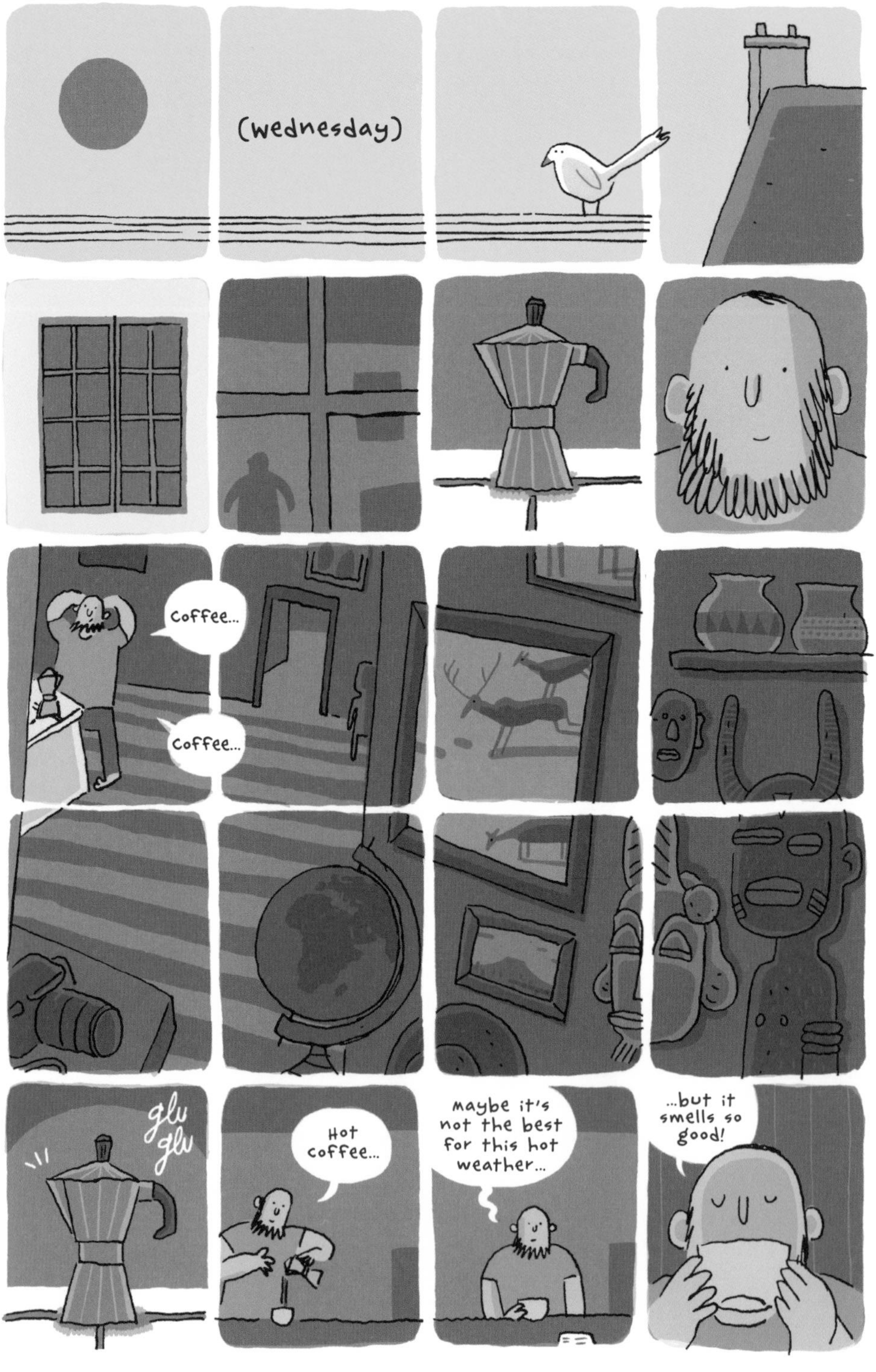
(wednesday)
coffee...
coffee...
glu glu
Hot coffee...
maybe it's not the best for this hot weather...
...but it smells so good!

In the beginning, there might have been Taranis, the celtic god of thunder, lightning, and sky.

Always represented with the lighting bolt...

...and the cosmic wheel, as a symbol of the passing of days and nights.

Worshipped in Britain, Gaul, and Asturias...

...he received the first acts of human sacrifice..

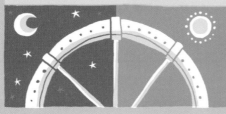

...performed by means of immolation.

Under the watchful eyes of the Druids, these sacrifices tried to appease his wrath.

Usually, they were prisoners captured in battle...

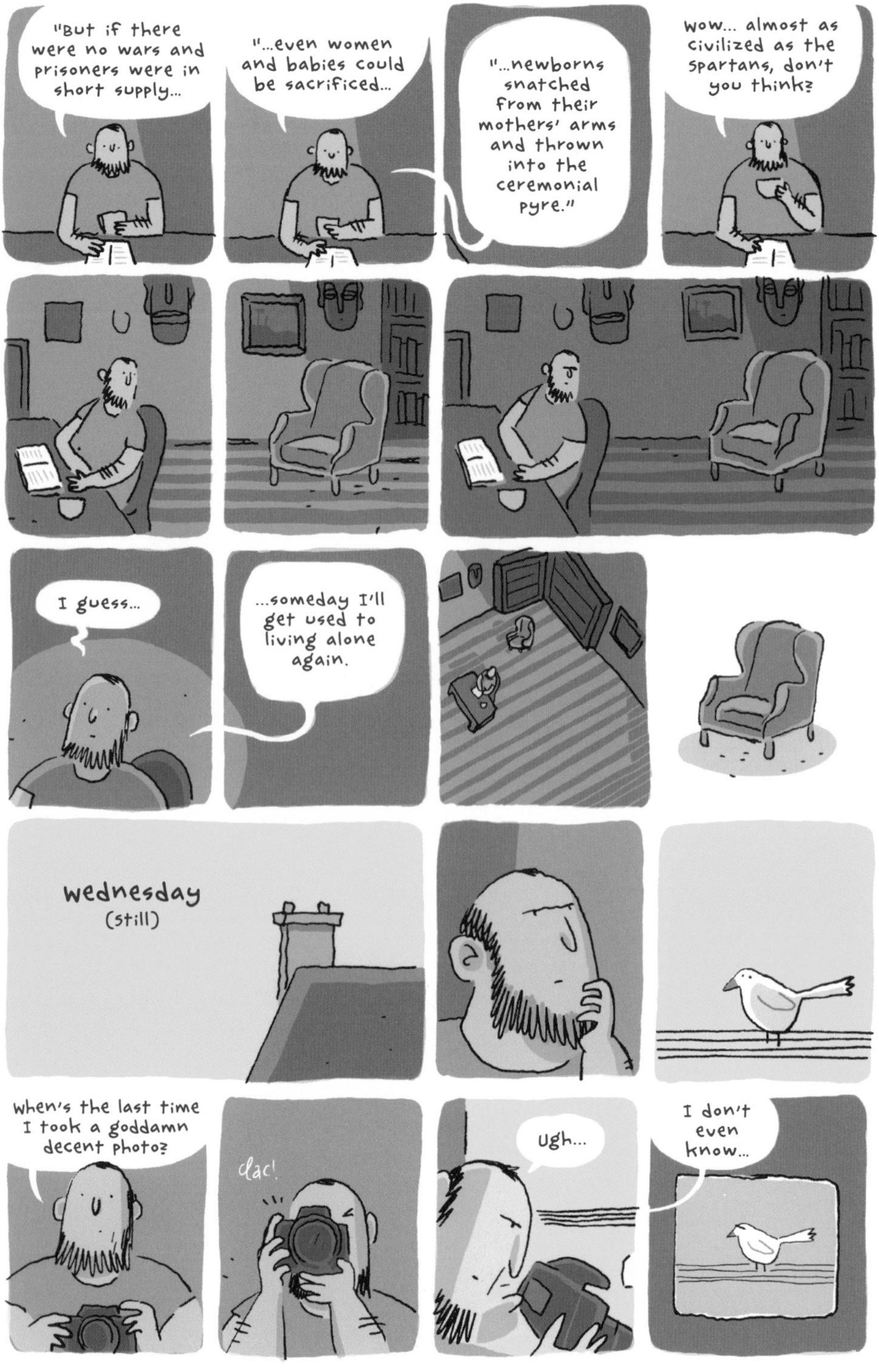
"But if there were no wars and prisoners were in short supply...
"...even women and babies could be sacrificed...
"...newborns snatched from their mothers' arms and thrown into the ceremonial pyre."
Wow... almost as civilized as the spartans, don't you think?
I guess...
...someday I'll get used to living alone again.
wednesday
(still)
When's the last time I took a goddamn decent photo?
clac!
Ugh...
I don't even know...

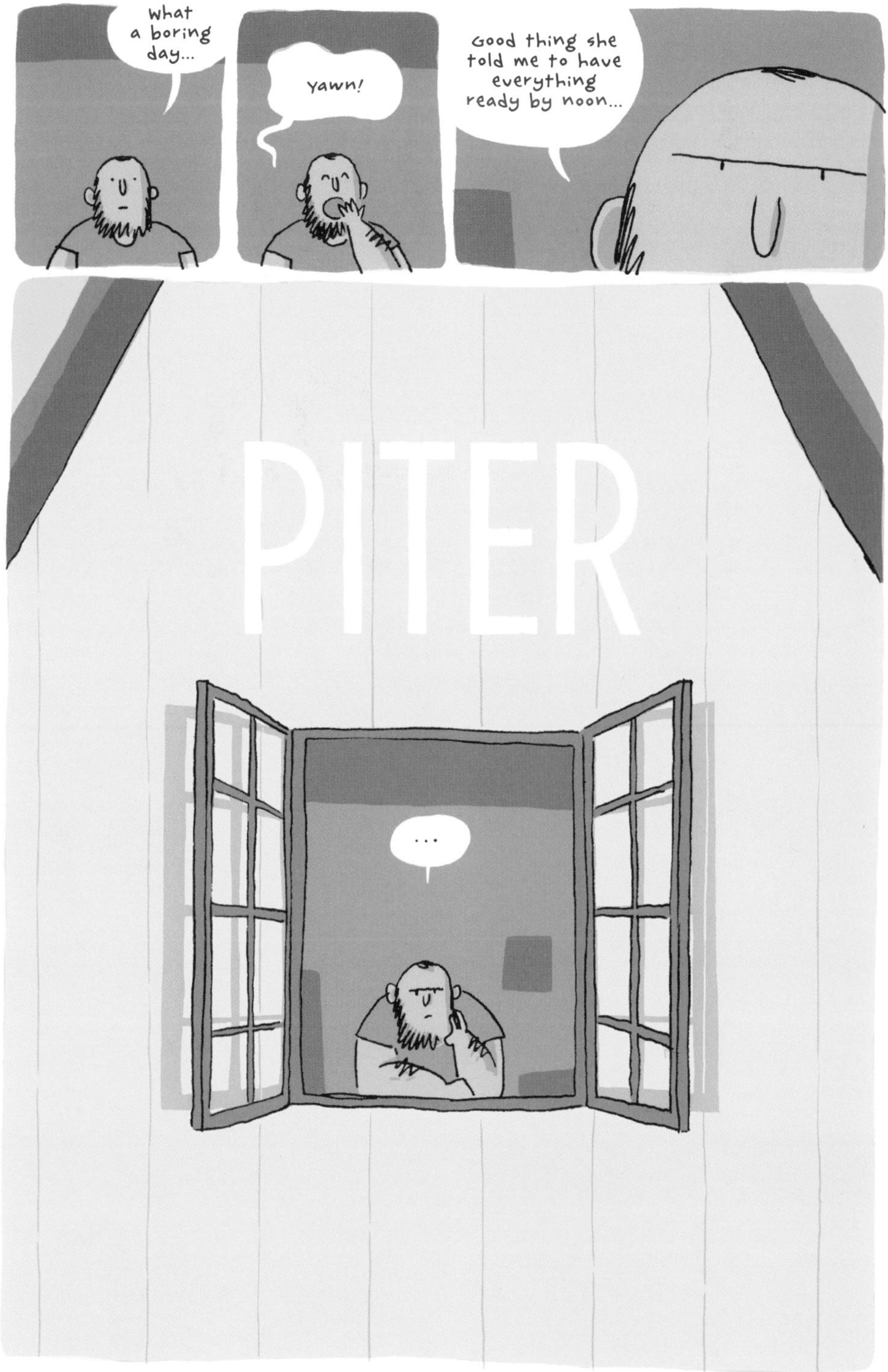

What a boring day...
Yawn!
Good thing she told me to have everything ready by noon...
PITER
...

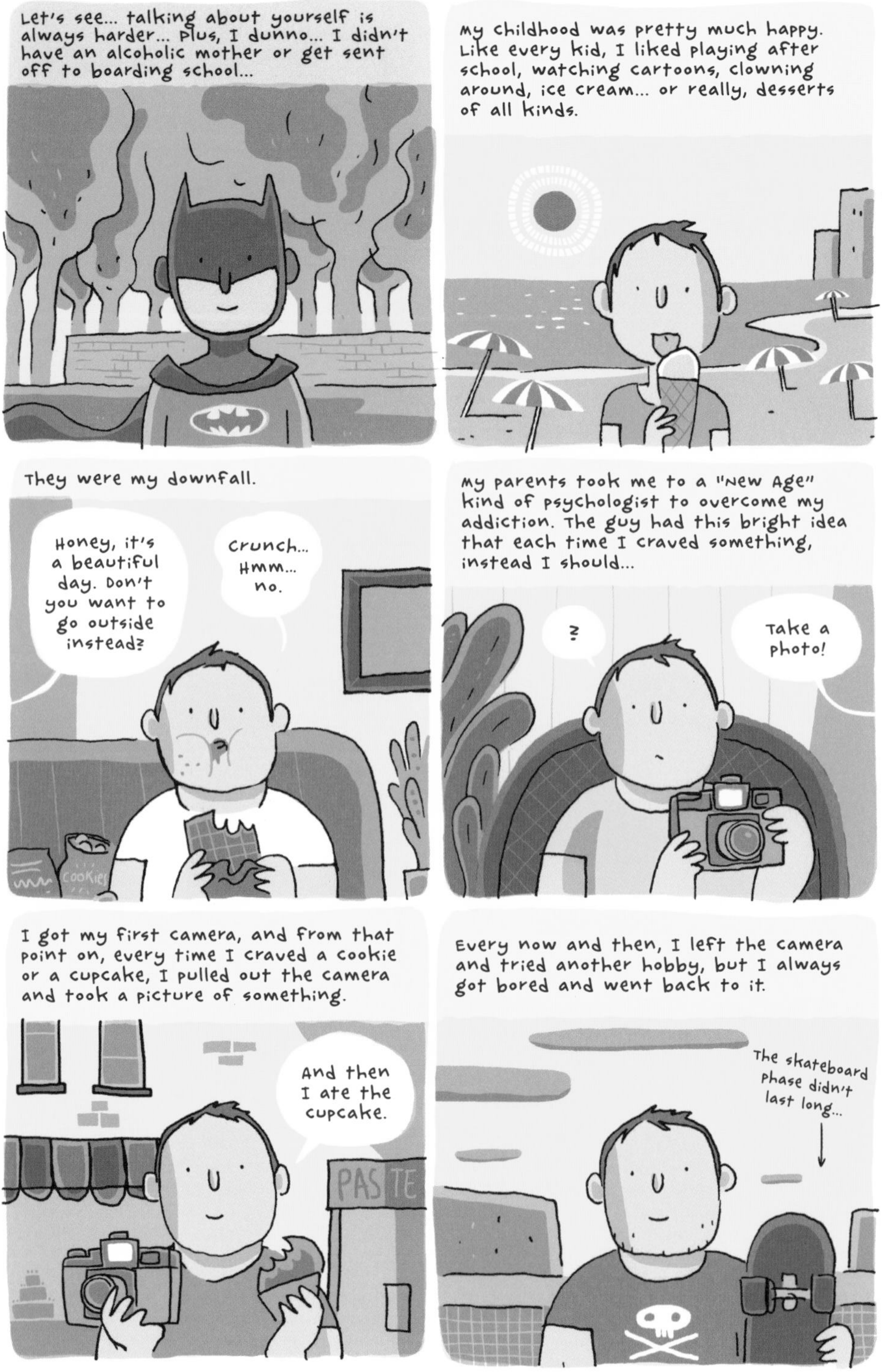
Let's see... talking about yourself is always harder... Plus, I dunno... I didn't have an alcoholic mother or get sent off to boarding school...
My childhood was pretty much happy. Like every kid, I liked playing after school, watching cartoons, clowning around, ice cream... or really, desserts of all kinds.
They were my downfall.
Honey, it's a beautiful day. Don't you want to go outside instead?
Crunch... Hmm... no.
COOKIES
My parents took me to a "New Age" kind of psychologist to overcome my addiction. The guy had this bright idea that each time I craved something, instead I should...
?
Take a photo!
I got my first camera, and from that point on, every time I craved a cookie or a cupcake, I pulled out the camera and took a picture of something.
And then I ate the cupcake.
PASTE
Every now and then, I left the camera and tried another hobby, but I always got bored and went back to it.
The skateboard phase didn't last long...

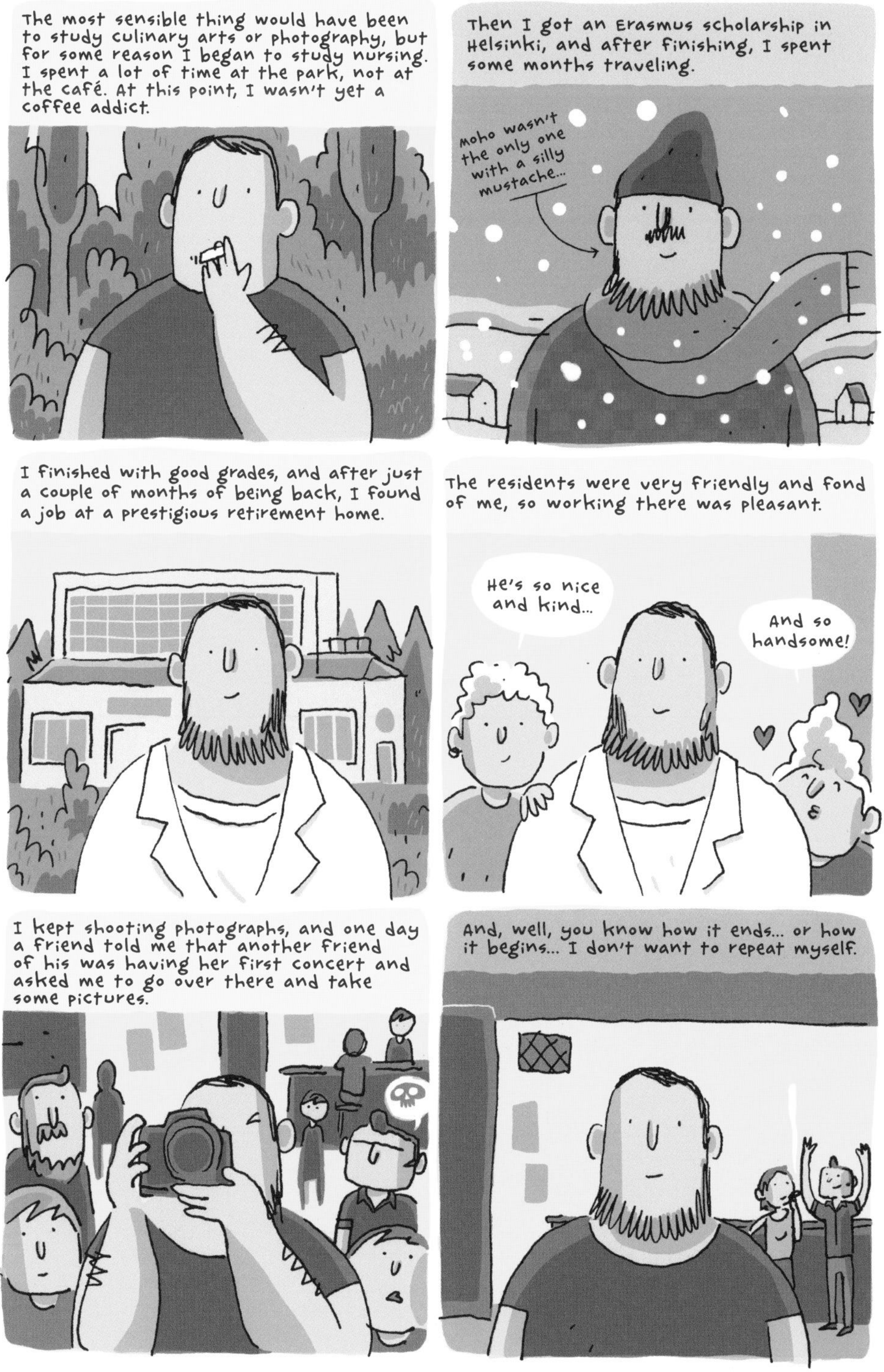
The most sensible thing would have been to study culinary arts or photography, but for some reason I began to study nursing. I spent a lot of time at the park, not at the café. At this point, I wasn't yet a coffee addict.
Then I got an Erasmus scholarship in Helsinki, and after finishing, I spent some months traveling.
Moho wasn't the only one with a silly mustache...
I finished with good grades, and after just a couple of months of being back, I found a job at a prestigious retirement home.
The residents were very friendly and fond of me, so working there was pleasant.
He's so nice and kind...
And so handsome!
I kept shooting photographs, and one day a friend told me that another friend of his was having her first concert and asked me to go over there and take some pictures.
And, well, you know how it ends... or how it begins... I don't want to repeat myself.

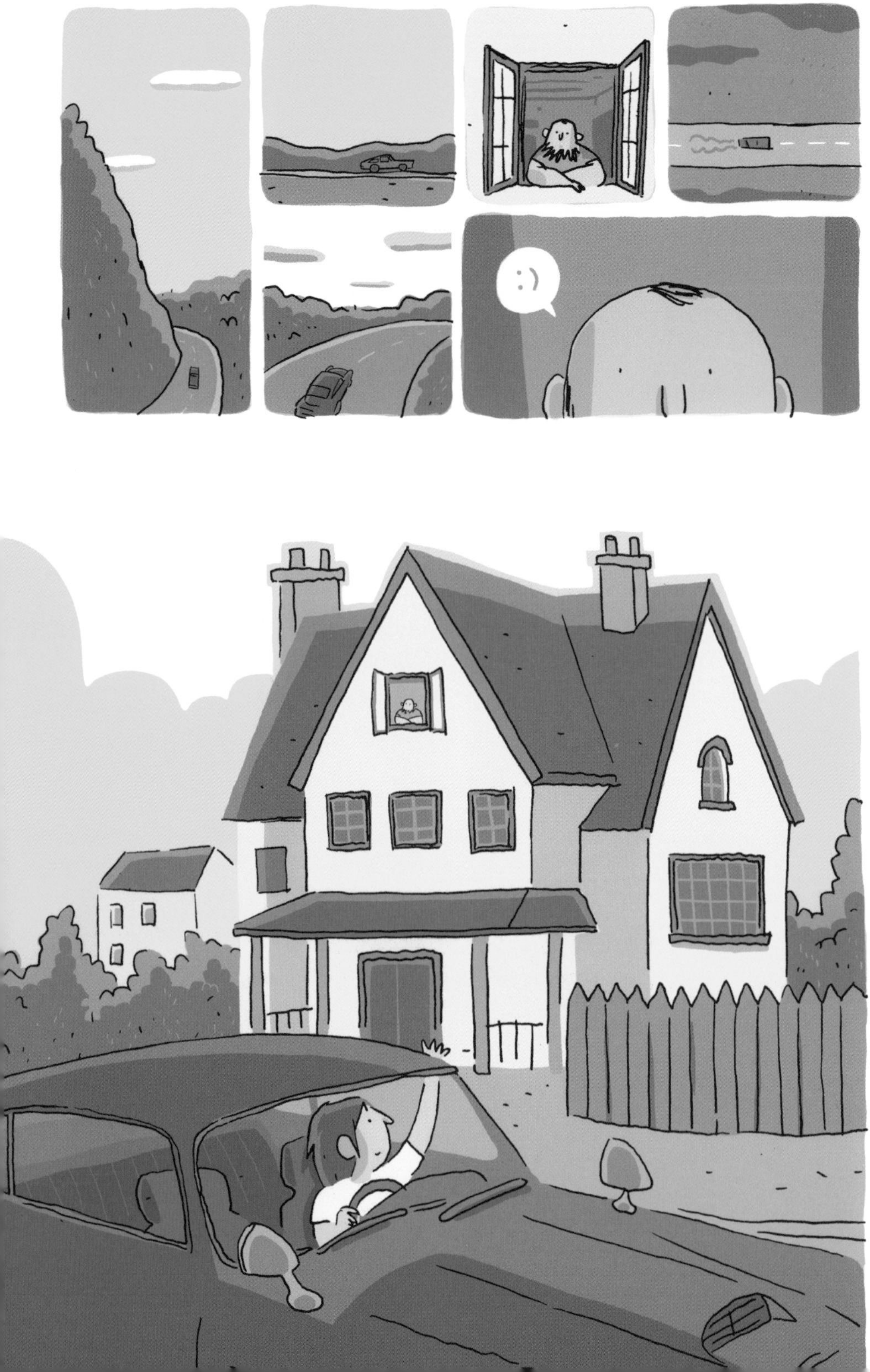
:)

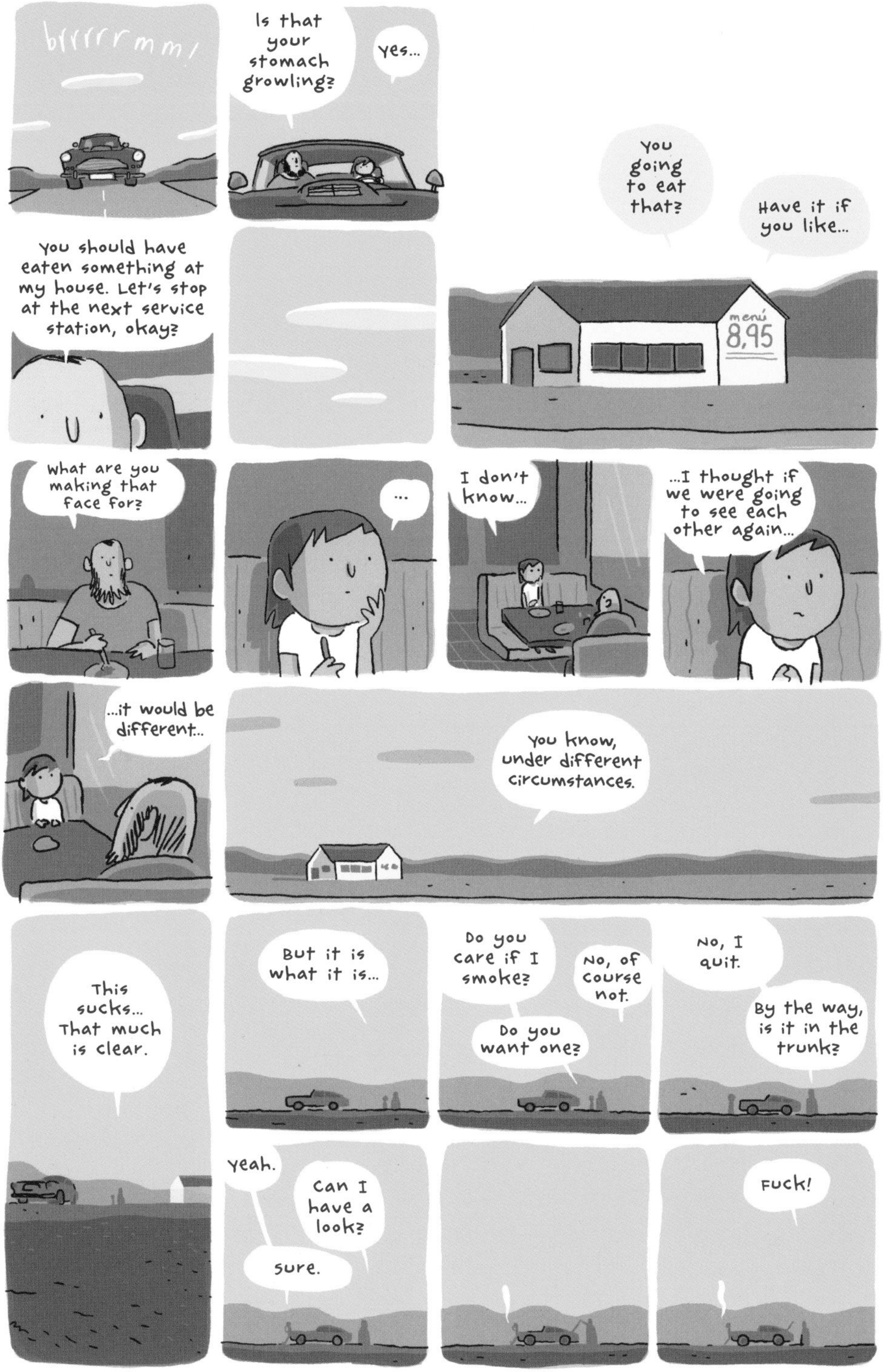
brrrrrmm!
Is that your stomach growling?
Yes...
You should have eaten something at my house. Let's stop at the next service station, okay?
You going to eat that?
Have it if you like...
menú 8,95
What are you making that face for?
...
I don't know...
...I thought if we were going to see each other again...
...it would be different...
You know, under different circumstances.
This sucks... That much is clear.
But it is what it is...
Do you care if I smoke?
No, of course not.
Do you want one?
No, I quit.
By the way, is it in the trunk?
Yeah.
Can I have a look?
Sure.
Fuck!

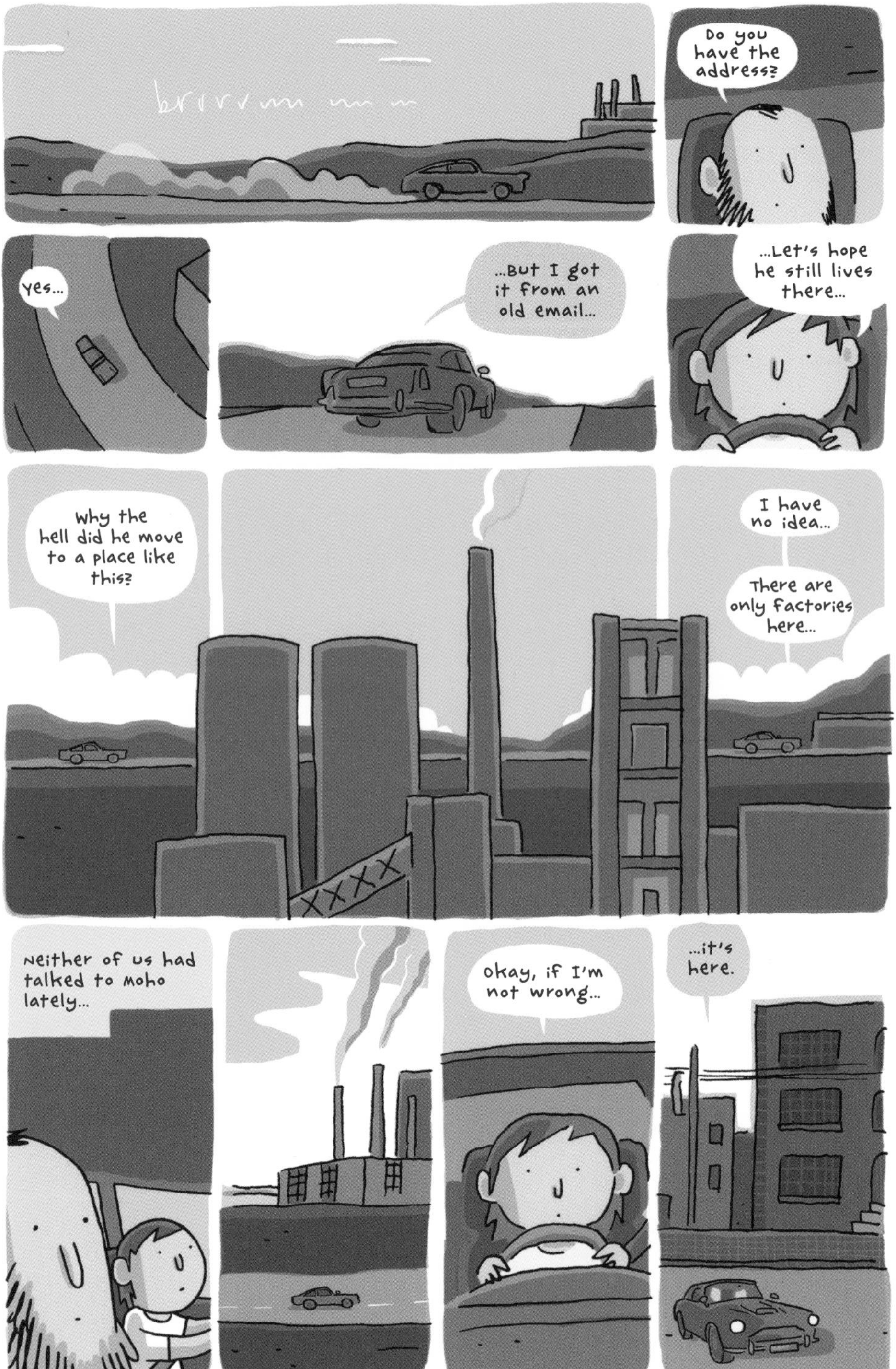
brrrvmm mm m
Do you have the address?
yes...
...But I got it from an old email...
...Let's hope he still lives there...
why the hell did he move to a place like this?
I have no idea...
There are only factories here...
Neither of us had talked to Moho lately...
okay, if I'm not wrong...
...it's here.

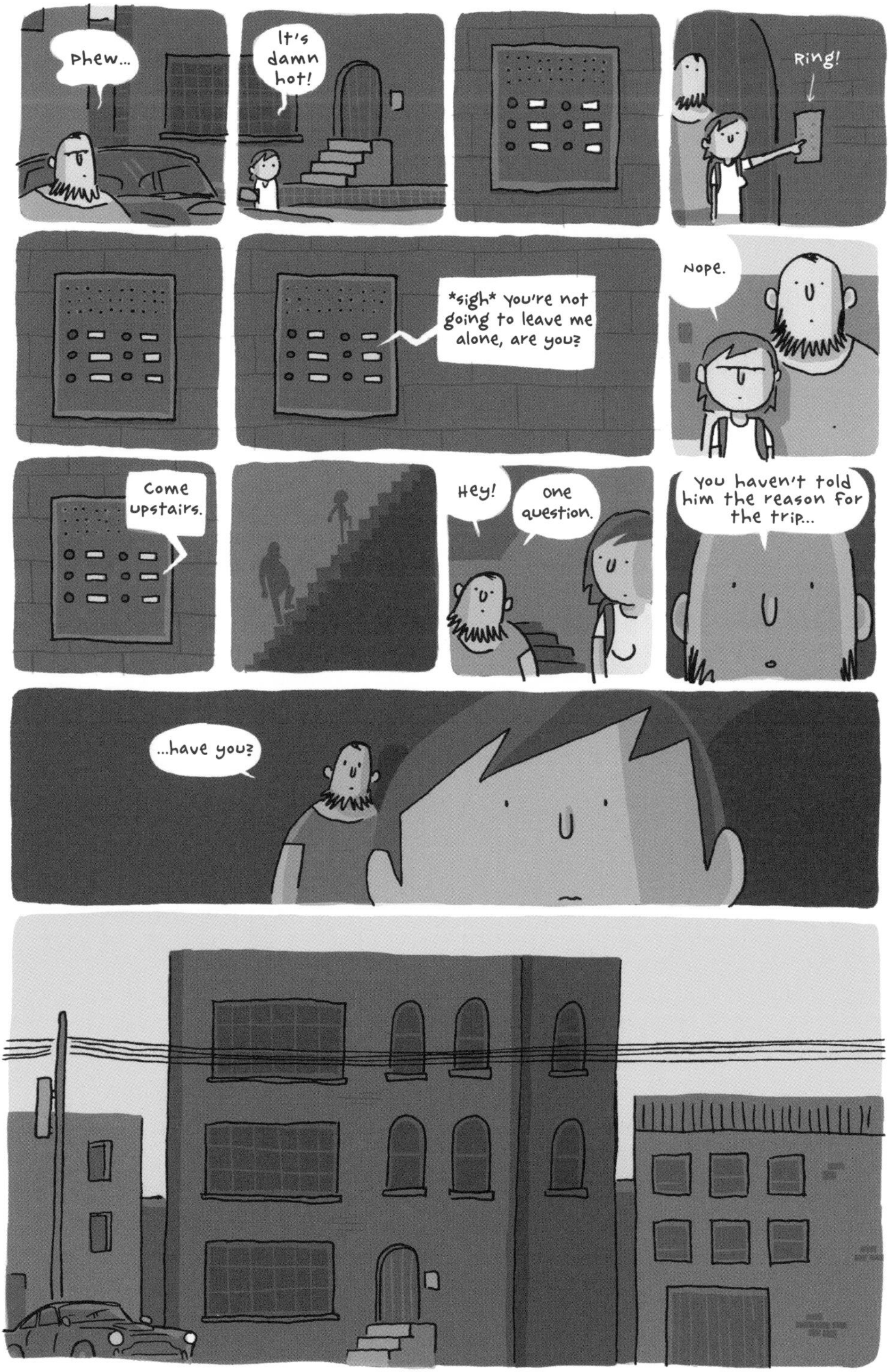
Phew...
It's damn hot!
Ring!
sigh You're not going to leave me alone, are you?
Nope.
Come upstairs.
Hey!
One question.
You haven't told him the reason for the trip...
...have you?

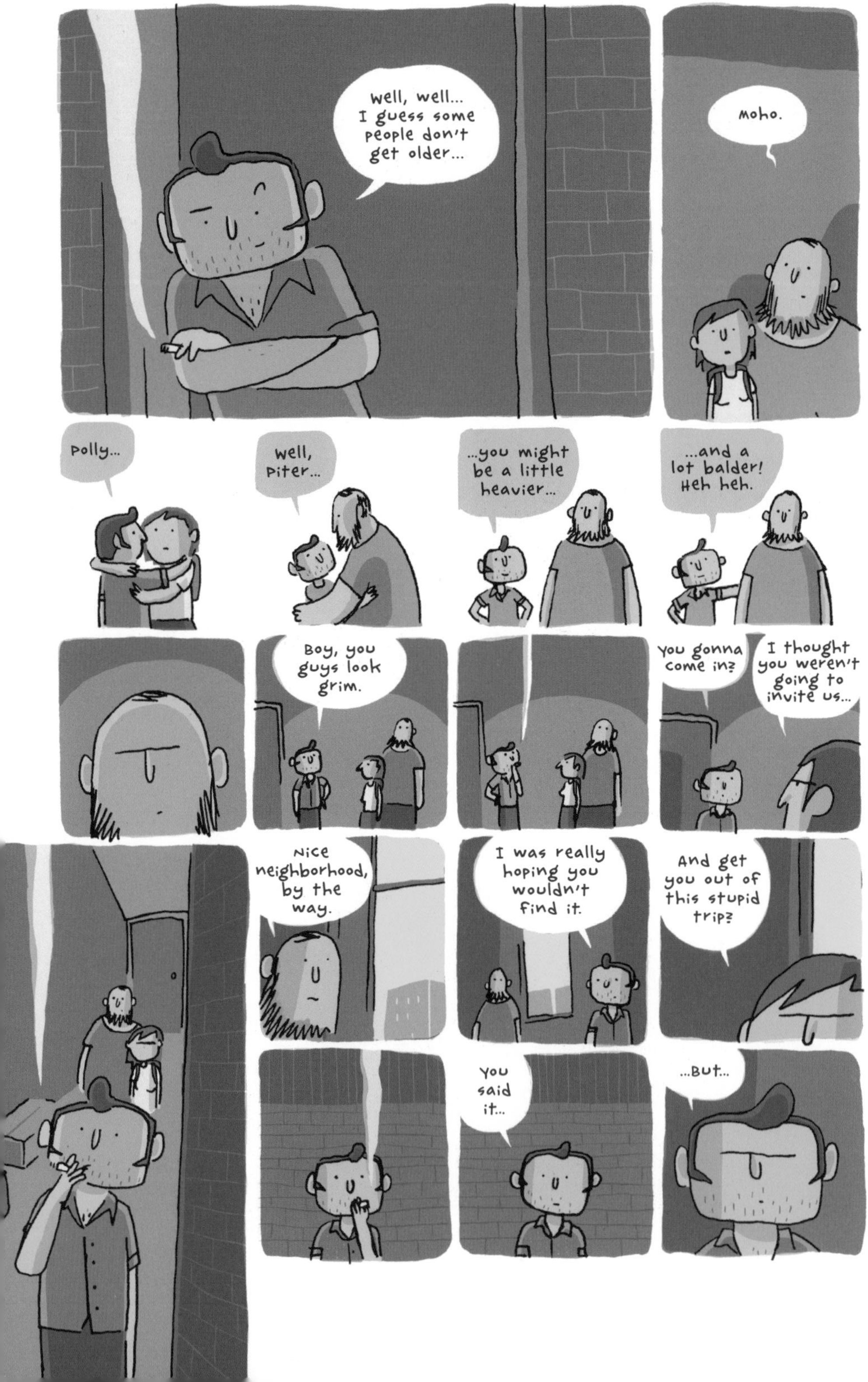
Well, well... I guess some people don't get older...
Moho.
Polly...
Well, Piter...
...you might be a little heavier...
...and a lot balder! Heh heh.
Boy, you guys look grim.
You gonna come in?
I thought you weren't going to invite us...
Nice neighborhood, by the way.
I was really hoping you wouldn't find it.
And get you out of this stupid trip?
You said it...
...But...

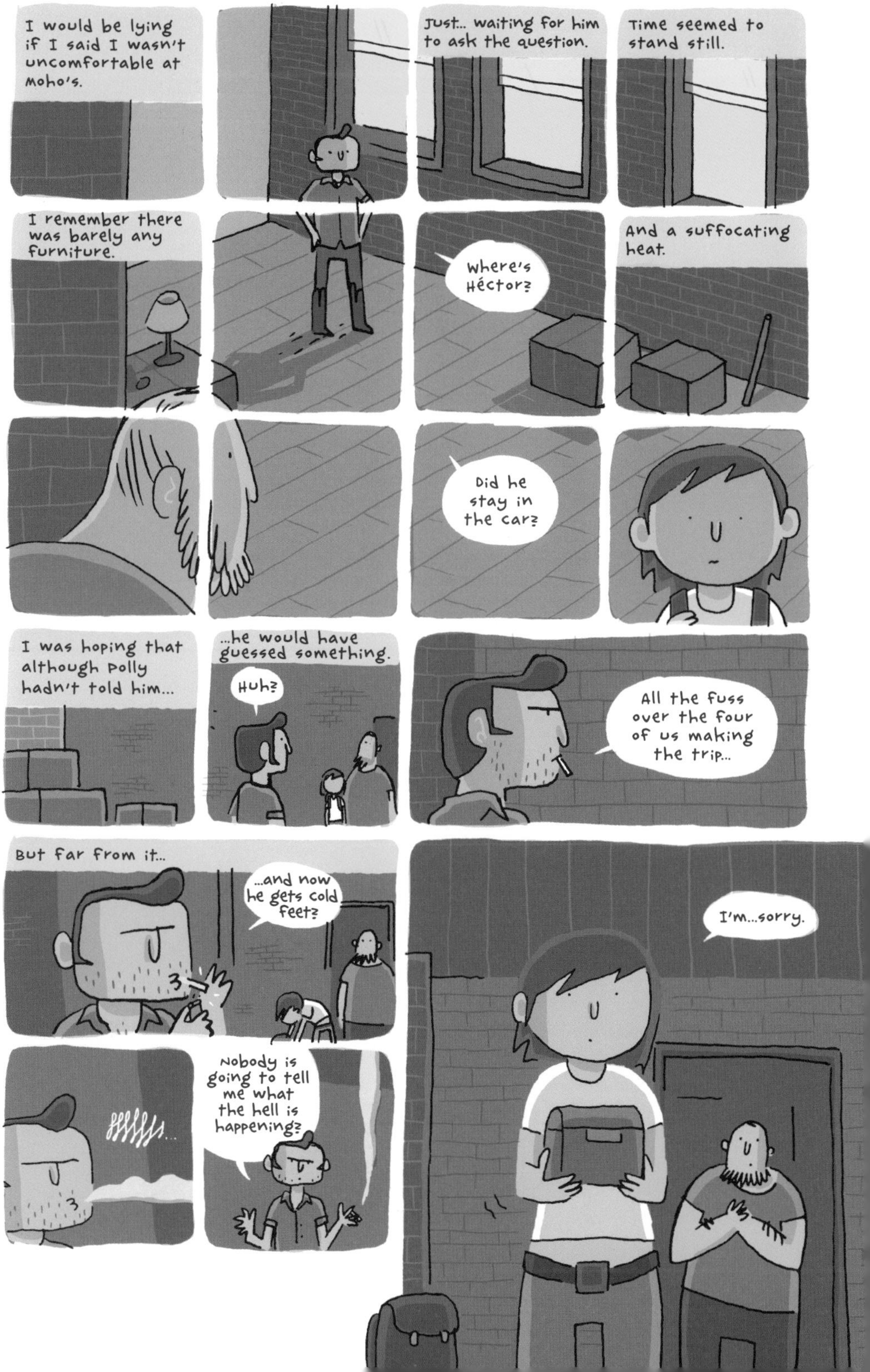
I would be lying if I said I wasn't uncomfortable at Moho's.
Just... waiting for him to ask the question.
Time seemed to stand still.
I remember there was barely any furniture.
Where's Héctor?
And a suffocating heat.
Did he stay in the car?
I was hoping that although Polly hadn't told him...
...he would have guessed something.
Huh?
All the fuss over the four of us making the trip...
But far from it...
...and now he gets cold feet?
ssssss...
Nobody is going to tell me what the hell is happening?
I'm...sorry.

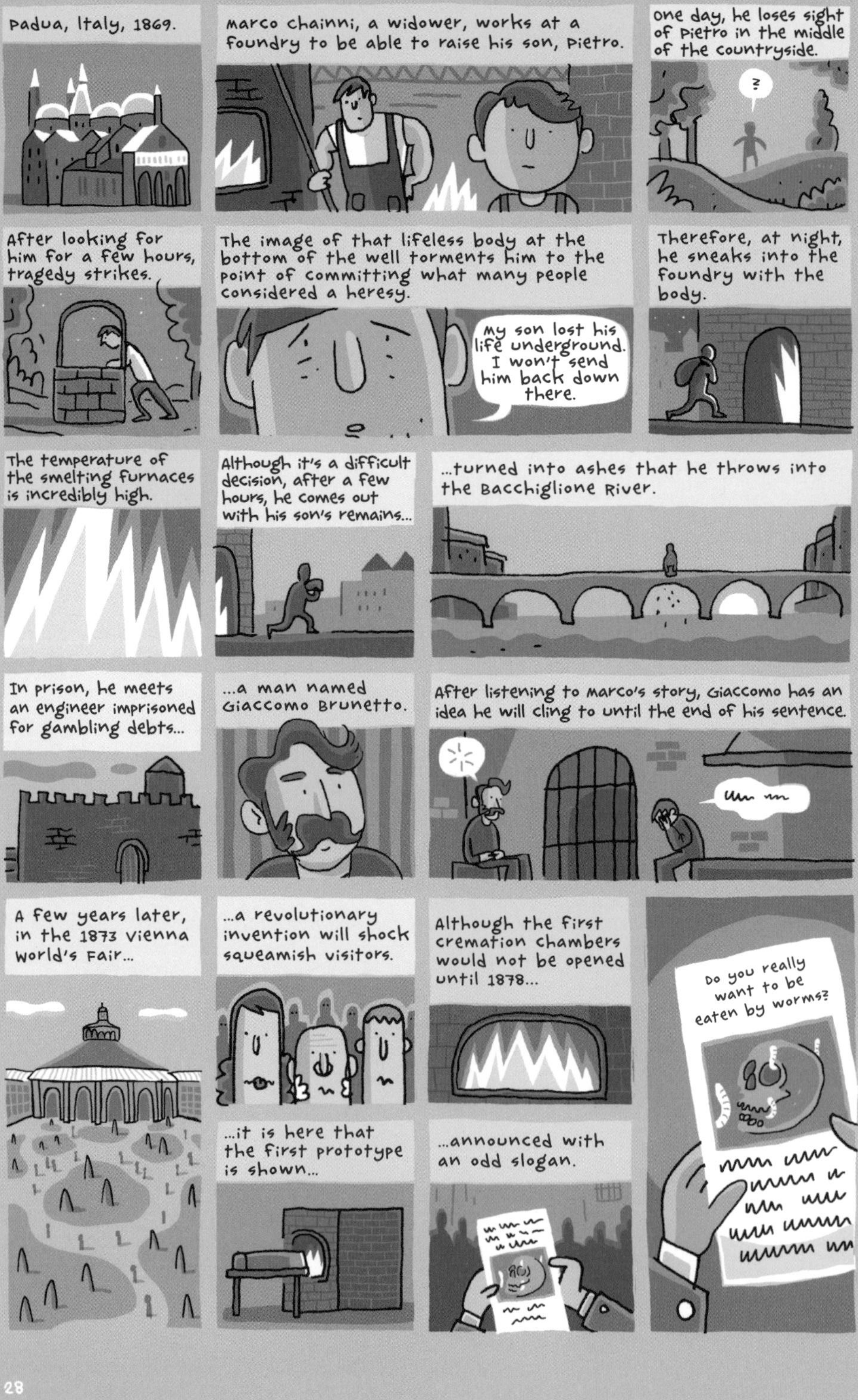
Padua, Italy, 1869.
Marco Chainni, a widower, works at a foundry to be able to raise his son, Pietro.
One day, he loses sight of Pietro in the middle of the countryside.
After looking for him for a few hours, tragedy strikes.
The image of that lifeless body at the bottom of the well torments him to the point of committing what many people considered a heresy.
My son lost his life underground. I won't send him back down there.
Therefore, at night, he sneaks into the foundry with the body.
The temperature of the smelting furnaces is incredibly high.
Although it's a difficult decision, after a few hours, he comes out with his son's remains...
...turned into ashes that he throws into the Bacchiglione River.
In prison, he meets an engineer imprisoned for gambling debts...
...a man named Giaccomo Brunetto.
After listening to Marco's story, Giaccomo has an idea he will cling to until the end of his sentence.
A few years later, in the 1873 Vienna World's Fair...
...a revolutionary invention will shock squeamish visitors.
Although the first cremation chambers would not be opened until 1878...
...it is here that the first prototype is shown...
...announced with an odd slogan.
Do you really want to be eaten by worms?

I don't understand why you didn't tell me before...

I don't know.

I guess I was ashamed...

...or something...

Yeah, sure, but you told him, didn't you?

...

Yes, well...

But...

Forget it...

...It makes no difference now.

Then Polly starts telling him what she told me a few days ago.

That she received a call from Héctor's mom.

And she immediately knew it was something bad...

...but not this bad.

A stupid accident...

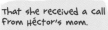

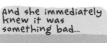

29

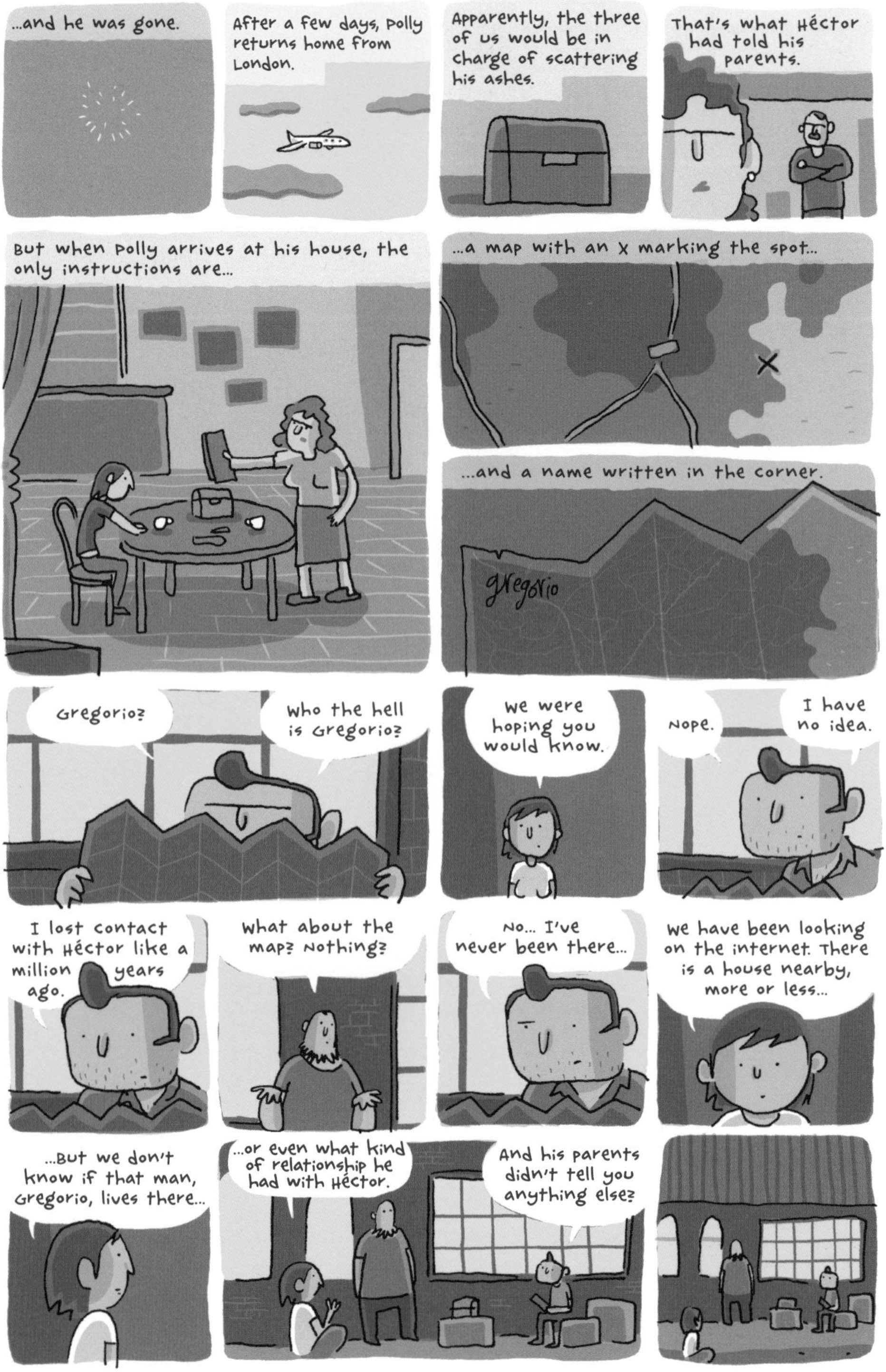
...and he was gone.
After a few days, Polly returns home from London.
Apparently, the three of us would be in charge of scattering his ashes.
That's what Héctor had told his parents.
But when Polly arrives at his house, the only instructions are...
...a map with an x marking the spot...
...and a name written in the corner.
Gregorio
Gregorio?
Who the hell is Gregorio?
We were hoping you would know.
Nope.
I have no idea.
I lost contact with Héctor like a million years ago.
What about the map? Nothing?
No... I've never been there...
We have been looking on the internet. There is a house nearby, more or less...
...But we don't know if that man, Gregorio, lives there...
...or even what kind of relationship he had with Héctor.
And his parents didn't tell you anything else?

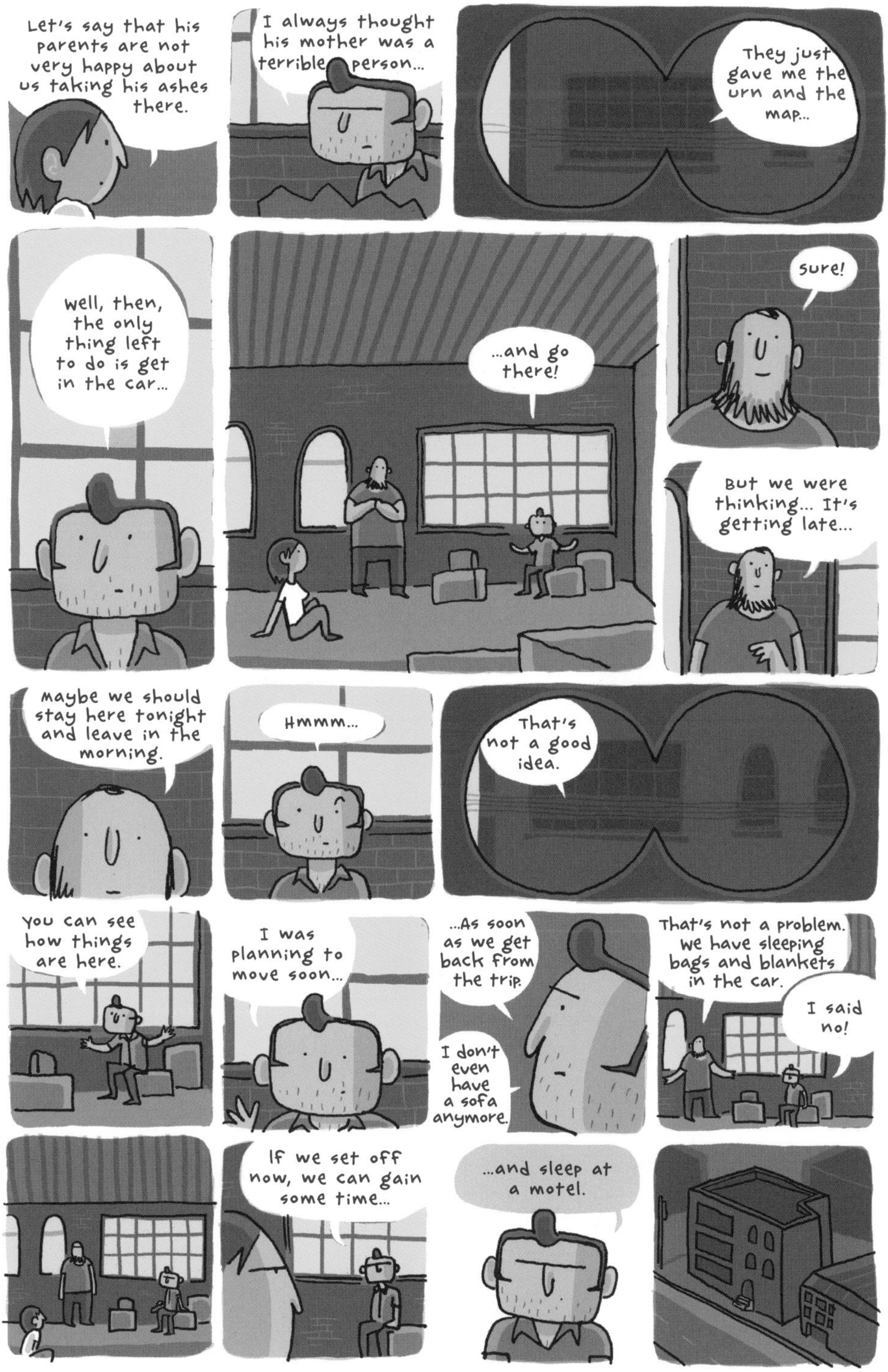
Let's say that his parents are not very happy about us taking his ashes there.
I always thought his mother was a terrible person...
They just gave me the urn and the map...
Well, then, the only thing left to do is get in the car...
...and go there!
Sure!
But we were thinking... It's getting late...
Maybe we should stay here tonight and leave in the morning.
Hmmm...
That's not a good idea.
You can see how things are here.
I was planning to move soon...
...As soon as we get back from the trip.
I don't even have a sofa anymore.
That's not a problem. We have sleeping bags and blankets in the car.
I said no!
If we set off now, we can gain some time...
...and sleep at a motel.

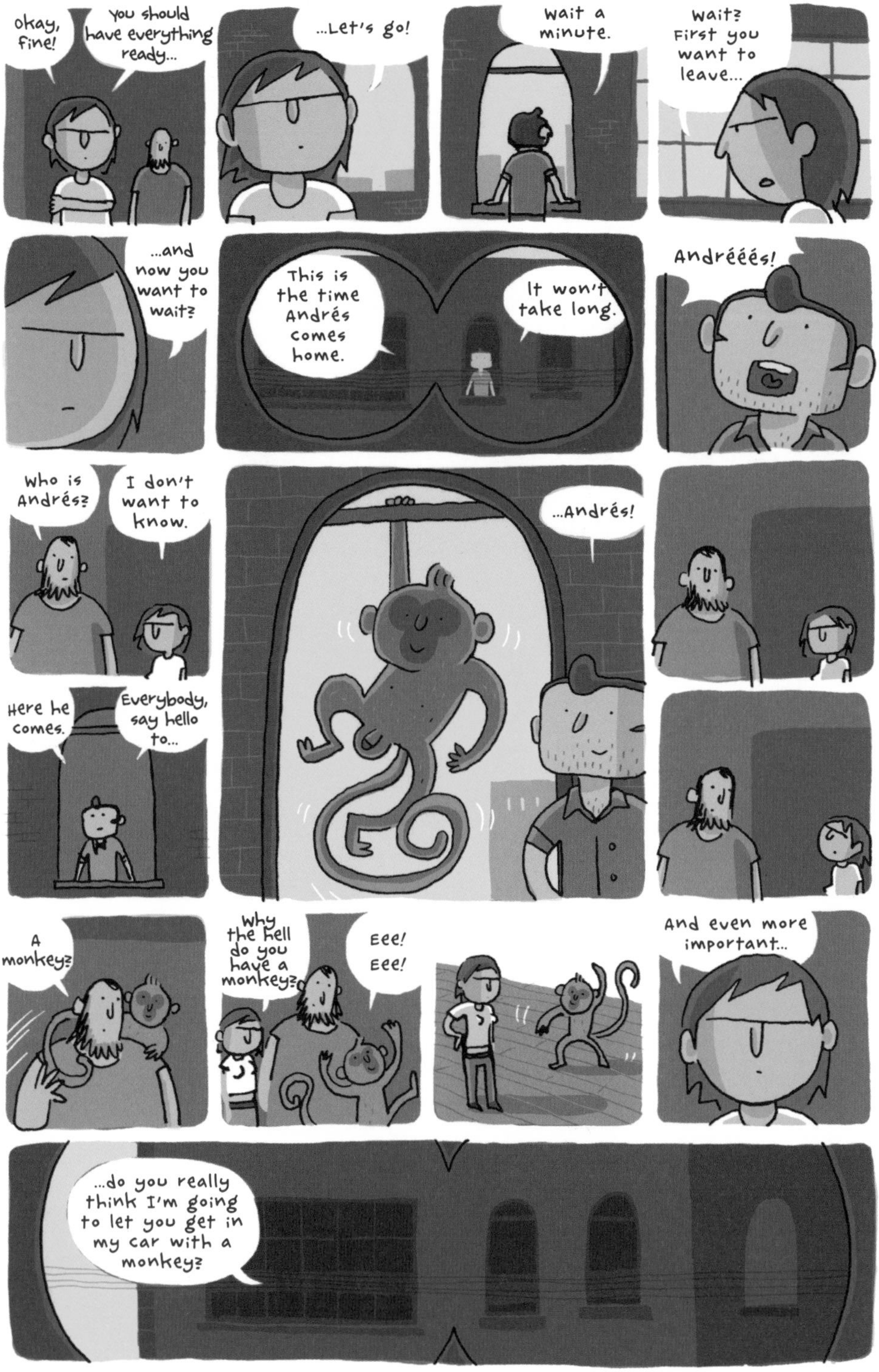
Okay, fine!
You should have everything ready...
...Let's go!
Wait a minute.
Wait? First you want to leave...
...and now you want to wait?
This is the time Andrés comes home.
It won't take long.
Andrééés!
Who is Andrés?
I don't want to know.
...Andrés!
Here he comes.
Everybody, say hello to...
A monkey?
Why the hell do you have a monkey?
Eee! Eee!
And even more important...
...do you really think I'm going to let you get in my car with a monkey?

DAY 1

· ·

(although there is really
not much of the day left)

· ·

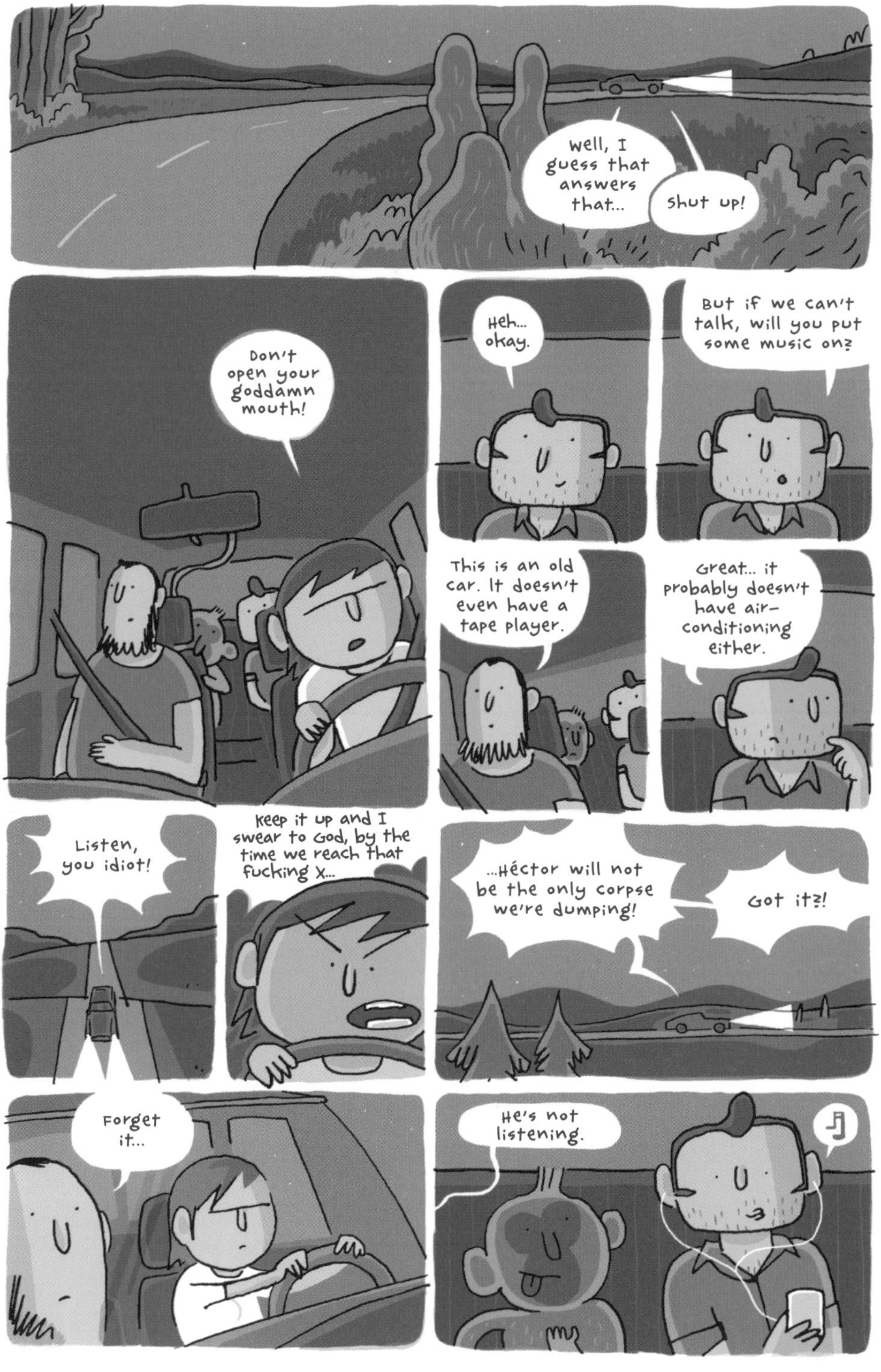
Well, I guess that answers that...
Shut up!
Don't open your goddamn mouth!
Heh... okay.
But if we can't talk, will you put some music on?
This is an old car. It doesn't even have a tape player.
Great... it probably doesn't have air-conditioning either.
Listen, you idiot!
Keep it up and I swear to God, by the time we reach that fucking X...
...Héctor will not be the only corpse we're dumping!
Got it?!
Forget it...
He's not listening.

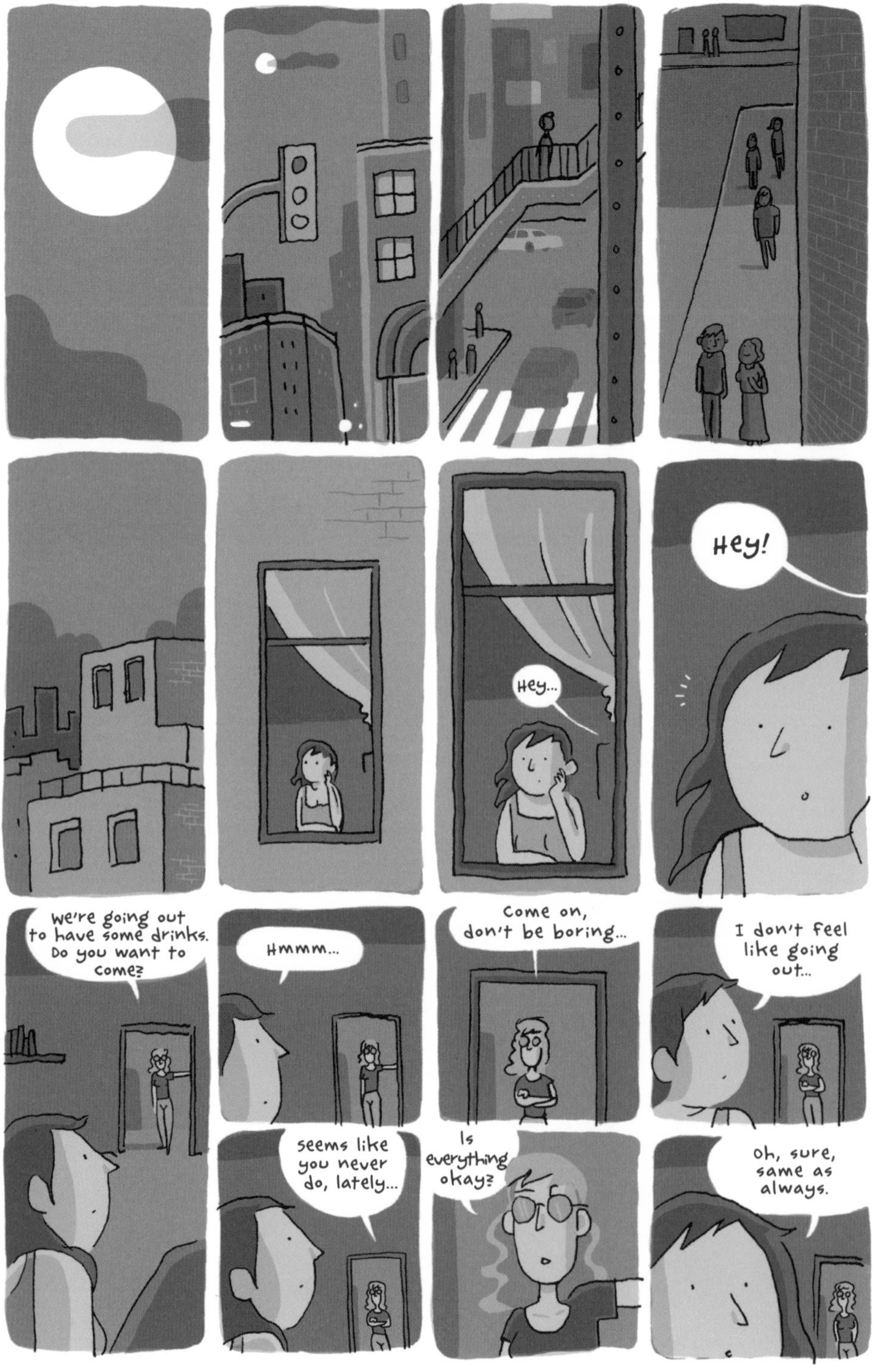
Hey!
Hey...
We're going out to have some drinks. Do you want to come?
Hmmm...
Come on, don't be boring...
I don't feel like going out...
Seems like you never do, lately...
Is everything okay?
Oh, sure, same as always.

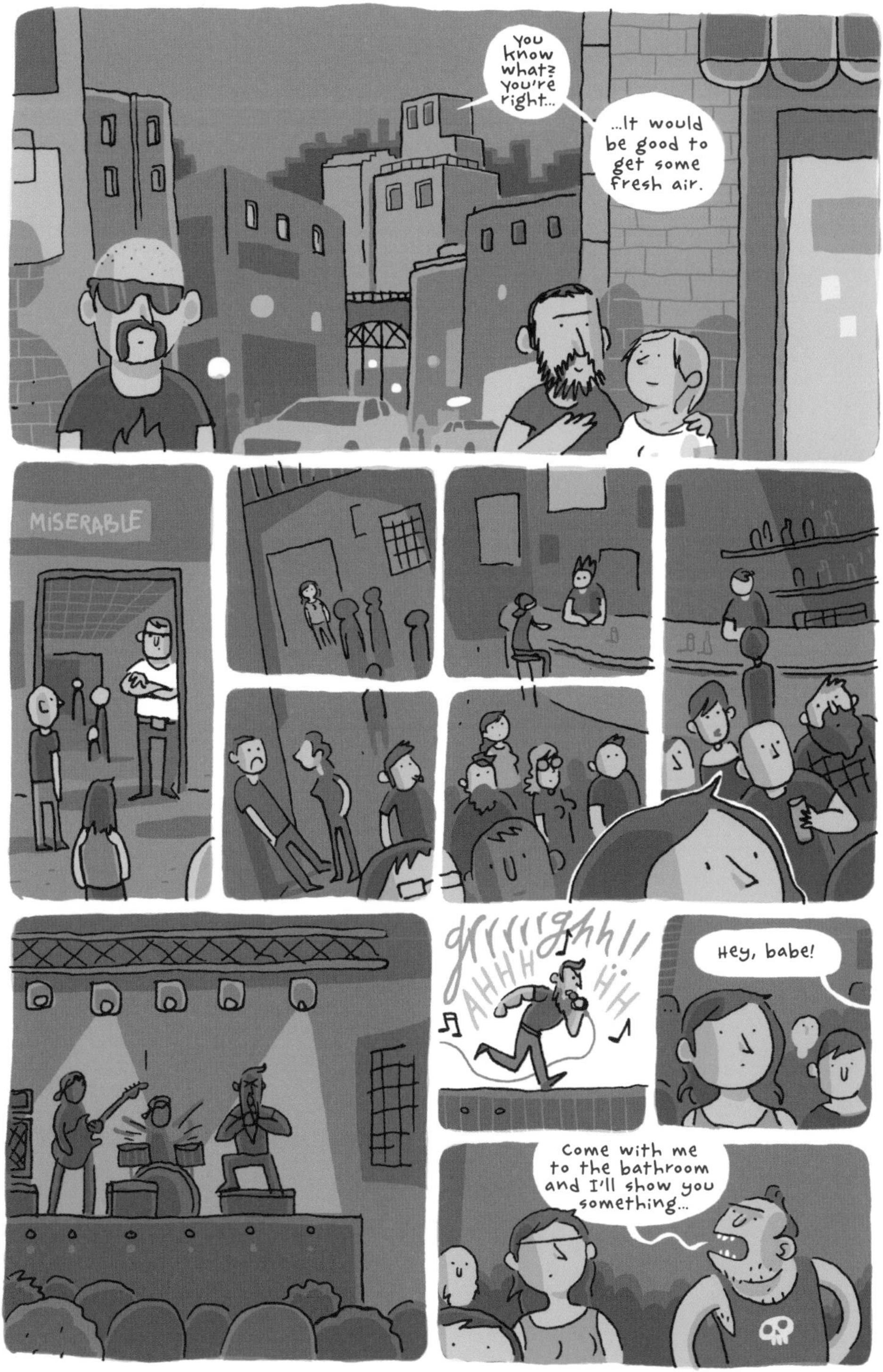
You know what? You're right...
...It would be good to get some fresh air.
MISERABLE
grrrrrghhh!!
AHHHHHH
Hey, babe!
Come with me to the bathroom and I'll show you something...

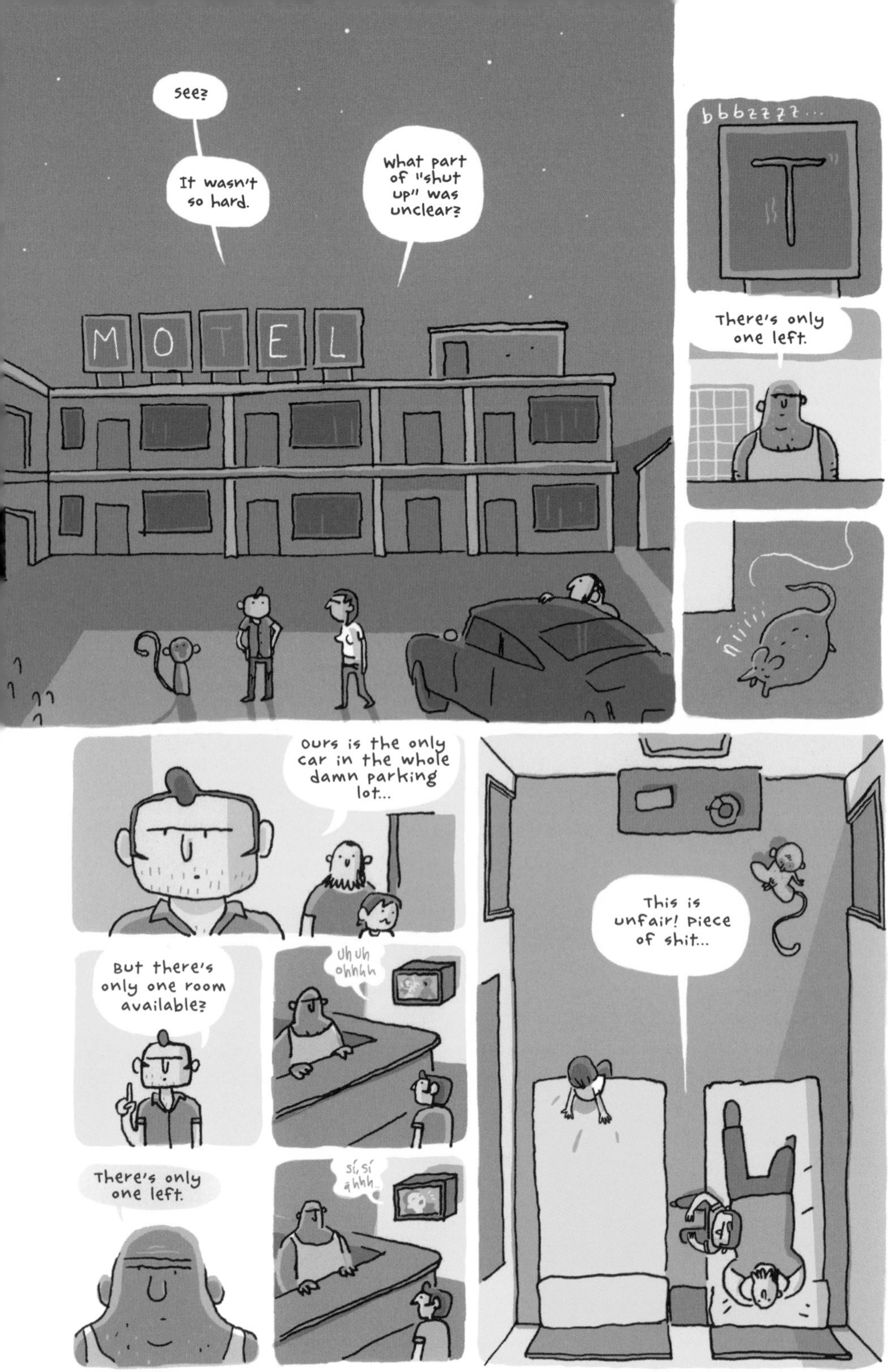
See?
It wasn't so hard.
What part of "shut up" was unclear?
MOTEL
bbbzzzz...
T
There's only one left.
Ours is the only car in the whole damn parking lot...
But there's only one room available?
Uh uh ohhhh
There's only one left.
Sí, sí ahhh..
This is unfair! Piece of shit...

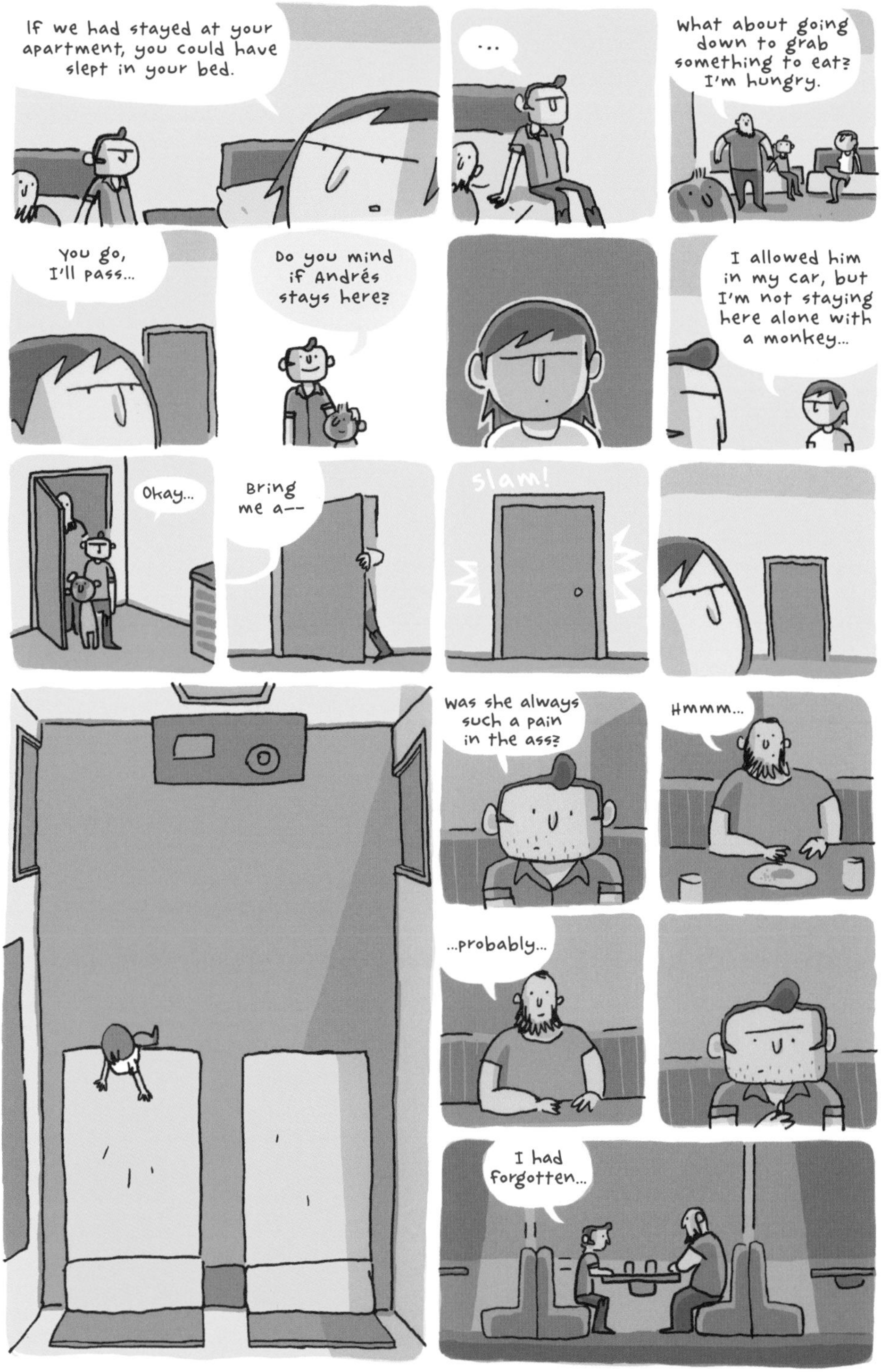
If we had stayed at your apartment, you could have slept in your bed.
...
What about going down to grab something to eat? I'm hungry.
You go, I'll pass...
Do you mind if Andrés stays here?
I allowed him in my car, but I'm not staying here alone with a monkey...
Okay...
Bring me a--
slam!
Was she always such a pain in the ass?
Hmmm...
...probably...
I had forgotten...

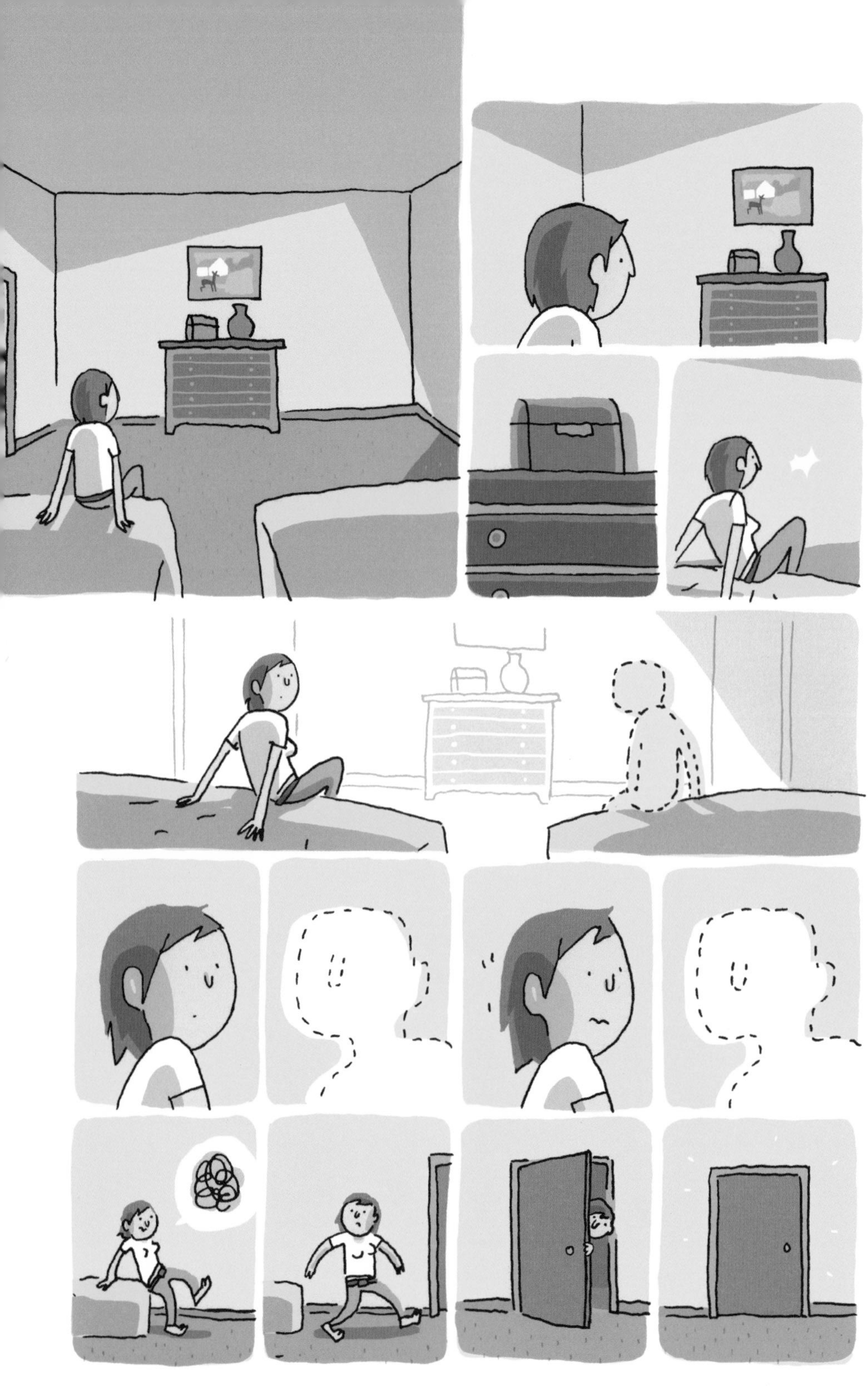

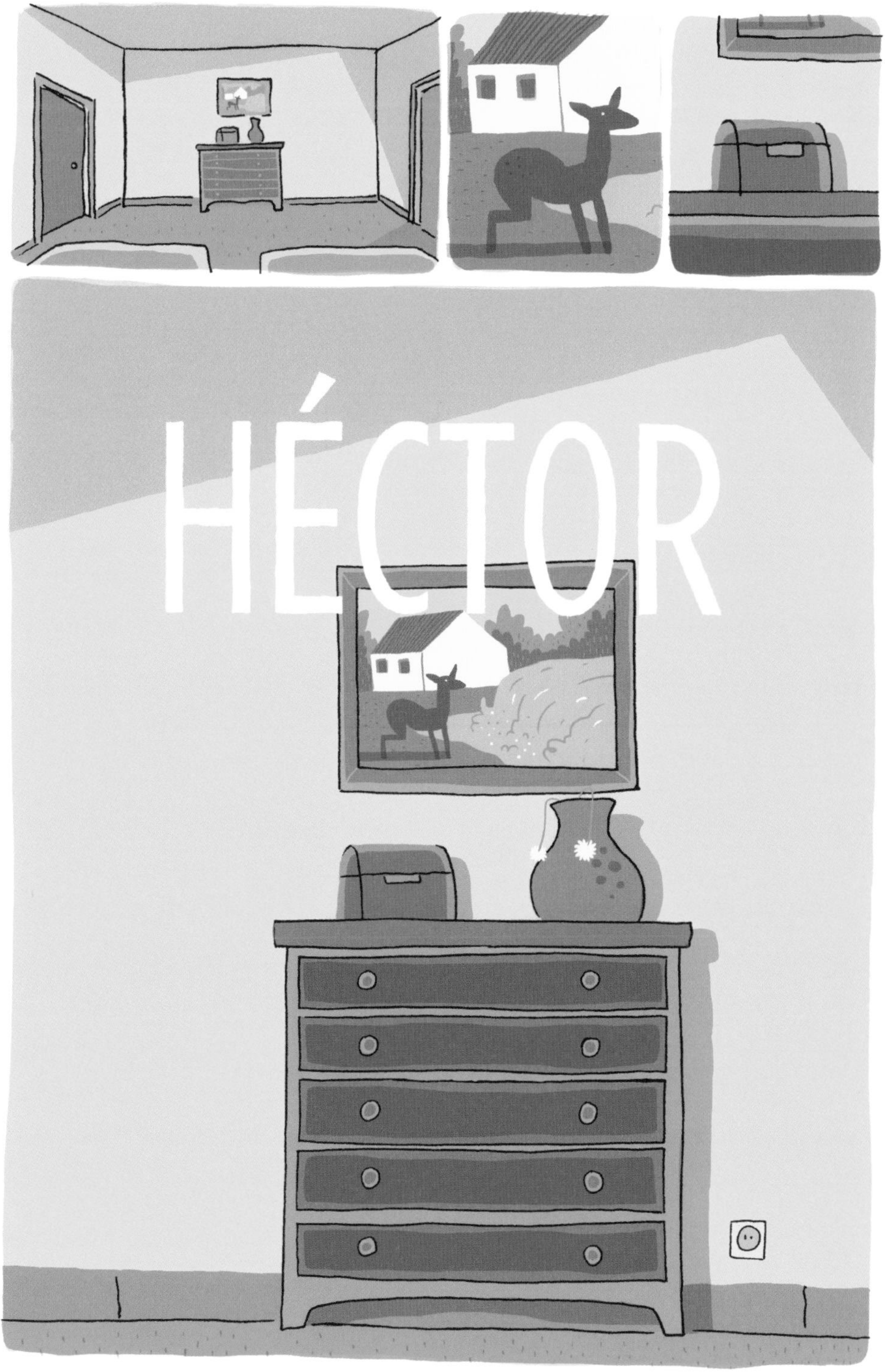
HÉCTOR

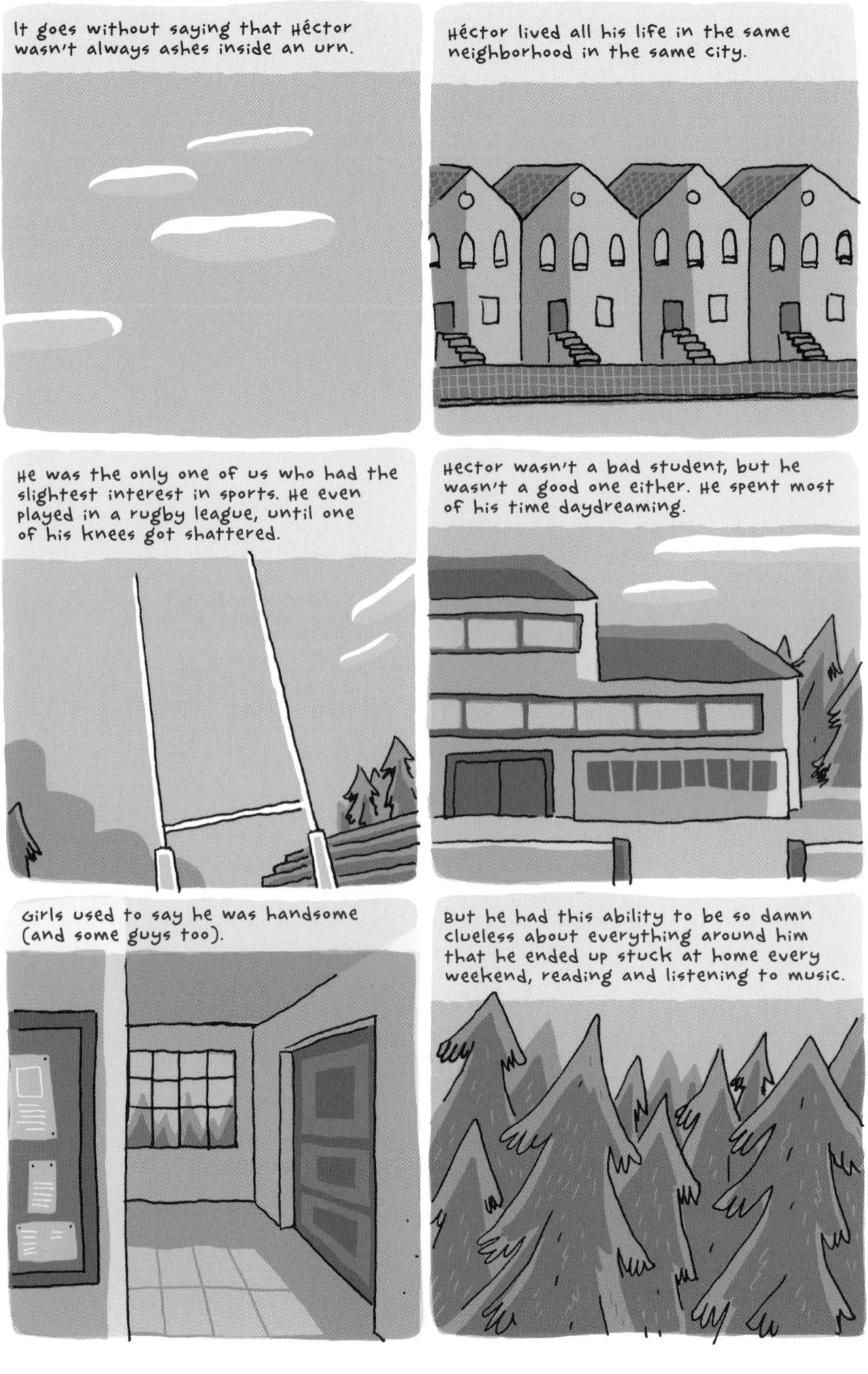
It goes without saying that Héctor wasn't always ashes inside an urn.
Héctor lived all his life in the same neighborhood in the same city.
He was the only one of us who had the slightest interest in sports. He even played in a rugby league, until one of his knees got shattered.
Hector wasn't a bad student, but he wasn't a good one either. He spent most of his time daydreaming.
Girls used to say he was handsome (and some guys too).
But he had this ability to be so damn clueless about everything around him that he ended up stuck at home every weekend, reading and listening to music.

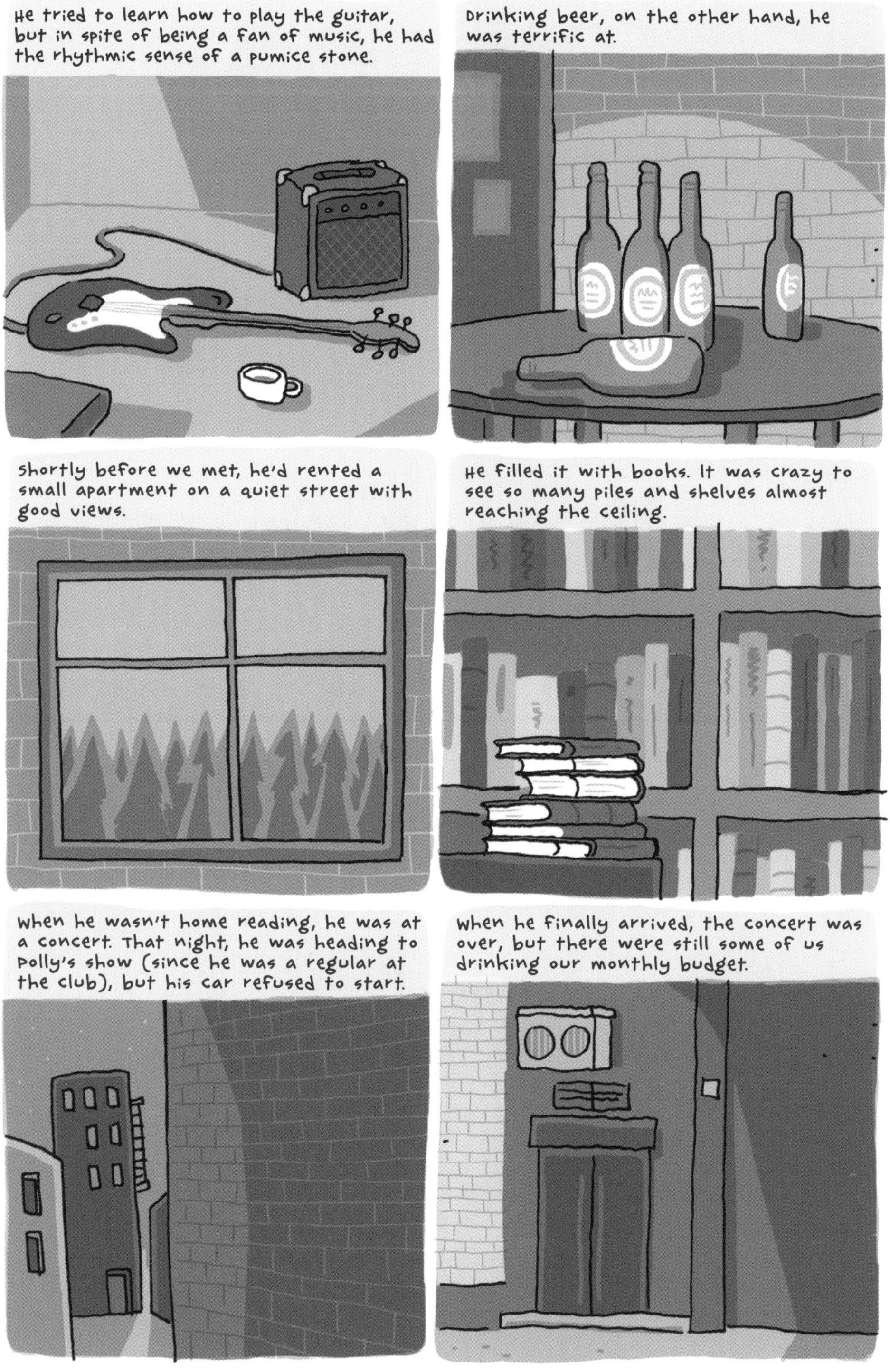
He tried to learn how to play the guitar, but in spite of being a fan of music, he had the rhythmic sense of a pumice stone.
Drinking beer, on the other hand, he was terrific at.
Shortly before we met, he'd rented a small apartment on a quiet street with good views.
He filled it with books. It was crazy to see so many piles and shelves almost reaching the ceiling.
When he wasn't home reading, he was at a concert. That night, he was heading to Polly's show (since he was a regular at the club), but his car refused to start.
When he finally arrived, the concert was over, but there were still some of us drinking our monthly budget.

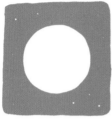

Uh...

...Are you still working in that nursing home?

I didn't know what to talk about, and silence was awkward, so I just started telling him about my life.

No...

About how I'd left the retirement home to assist one particular widow.

I told him about Azah...

...and how close we were.

About Pierre, her late husband.

How they had met, a long time ago.

And how bad I felt when she also died some months ago.

Wow, I'm sorry...

You see...

...everybody is dying lately.

Are you saying that huge house where I picked you up...

And to tone down the drama, I told him about the inheritance of the house...

So, they didn't have any heirs?

None.

Daaamn, what a lucky break, eh?

44

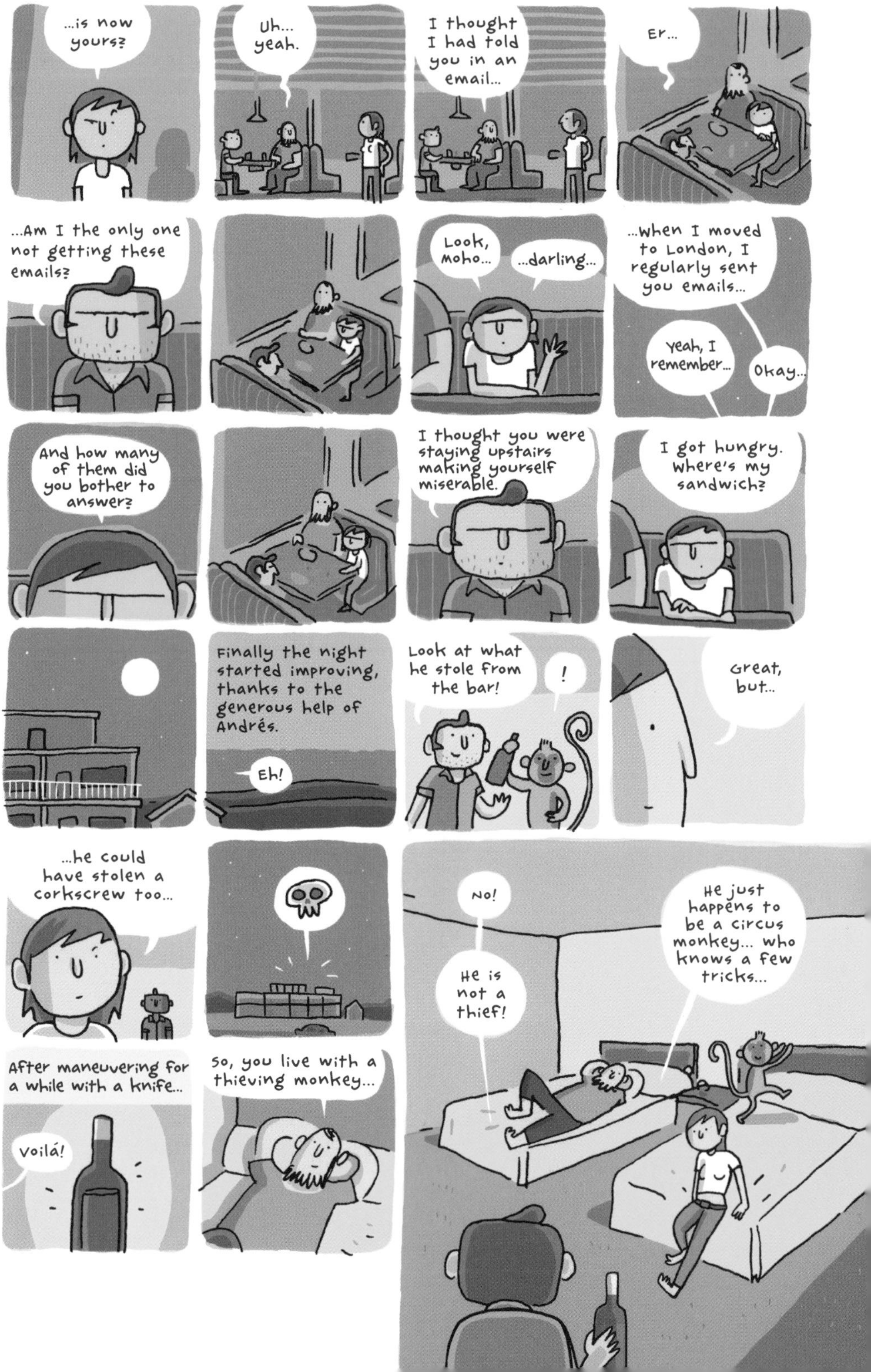
...is now yours?
Uh... yeah.
I thought I had told you in an email...
Er...
...Am I the only one not getting these emails?
Look, Moho...
...darling...
...when I moved to London, I regularly sent you emails...
Yeah, I remember...
Okay...
And how many of them did you bother to answer?
I thought you were staying upstairs making yourself miserable.
I got hungry. Where's my sandwich?
Finally the night started improving, thanks to the generous help of Andrés.
Eh!
Look at what he stole from the bar!
!
Great, but...
...he could have stolen a corkscrew too...
After maneuvering for a while with a knife...
Voilá!
So, you live with a thieving monkey...
No!
He is not a thief!
He just happens to be a circus monkey... who knows a few tricks...

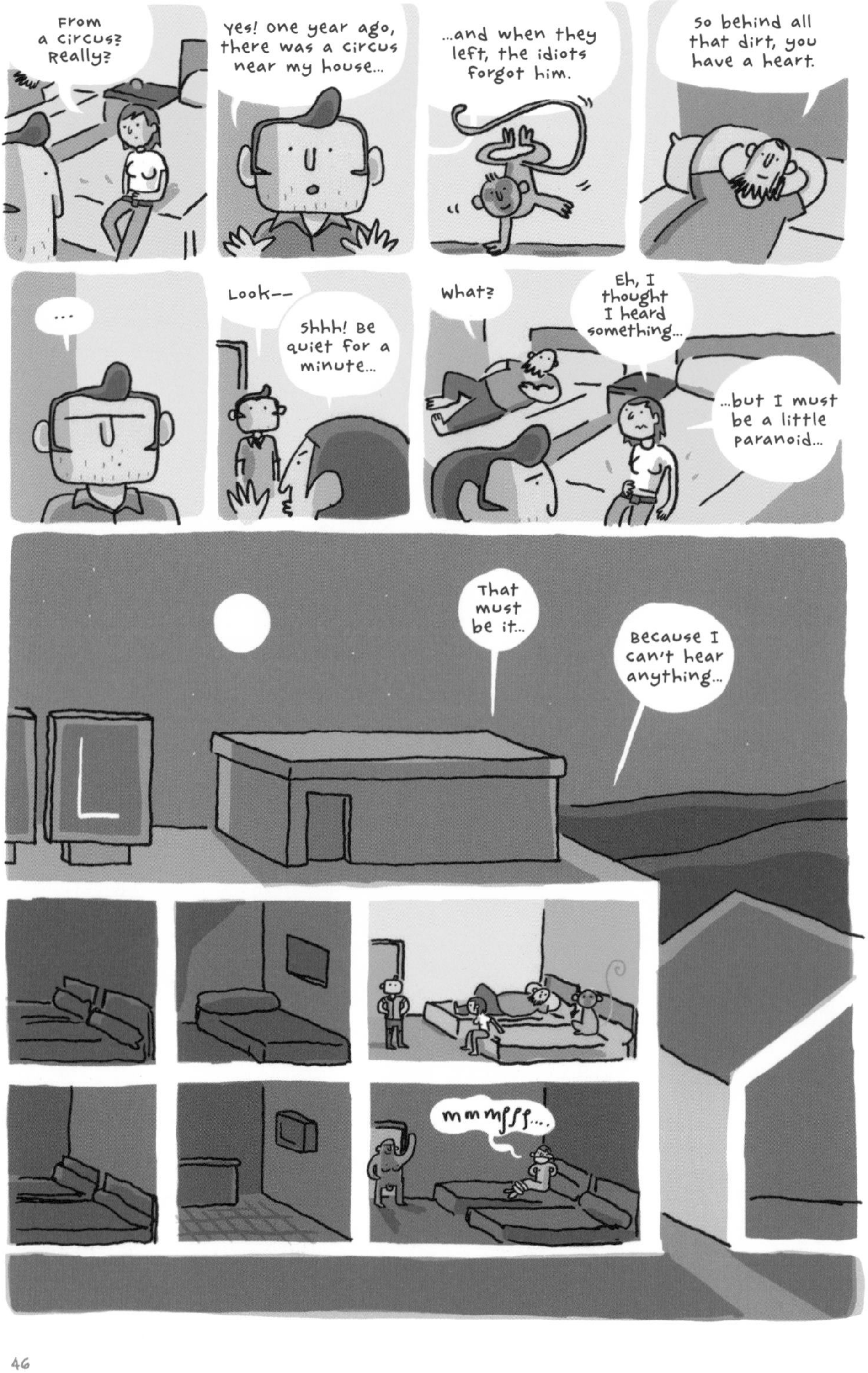
From a circus? Really?
Yes! One year ago, there was a circus near my house...
...and when they left, the idiots forgot him.
So behind all that dirt, you have a heart.
...
Look--
Shhh! Be quiet for a minute...
What?
Eh, I thought I heard something...
...but I must be a little paranoid...
That must be it...
Because I can't hear anything...
mmmfff....

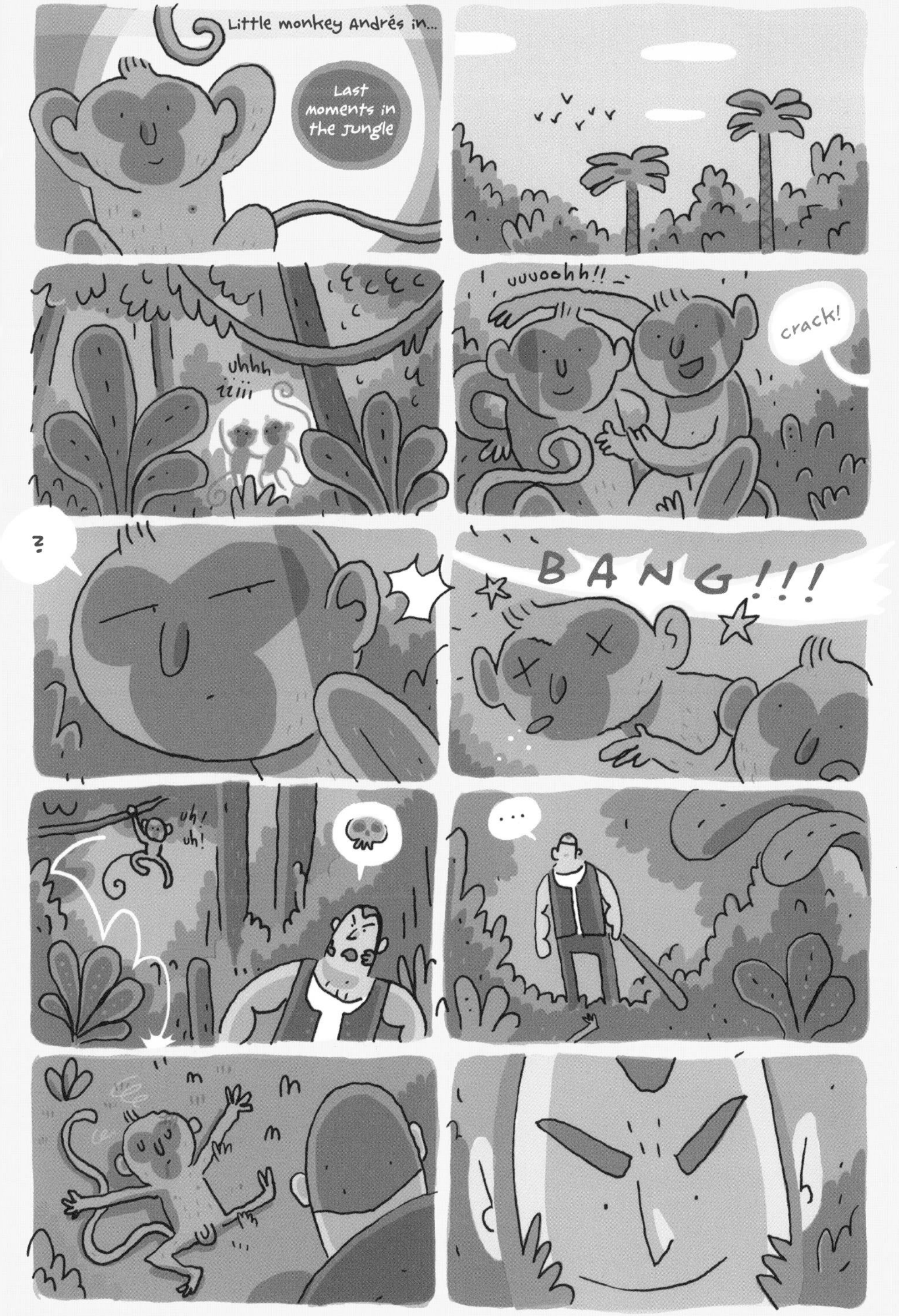

Little monkey Andrés in...
Last moments in the jungle
uhhh iiiii
uuuoohh!!
crack!
?
BANG!!!
uh! uh!
...

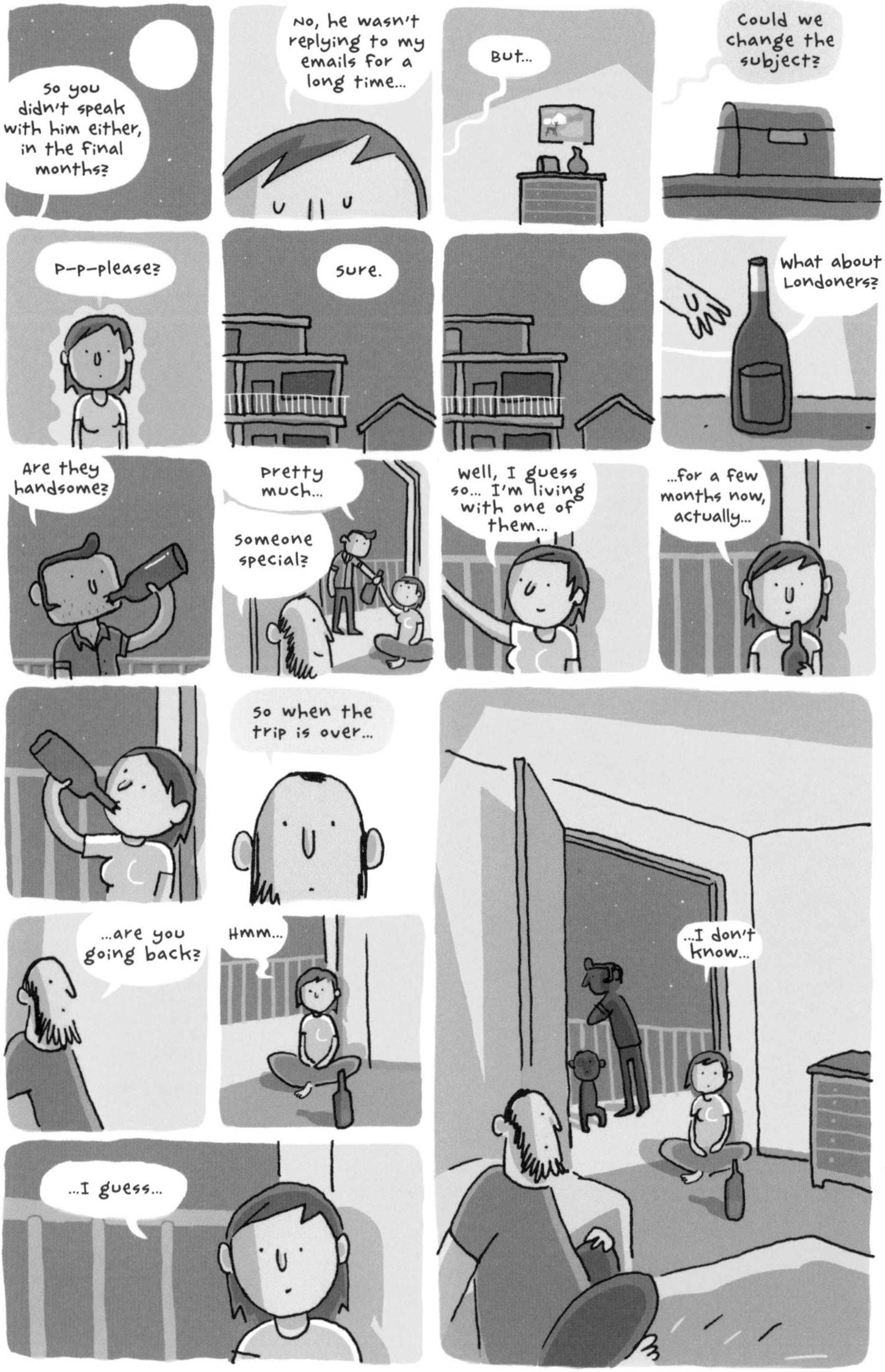
So you didn't speak with him either, in the final months?
No, he wasn't replying to my emails for a long time...
But...
Could we change the subject?
P-p-please?
Sure.
What about Londoners?
Are they handsome?
Pretty much...
Someone special?
Well, I guess so... I'm living with one of them...
...for a few months now, actually...
So when the trip is over...
...are you going back?
Hmm...
...I don't know...
...I guess...

DAY 2

(in which the trip
actually begins)

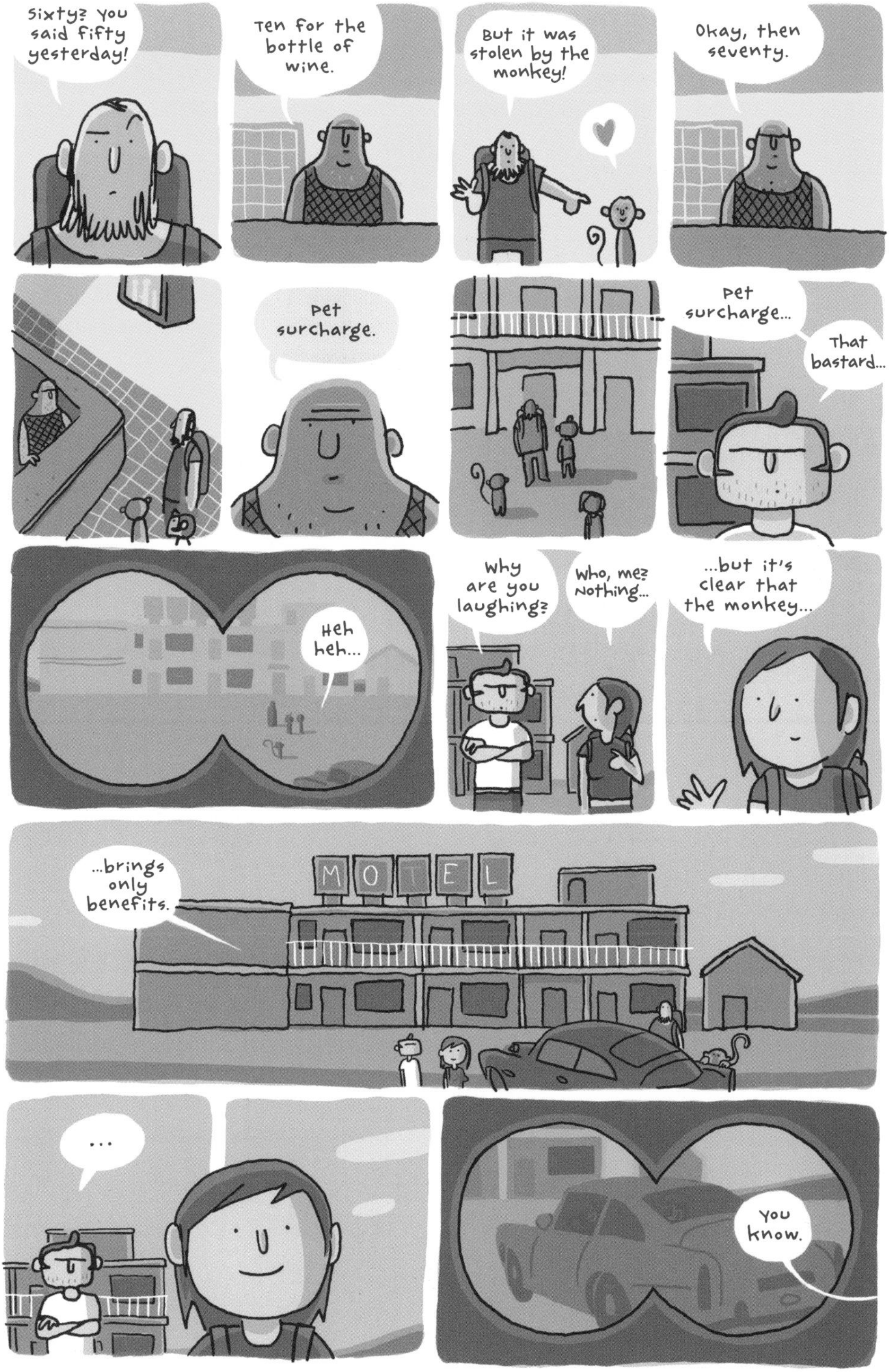
Sixty? You said fifty yesterday!
Ten for the bottle of wine.
But it was stolen by the monkey!
Okay, then seventy.
Pet surcharge.
Pet surcharge...
That bastard...
Heh heh...
Why are you laughing?
Who, me? Nothing...
...but it's clear that the monkey...
MOTEL
...brings only benefits.
...
You know.

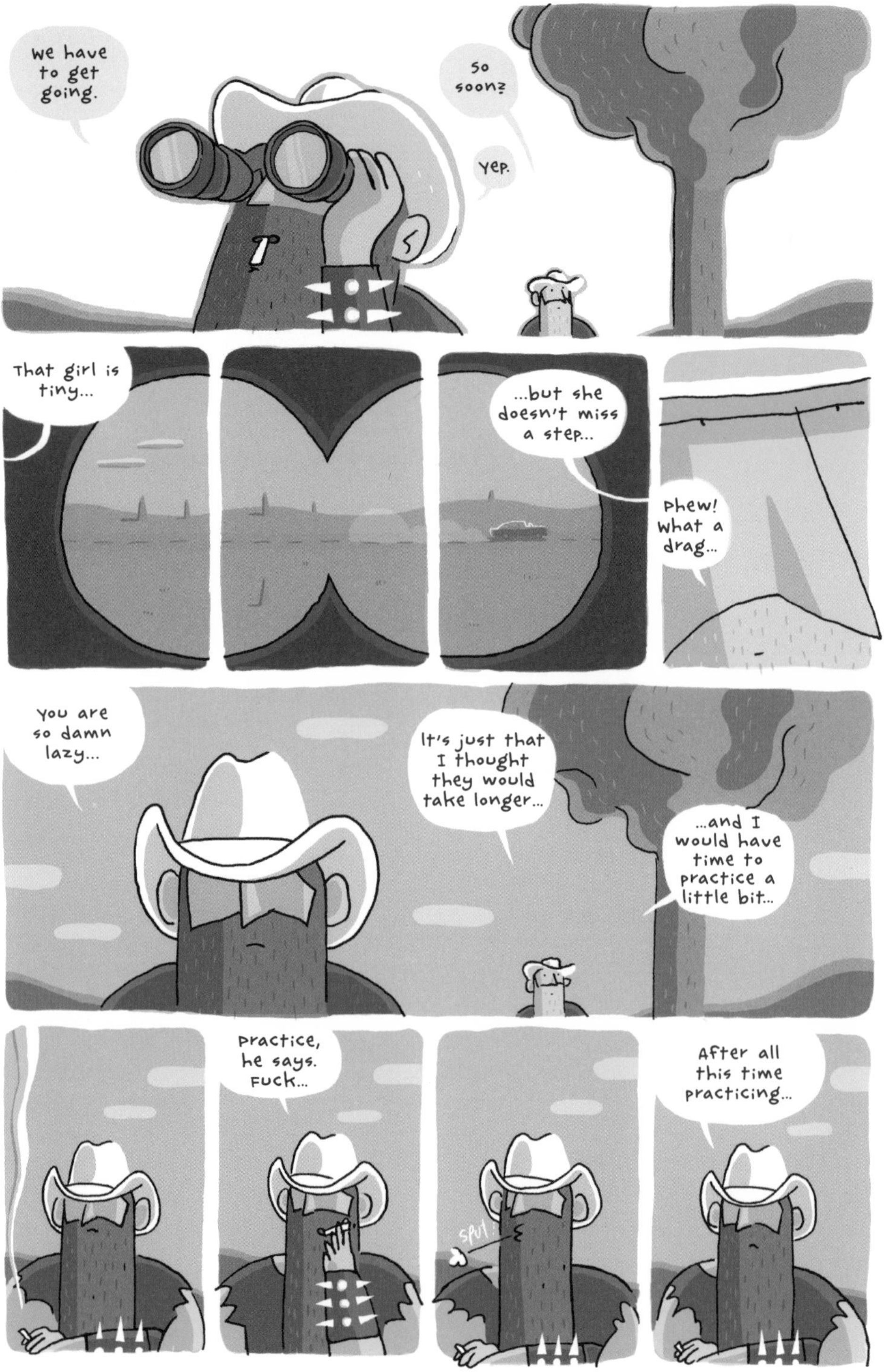
We have to get going.
So soon?
Yep.
That girl is tiny...
...but she doesn't miss a step...
Phew! What a drag...
You are so damn lazy...
It's just that I thought they would take longer...
...and I would have time to practice a little bit...
Practice, he says. Fuck...
SPUT!
After all this time practicing...

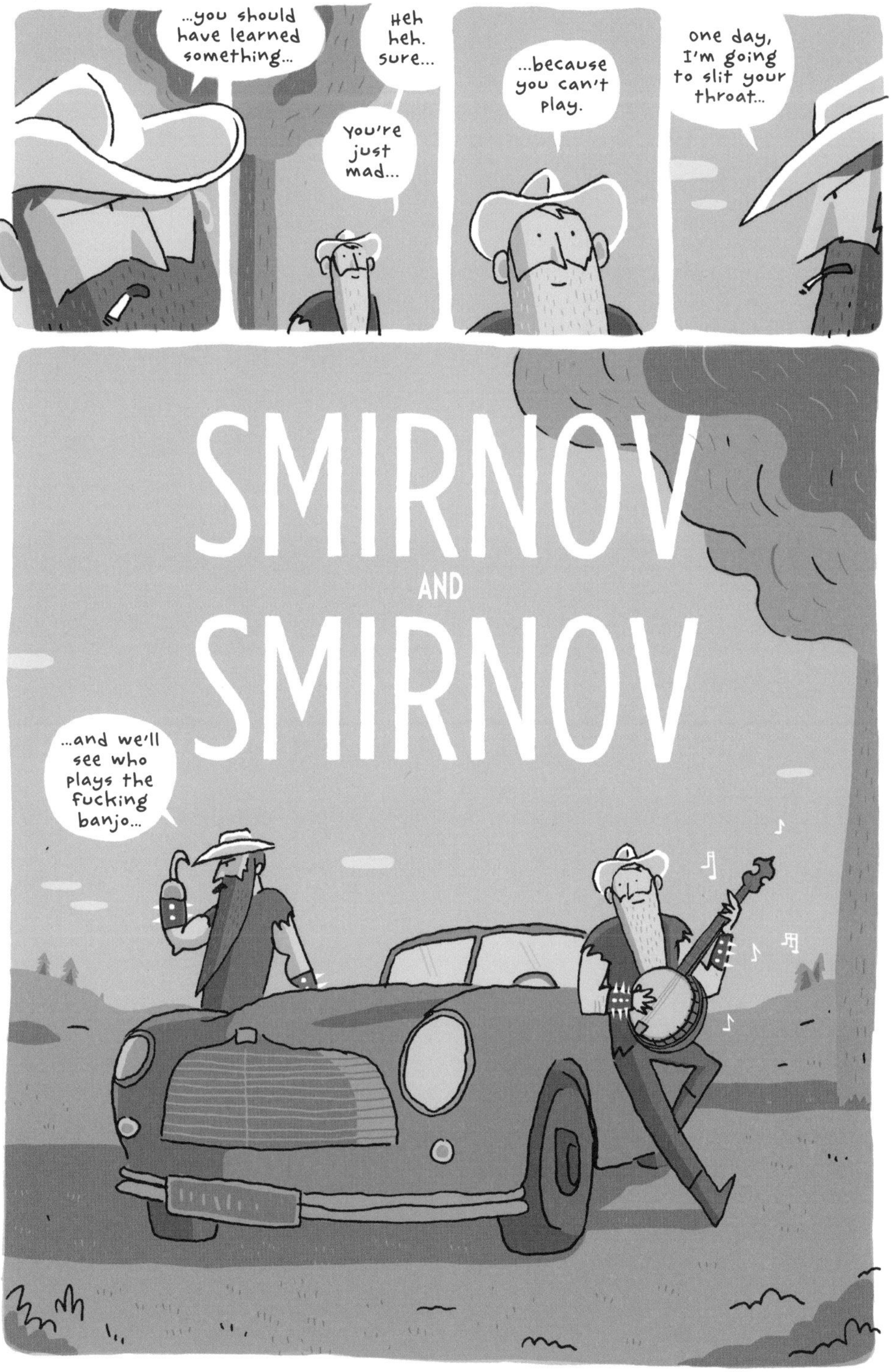

...you should have learned something...
Heh heh. sure...
You're just mad...
...because you can't play.
one day, I'm going to slit your throat...
SMIRNOV AND SMIRNOV
...and we'll see who plays the fucking banjo...

Smirnov and Smirnov were born on the same day, at almost the same hour, and of course, from the same mother.

Their grandparents were gold diggers, and their parents bred cattle. So they grow up on a small farm in the middle of nowhere.

The only possible entertainment in the area is going night after night to Joe's Bar, about three miles from the farm.

There, they drink their first beers and throw their first punches. Two out of every three nights end up in a fight.

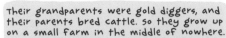

Apart from the evening brawls, life is peaceful there, and when they aren't at Joe's Bar, the brothers like to go on quiet walks through the desolate landscape.

On one such night they have an almost mystical revelation, realizing that the world is vast and that perhaps they should see more of it.

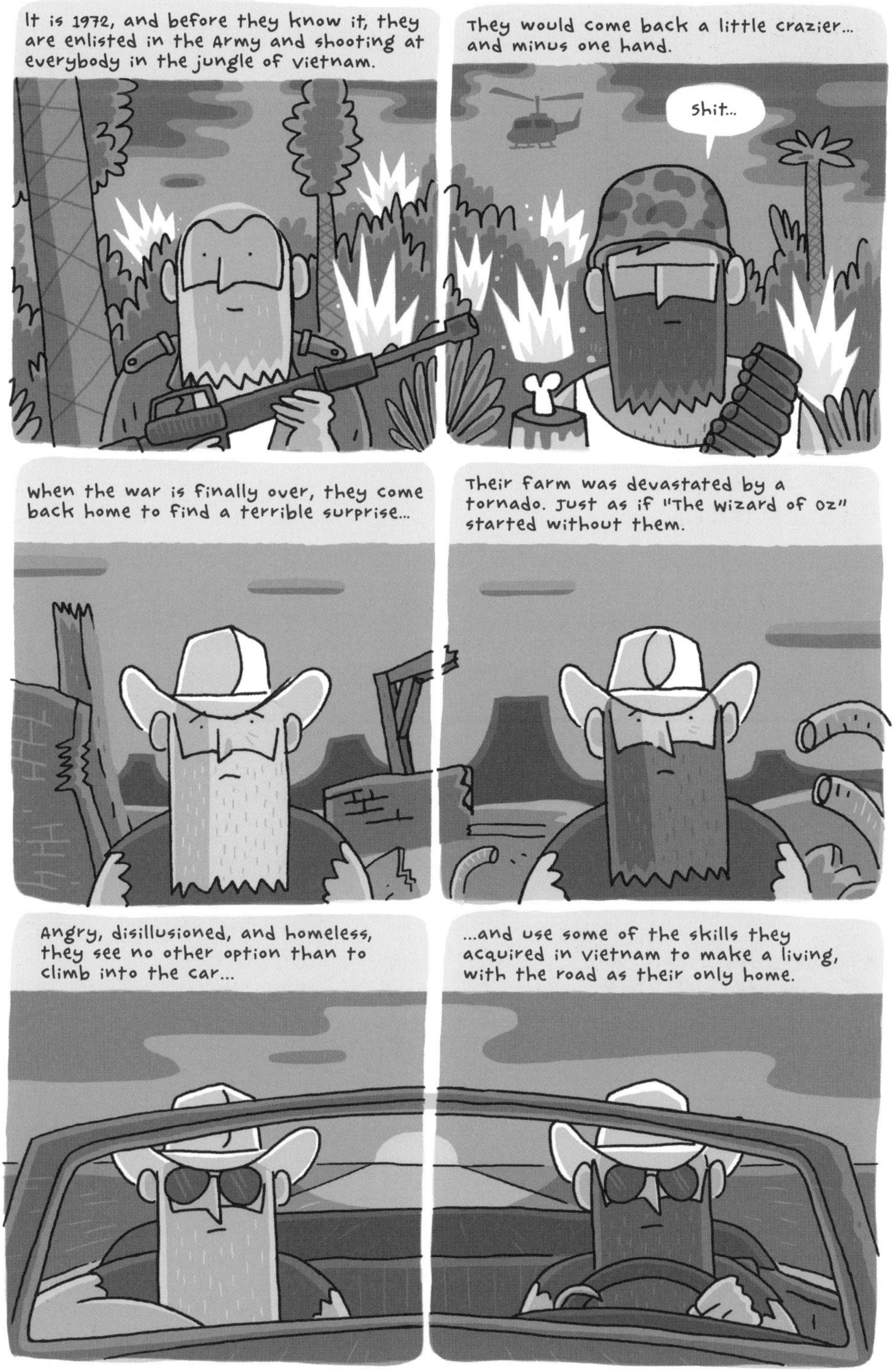

It is 1972, and before they know it, they are enlisted in the Army and shooting at everybody in the jungle of vietnam.
They would come back a little crazier... and minus one hand.
shit..
when the war is finally over, they come back home to find a terrible surprise...
Their farm was devastated by a tornado. Just as if "The Wizard of Oz" started without them.
Angry, disillusioned, and homeless, they see no other option than to climb into the car...
...and use some of the skills they acquired in vietnam to make a living, with the road as their only home.

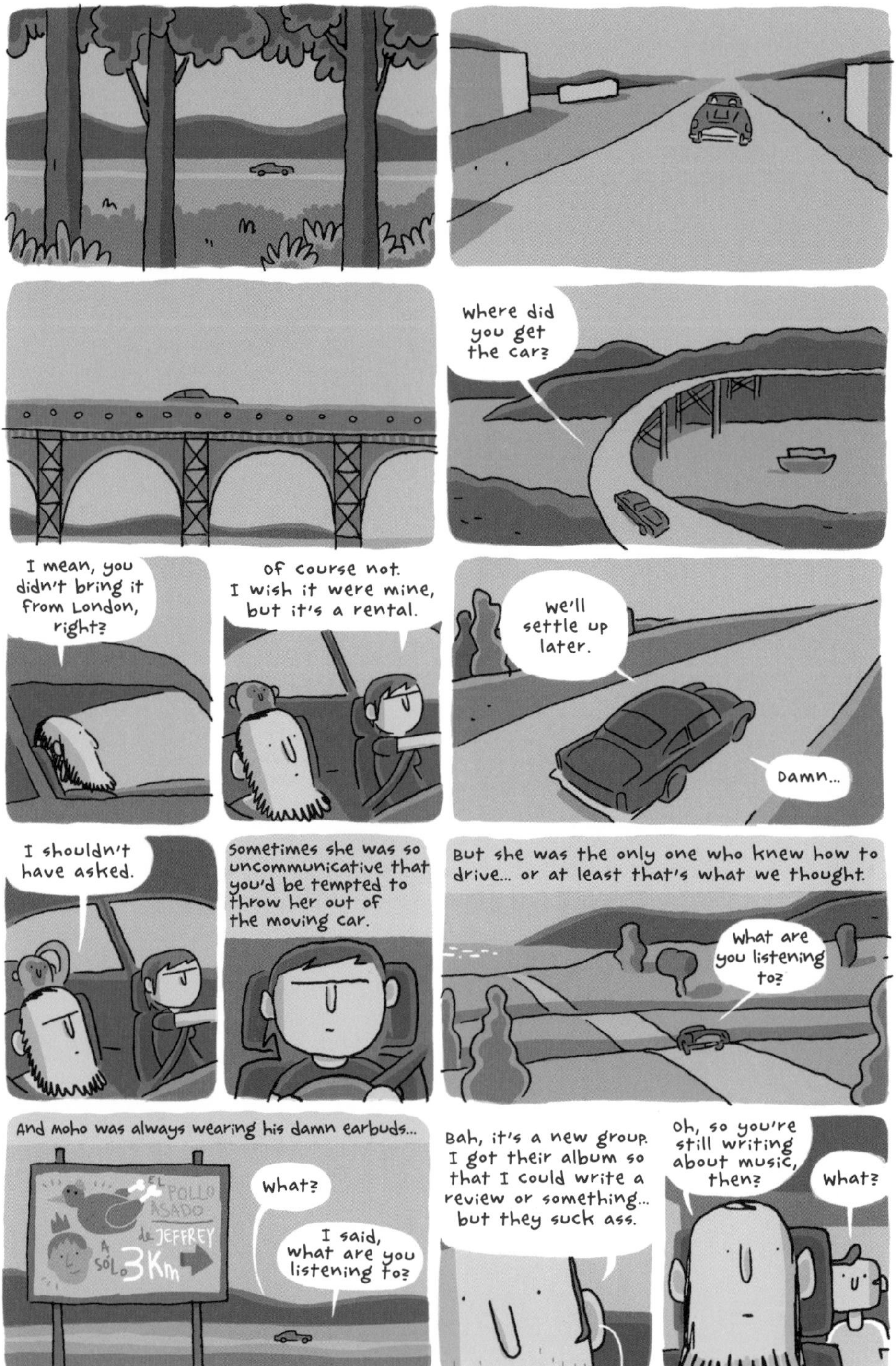
Where did you get the car?
I mean, you didn't bring it from London, right?
Of course not. I wish it were mine, but it's a rental.
We'll settle up later.
Damn...
I shouldn't have asked.
Sometimes she was so uncommunicative that you'd be tempted to throw her out of the moving car.
But she was the only one who knew how to drive... or at least that's what we thought.
What are you listening to?
And Moho was always wearing his damn earbuds...
EL POLLO ASADO de JEFFREY A SÓLO 3Km
What?
I said, what are you listening to?
Bah, it's a new group. I got their album so that I could write a review or something... but they suck ass.
Oh, so you're still writing about music, then?
What?

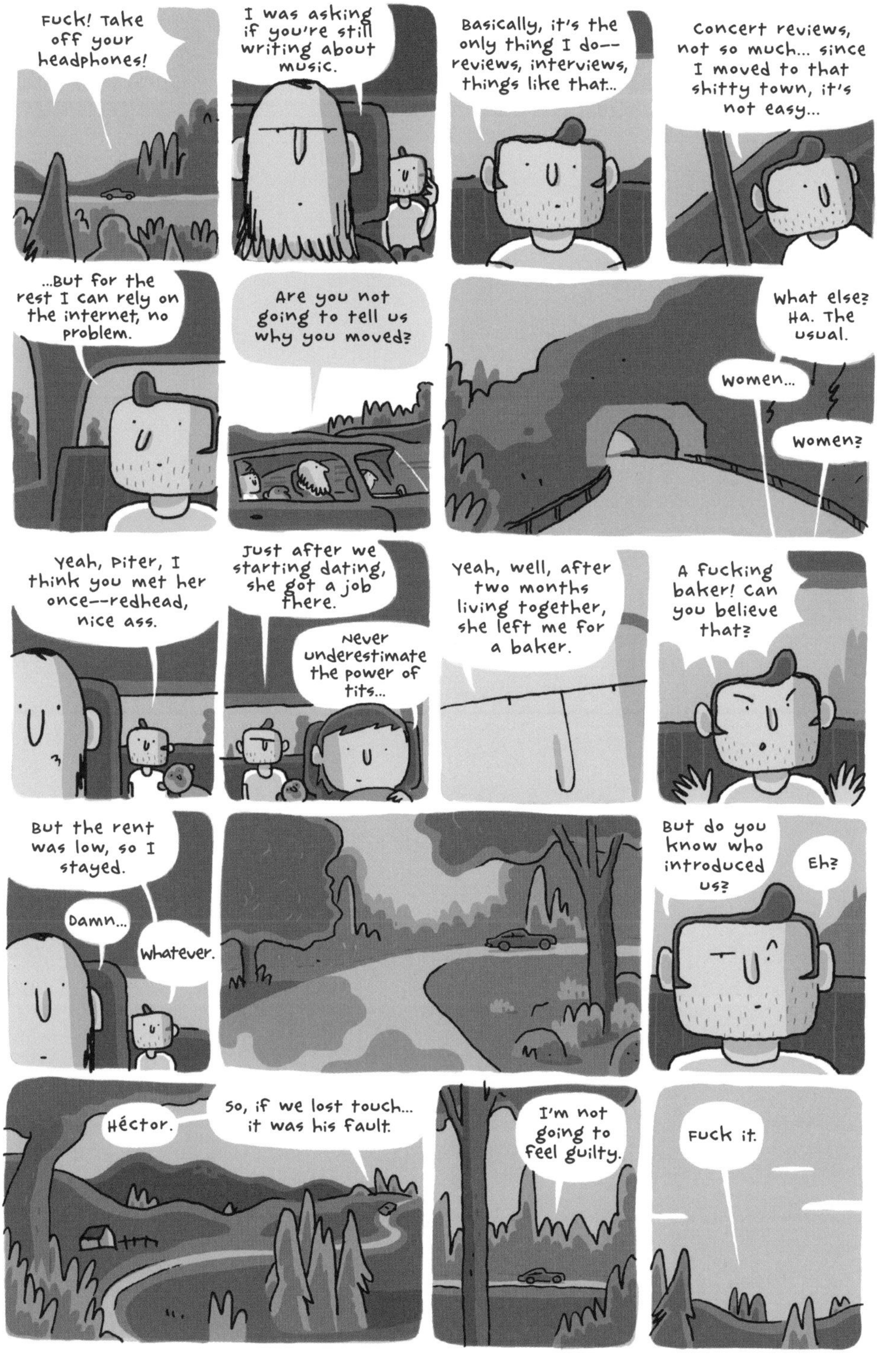
Fuck! Take off your headphones!
I was asking if you're still writing about music.
Basically, it's the only thing I do--reviews, interviews, things like that...
Concert reviews, not so much... since I moved to that shitty town, it's not easy...
...But for the rest I can rely on the internet, no problem.
Are you not going to tell us why you moved?
What else? Ha. The usual.
Women...
Women?
Yeah, Piter, I think you met her once--redhead, nice ass.
Just after we starting dating, she got a job there.
Never underestimate the power of tits...
Yeah, well, after two months living together, she left me for a baker.
A fucking baker! Can you believe that?
But the rent was low, so I stayed.
Damn...
Whatever.
But do you know who introduced us?
Eh?
Héctor.
So, if we lost touch... it was his fault.
I'm not going to feel guilty.
Fuck it.

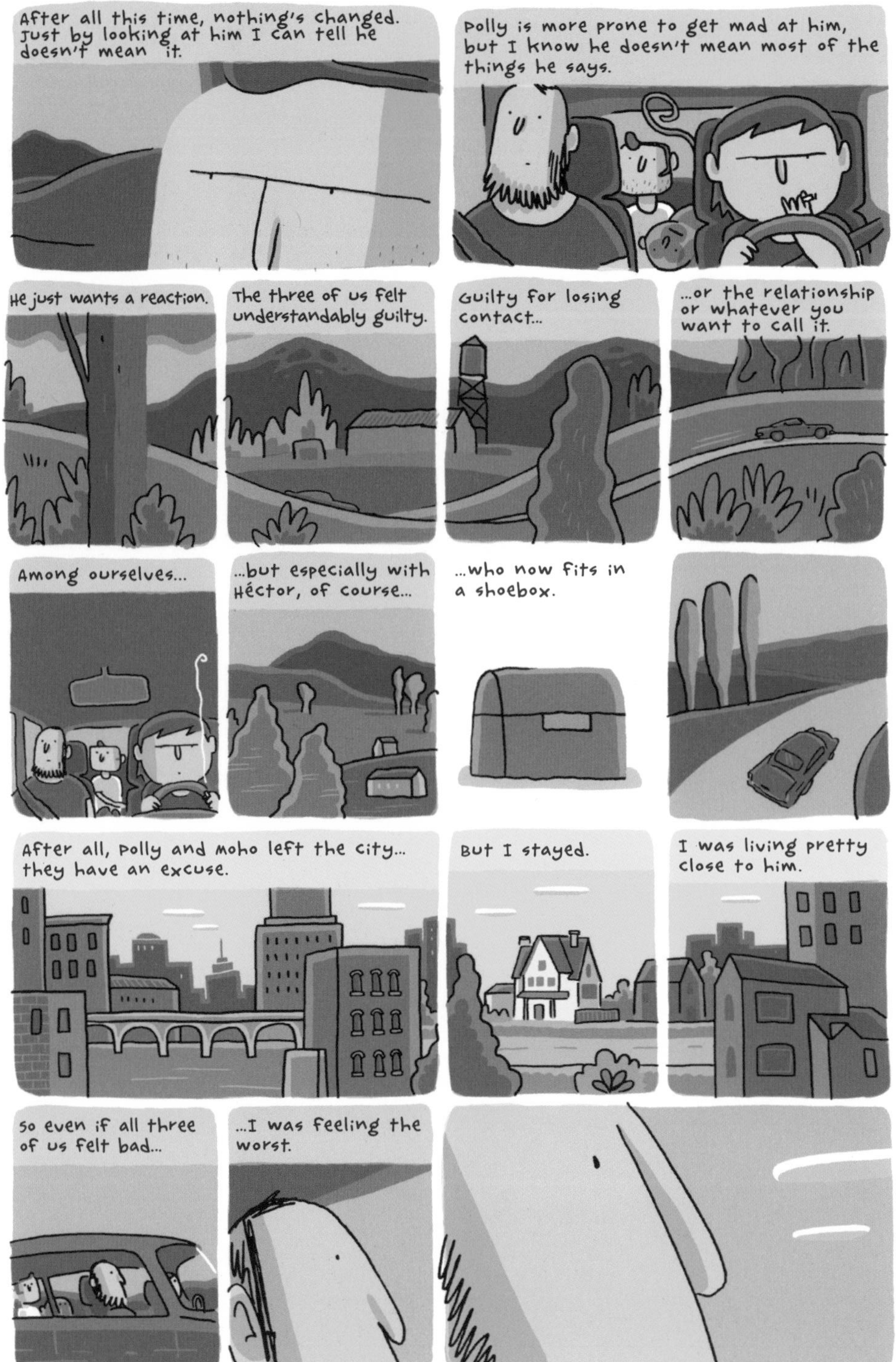
After all this time, nothing's changed. Just by looking at him I can tell he doesn't mean it.
Polly is more prone to get mad at him, but I know he doesn't mean most of the things he says.
He just wants a reaction.
The three of us felt understandably guilty.
Guilty for losing contact...
...or the relationship or whatever you want to call it.
Among ourselves...
...but especially with Héctor, of course...
...who now fits in a shoebox.
After all, Polly and Moho left the city... they have an excuse.
But I stayed.
I was living pretty close to him.
So even if all three of us felt bad...
...I was feeling the worst.

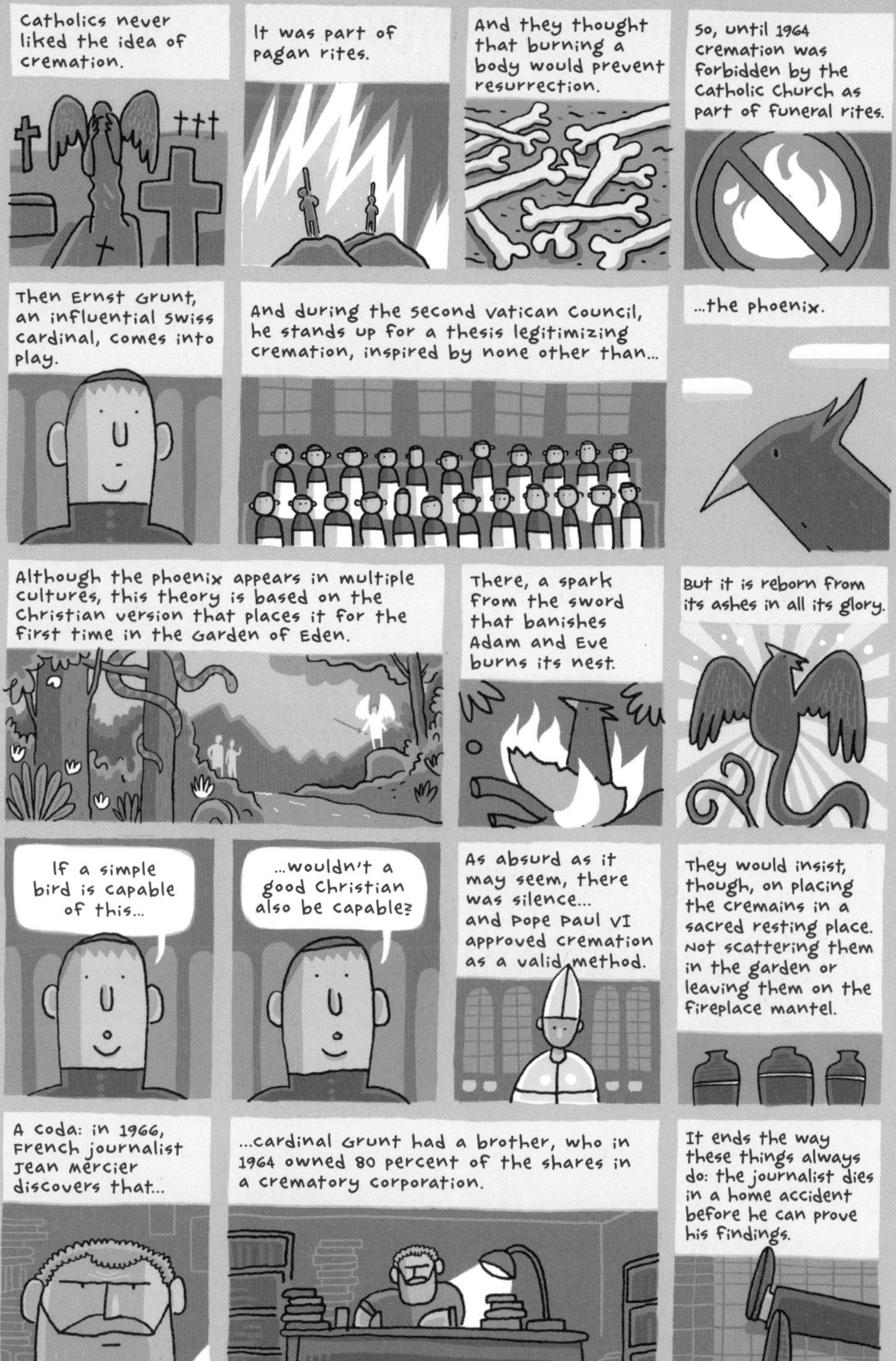
Catholics never liked the idea of cremation.
It was part of pagan rites.
And they thought that burning a body would prevent resurrection.
So, until 1964 cremation was forbidden by the Catholic Church as part of funeral rites.
Then Ernst Grunt, an influential Swiss cardinal, comes into play.
And during the Second Vatican Council, he stands up for a thesis legitimizing cremation, inspired by none other than...
...the phoenix.
Although the phoenix appears in multiple cultures, this theory is based on the Christian version that places it for the first time in the Garden of Eden.
There, a spark from the sword that banishes Adam and Eve burns its nest.
But it is reborn from its ashes in all its glory.
If a simple bird is capable of this...
...wouldn't a good Christian also be capable?
As absurd as it may seem, there was silence... and Pope Paul VI approved cremation as a valid method.
They would insist, though, on placing the cremains in a sacred resting place. Not scattering them in the garden or leaving them on the fireplace mantel.
A coda: in 1966, French journalist Jean Mercier discovers that...
...Cardinal Grunt had a brother, who in 1964 owned 80 percent of the shares in a crematory corporation.
It ends the way these things always do: the journalist dies in a home accident before he can prove his findings.

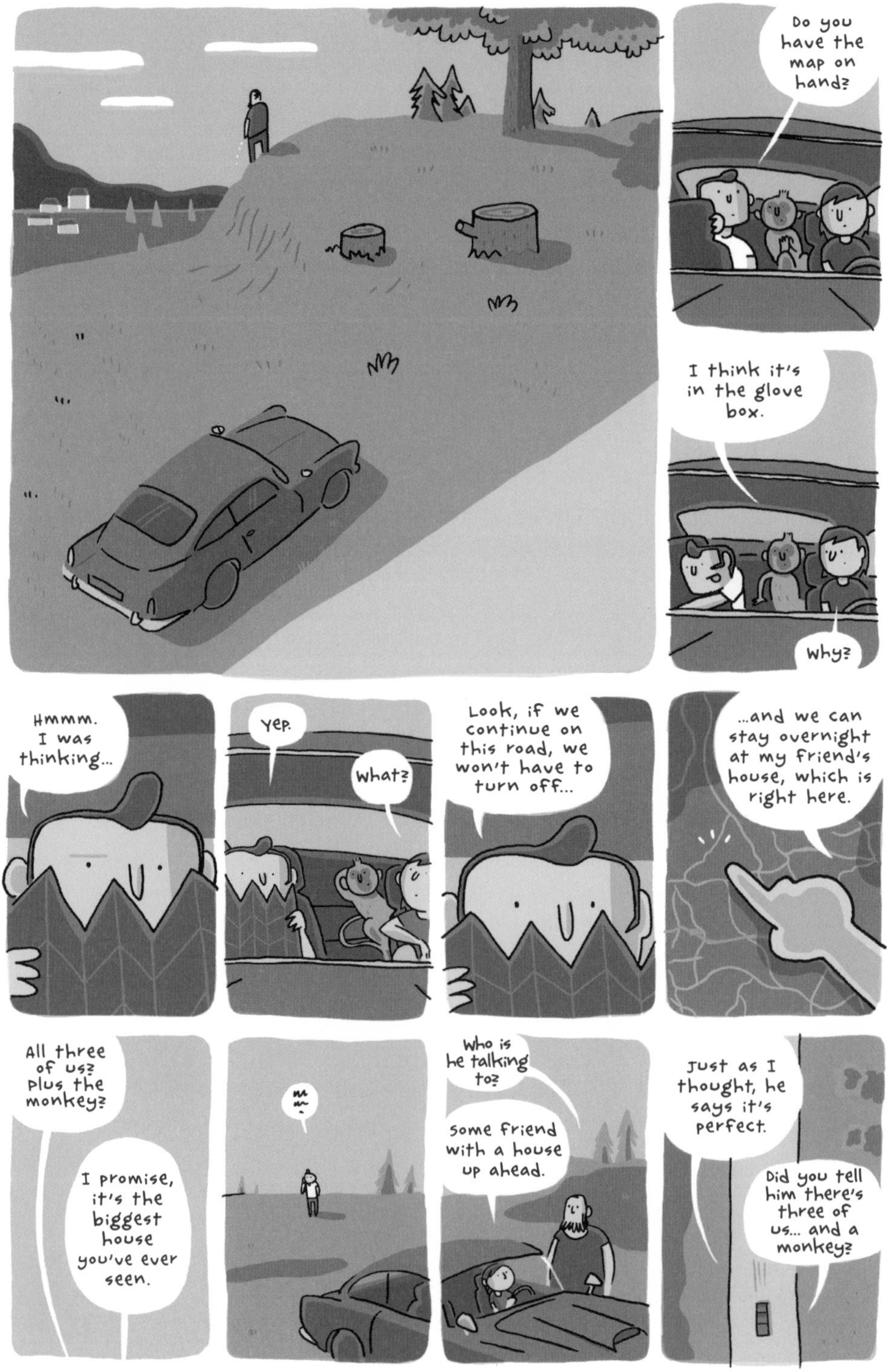

Do you have the map on hand?
I think it's in the glove box.
Why?
Hmmm. I was thinking...
Yep.
What?
Look, if we continue on this road, we won't have to turn off...
...and we can stay overnight at my friend's house, which is right here.
All three of us? Plus the monkey?
I promise, it's the biggest house you've ever seen.
Who is he talking to?
Some friend with a house up ahead.
Just as I thought, he says it's perfect.
Did you tell him there's three of us... and a monkey?

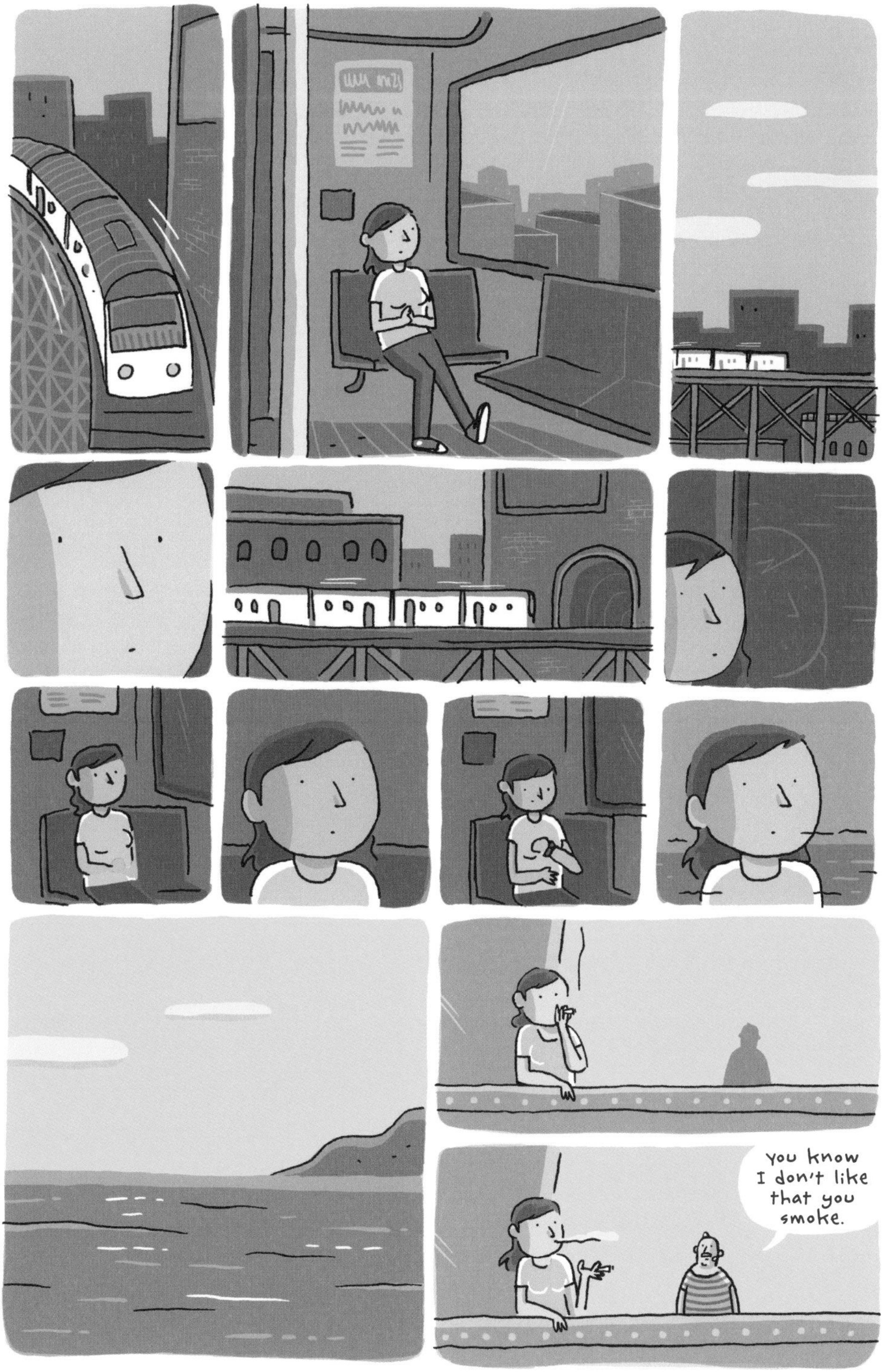
you know I don't like that you smoke.

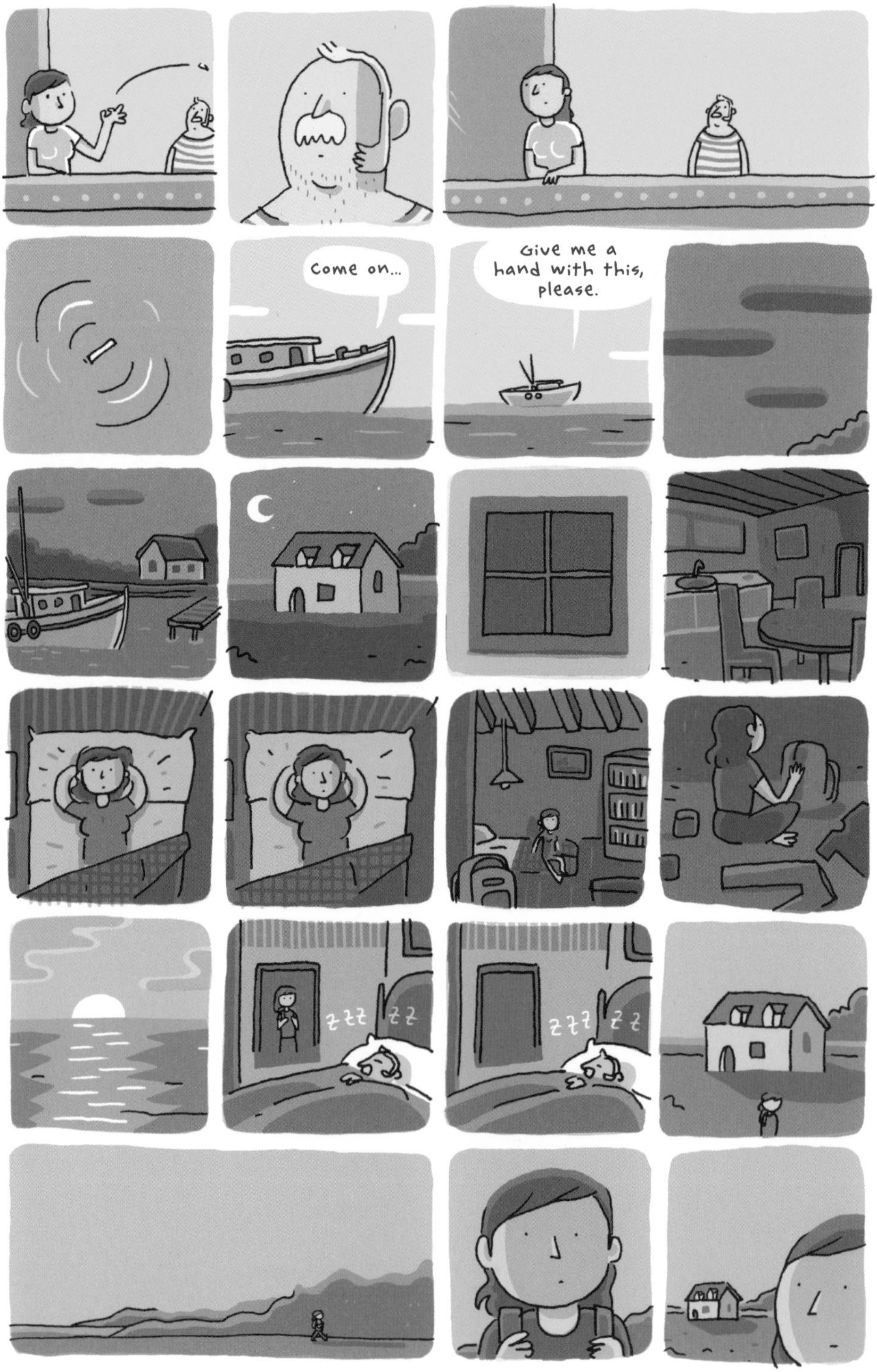
Come on...
Give me a hand with this, please.
z z z z z
z z z z z

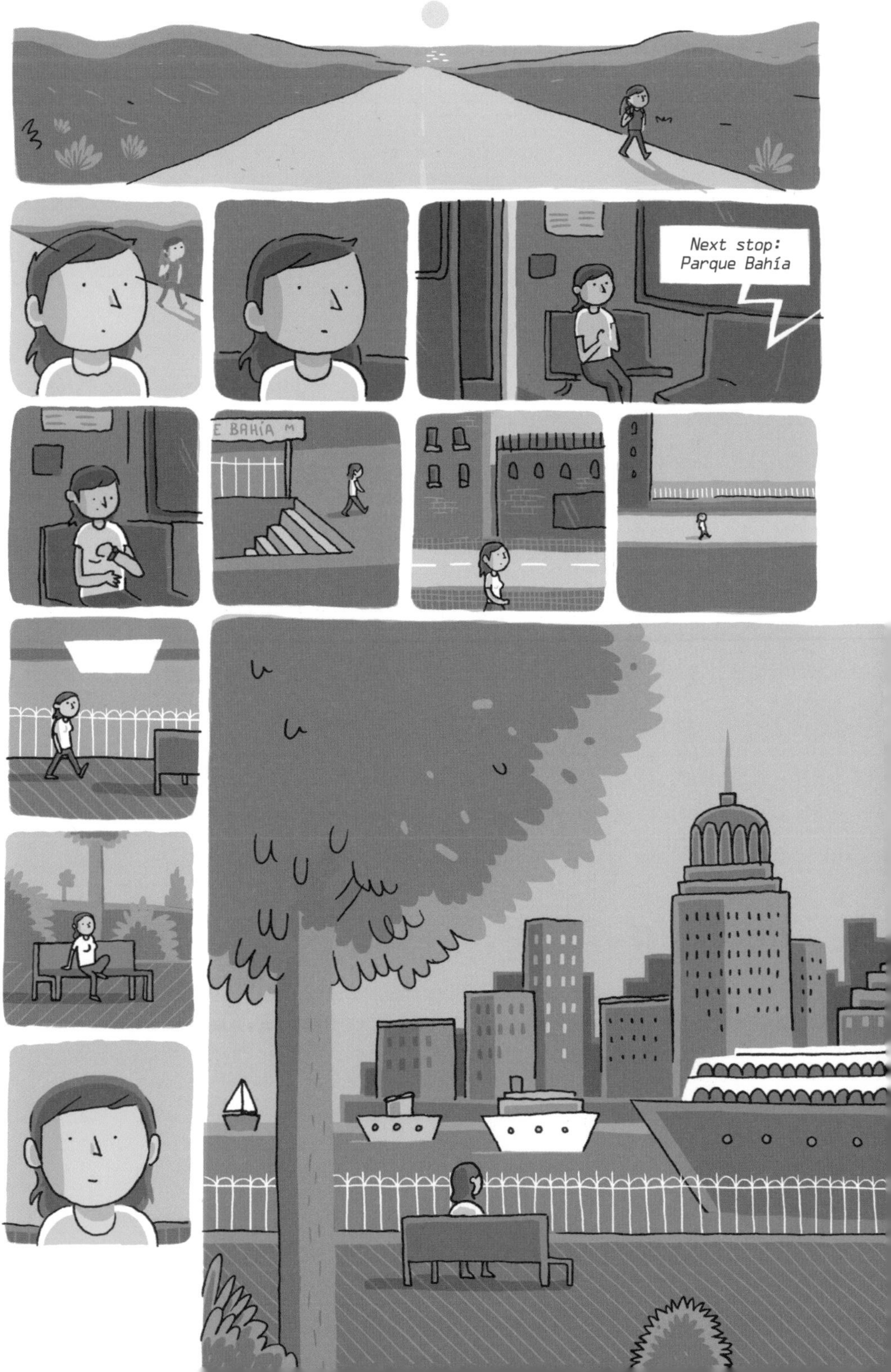
Next stop:
Parque Bahía
E BAHÍA M

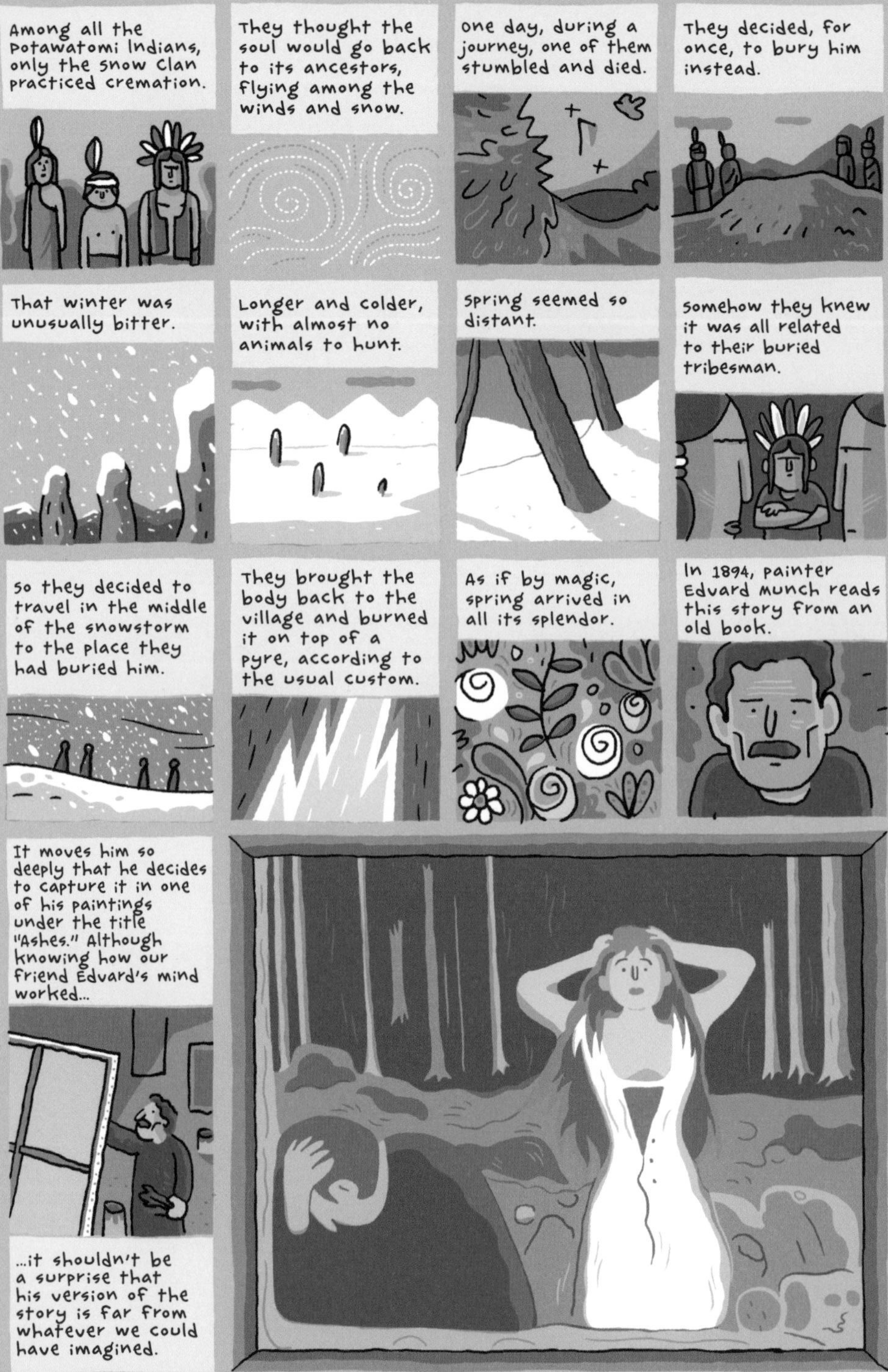
Among all the Potawatomi Indians, only the Snow Clan practiced cremation.
They thought the soul would go back to its ancestors, flying among the winds and snow.
One day, during a journey, one of them stumbled and died.
They decided, for once, to bury him instead.
That winter was unusually bitter.
Longer and colder, with almost no animals to hunt.
Spring seemed so distant.
Somehow they knew it was all related to their buried tribesman.
So they decided to travel in the middle of the snowstorm to the place they had buried him.
They brought the body back to the village and burned it on top of a pyre, according to the usual custom.
As if by magic, spring arrived in all its splendor.
In 1894, painter Edvard Munch reads this story from an old book.
It moves him so deeply that he decides to capture it in one of his paintings under the title "Ashes." Although knowing how our friend Edvard's mind worked...
...it shouldn't be a surprise that his version of the story is far from whatever we could have imagined.

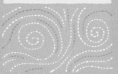

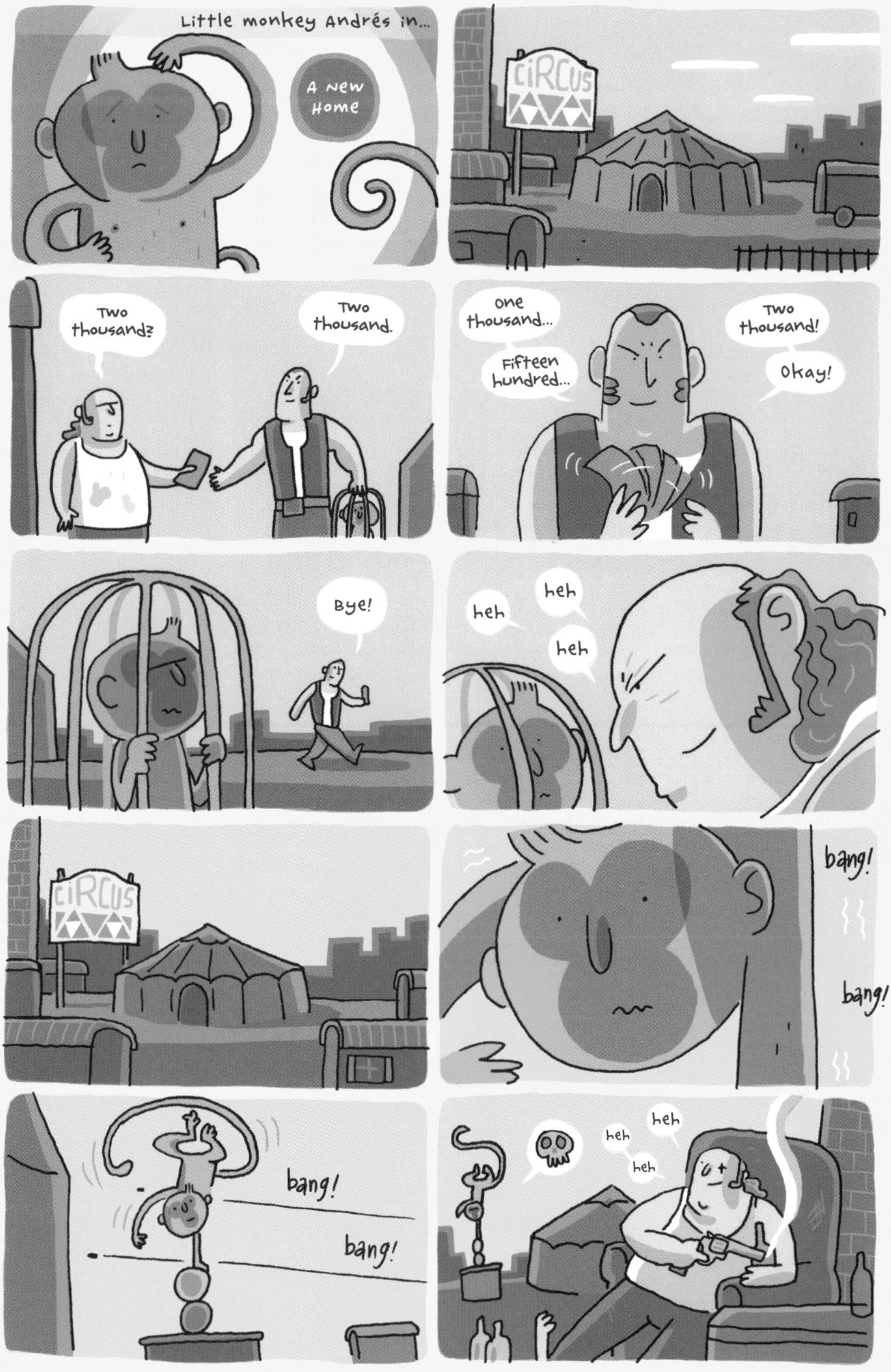
Little monkey Andrés in...
A New Home
CiRCUS
Two thousand?
Two thousand.
One thousand...
Fifteen hundred...
Two thousand!
Okay!
Bye!
heh
heh
heh
CiRCUS
bang!
bang!
bang!
bang!
heh
heh
heh

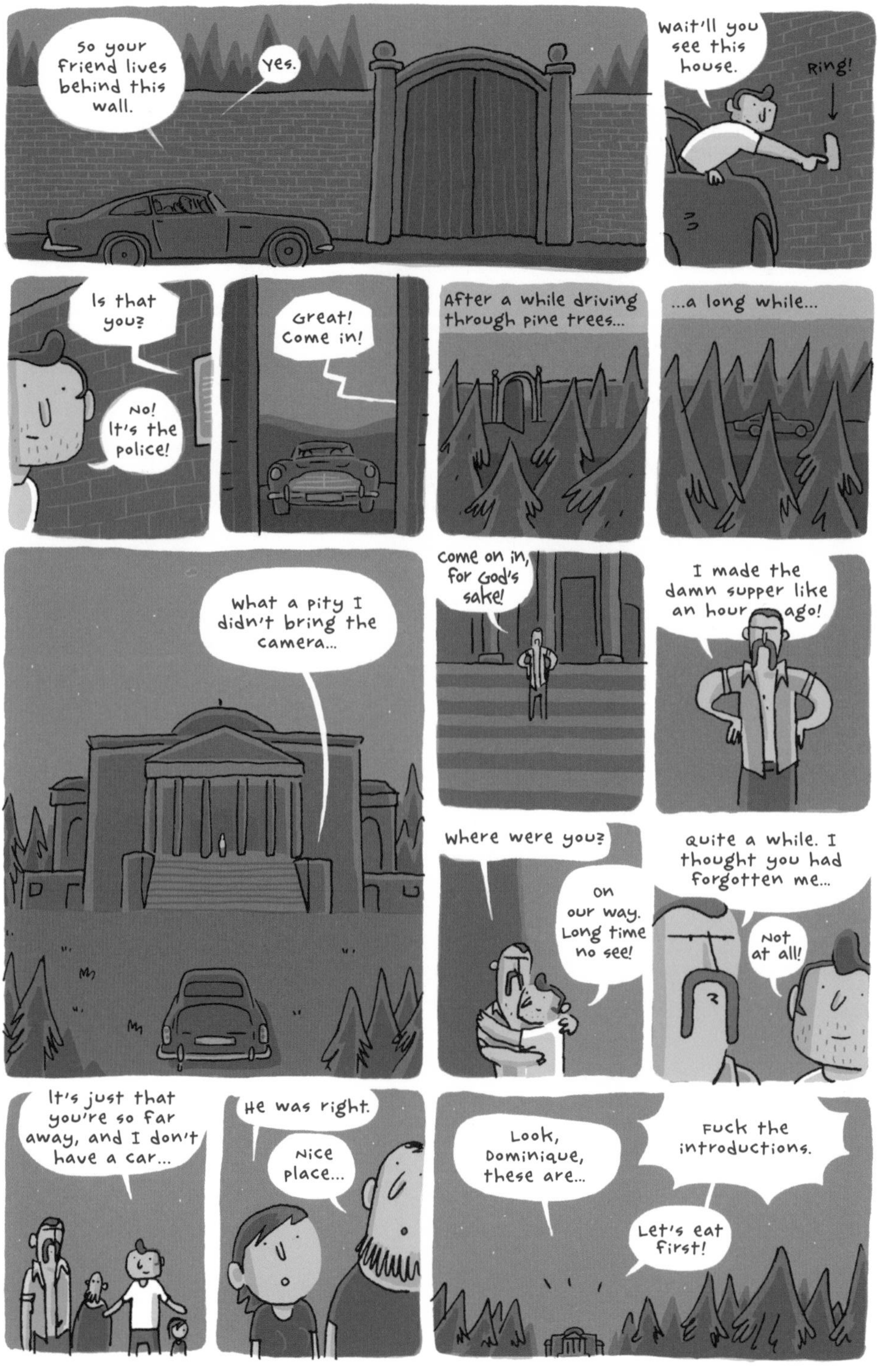
So your friend lives behind this wall.
Yes.
Wait'll you see this house.
Ring!
Is that you?
No! It's the police!
Great! Come in!
After a while driving through pine trees...
...a long while...
What a pity I didn't bring the camera...
Come on in, for God's sake!
I made the damn supper like an hour ago!
Where were you?
On our way. Long time no see!
Quite a while. I thought you had forgotten me...
Not at all!
It's just that you're so far away, and I don't have a car...
He was right.
Nice place...
Look, Dominique, these are...
Fuck the introductions.
Let's eat first!

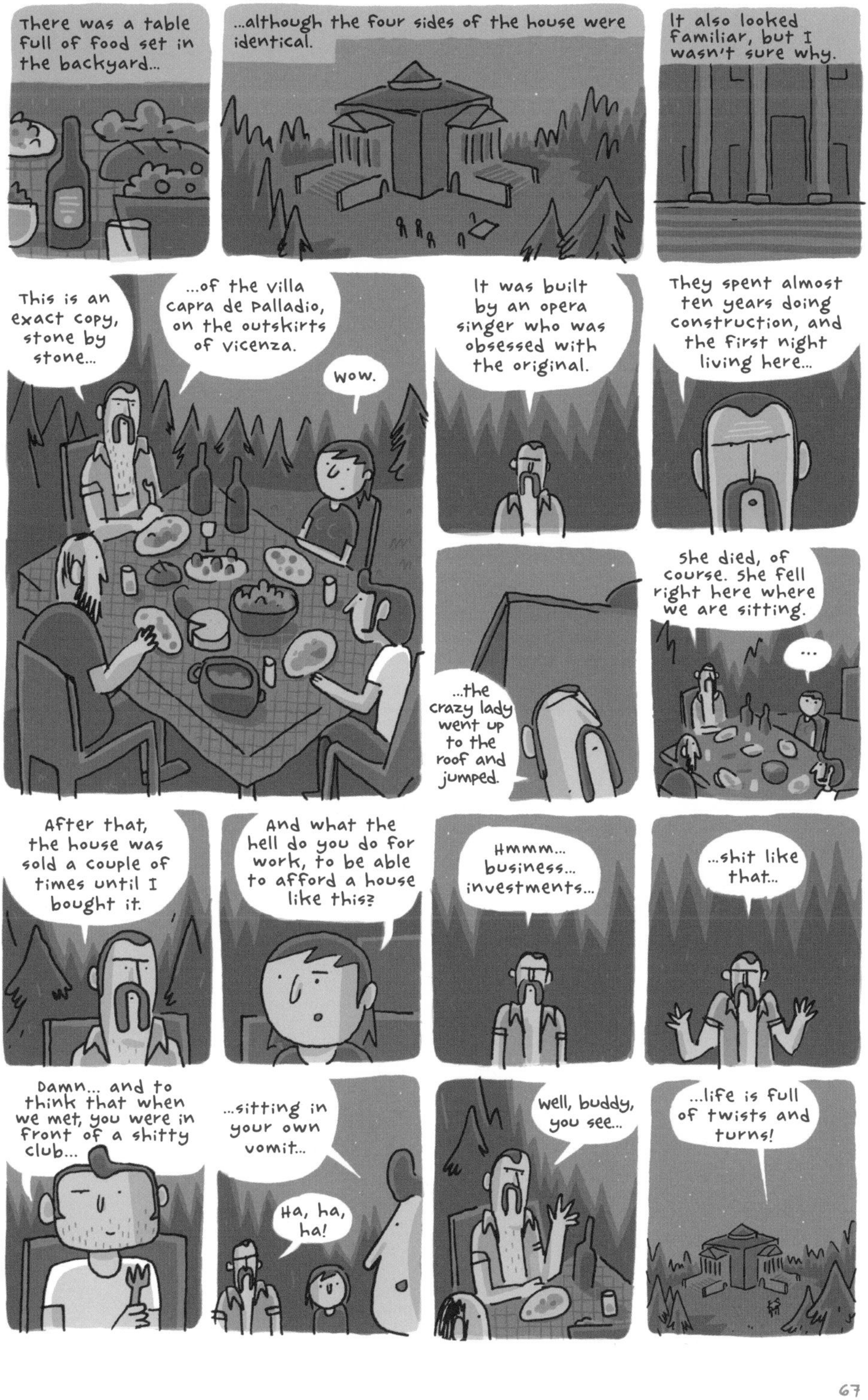
There was a table full of food set in the backyard...
...although the four sides of the house were identical.
It also looked familiar, but I wasn't sure why.
This is an exact copy, stone by stone...
...of the villa capra de palladio, on the outskirts of vicenza.
Wow.
It was built by an opera singer who was obsessed with the original.
They spent almost ten years doing construction, and the first night living here...
...the crazy lady went up to the roof and jumped.
She died, of course. She fell right here where we are sitting.
...
After that, the house was sold a couple of times until I bought it.
And what the hell do you do for work, to be able to afford a house like this?
Hmmm... business... investments...
...shit like that...
Damn... and to think that when we met, you were in front of a shitty club...
...sitting in your own vomit...
Ha, ha, ha!
Well, buddy, you see...
...life is full of twists and turns!

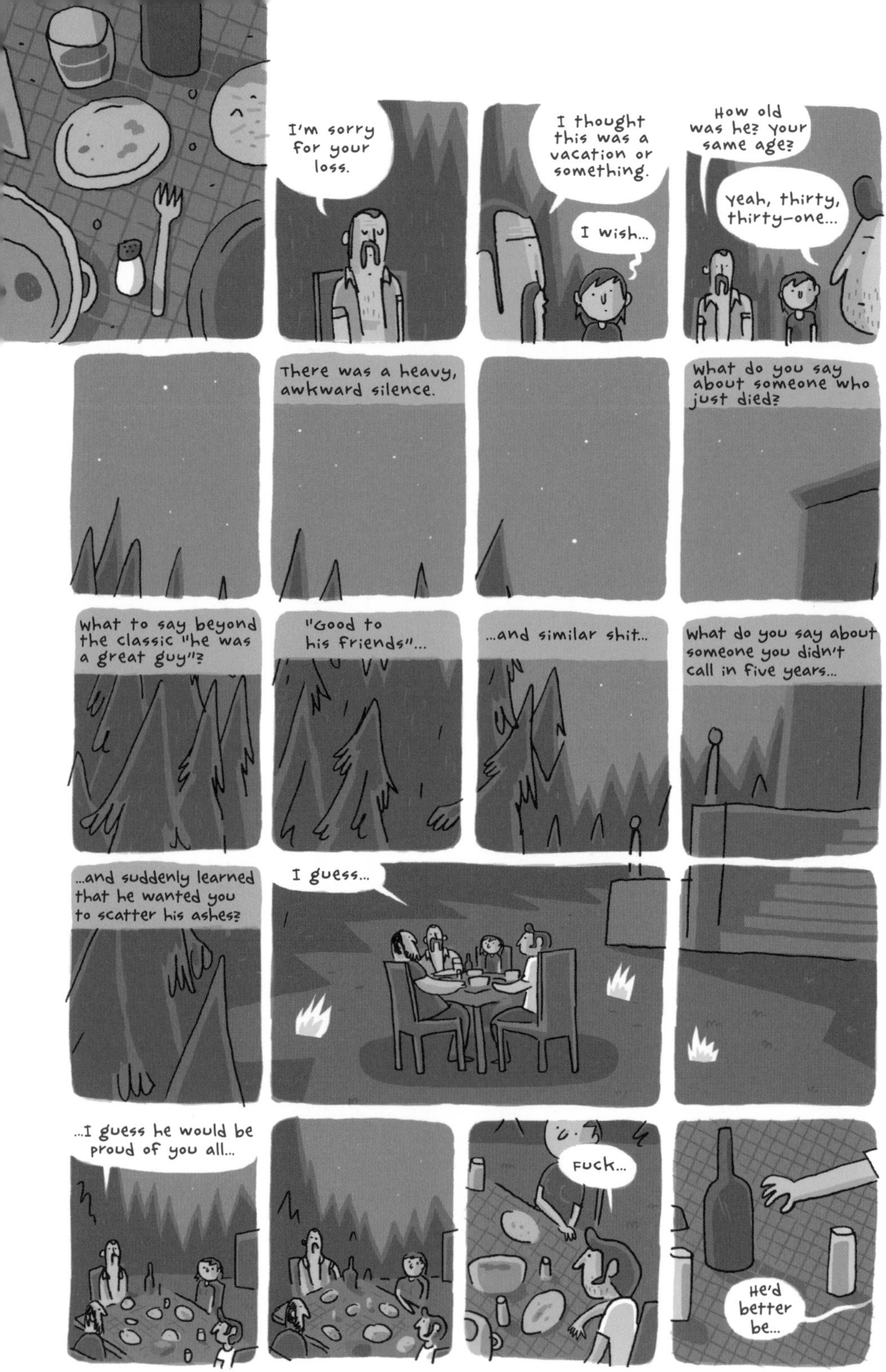
I'm sorry for your loss.
I thought this was a vacation or something.
I wish...
How old was he? Your same age?
Yeah, thirty, thirty-one...
There was a heavy, awkward silence.
What do you say about someone who just died?
What to say beyond the classic "he was a great guy"?
"Good to his friends"...
...and similar shit...
What do you say about someone you didn't call in five years...
...and suddenly learned that he wanted you to scatter his ashes?
I guess...
...I guess he would be proud of you all...
Fuck...
He'd better be...

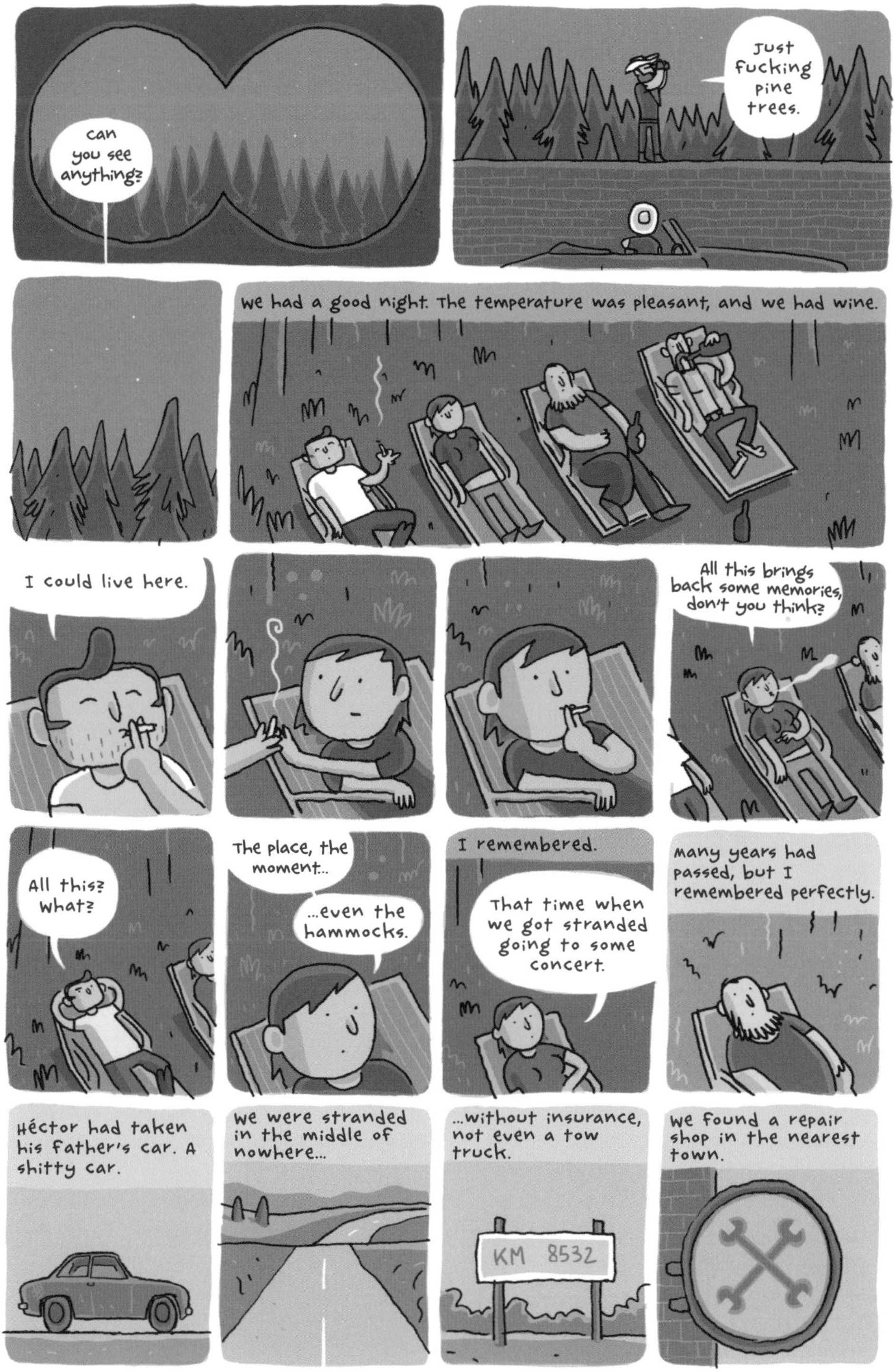
Can you see anything?
Just fucking pine trees.
We had a good night. The temperature was pleasant, and we had wine.
I could live here.
All this brings back some memories, don't you think?
All this? What?
The place, the moment...
...even the hammocks.
I remembered.
That time when we got stranded going to some concert.
Many years had passed, but I remembered perfectly.
Héctor had taken his father's car. A shitty car.
We were stranded in the middle of nowhere...
...without insurance, not even a tow truck.
KM 8532
We found a repair shop in the nearest town.

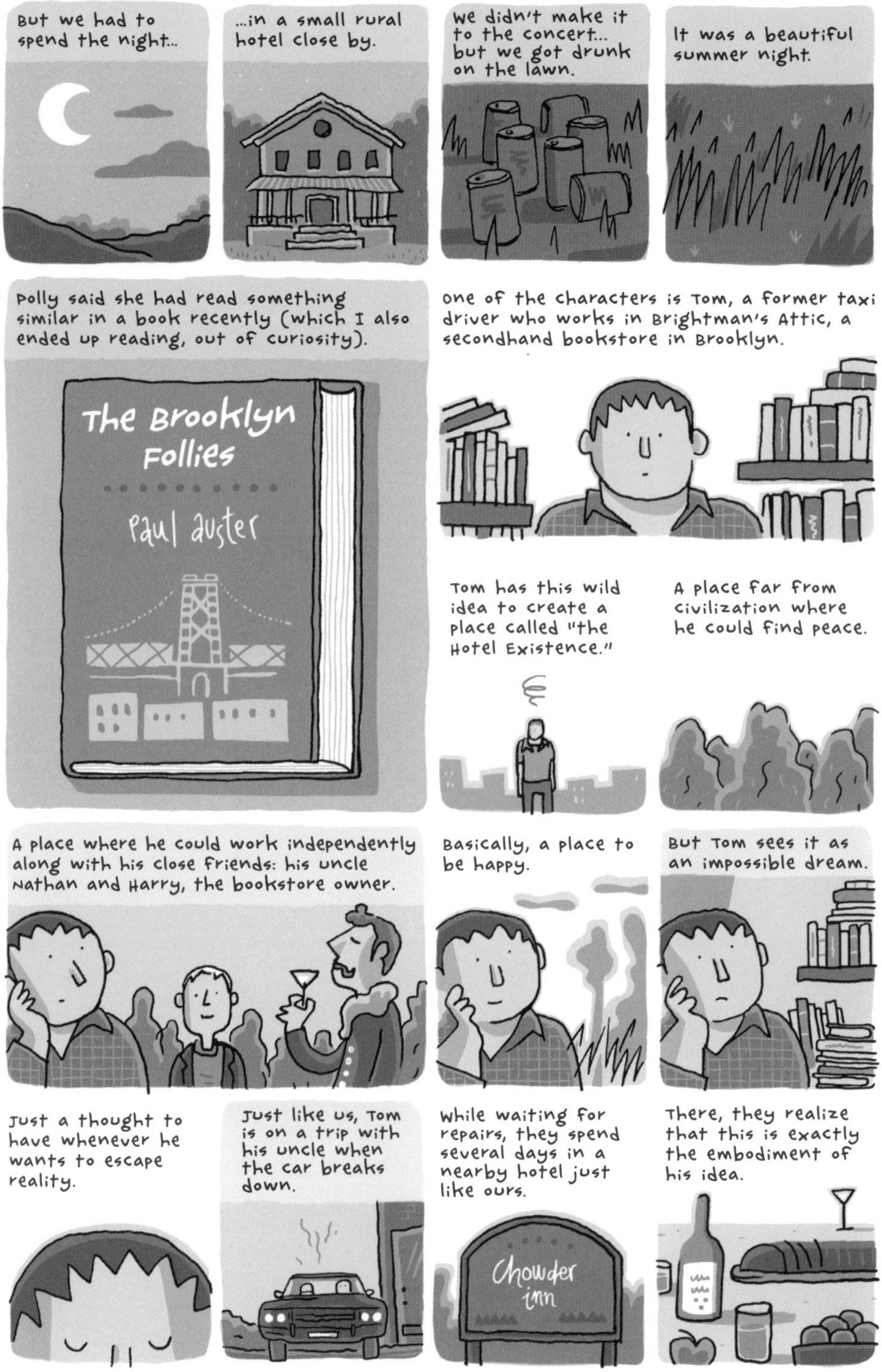
But we had to spend the night...
...in a small rural hotel close by.
We didn't make it to the concert... but we got drunk on the lawn.
It was a beautiful summer night.
Polly said she had read something similar in a book recently (which I also ended up reading, out of curiosity).
The Brooklyn Follies
paul auster
One of the characters is Tom, a former taxi driver who works in Brightman's Attic, a secondhand bookstore in Brooklyn.
Tom has this wild idea to create a place called "the Hotel Existence."
A place far from civilization where he could find peace.
A place where he could work independently along with his close friends: his uncle Nathan and Harry, the bookstore owner.
Basically, a place to be happy.
But Tom sees it as an impossible dream.
Just a thought to have whenever he wants to escape reality.
Just like us, Tom is on a trip with his uncle when the car breaks down.
While waiting for repairs, they spend several days in a nearby hotel just like ours.
Chowder inn
There, they realize that this is exactly the embodiment of his idea.

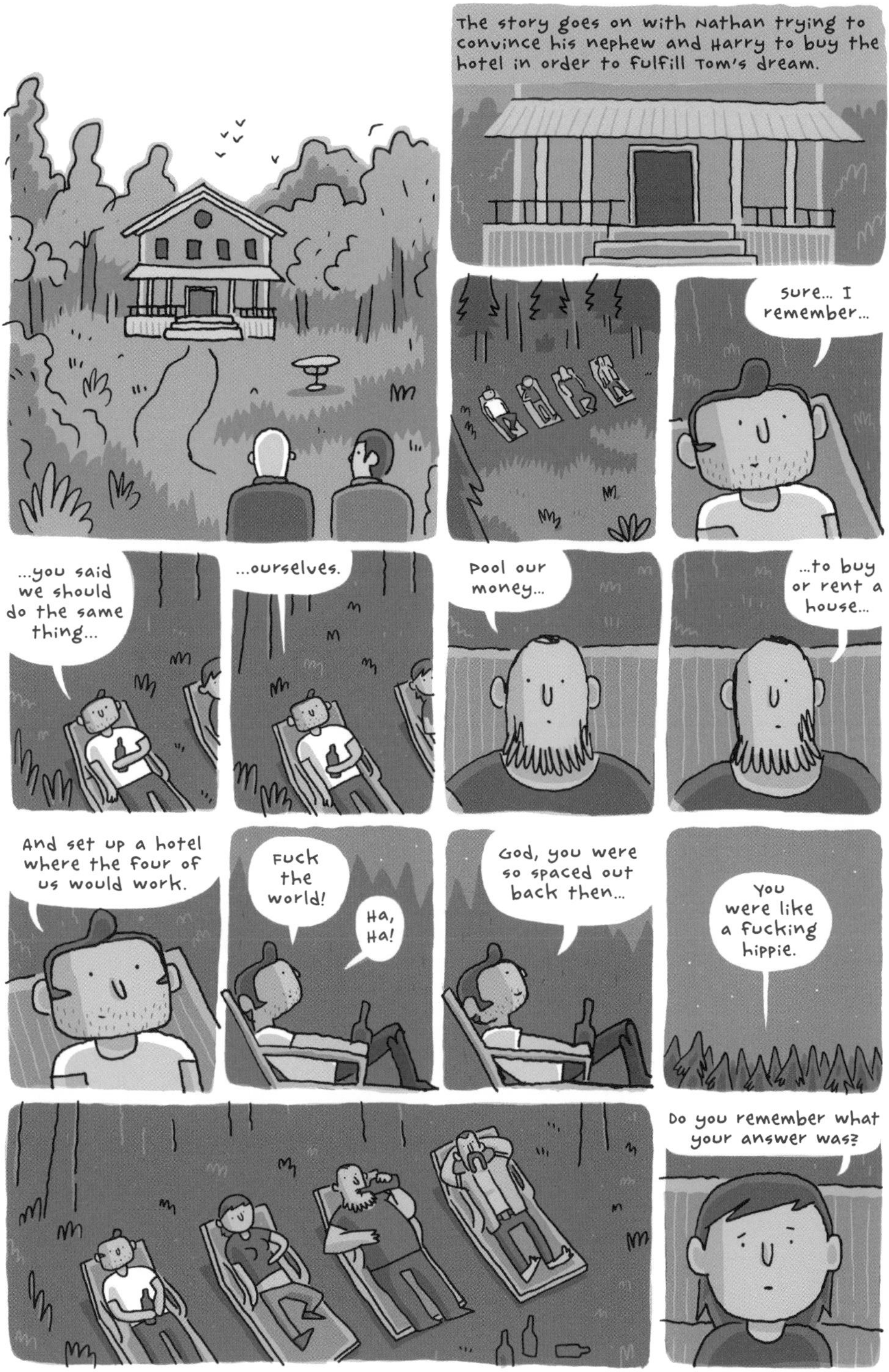
The story goes on with Nathan trying to convince his nephew and Harry to buy the hotel in order to fulfill Tom's dream.
Sure... I remember...
...you said we should do the same thing...
...ourselves.
Pool our money...
...to buy or rent a house...
And set up a hotel where the four of us would work.
Fuck the world!
Ha, Ha!
God, you were so spaced out back then...
You were like a fucking hippie.
Do you remember what your answer was?

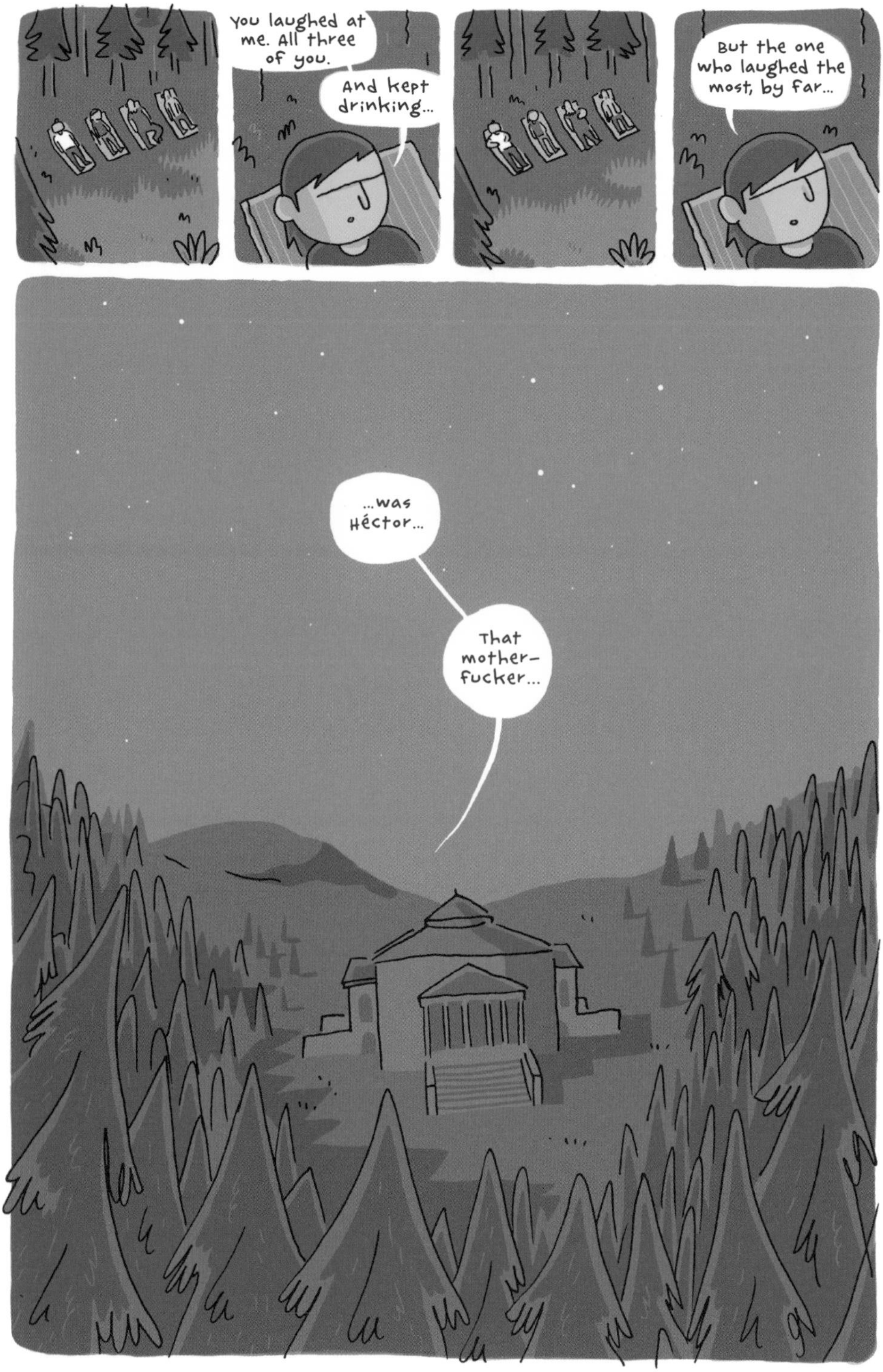
You laughed at me. All three of you.
And kept drinking...
But the one who laughed the most, by far...
...was Héctor...
That mother-fucker...

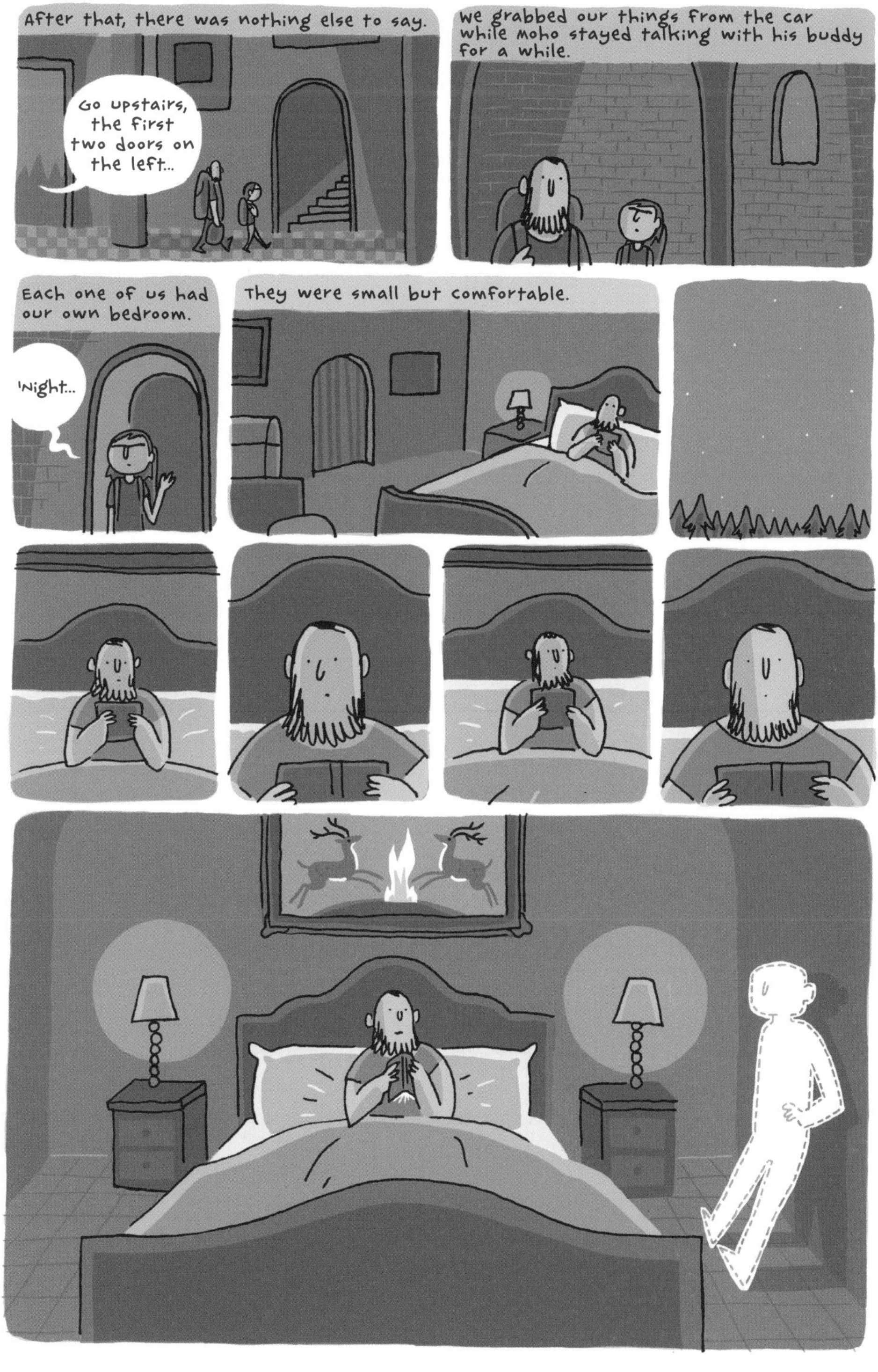
After that, there was nothing else to say.
Go upstairs, the first two doors on the left...
We grabbed our things from the car while Moho stayed talking with his buddy for a while.
Each one of us had our own bedroom.
'Night...
They were small but comfortable.

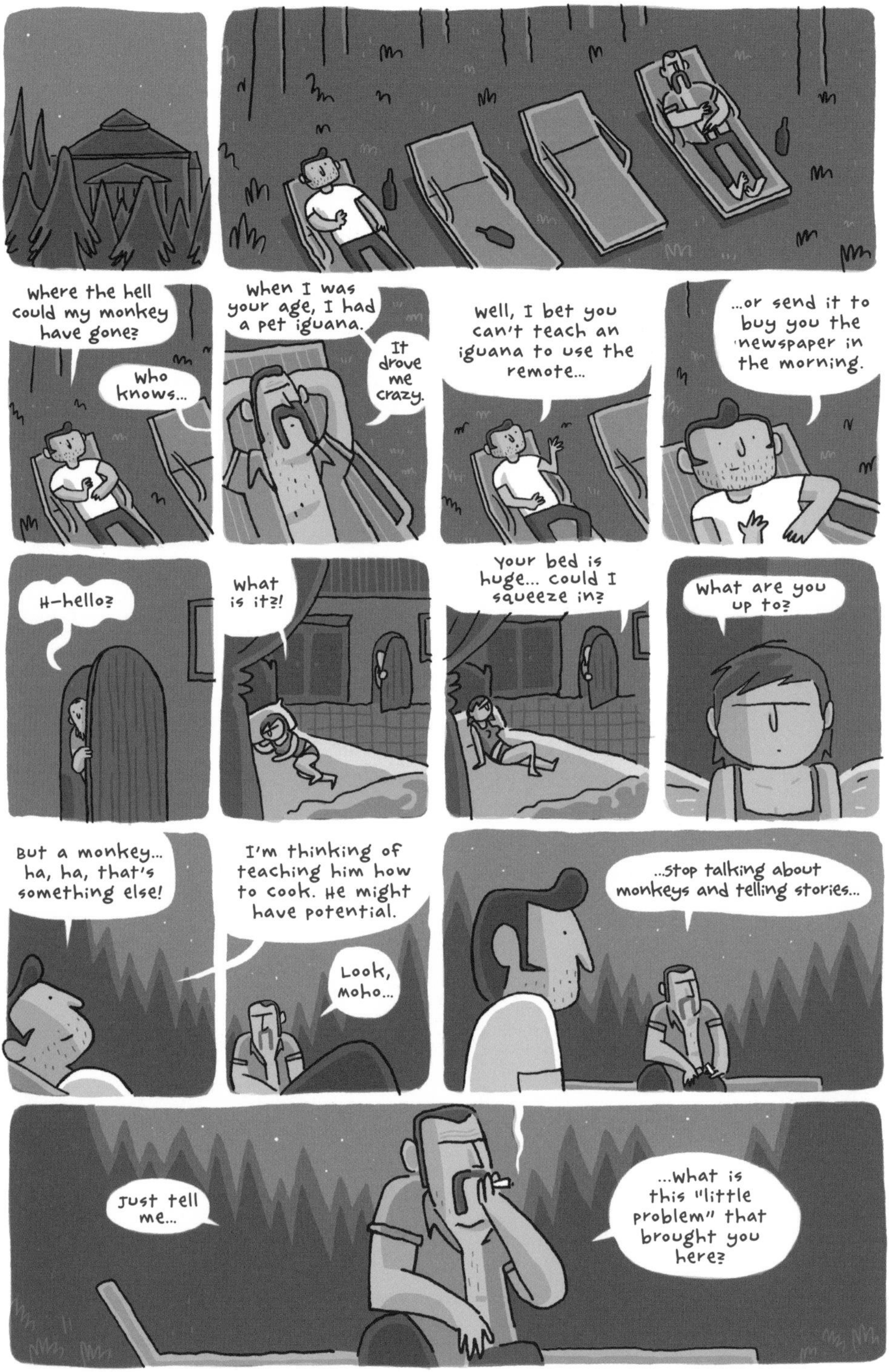
Where the hell could my monkey have gone?
Who knows...
When I was your age, I had a pet iguana.
It drove me crazy.
Well, I bet you can't teach an iguana to use the remote...
...or send it to buy you the newspaper in the morning.
H-hello?
What is it?!
Your bed is huge... could I squeeze in?
What are you up to?
But a monkey... ha, ha, that's something else!
I'm thinking of teaching him how to cook. He might have potential.
Look, Moho...
...stop talking about monkeys and telling stories...
Just tell me...
...what is this "little problem" that brought you here?

DAY 3

(in which things
start to go wrong)

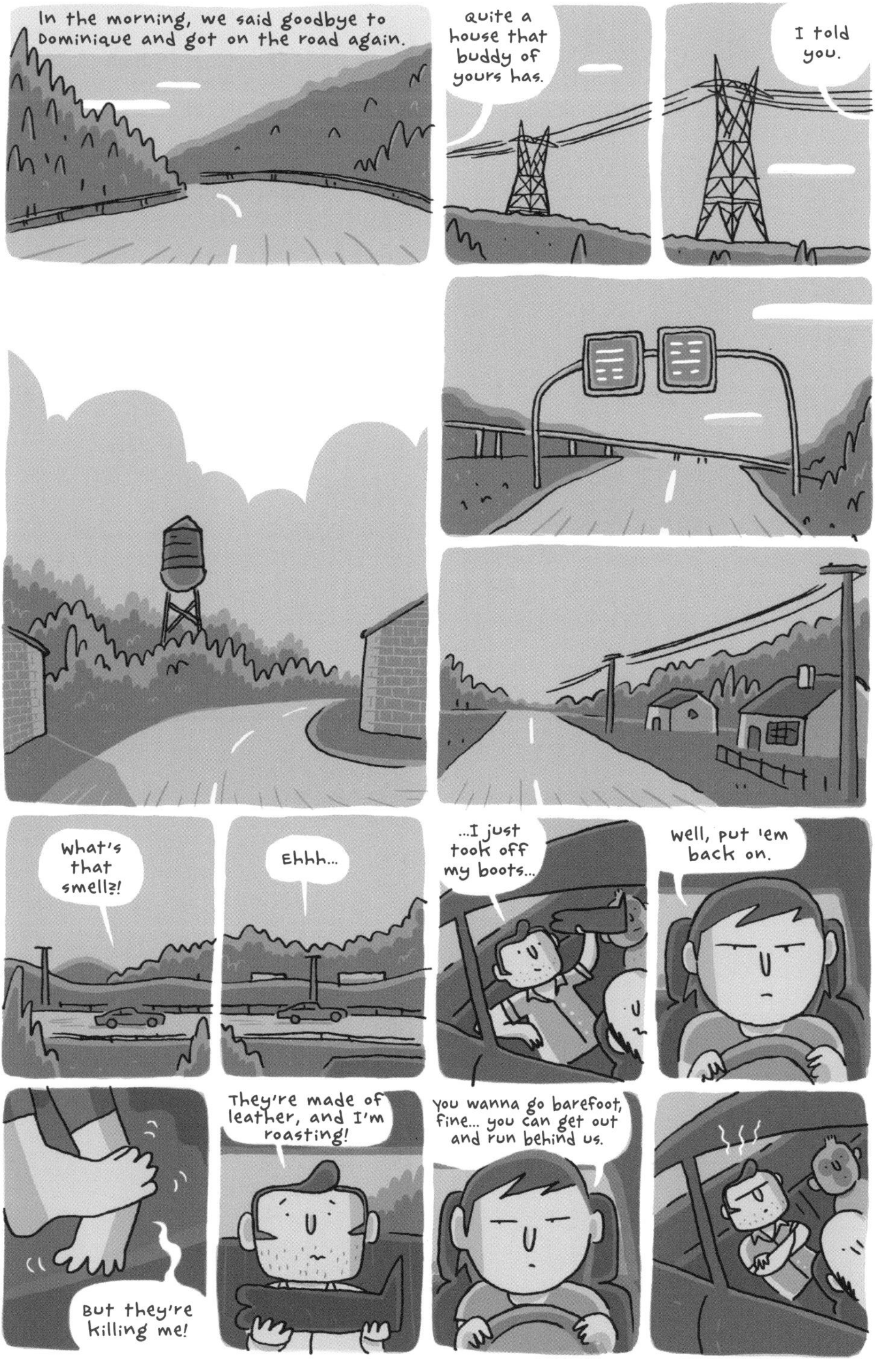
In the morning, we said goodbye to Dominique and got on the road again.
Quite a house that buddy of yours has.
I told you.
What's that smell?!
Ehhh...
...I just took off my boots...
Well, put 'em back on.
But they're killing me!
They're made of leather, and I'm roasting!
You wanna go barefoot, fine... you can get out and run behind us.

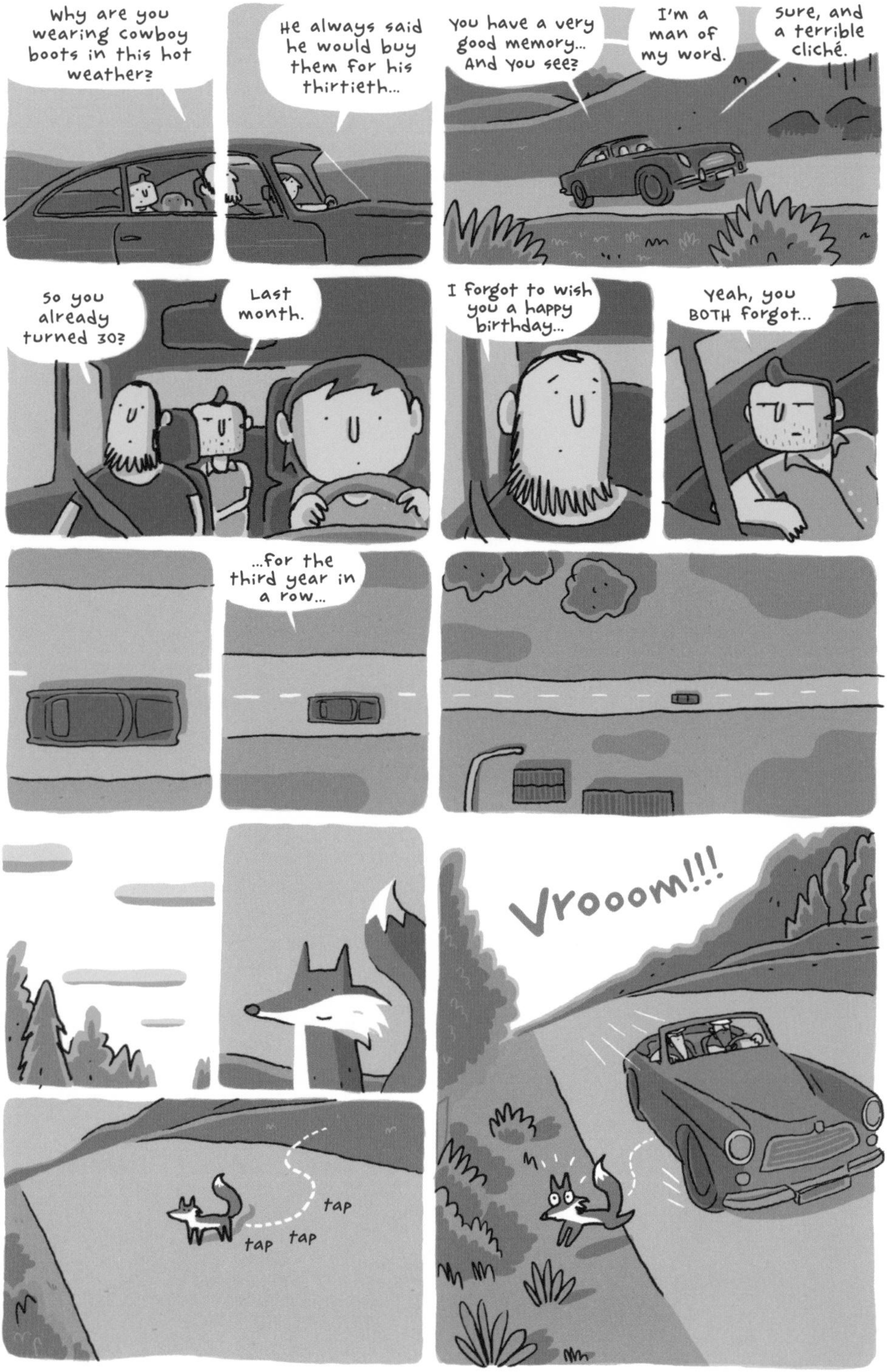
Why are you wearing cowboy boots in this hot weather?
He always said he would buy them for his thirtieth...
You have a very good memory... And you see?
I'm a man of my word.
Sure, and a terrible cliché.
So you already turned 30?
Last month.
I forgot to wish you a happy birthday...
Yeah, you BOTH forgot...
...for the third year in a row...
Vrooom!!!
tap
tap
tap

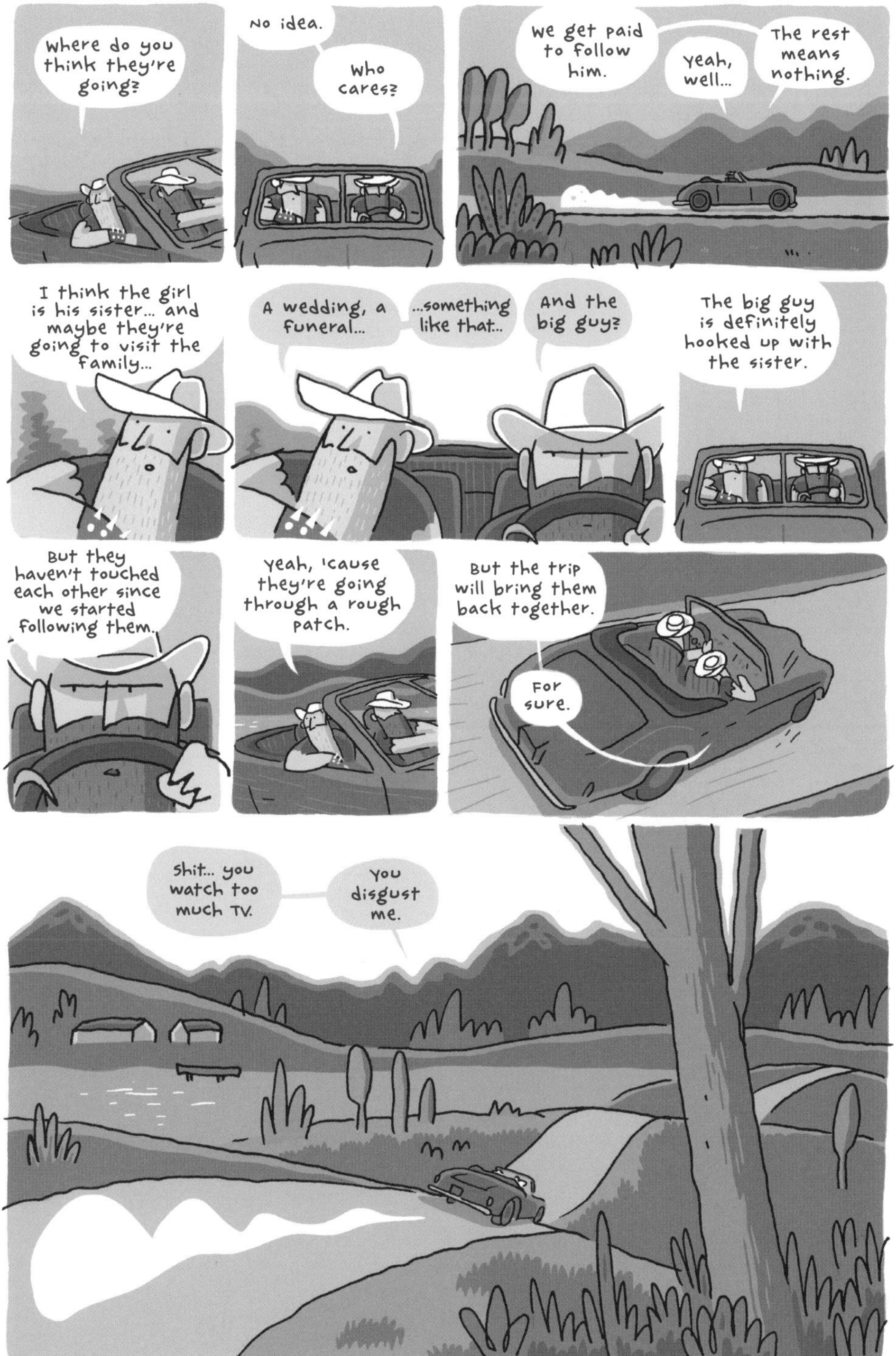
Where do you think they're going?
No idea.
Who cares?
We get paid to follow him.
Yeah, well...
The rest means nothing.
I think the girl is his sister... and maybe they're going to visit the family...
A wedding, a funeral...
...something like that...
And the big guy?
The big guy is definitely hooked up with the sister.
But they haven't touched each other since we started following them.
Yeah, 'cause they're going through a rough patch.
But the trip will bring them back together.
For sure.
Shit... you watch too much TV.
You disgust me.

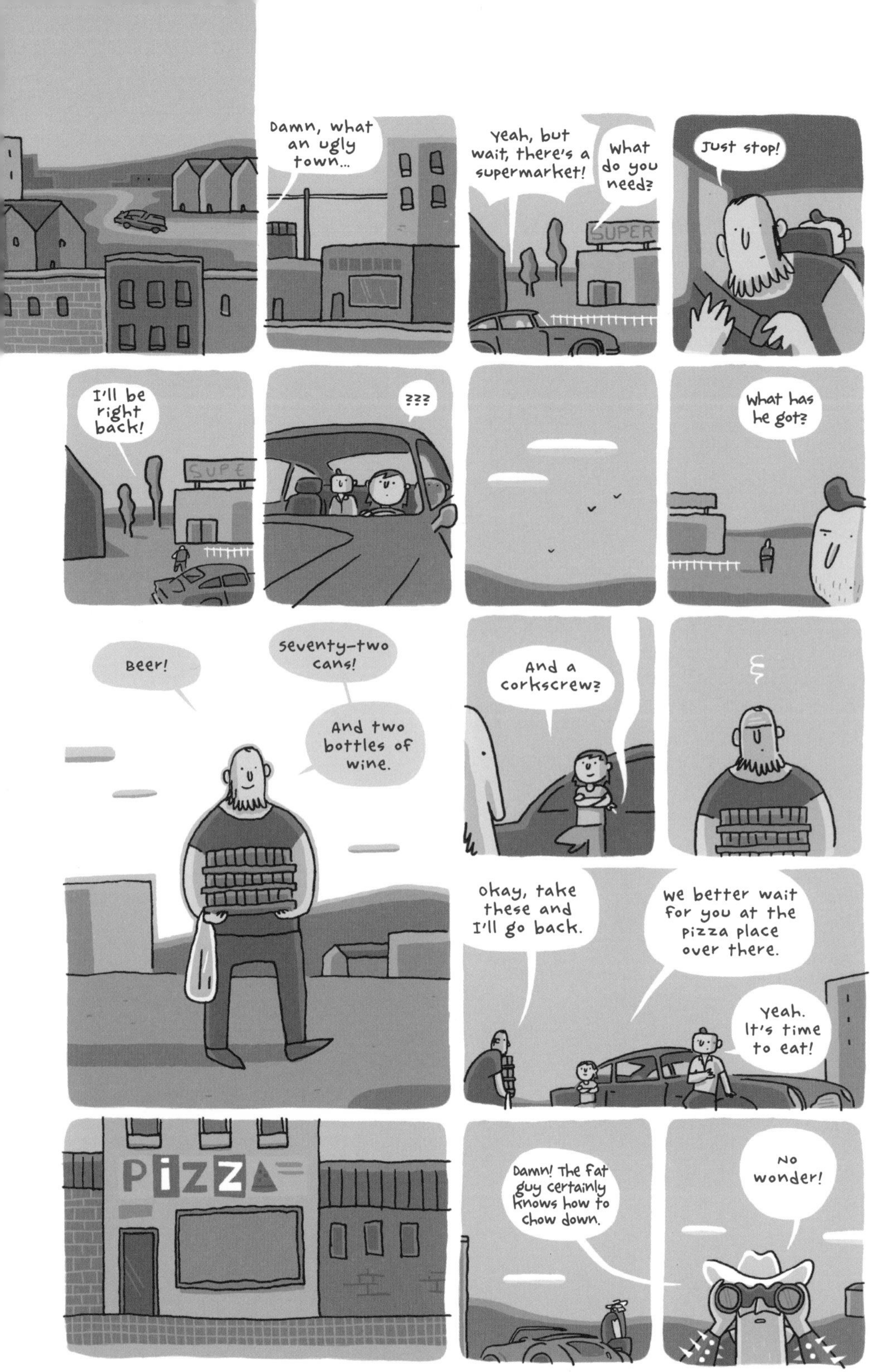
Damn, what an ugly town...
Yeah, but wait, there's a supermarket!
What do you need?
Just stop!
I'll be right back!
???
What has he got?
Beer!
Seventy-two cans!
And two bottles of wine.
And a corkscrew?
Okay, take these and I'll go back.
We better wait for you at the pizza place over there.
Yeah. It's time to eat!
PIZZA
Damn! The fat guy certainly knows how to chow down.
No wonder!

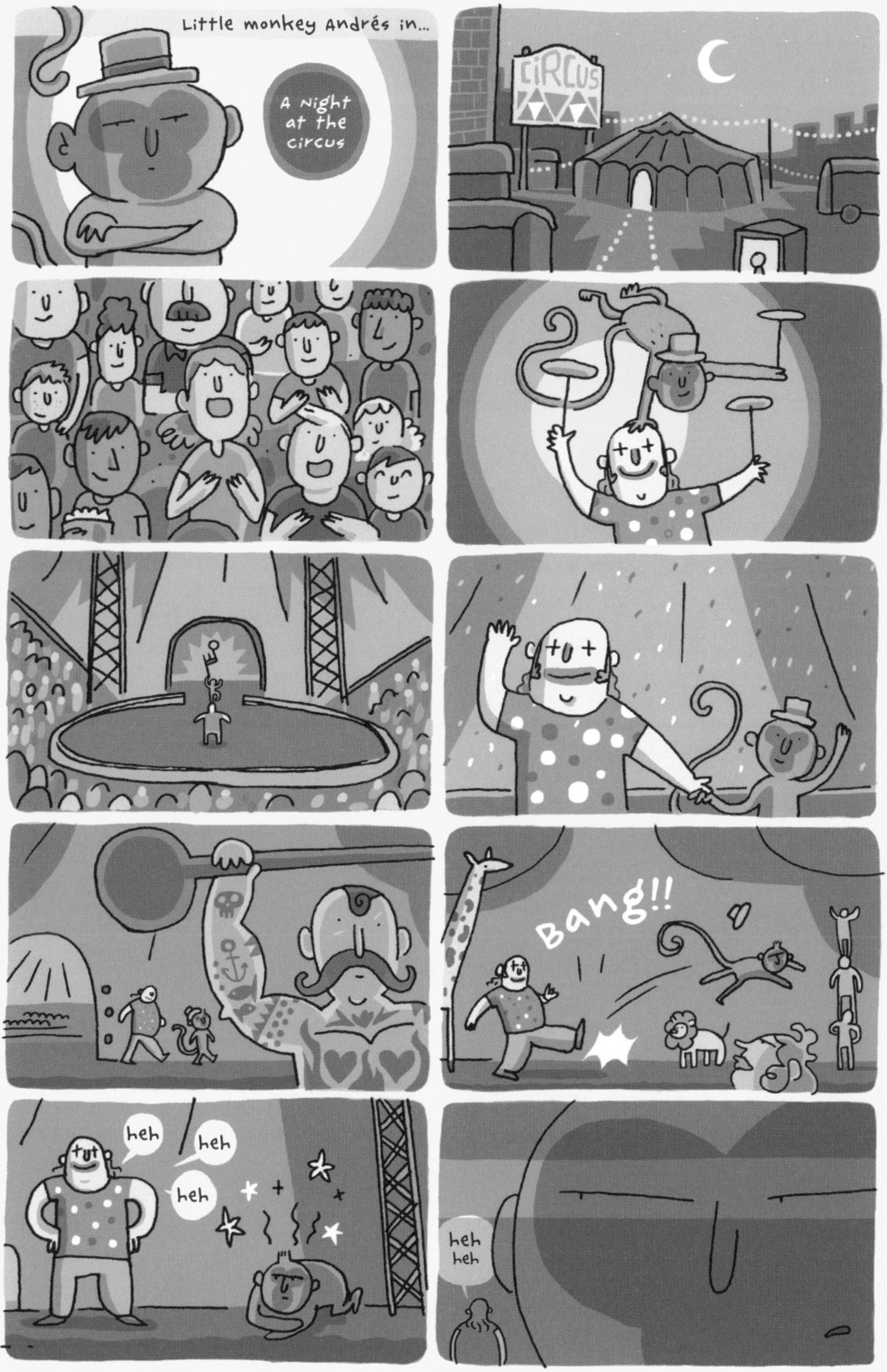
Little monkey Andrés in...
A Night at the circus
CiRCUS
Bang!!
heh
heh
heh
heh heh

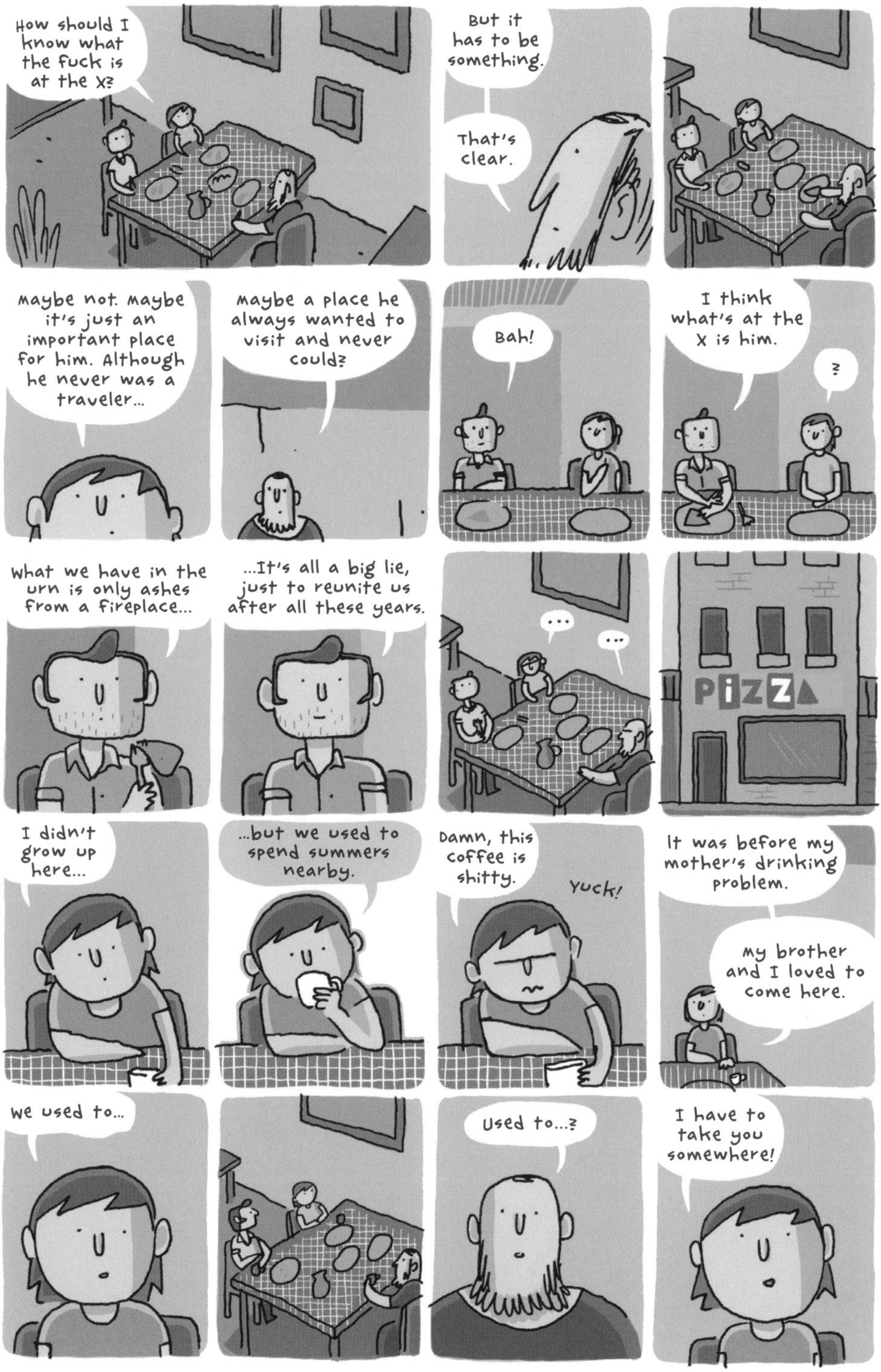
How should I know what the fuck is at the X?
But it has to be something.
That's clear.
Maybe not. Maybe it's just an important place for him. Although he never was a traveler...
Maybe a place he always wanted to visit and never could?
Bah!
I think what's at the X is him.
?
What we have in the urn is only ashes from a fireplace...
...It's all a big lie, just to reunite us after all these years.
...
...
PIZZA
I didn't grow up here...
...but we used to spend summers nearby.
Damn, this coffee is shitty.
YUCK!
It was before my mother's drinking problem.
My brother and I loved to come here.
We used to...
Used to...?
I have to take you somewhere!

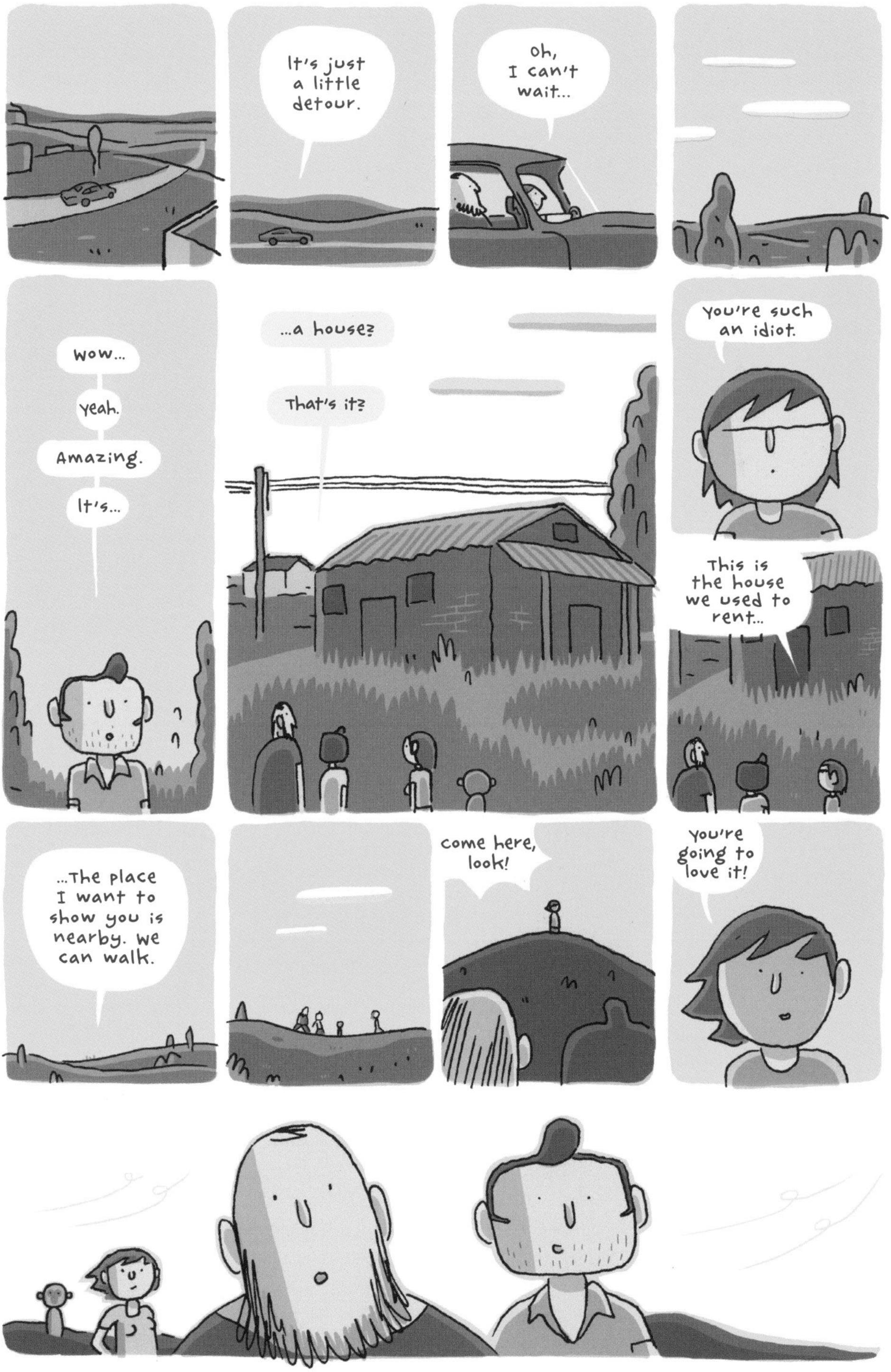
It's just a little detour.
Oh, I can't wait...
Wow...
Yeah.
Amazing.
It's...
...a house?
That's it?
You're such an idiot.
This is the house we used to rent...
...The place I want to show you is nearby. We can walk.
Come here, look!
You're going to love it!

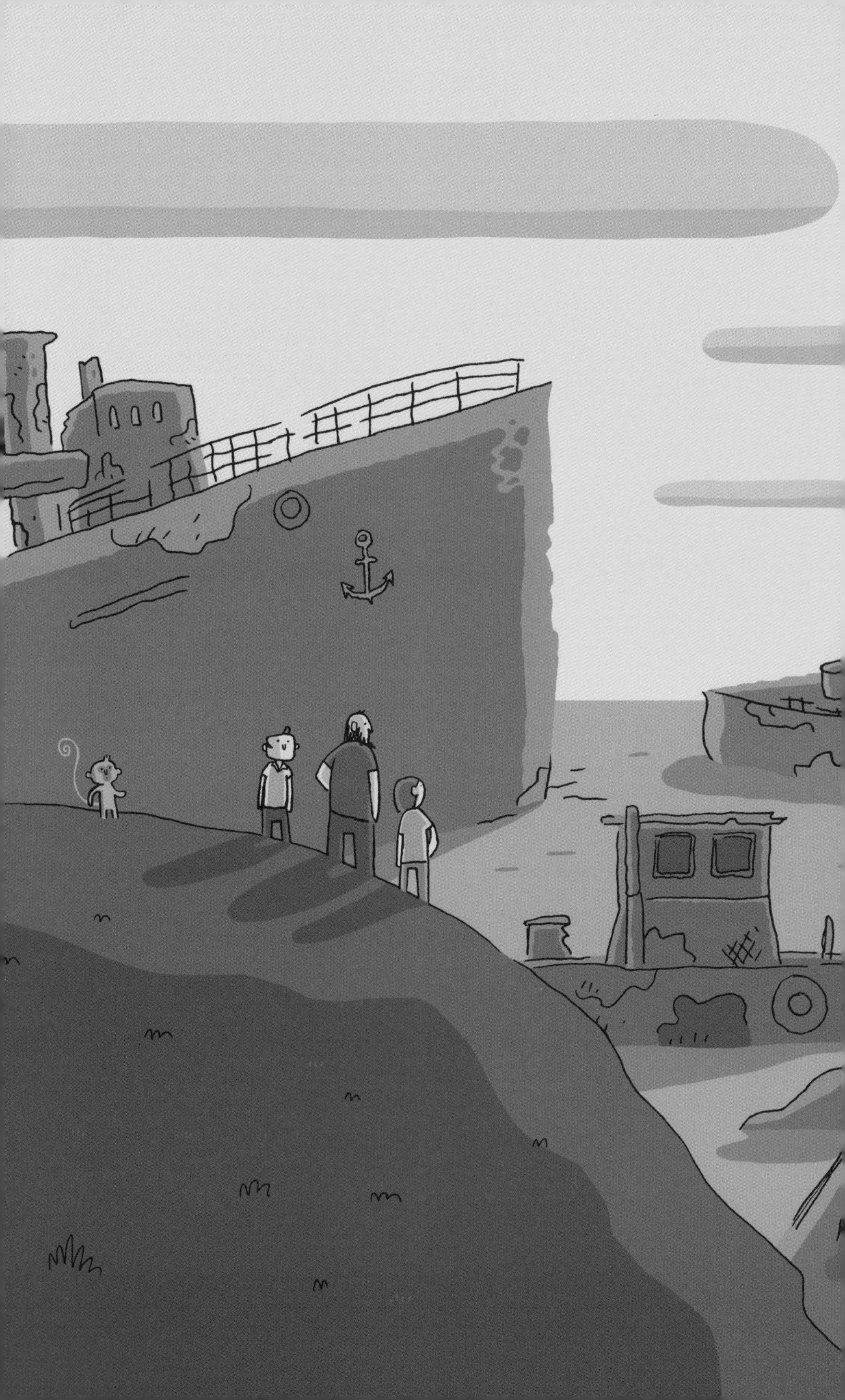

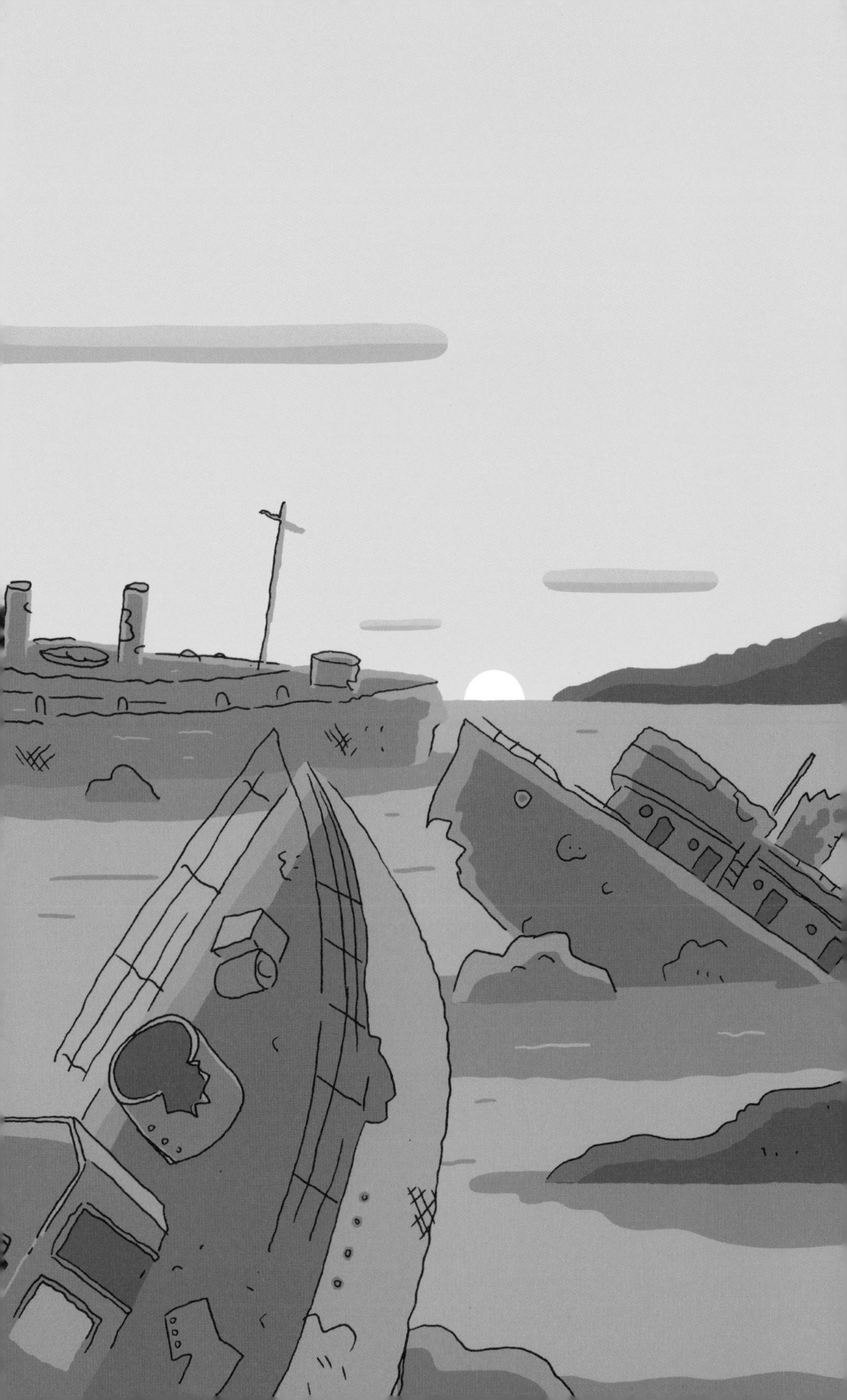

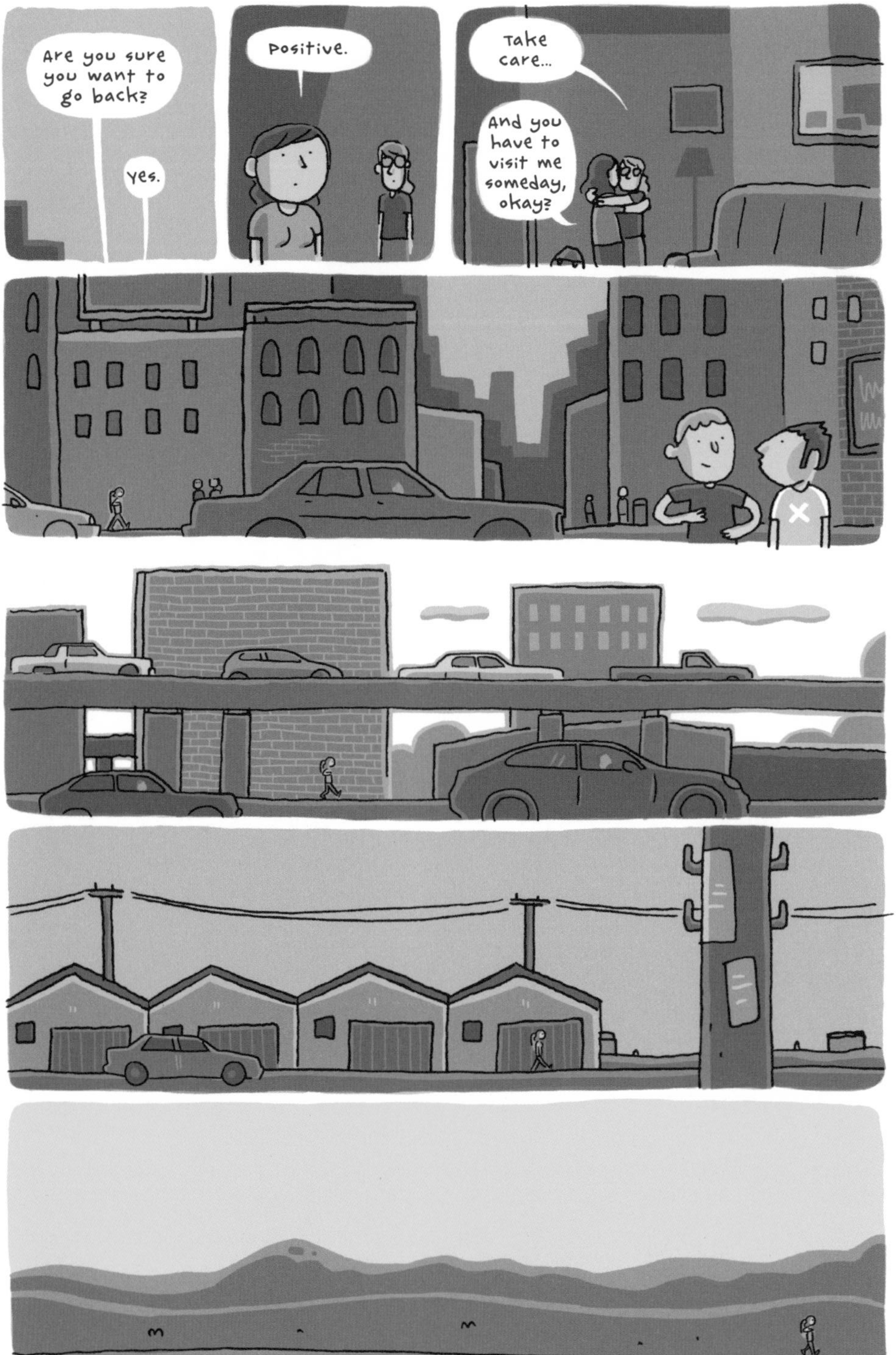
Are you sure you want to go back?
Yes.
Positive.
Take care...
And you have to visit me someday, okay?

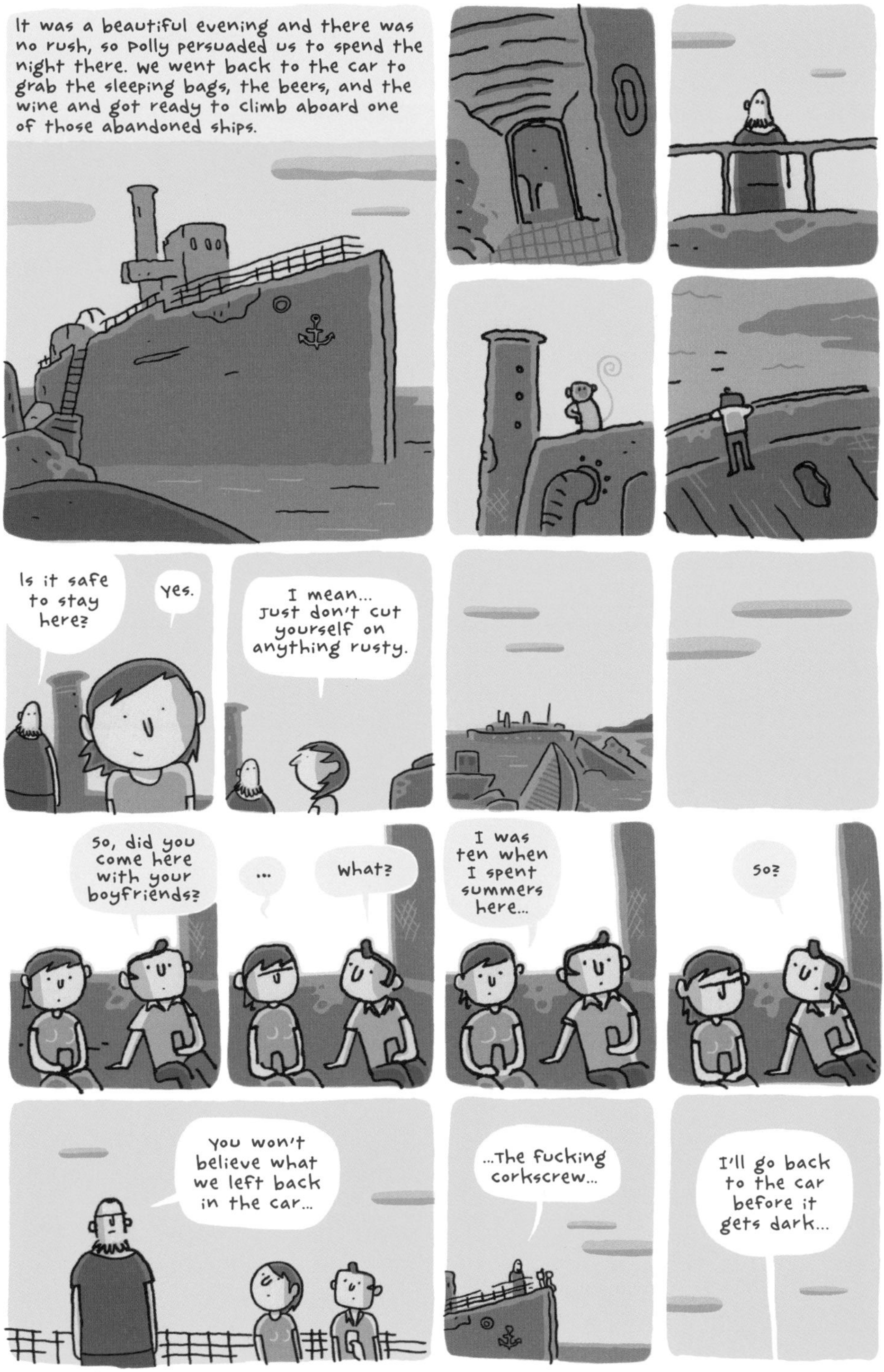

It was a beautiful evening and there was no rush, so Polly persuaded us to spend the night there. We went back to the car to grab the sleeping bags, the beers, and the wine and got ready to climb aboard one of those abandoned ships.
Is it safe to stay here?
Yes.
I mean... Just don't cut yourself on anything rusty.
So, did you come here with your boyfriends?
...
What?
I was ten when I spent summers here...
So?
You won't believe what we left back in the car...
...The fucking corkscrew...
I'll go back to the car before it gets dark...

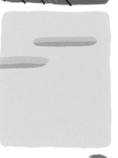

All this for a damn corkscrew...

Besides, I hardly drink any wine...

Let's see where it is...

...Hmmm...

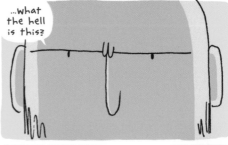

...what the hell is this?

Ahem! Ahem!

Sorry to interrupt...

...well, actually I'm not sorry.

may I ask what the fuck is this?

You fucking asshole!

plaf!

shit!

This is full of coke!

And cash... This is a lot of money!

...

Why do you have that? Is it yours?

...

Apparently music journalism was not the only job moho had...

Did you bring us to a drug dealer's house?

Did you see that house?! c'mon, you could've guessed...

stop messing around...

okay, okay, I'm not proud of it, but such is life...

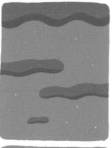

...some of us have changed more than others.

And what are you supposed to do with all this?

Just deliver it to some guy. It's almost on our way...

we wouldn't have to make a big detour.

I'm sorry, "we"?

Not a chance.

Eh?

What about that whole tearjerker of scattering Héctor's ashes together?

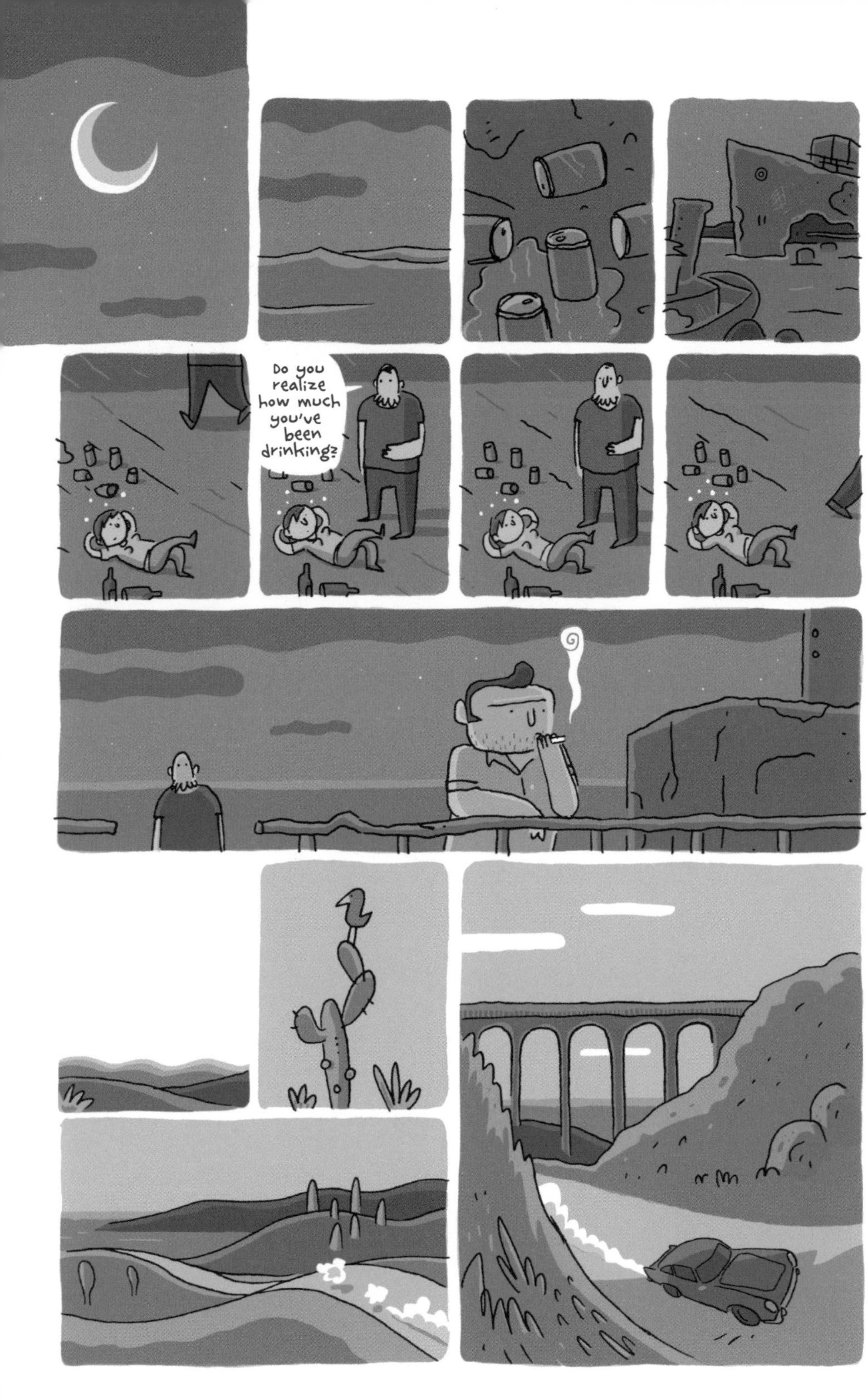
Do you realize how much you've been drinking?

DAY 4

(the one that could not
have gone any worse)

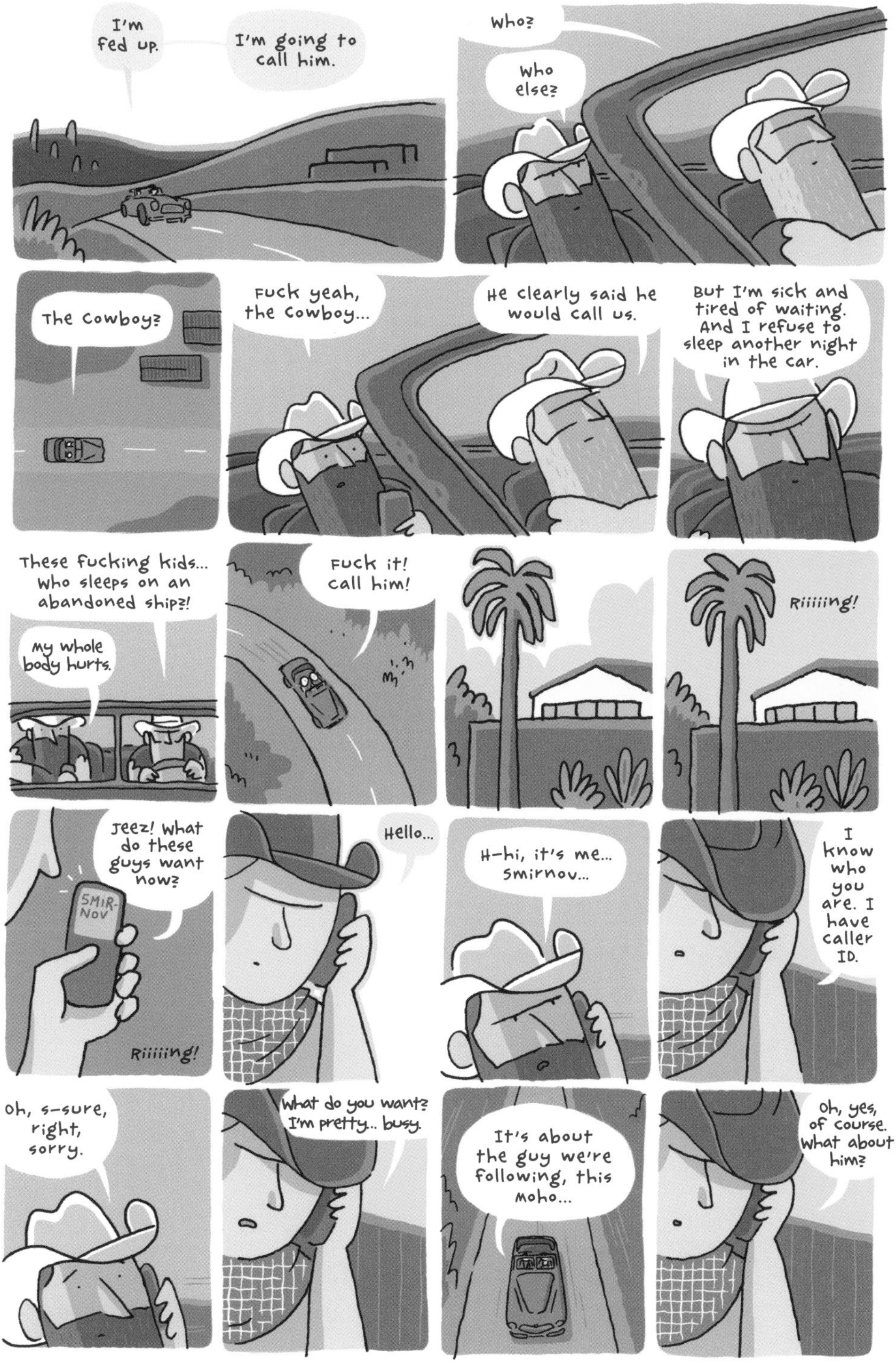
I'm fed up.
I'm going to call him.
Who?
Who else?
The cowboy?
Fuck yeah, the cowboy...
He clearly said he would call us.
But I'm sick and tired of waiting. And I refuse to sleep another night in the car.
These fucking kids... who sleeps on an abandoned ship?!
My whole body hurts.
Fuck it! Call him!
Riiiing!
Jeez! What do these guys want now?
SMIR-NOV
Riiiing!
Hello...
H-hi, it's me... Smirnov...
I know who you are. I have caller ID.
Oh, s-sure, right, sorry.
What do you want? I'm pretty... busy.
It's about the guy we're following, this Moho...
Oh, yes, of course. What about him?

 We are hot on his heels...

...and we think it's time for some action...

Great, that's fine with me... But I haven't decided yet what you should do to him...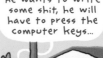

We already talked about breaking some fingers.

or better yet: all his fingers!

And his legs, of course.

So that next time he wants to write some shit, he will have to press the computer keys...

...with a stick in his mouth! Ha, ha, ha!

 Okay?

Okay, that's it. We'll break his legs and all his fingers. Have a good day.

Same to you, Smirnov. Say hello to your brother, and keep me posted.

Okay, guys...

click

Where were we?

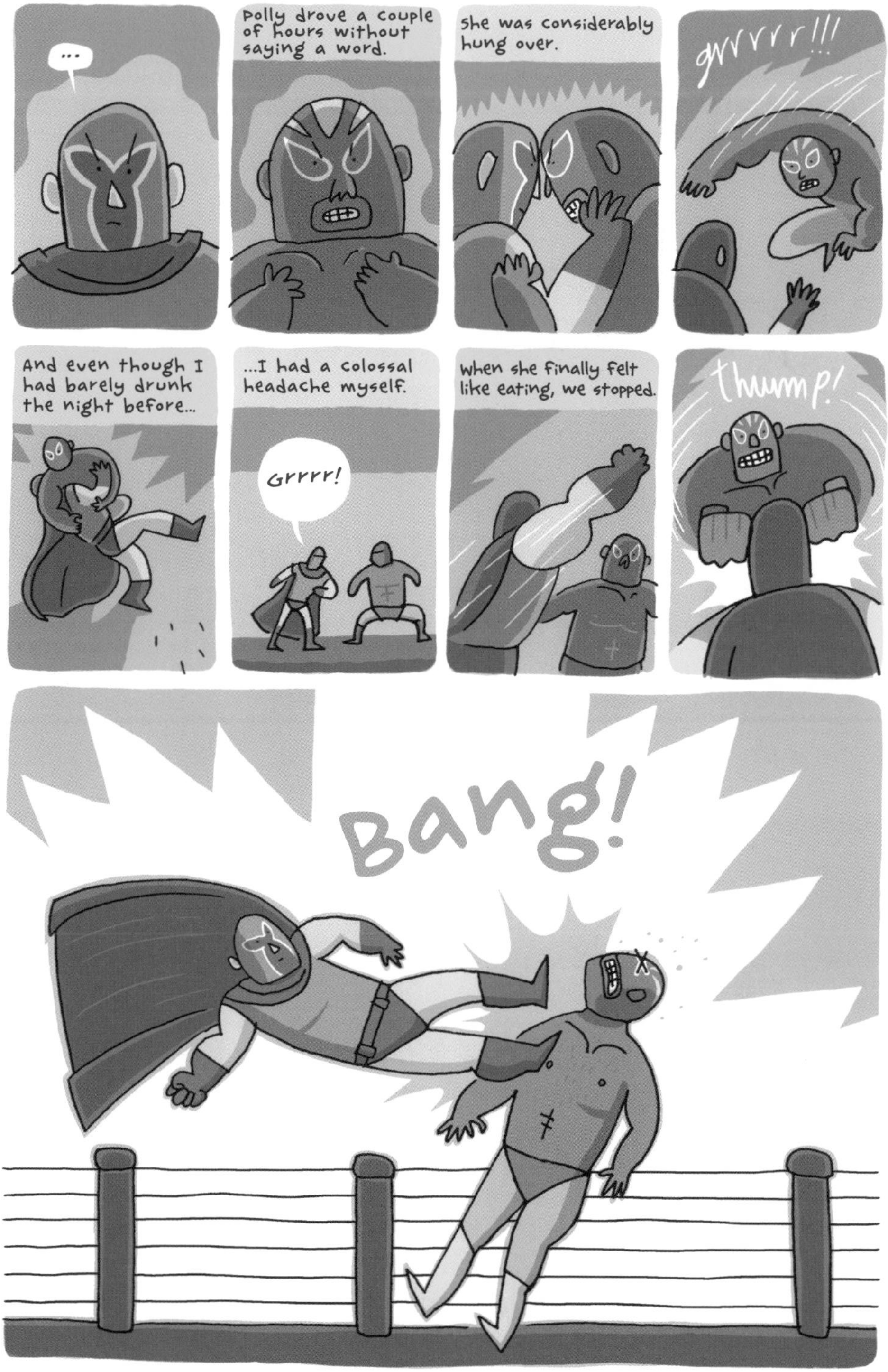
...
Polly drove a couple of hours without saying a word.
She was considerably hung over.
grrrrr!!!
And even though I had barely drunk the night before...
...I had a colossal headache myself.
Grrrr!
When she finally felt like eating, we stopped.
thuump!
Bang!

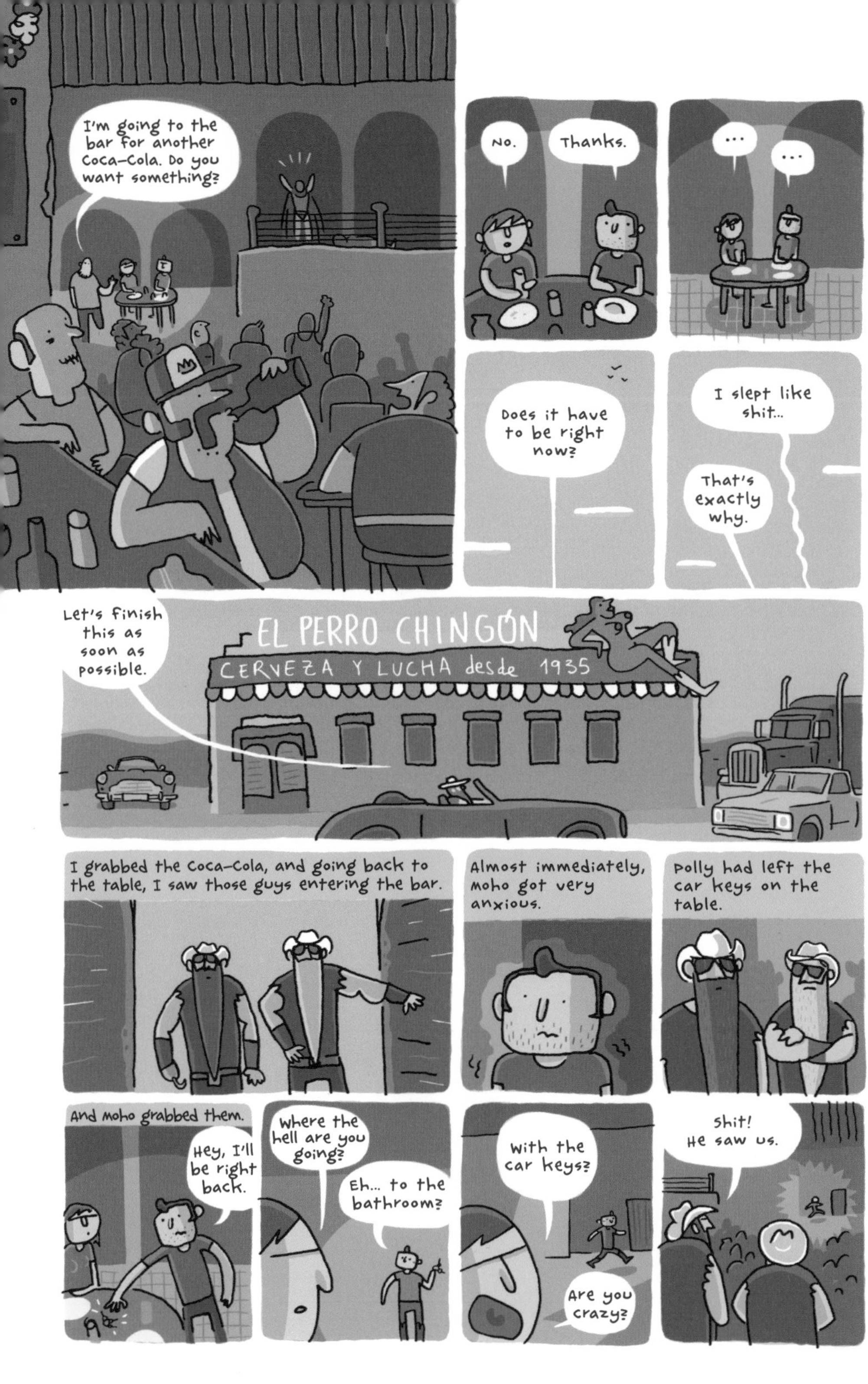
I'm going to the bar for another Coca-Cola. Do you want something?
No.
Thanks.
...
...
Does it have to be right now?
I slept like shit...
That's exactly why.
Let's finish this as soon as possible.
EL PERRO CHINGÓN
CERVEZA Y LUCHA desde 1935
I grabbed the Coca-Cola, and going back to the table, I saw those guys entering the bar.
Almost immediately, Moho got very anxious.
Polly had left the car keys on the table.
And Moho grabbed them.
Hey, I'll be right back.
Where the hell are you going?
Eh... to the bathroom?
With the car keys?
Are you crazy?
Shit! He saw us.

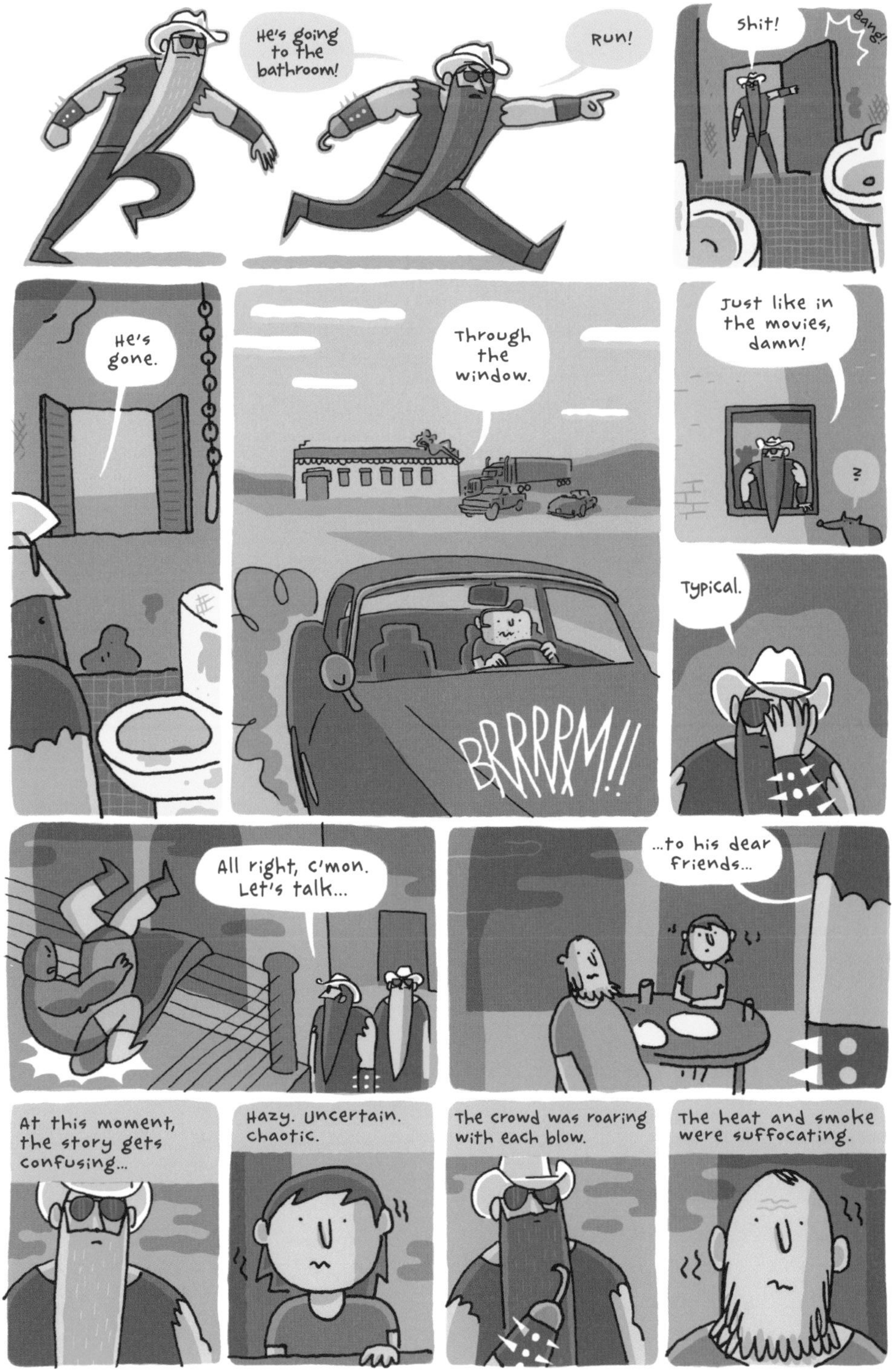
He's going to the bathroom!
Run!
Shit!
Bang!
He's gone.
Through the window.
BRRRRM!!
Just like in the movies, damn!
?
Typical.
All right, c'mon. Let's talk...
...to his dear friends...
At this moment, the story gets confusing...
Hazy. Uncertain. Chaotic.
The crowd was roaring with each blow.
The heat and smoke were suffocating.

Hello, lovebirds.

H-hello...

It seems your buddy was in a hurry...

And we wanted to talk to him.

We really don't know where he went...

Well, if he continues to be so slippery, maybe next time...

...we won't be talking.

So if you could tell him we are looking for him...

...we would appreciate it.

Okay?

Sluuuurp

Okay, s-sure...

Of course...

That's the spirit.

Bye.

Then they walked out.

And we stayed put, trembling.

Should we follow him?

No.

He'll come back for them.

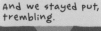
If not, we'll follow these two when they leave.

They'll eventually meet up.

Son of a fucking bitch.

I'm going to kill him! I mean it!

I'M GOING TO KILL HIM!

I mean, I could kill him too...

...but...

Yeah, I know...

...he took the car...

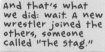

And on top of that, he left us the monkey.

Wait, let's call him.

Ring... ring... ring...

He didn't answer. We'll have to wait.

And that's what we did: wait. A new wrestler joined the others, someone called "The Stag."

The crowd started really going crazy.

WOOOOOO!!!

Then the punches and slams resumed.

Ring... ring...

It's him.

Where the hell are you?

Not far... hidden in an alley. Do you remember the last town we passed through?

I told him to pick us up, but he said it was better if we came to him. He was afraid to drive back.

You are an idiot too.

I'm sorry...

...You know how convincing Moho can be.

Sure, walking for more than an hour in the hot sun was not a great idea.

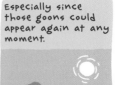
Especially since those goons could appear again at any moment.

Luckily, we managed to get to the town without any problems...

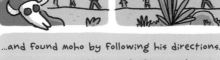
...and found Moho by following his directions.

You see? It didn't take you too long...

Slap!!!

c'mon, you're over-reacting.

I'm overreacting?

Some ZZ Top creep scrapes his hook on my face after you steal our car and disappear...

...And you dare to tell me that I'm overreacting?!

Now this part of the story happened too fast.

You might be right...

One moment Moho was taking his stuff out of the car trunk.

It will be better if I go.

And the next, Polly and I were leaving the town in the car alone.

As far as I'm concerned, you can fall off a cliff...

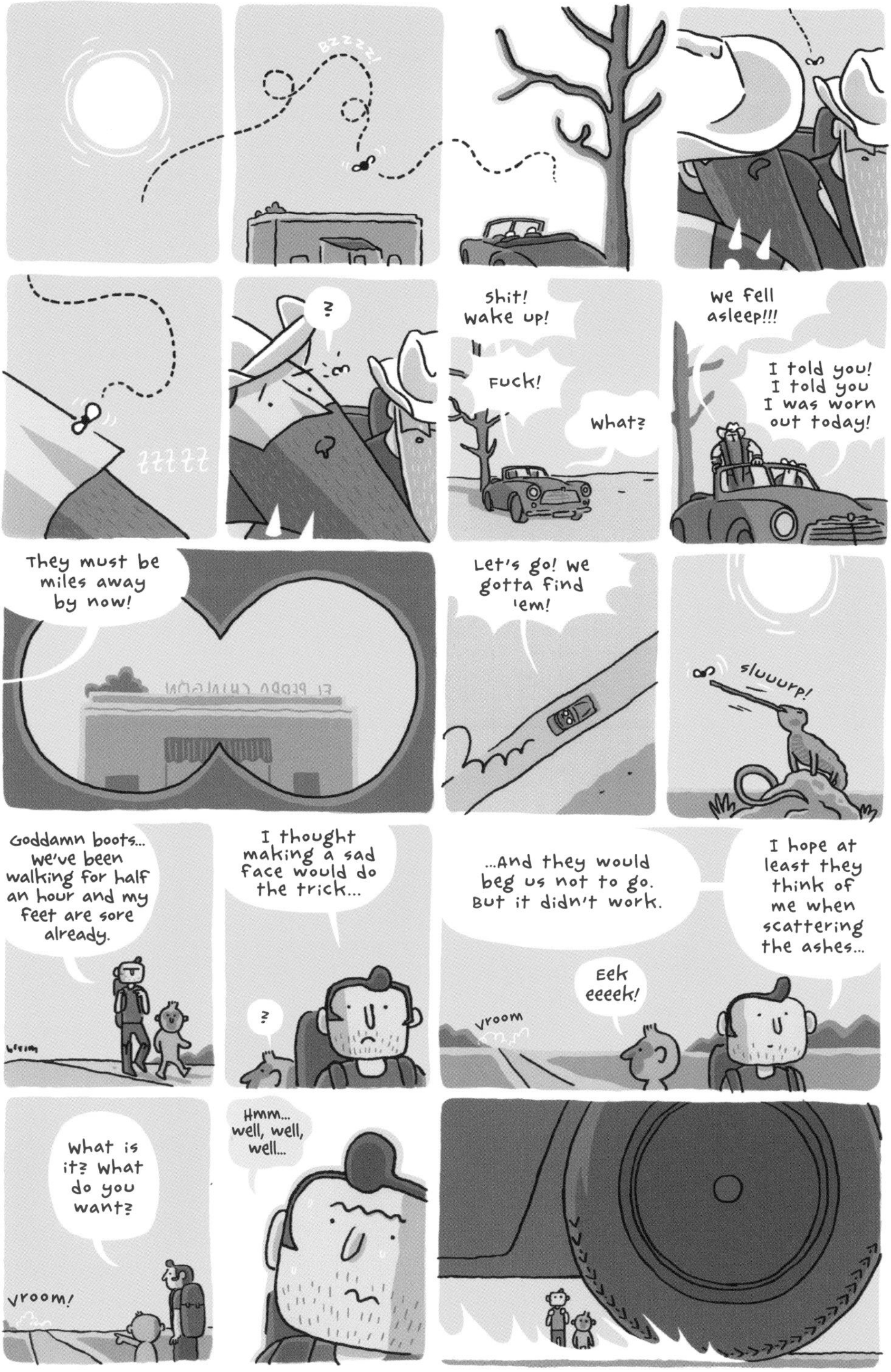
Bzzzz!
zzzzz
?
Shit! Wake up!
Fuck!
What?
We fell asleep!!!
I told you! I told you I was worn out today!
They must be miles away by now!
Let's go! We gotta find 'em!
sluuurp!
Goddamn boots... we've been walking for half an hour and my feet are sore already.
I thought making a sad face would do the trick...
?
...And they would beg us not to go. But it didn't work.
I hope at least they think of me when scattering the ashes...
vroom
Eek eeeek!
What is it? What do you want?
vroom!
Hmm... well, well, well...

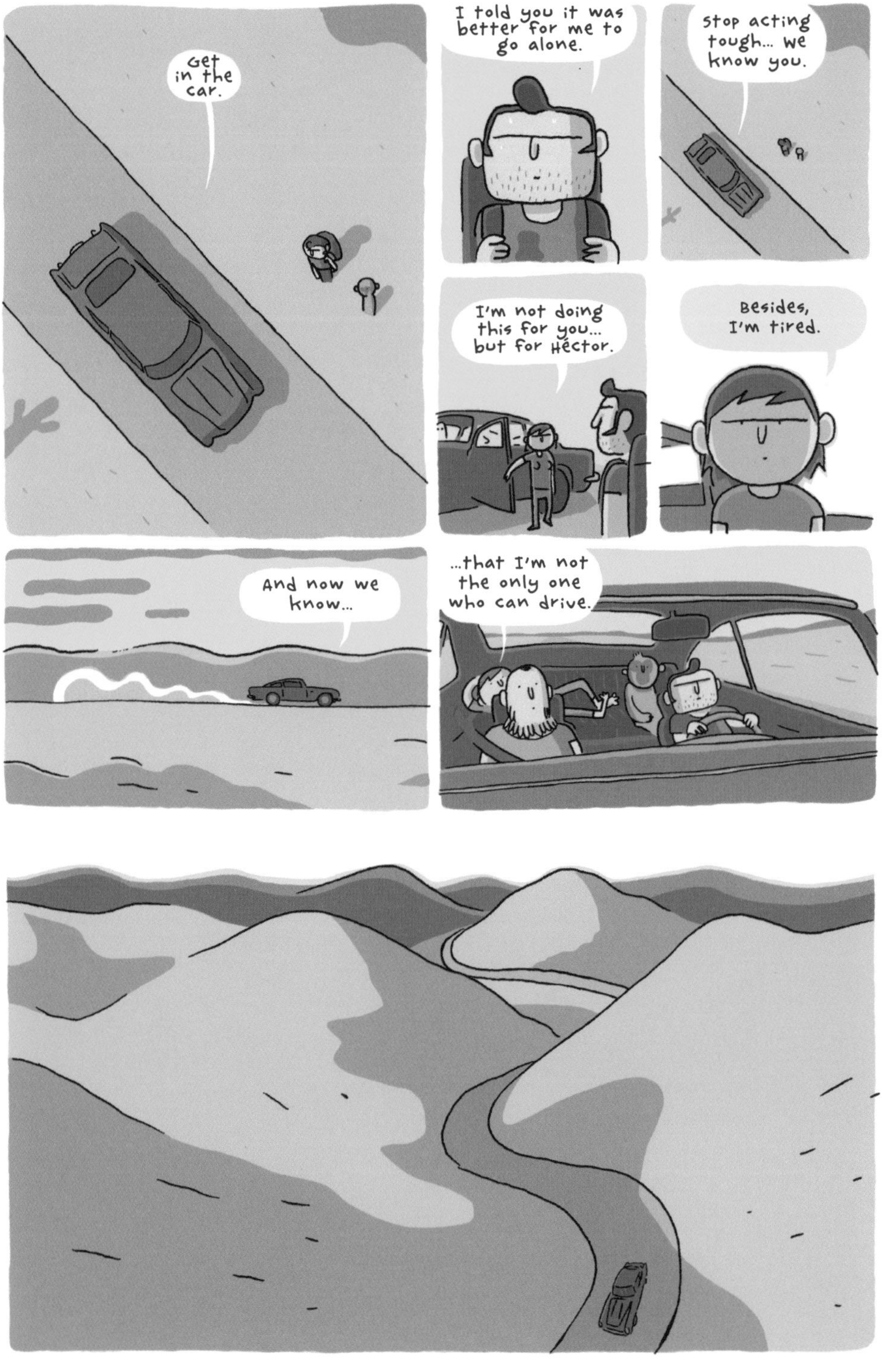
Get in the car.
I told you it was better for me to go alone.
Stop acting tough... we know you.
I'm not doing this for you... but for Héctor.
Besides, I'm tired.
And now we know...
...that I'm not the only one who can drive.

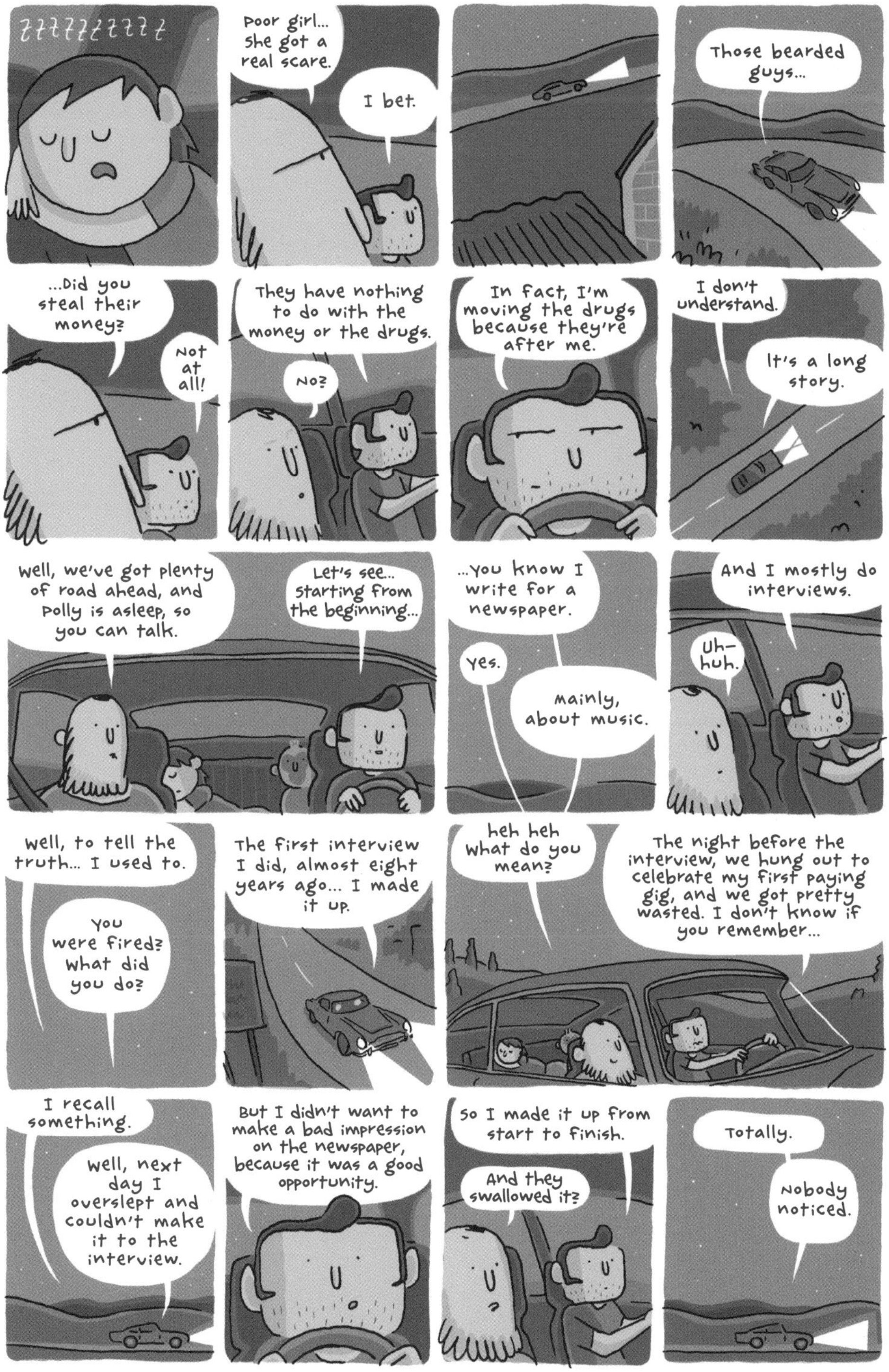
ZZZZZZZZZZ
Poor girl... she got a real scare.
I bet.
Those bearded guys...
...Did you steal their money?
Not at all!
They have nothing to do with the money or the drugs.
No?
In fact, I'm moving the drugs because they're after me.
I don't understand.
It's a long story.
Well, we've got plenty of road ahead, and Polly is asleep, so you can talk.
Let's see... starting from the beginning...
...You know I write for a newspaper.
Yes.
Mainly, about music.
And I mostly do interviews.
Uh-huh.
Well, to tell the truth... I used to.
You were fired? What did you do?
The first interview I did, almost eight years ago... I made it up.
heh heh What do you mean?
The night before the interview, we hung out to celebrate my first paying gig, and we got pretty wasted. I don't know if you remember...
I recall something.
Well, next day I overslept and couldn't make it to the interview.
But I didn't want to make a bad impression on the newspaper, because it was a good opportunity.
So I made it up from start to finish.
And they swallowed it?
Totally.
Nobody noticed.

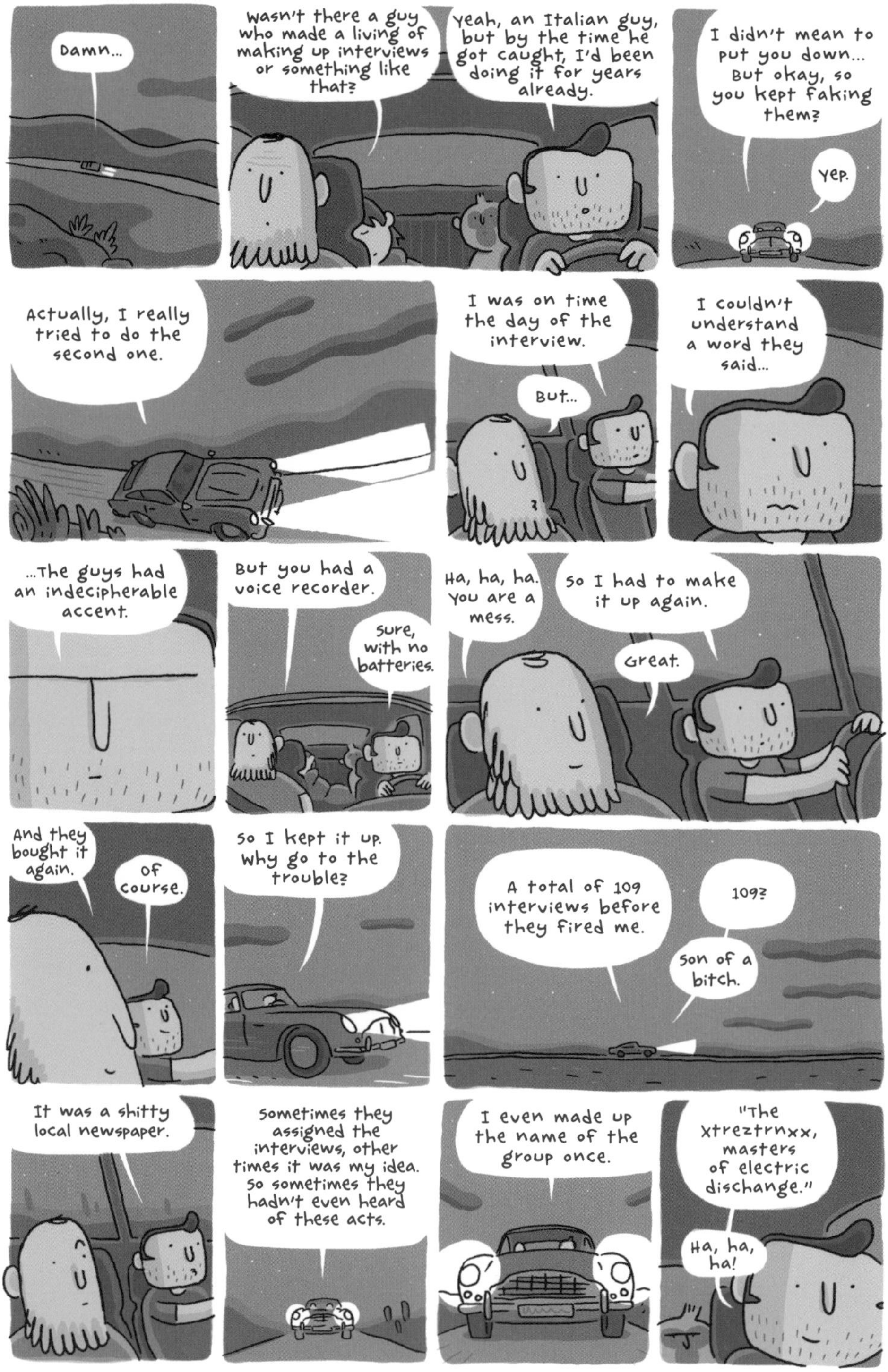
Damn...
Wasn't there a guy who made a living of making up interviews or something like that?
Yeah, an Italian guy, but by the time he got caught, I'd been doing it for years already.
I didn't mean to put you down... But okay, so you kept faking them?
Yep.
Actually, I really tried to do the second one.
I was on time the day of the interview.
But...
I couldn't understand a word they said...
...The guys had an indecipherable accent.
But you had a voice recorder.
Sure, with no batteries.
Ha, ha, ha. You are a mess.
So I had to make it up again.
Great.
And they bought it again.
Of course.
So I kept it up. Why go to the trouble?
A total of 109 interviews before they fired me.
109?
Son of a bitch.
It was a shitty local newspaper.
Sometimes they assigned the interviews, other times it was my idea. So sometimes they hadn't even heard of these acts.
I even made up the name of the group once.
"The Xtreztrnxx, masters of electric dischange."
Ha, ha, ha!

of course, it couldn't last forever...

...One day they asked me to interview a country singer who was rising to fame.

The bastard calls himself "the Cowboy."

His music is fucking dogshit...

"...But this asshole thinks he's some kind of savior of country music."

From the Cross to Your Heart ♡

THE COWBOY

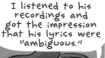

I listened to his recordings and got the impression that his lyrics were "ambiguous."

So I mentioned that some songs were a little bit like "Brokeback Mountain."

Long story short, "the cowboy" sees this interview, gets pissed, contacts the paper.

It seemed that what annoyed him the most was the insinuation of the homosexual lyrics.

Even more than the fact that I made up the whole damn interview!

When they called me from the newspaper, I denied everything.

But in the end I confessed.

They were super pissed and fired me. Tough luck! And I thought it was the end of it.

But then I started getting these nasty threats over email.

At first, I didn't take them seriously, but they kept getting worse. And the other day I got a text on my cell phone.

They had my address.

And it freaked me out.

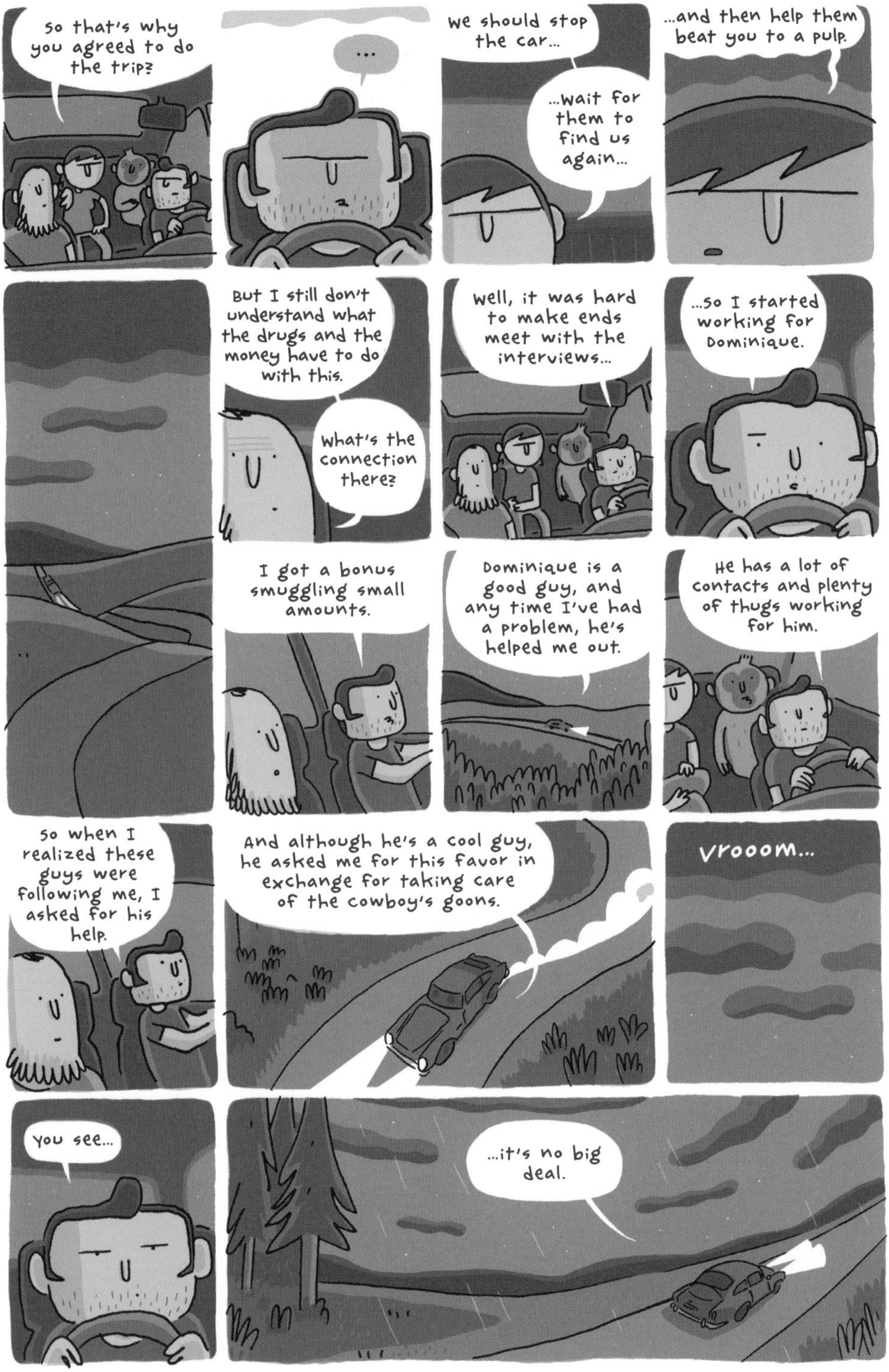
So that's why you agreed to do the trip?
...
We should stop the car...
...wait for them to find us again...
...and then help them beat you to a pulp.
But I still don't understand what the drugs and the money have to do with this.
What's the connection there?
Well, it was hard to make ends meet with the interviews...
...so I started working for Dominique.
I got a bonus smuggling small amounts.
Dominique is a good guy, and any time I've had a problem, he's helped me out.
He has a lot of contacts and plenty of thugs working for him.
So when I realized these guys were following me, I asked for his help.
And although he's a cool guy, he asked me for this favor in exchange for taking care of the cowboy's goons.
VROOOM...
You see...
...it's no big deal.

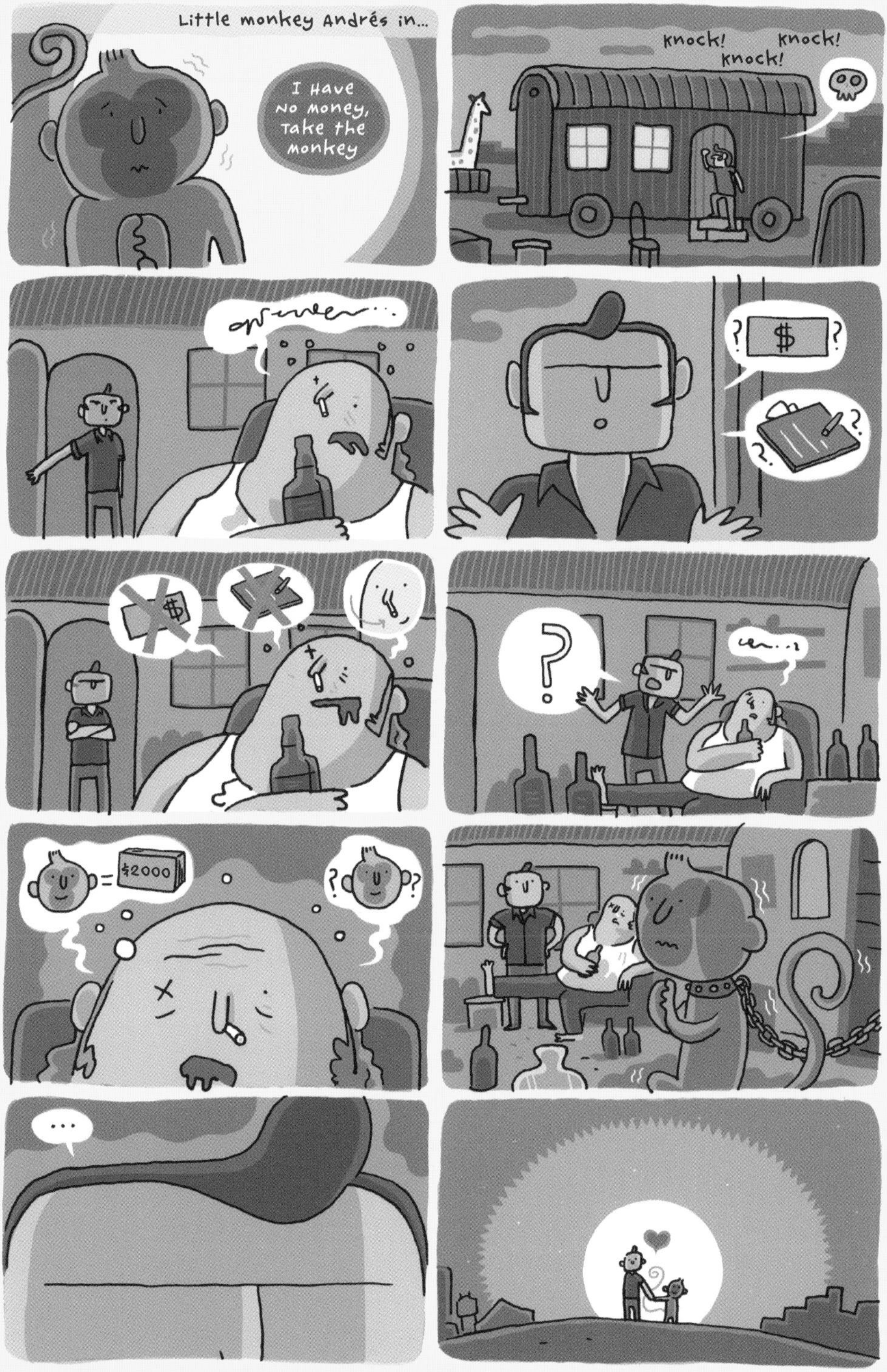
Little monkey Andrés in...
I Have No money, Take the monkey
Knock! Knock! Knock!
$2000

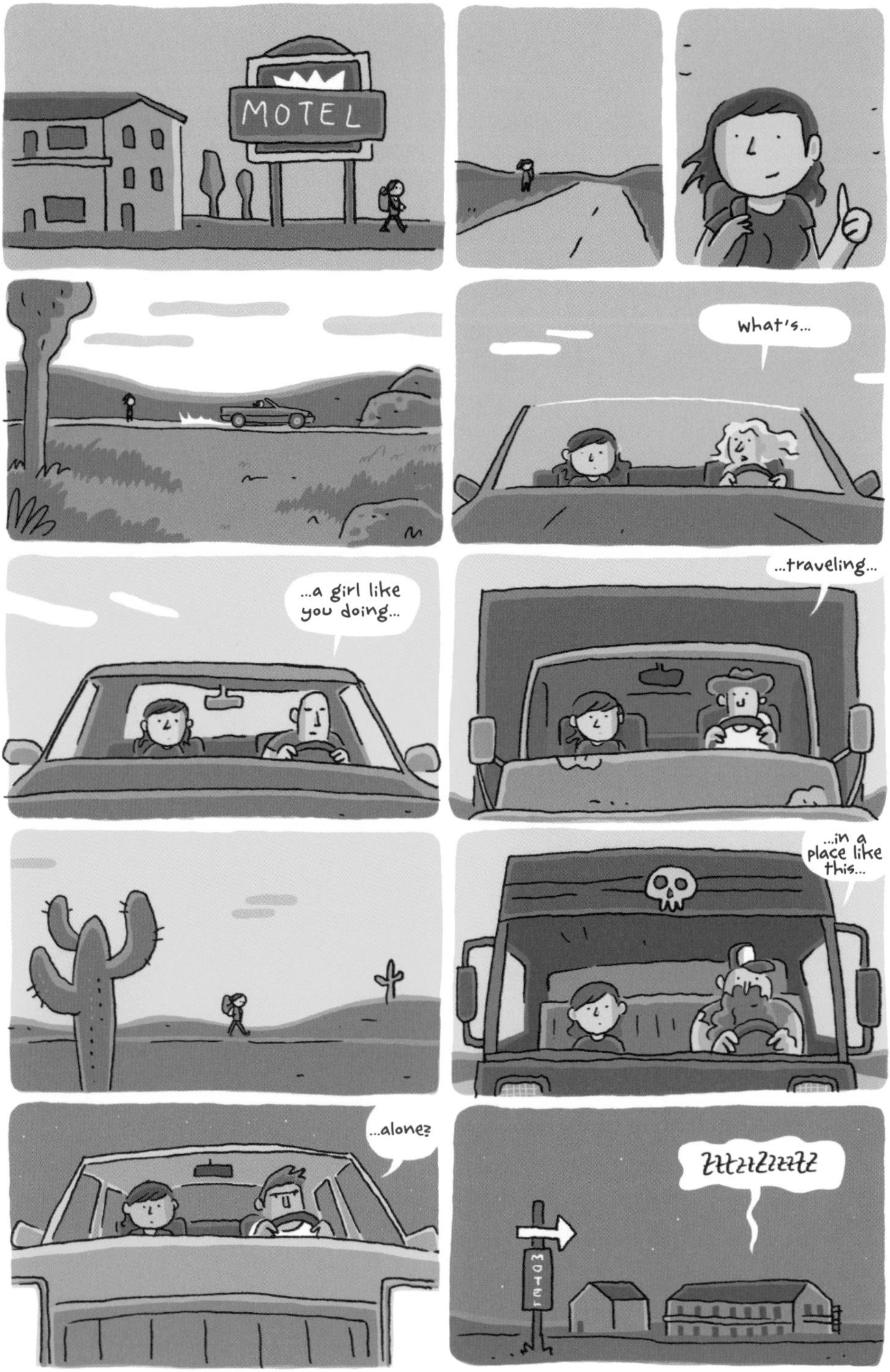
MOTEL
what's...
...a girl like you doing...
...traveling...
...in a place like this...
...alone?
ZZZZZZZZZZZ
MOTEL

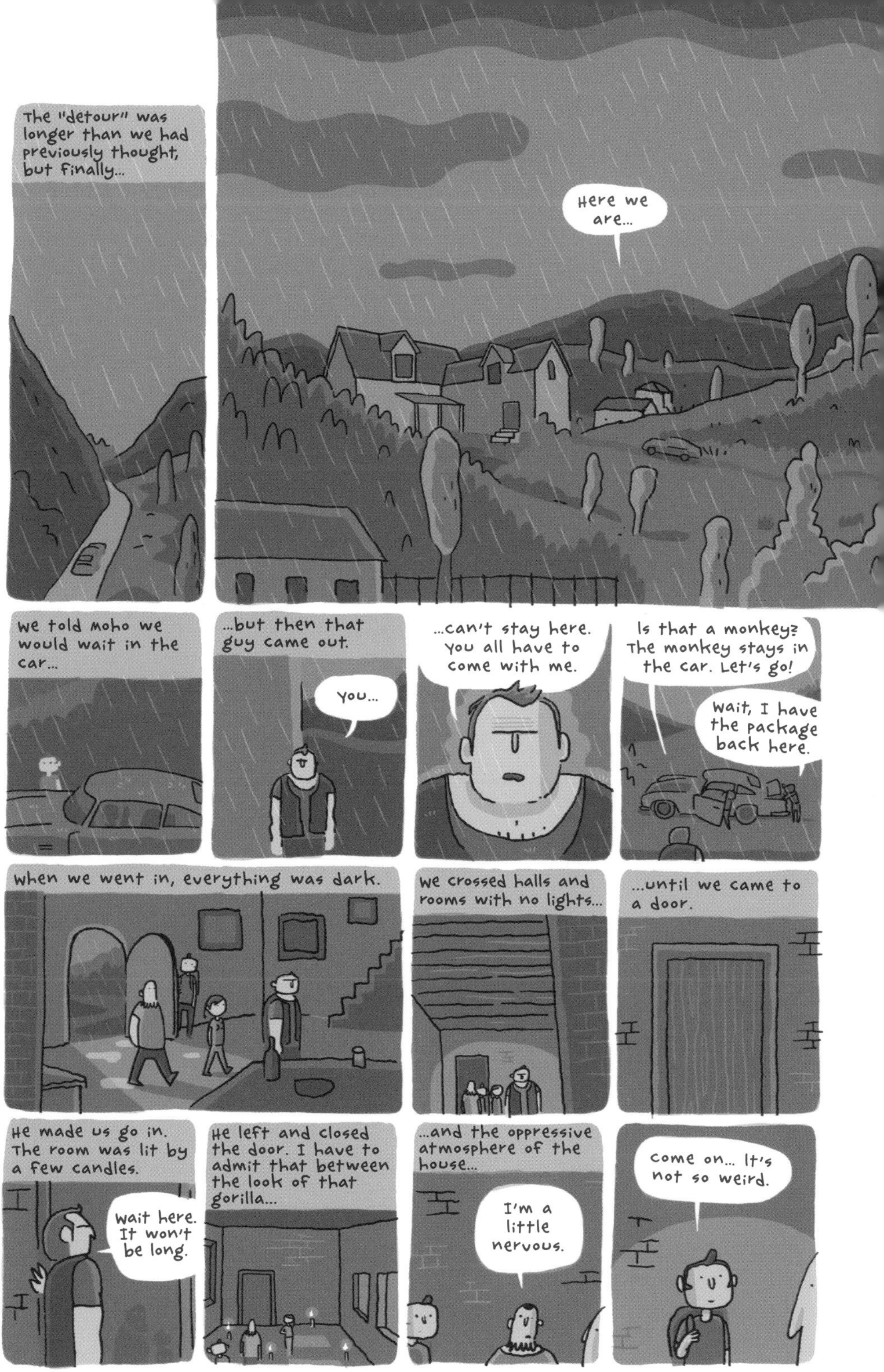
The "detour" was longer than we had previously thought, but finally...
Here we are...
We told Moho we would wait in the car...
...but then that guy came out.
You...
...can't stay here. You all have to come with me.
Is that a monkey? The monkey stays in the car. Let's go!
Wait, I have the package back here.
When we went in, everything was dark.
We crossed halls and rooms with no lights...
...until we came to a door.
He made us go in. The room was lit by a few candles.
Wait here. It won't be long.
He left and closed the door. I have to admit that between the look of that gorilla...
...and the oppressive atmosphere of the house...
I'm a little nervous.
Come on... It's not so weird.

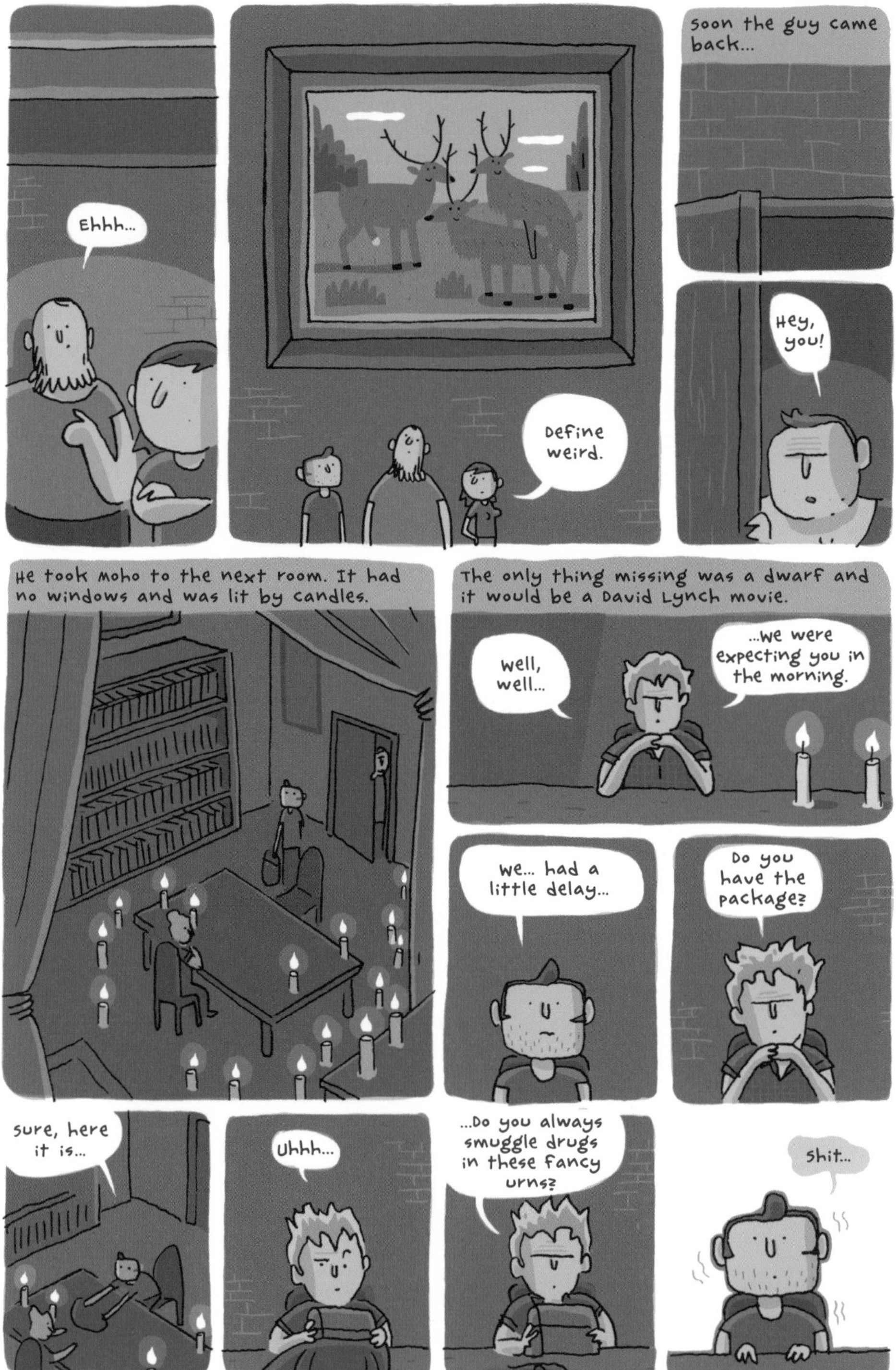
Ehhh...
Define weird.
Soon the guy came back...
Hey, you!
He took Moho to the next room. It had no windows and was lit by candles.
The only thing missing was a dwarf and it would be a David Lynch movie.
Well, well...
...we were expecting you in the morning.
We... had a little delay...
Do you have the package?
Sure, here it is...
Uhhh...
...Do you always smuggle drugs in these fancy urns?
Shit...

malibu, sometime in the late nineties.

Journalist Neil Strauss interviews Courtney Love...

...she stands up and goes to the armoire...

...and comes back with a bag full of ashes.

Do you want to snort Kurt?

She looks serious, and it doesn't seem like a joke, but neither of them ends up snorting the ashes of the grunge icon.

But there was someone else who snorted the ashes of a deceased...

...Her satanic majesty Keith Richards.

In particular, those of his father who died in 2002.

Although he would deny it later.

I would never snort my own father.

"His ashes are resting under an oak I planted myself."

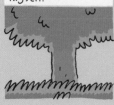

Okay?

But you don't have to be a rock star to snort ashes.

In 2011, four young guys were arrested in Florida for inhaling...

...the ashes of the father of the owner of the house they broke into.

We thought it was cocaine.

said one of the guys...

...after they were arrested and got rid of the urn by throwing it in a nearby lake.

Those... those are the ashes of a friend...

...I must have mixed up the two packages, but I can go back to pick it up.

You stay here.

I'll go.

the dude locks the door after leaving.

But when he gets to the car, he realizes it is also locked.

Fucking Dominique!

He uses the most worthless people.

And what the hell is a monkey doing inside the car?

Fuck!

Back in the room, Moho has the same experience Polly and I already had, but neither of us wanted to talk about.

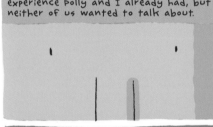

Wellll...

...I'm not staying here...

clunk!

?

Oops...

Fssshh!

Shit! Shit!

And the fucking door is locked!

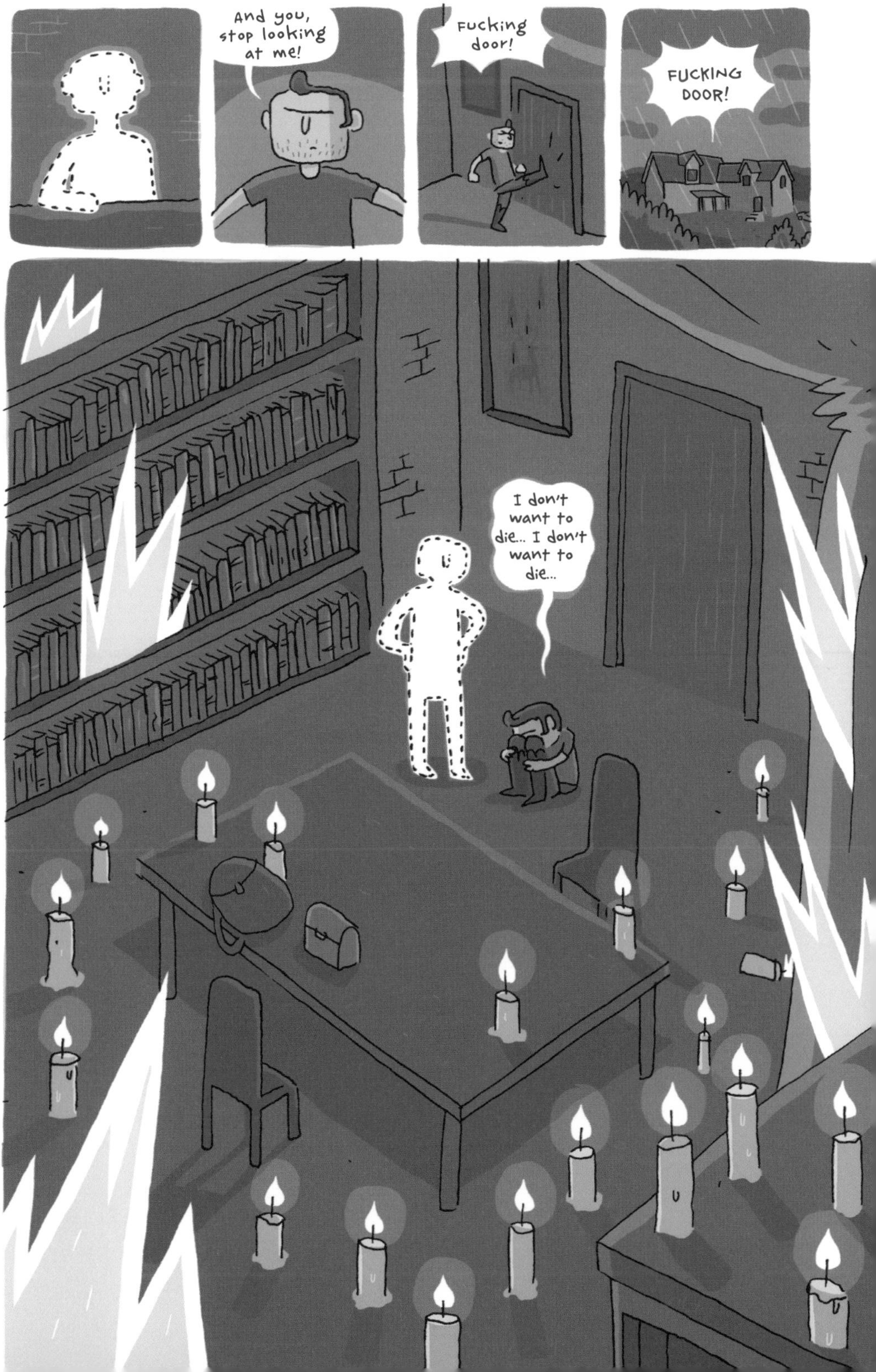
And you, stop looking at me!
Fucking door!
FUCKING DOOR!
I don't want to die... I don't want to die...

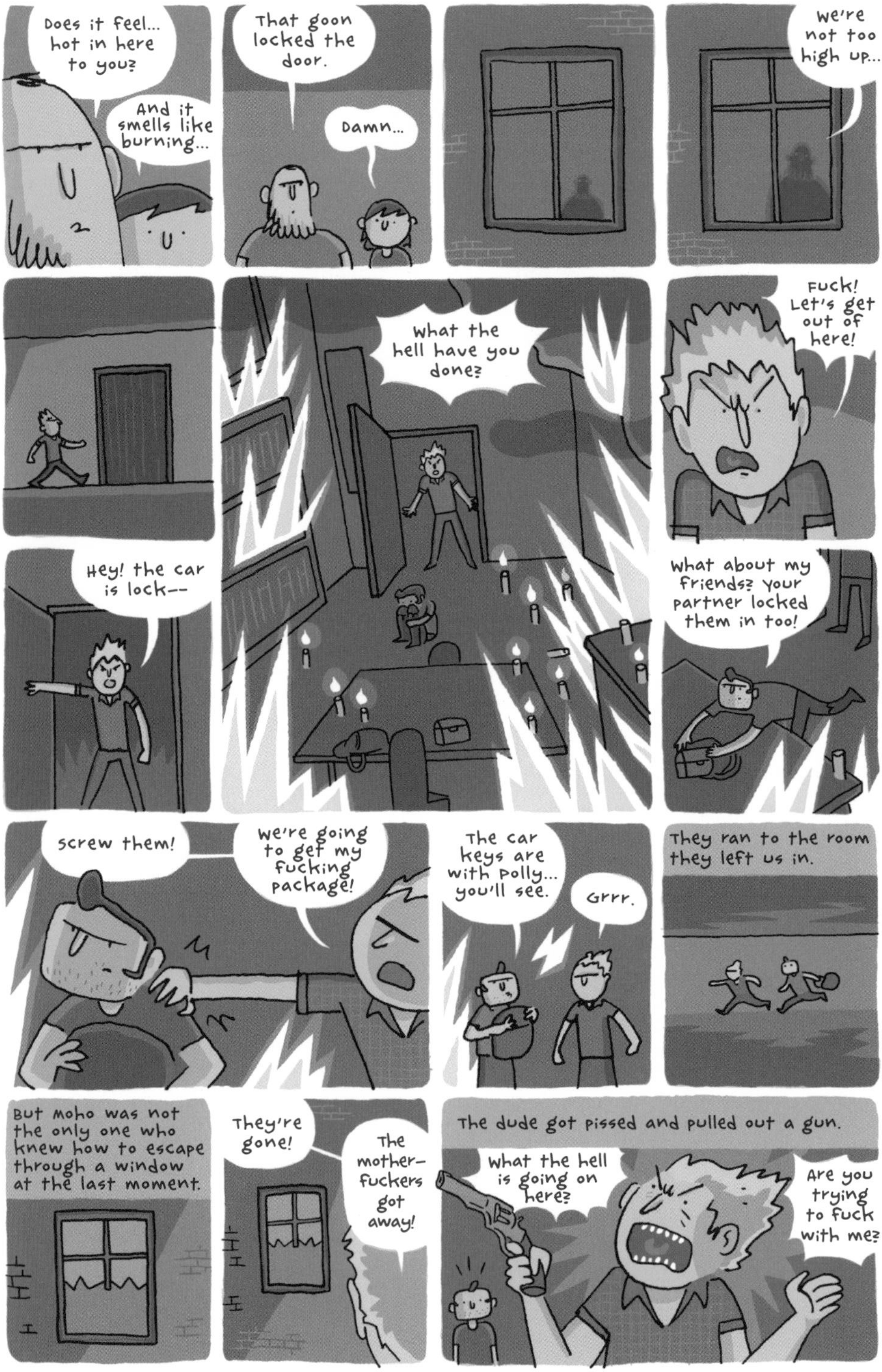
Does it feel... hot in here to you?
And it smells like burning...
That goon locked the door.
Damn...
We're not too high up...
What the hell have you done?
Fuck! Let's get out of here!
Hey! the car is lock--
What about my friends? Your partner locked them in too!
Screw them!
We're going to get my fucking package!
The car keys are with Polly... you'll see.
Grrr.
They ran to the room they left us in.
But Moho was not the only one who knew how to escape through a window at the last moment.
They're gone!
The mother-fuckers got away!
The dude got pissed and pulled out a gun.
What the hell is going on here?
Are you trying to fuck with me?

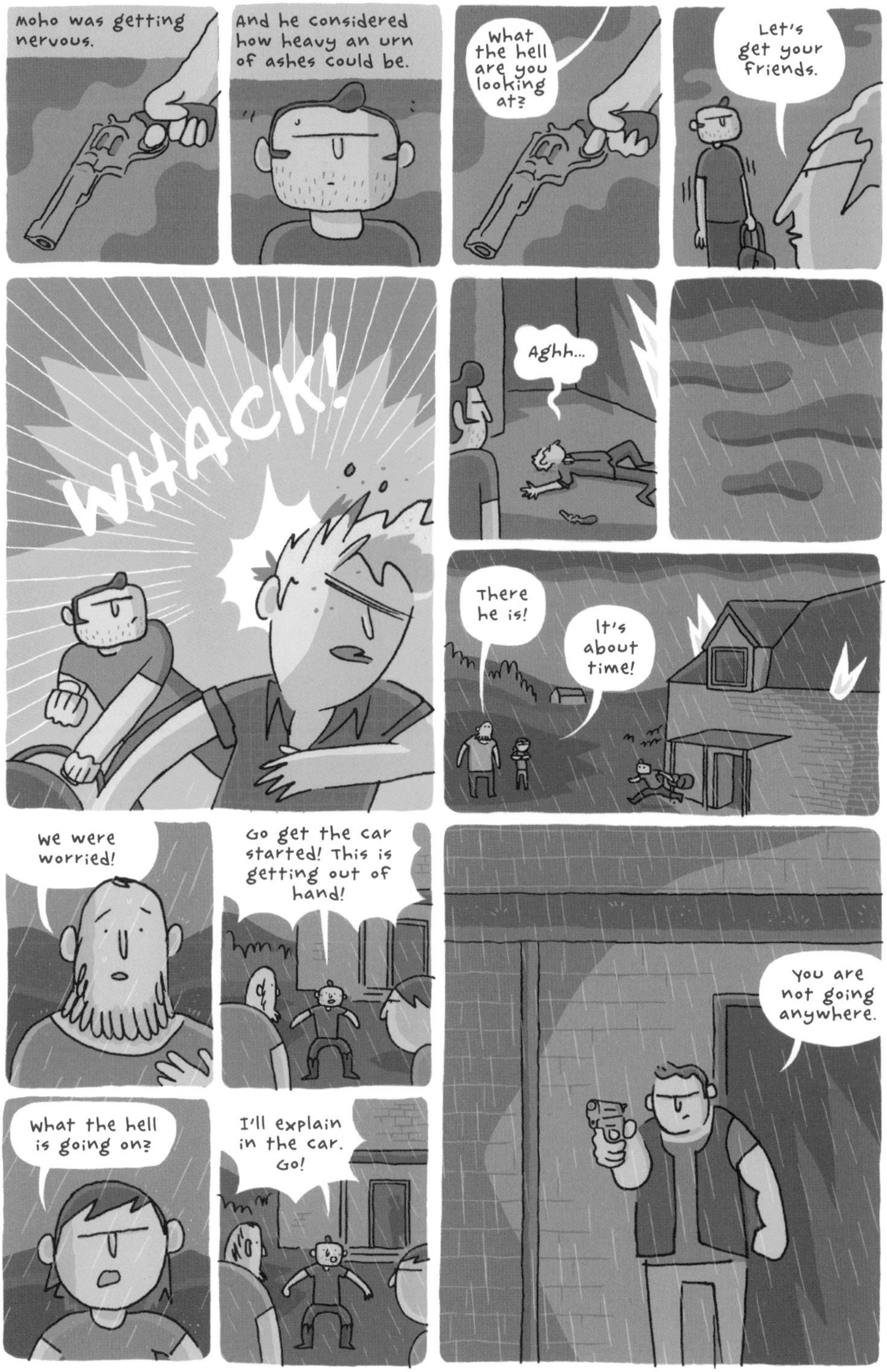
Moho was getting nervous.
And he considered how heavy an urn of ashes could be.
What the hell are you looking at?
Let's get your friends.
WHACK!
Aghh...
There he is!
It's about time!
We were worried!
Go get the car started! This is getting out of hand!
What the hell is going on?
I'll explain in the car. Go!
You are not going anywhere.

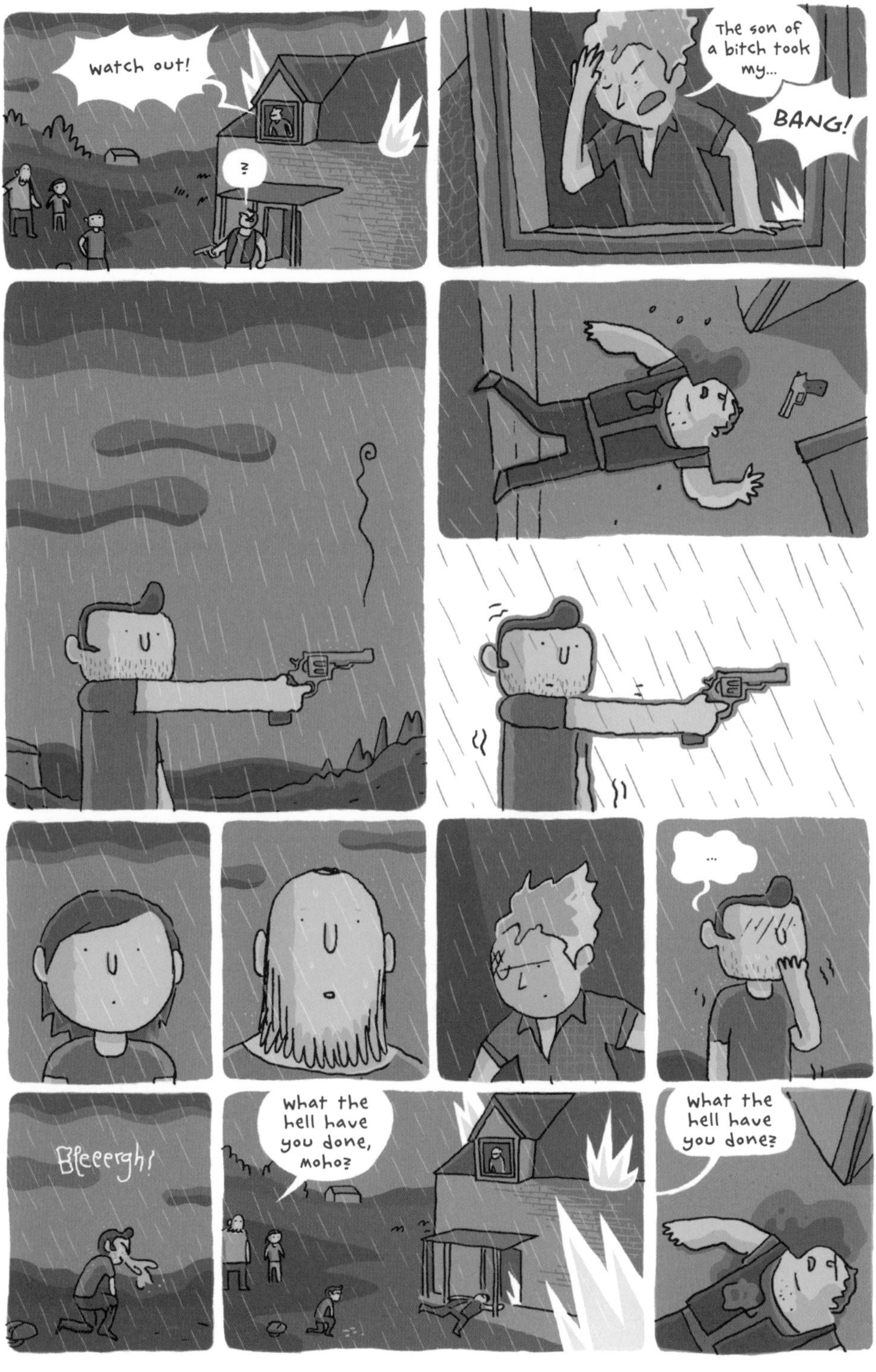
watch out!
?
The son of a bitch took my...
BANG!
...
Bleeergh!
what the hell have you done, moho?
what the hell have you done?

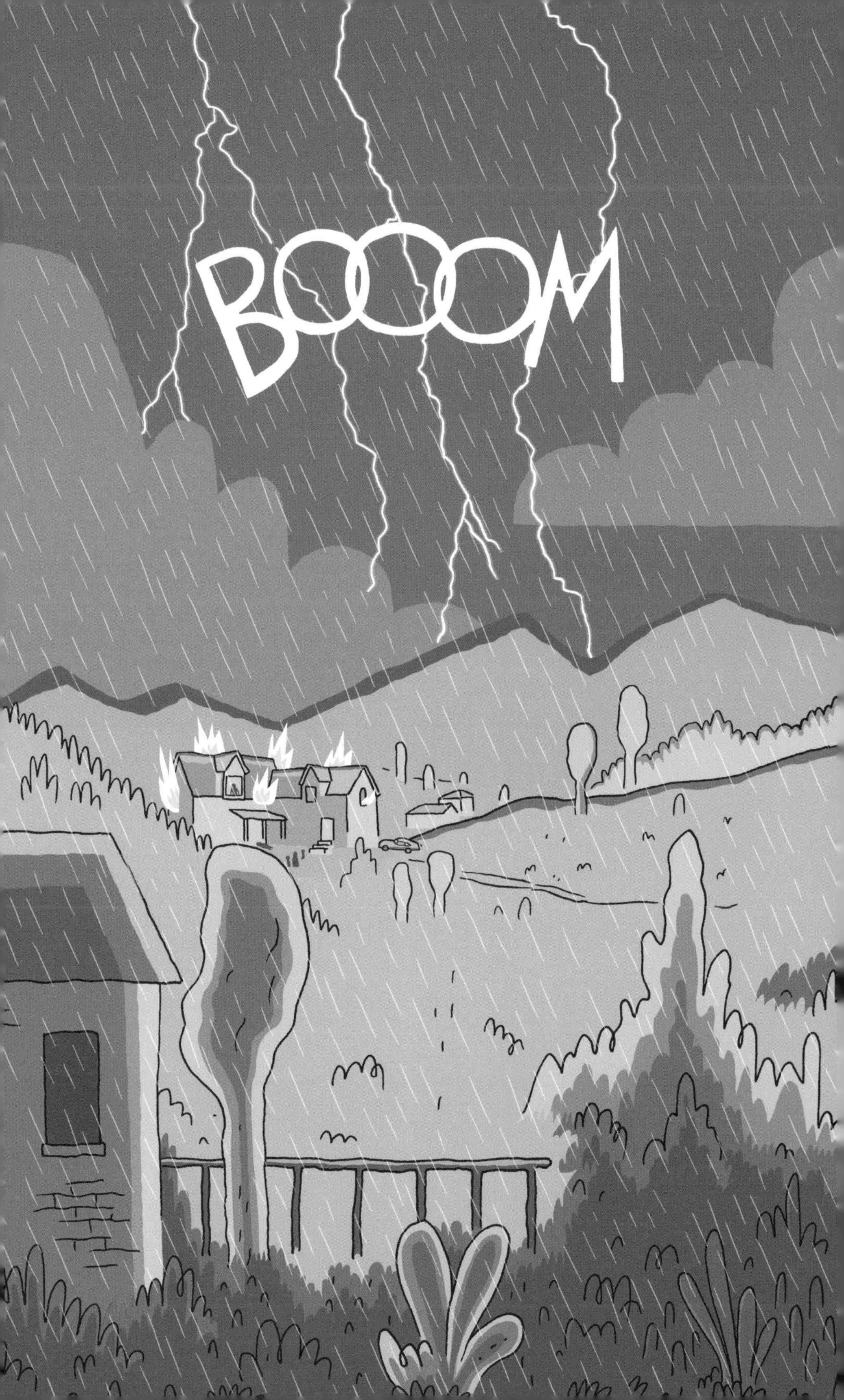
BOOOM

we saw the glare of the blazing house in the rearview mirror until we took the first turn.

moho threw the revolver out the window. Nobody said a word.

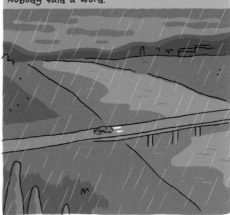

I couldn't stop thinking about everything that had just happened.

After the big guy was shot, the other one jumped out the window. The fall was bad, and the noise was even worse. He didn't move or scream anymore, after that.

we ran away like bats out of hell.

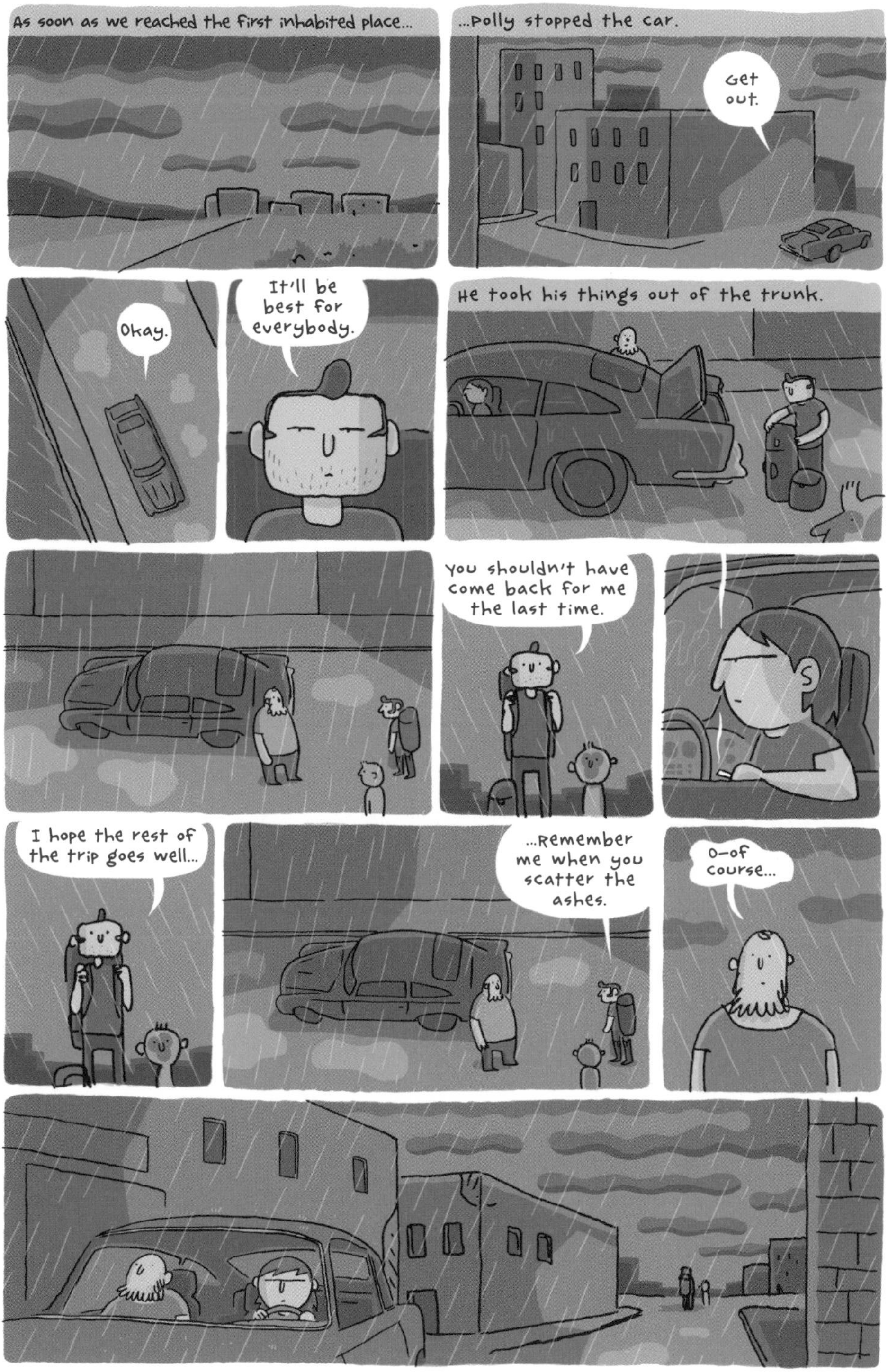
As soon as we reached the first inhabited place...
...Polly stopped the car.
Get out.
Okay.
It'll be best for everybody.
He took his things out of the trunk.
You shouldn't have come back for me the last time.
I hope the rest of the trip goes well...
...Remember me when you scatter the ashes.
O-of course...

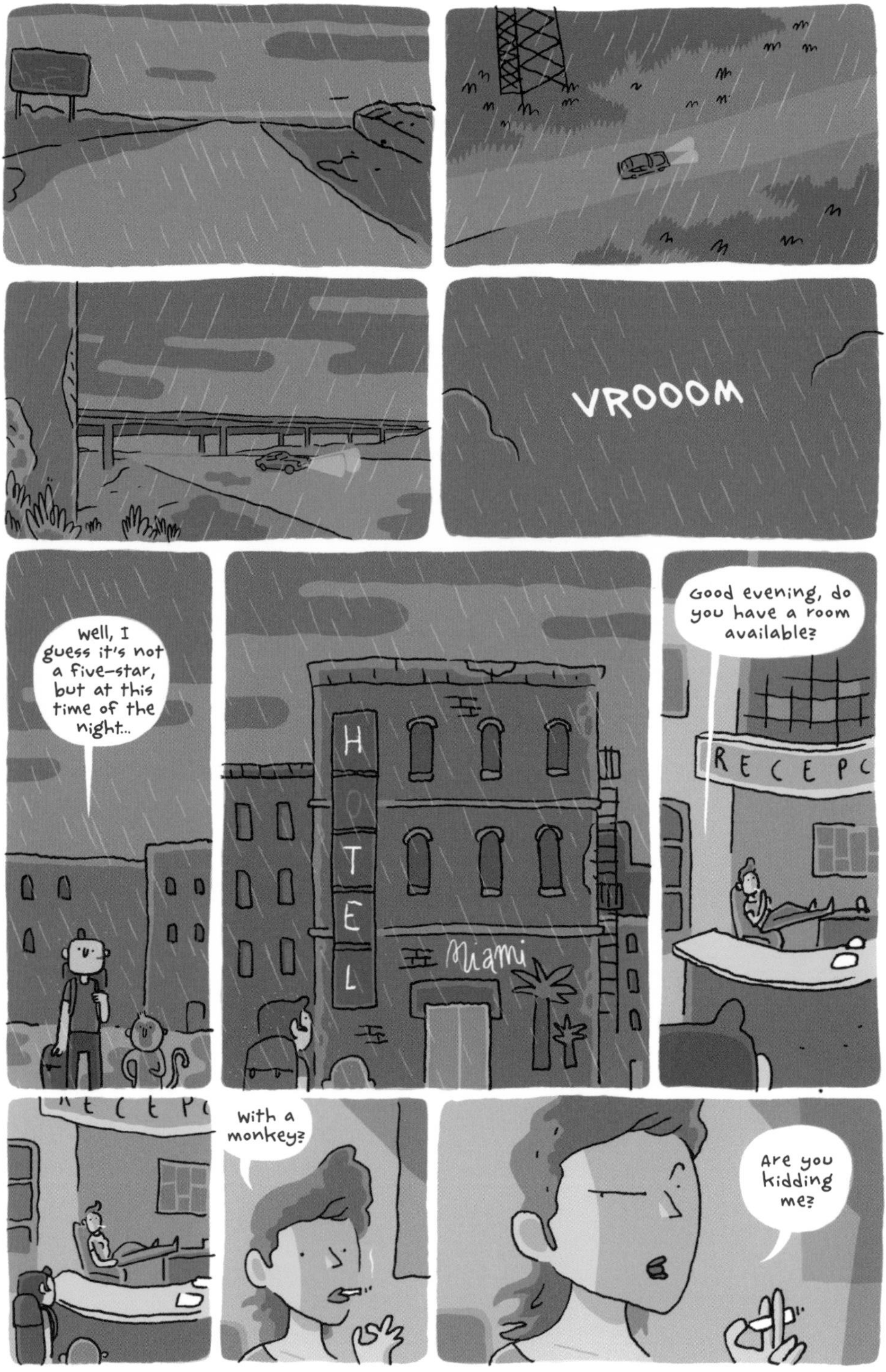
VROOOM
Well, I guess it's not a five-star, but at this time of the night...
HOTEL
Miami
Good evening, do you have a room available?
RECEPC
RECEPC
With a monkey?
Are you kidding me?

DAY 4 (+)

·······························

(because it's not over yet)

·······························

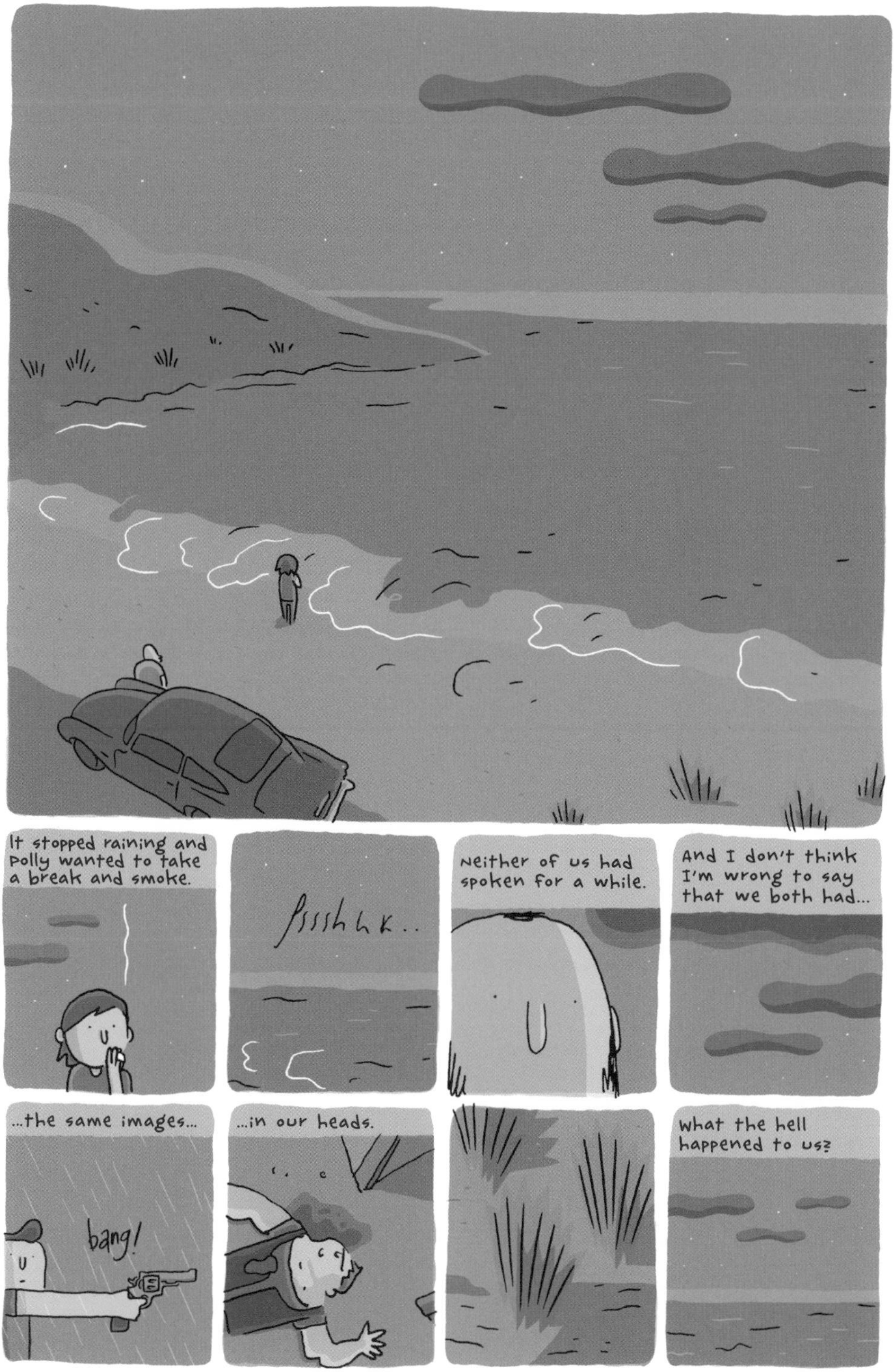
It stopped raining and Polly wanted to take a break and smoke.
Psssshhk..
Neither of us had spoken for a while.
And I don't think I'm wrong to say that we both had...
...the same images...
bang!
...in our heads.
What the hell happened to us?

There were some beers left in the trunk.

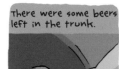

After a while, it started getting cooler...

...so, I got some sticks and lit a fire.

If you think about it...

...it's funny...

...Who would think something like this was going to happen?

...

I was only trying to play down the drama.

There's nothing funny about it.

Nothing.

And the trip's not over yet.

But I feel like taking the fucking boat...

...and scattering the ashes right here.

Maybe there's nothing at the X and he did it just to fuck with us.

Make us get into a car...

...and spend a week arguing...

Knowing him, I wouldn't be surprised.

Héctor's last practical joke.

So typical...

Then what do we do?

About what?

Should we scatter the ashes here?

This place isn't bad. He wanted a beach?

Here's a beach.

Besides, the three of us aren't together, so maybe the place is the least of it.

So what do we do? Scatter him and go back home?

...

At least you have a home to go back to...

But you're going back to London, right? With your boyfriend?

well...

...my boyfriend left me a couple of months ago.

Gosh... I'm sorry...

I don't care, he was an asshole, but I couldn't pay the rent...

...and now I'm living with two Chinese people whose names I can't pronounce...

...and another idiot who thinks he's Rasputin reincarnated...

My hours were cut at work, so I'm earning less.

And the manager is a fucking brat who doesn't even know who the Smiths are...

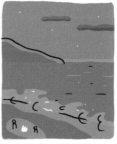

So the idea of going back is as attractive as a kick in the ovaries.

Would you rent a room to an eternal waitress?

I promise I play the guitar quietly...

well...

...Actually...

I don't really have a home either...

?

I inherited the house when Azah died.

Supposedly she didn't have any family left.

"But soon after, a distant nephew of her husband showed up. There was some irregularity in the will...

"...and after a few months of proceedings, he got to keep the house."

125

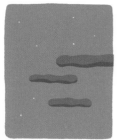

Damn... I had no idea.

Then the idiot calls to tell me not to worry...

"...that I could keep everything inside the house, because he doesn't want it."

I wish he were here so I could kick his head in.

It would fit with the day we've had...

That's true...

"So, I have like a million things--paintings, antique furniture, carvings, sculptures...

"All the mementos Azah and her husband collected during their lives. All their books."

What the heck should I do with all that? Let them rot in a landfill?

Sell them at auction on the internet?

I loved that house. I wish I could keep living there.

You would flip out if you saw the collection of African masks.

But now I have a month to leave and no job.

The only place I can afford with my savings will be some filthy room...

...with no space for even a quarter of Azah's things...

Goddd, what a mess...

Fuck...

Enough drama for one day.

How about going for a swim?

What?

I don't have a swimsuit...

Me neither.

126

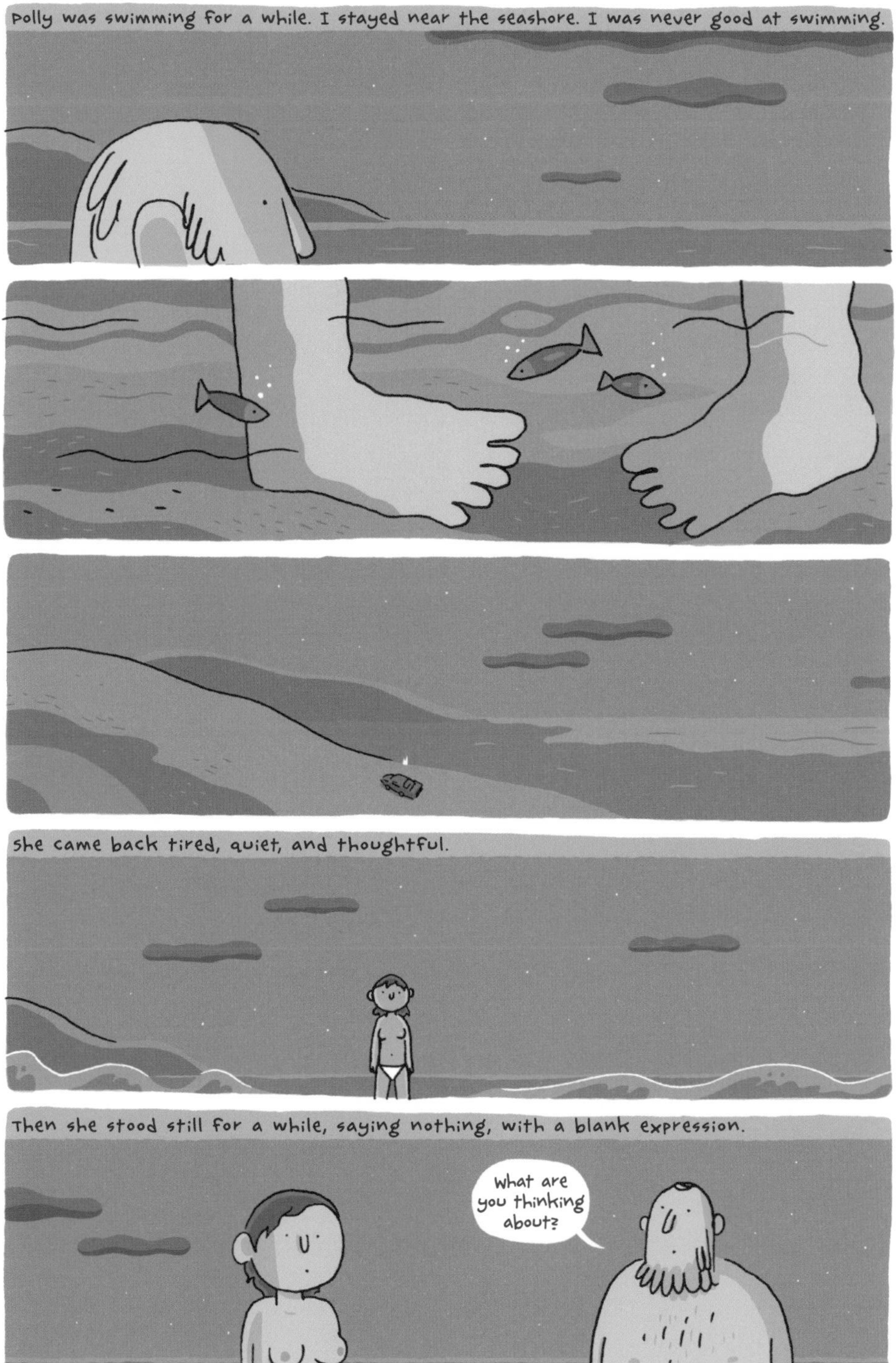
Polly was swimming for a while. I stayed near the seashore. I was never good at swimming.
She came back tired, quiet, and thoughtful.
Then she stood still for a while, saying nothing, with a blank expression.
What are you thinking about?

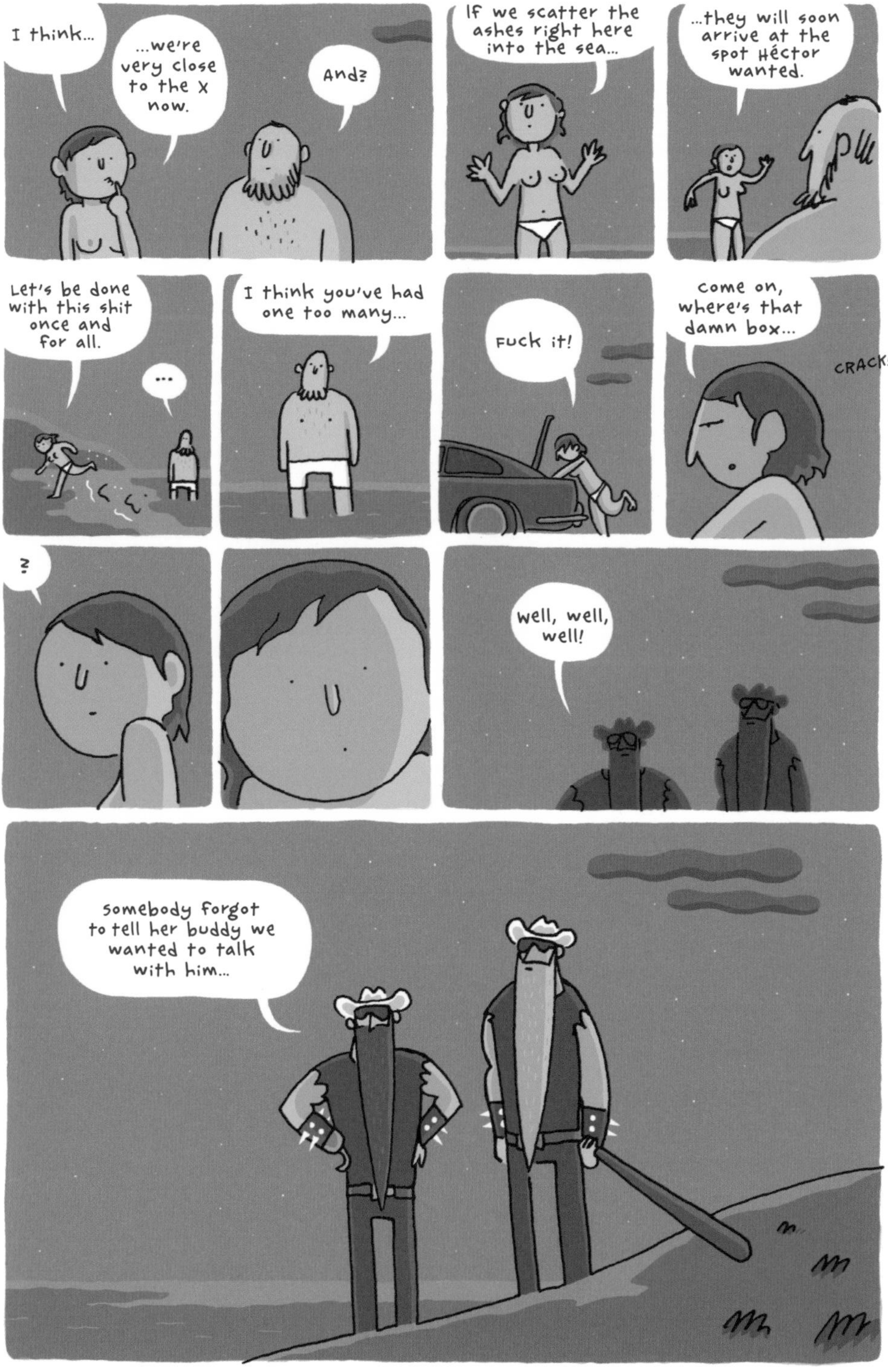
I think...
...we're very close to the X now.
And?
If we scatter the ashes right here into the sea...
...they will soon arrive at the spot Héctor wanted.
Let's be done with this shit once and for all.
...
I think you've had one too many...
Fuck it!
Come on, where's that damn box...
CRACK!
?
Well, well, well!
Somebody forgot to tell her buddy we wanted to talk with him...

DAY 5

(in which someone will
try to be a hero)

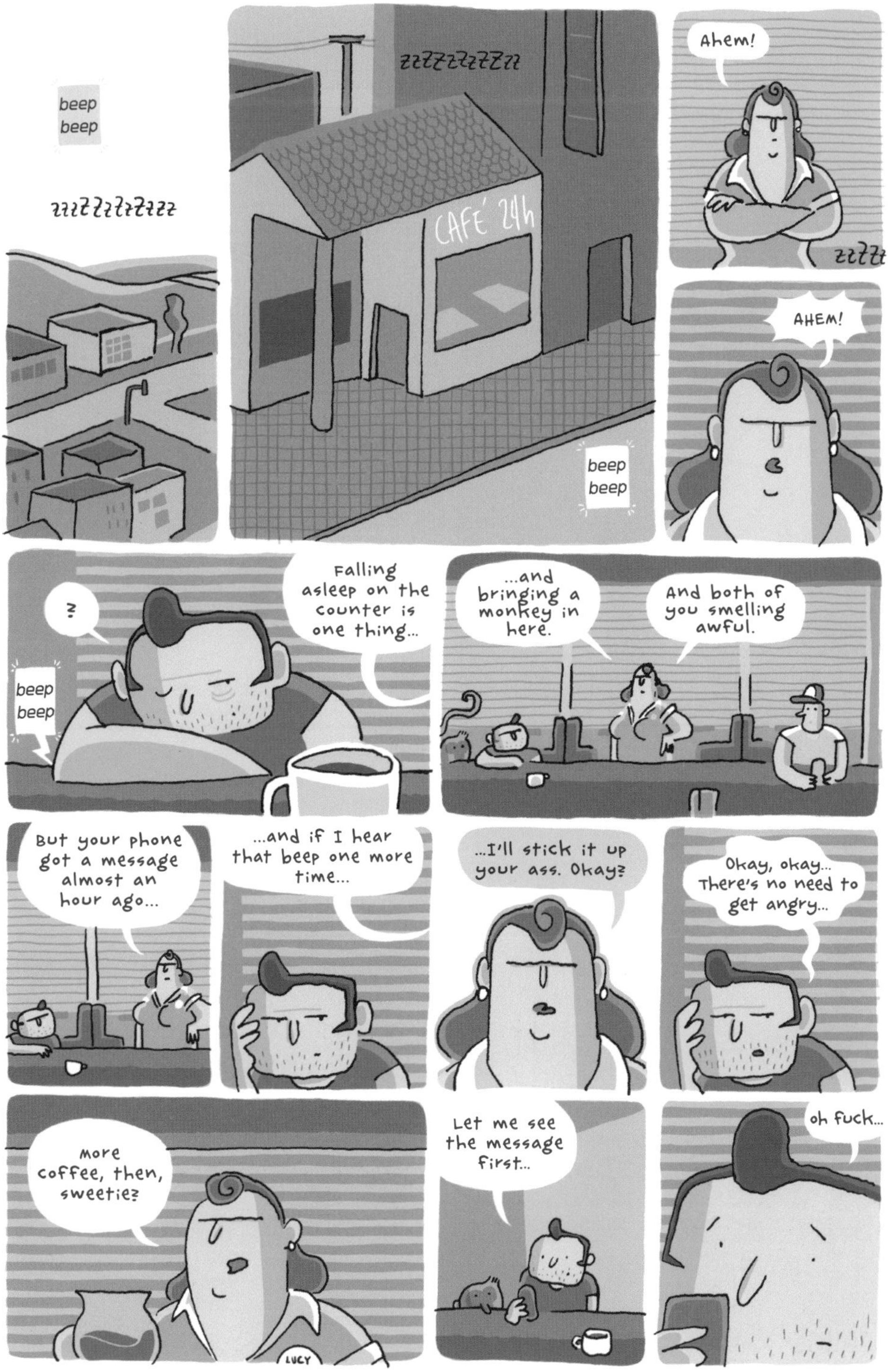
beep
beep
zzzZzzzZzzz
zzZZzzzzZzz
CAFÉ 24h
beep
beep
Ahem!
zzZZz
AHEM!
?
beep
beep
Falling asleep on the counter is one thing...
...and bringing a monkey in here.
And both of you smelling awful.
But your phone got a message almost an hour ago...
...and if I hear that beep one more time...
...I'll stick it up your ass. Okay?
Okay, okay... There's no need to get angry...
More coffee, then, sweetie?
LUCY
Let me see the message first...
oh fuck...

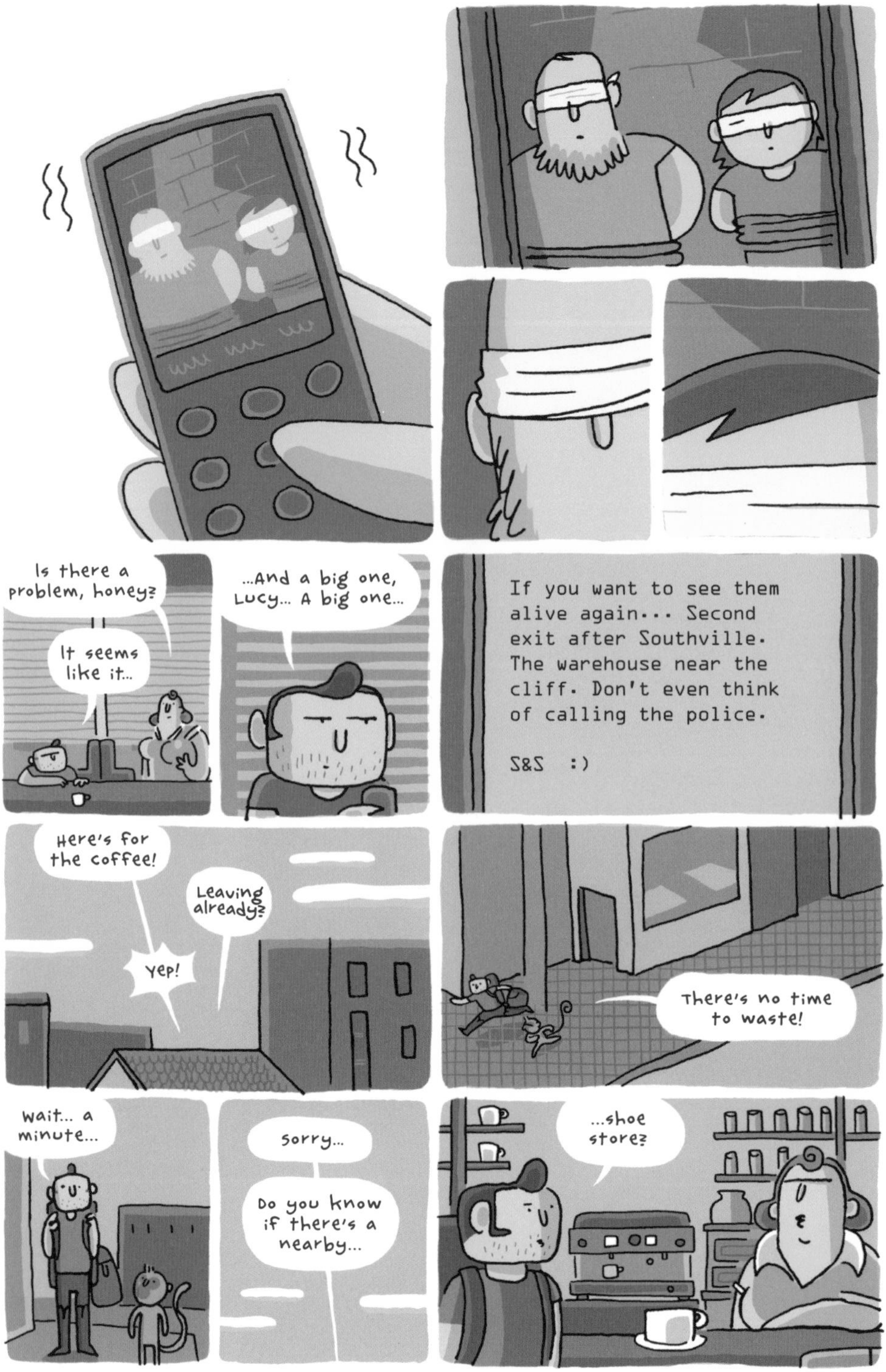

Is there a problem, honey?
It seems like it...
...And a big one, Lucy... A big one...
If you want to see them alive again... Second exit after Southville. The warehouse near the cliff. Don't even think of calling the police.
S&S :)
Here's for the coffee!
Leaving already?
Yep!
There's no time to waste!
Wait... a minute...
Sorry...
Do you know if there's a nearby...
...shoe store?

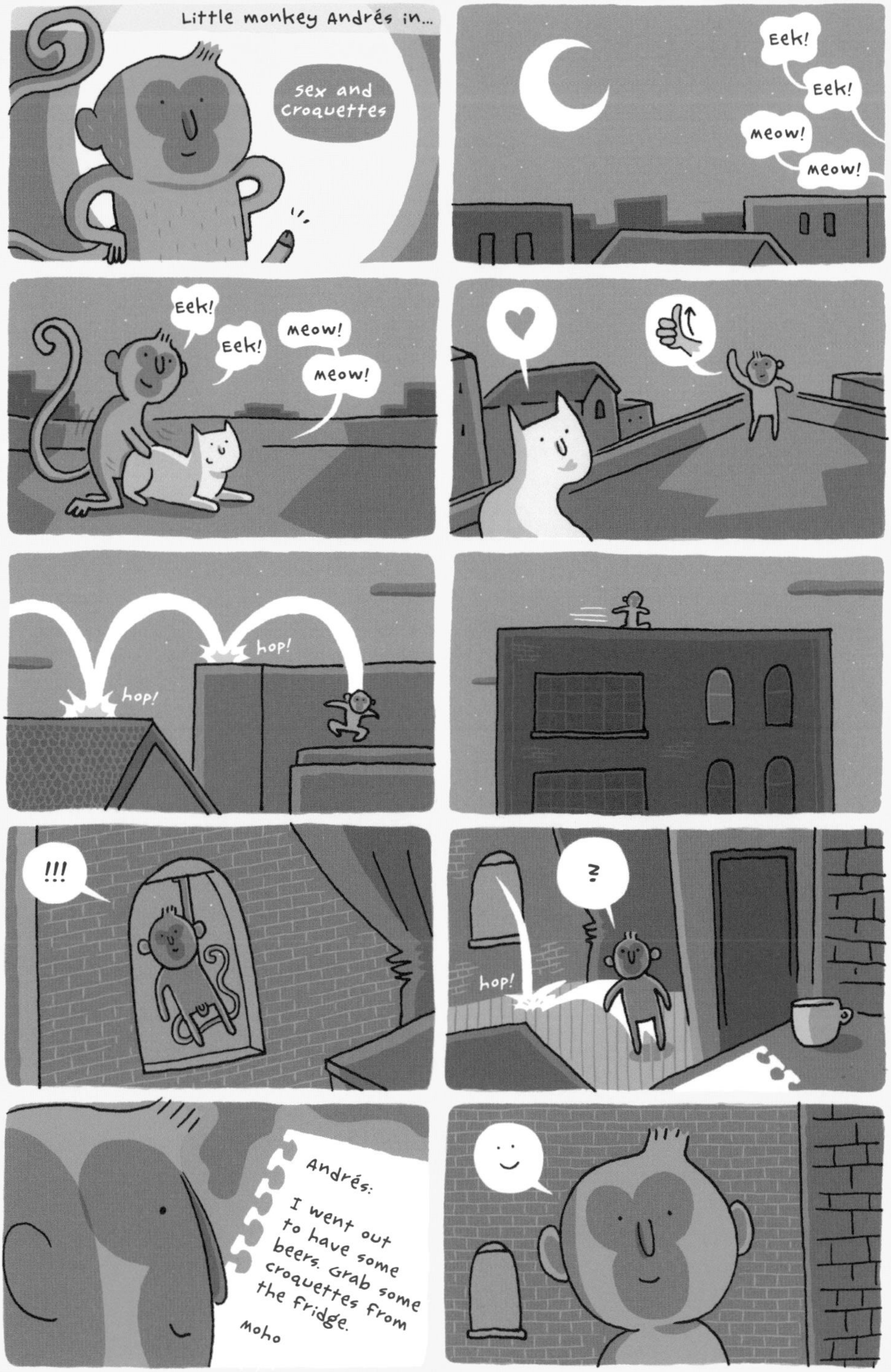
Little monkey Andrés in...
sex and croquettes
Eek!
Eek!
meow!
meow!
Eek!
Eek!
meow!
meow!
hop!
hop!
!!!
?
hop!
Andrés:
I went out to have some beers. Grab some croquettes from the fridge.
Moho

The first cremation chamber was invented in 1857, but people have found ways to be cremated for centuries.

Among the most bizarre reasons for doing so was the mass panic in the United Kingdom circa 1815.

It is known that the bodies of executed inmates were used for dissection in medical schools.

It was common that murderers and rapists were used to study the marvels of the human body.

But in 1815, thanks to human rights activist John Miles, the death penalty was abolished.

Therefore, there was a shortage of corpses available.

People with dubious morals saw a potential business.

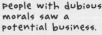

Some, like the infamous Burke and Hare, obtained their wares through murder...

...although most people were simply robbing fresh corpses.

The body snatchers spread terror in Victorian society.

Extra! Extra!

THEFT IN CEMETERY

Families had to keep watch at the tombs of the deceased for weeks...

...And cemeteries began to construct higher walls and hire security guards.

Still, a terrified public begged to be cremated. Anything to escape becoming an involuntary postmortem lab rat.

Frankenstein
or The Modern Prometheus

Mary Shelley

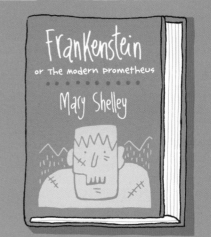

Of course, the 1818 publication of a book by young Mary Shelley did not help to ease their minds.

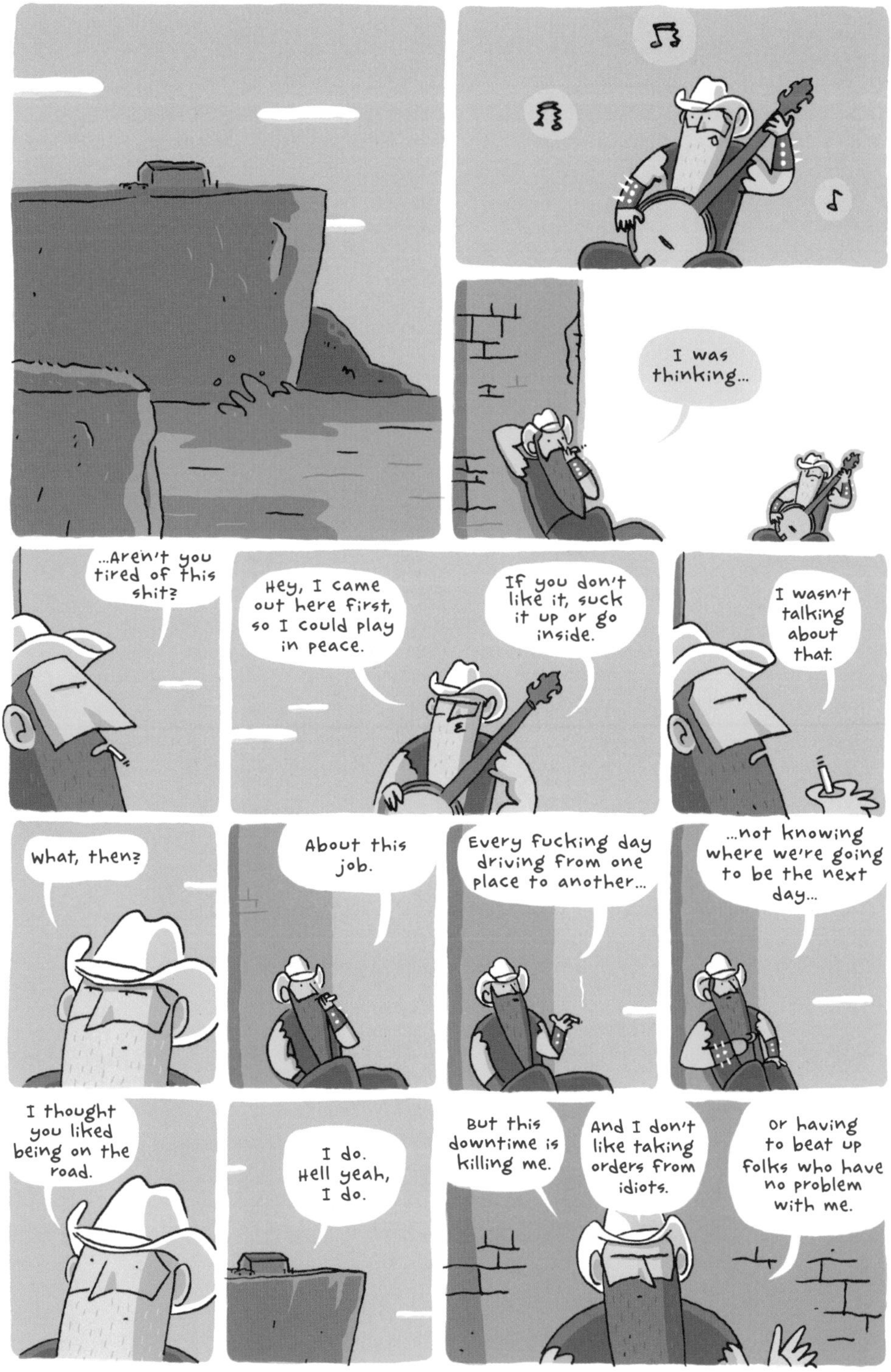
I was thinking...
...Aren't you tired of this shit?
Hey, I came out here first, so I could play in peace.
If you don't like it, suck it up or go inside.
I wasn't talking about that.
What, then?
About this job.
Every fucking day driving from one place to another...
...not knowing where we're going to be the next day...
I thought you liked being on the road.
I do. Hell yeah, I do.
But this downtime is killing me.
And I don't like taking orders from idiots.
Or having to beat up folks who have no problem with me.

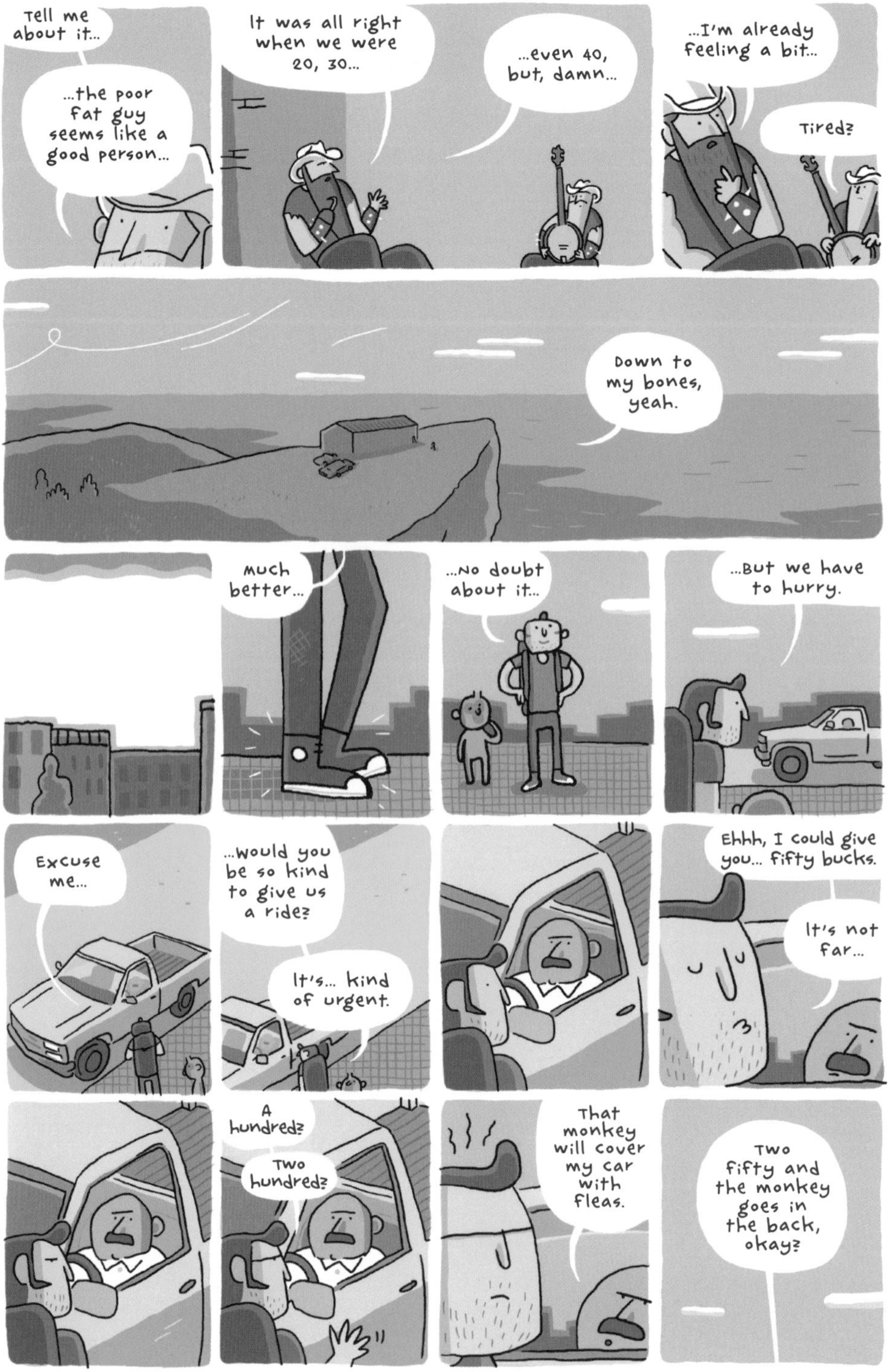
Tell me about it...
...the poor fat guy seems like a good person...
It was all right when we were 20, 30...
...even 40, but, damn...
...I'm already feeling a bit...
Tired?
Down to my bones, yeah.
Much better...
...No doubt about it...
...But we have to hurry.
Excuse me...
...would you be so kind to give us a ride?
It's... kind of urgent.
Ehhh, I could give you... fifty bucks.
It's not far...
A hundred?
Two hundred?
That monkey will cover my car with fleas.
Two fifty and the monkey goes in the back, okay?

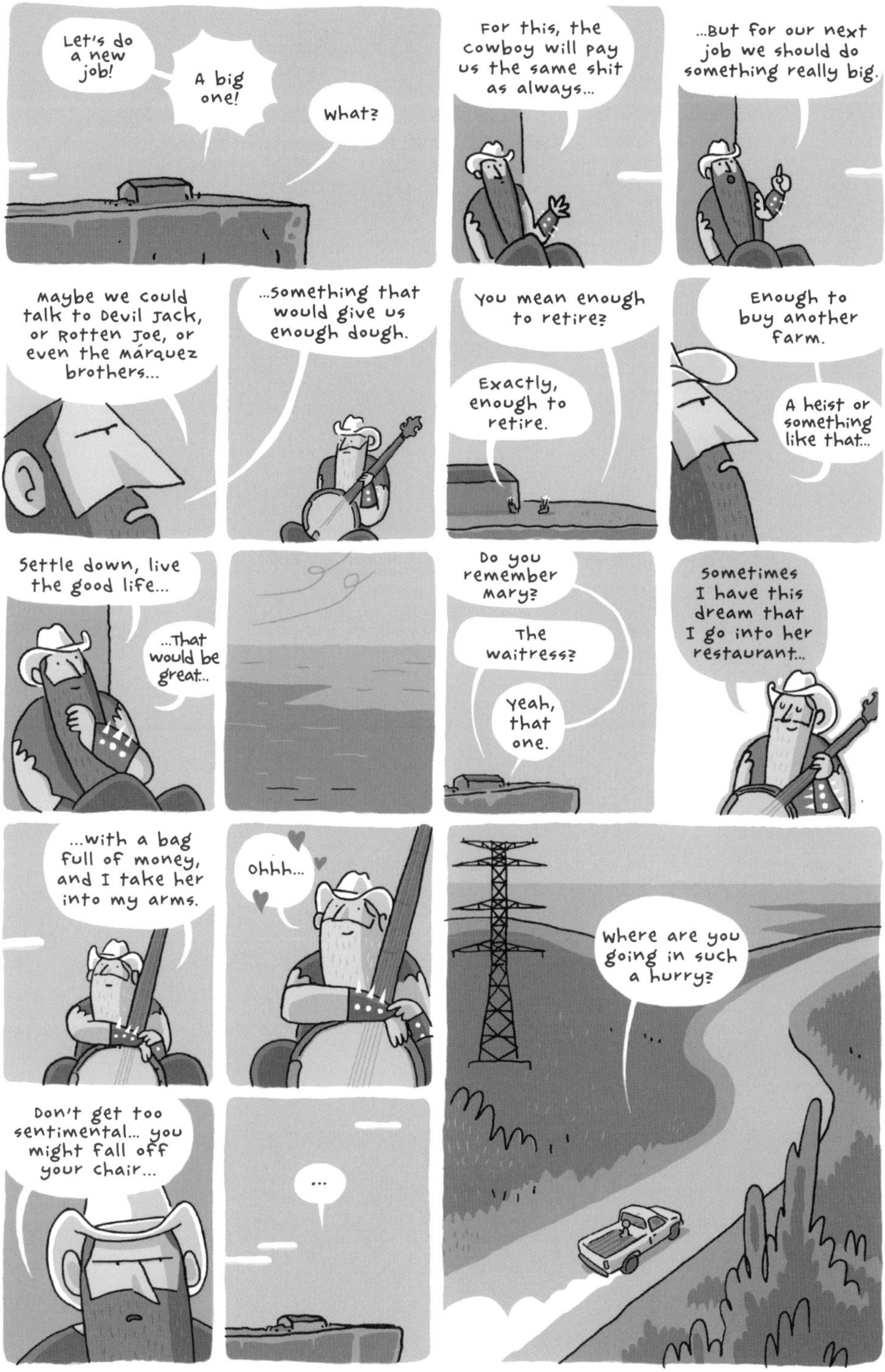
Let's do a new job!
A big one!
What?
For this, the cowboy will pay us the same shit as always...
...But for our next job we should do something really big.
Maybe we could talk to Devil Jack, or Rotten Joe, or even the Márquez brothers...
...something that would give us enough dough.
You mean enough to retire?
Exactly, enough to retire.
Enough to buy another farm.
A heist or something like that...
Settle down, live the good life...
...That would be great...
Do you remember Mary?
The waitress?
Yeah, that one.
Sometimes I have this dream that I go into her restaurant...
...with a bag full of money, and I take her into my arms.
Ohhh...
Where are you going in such a hurry?
Don't get too sentimental... you might fall off your chair...
...

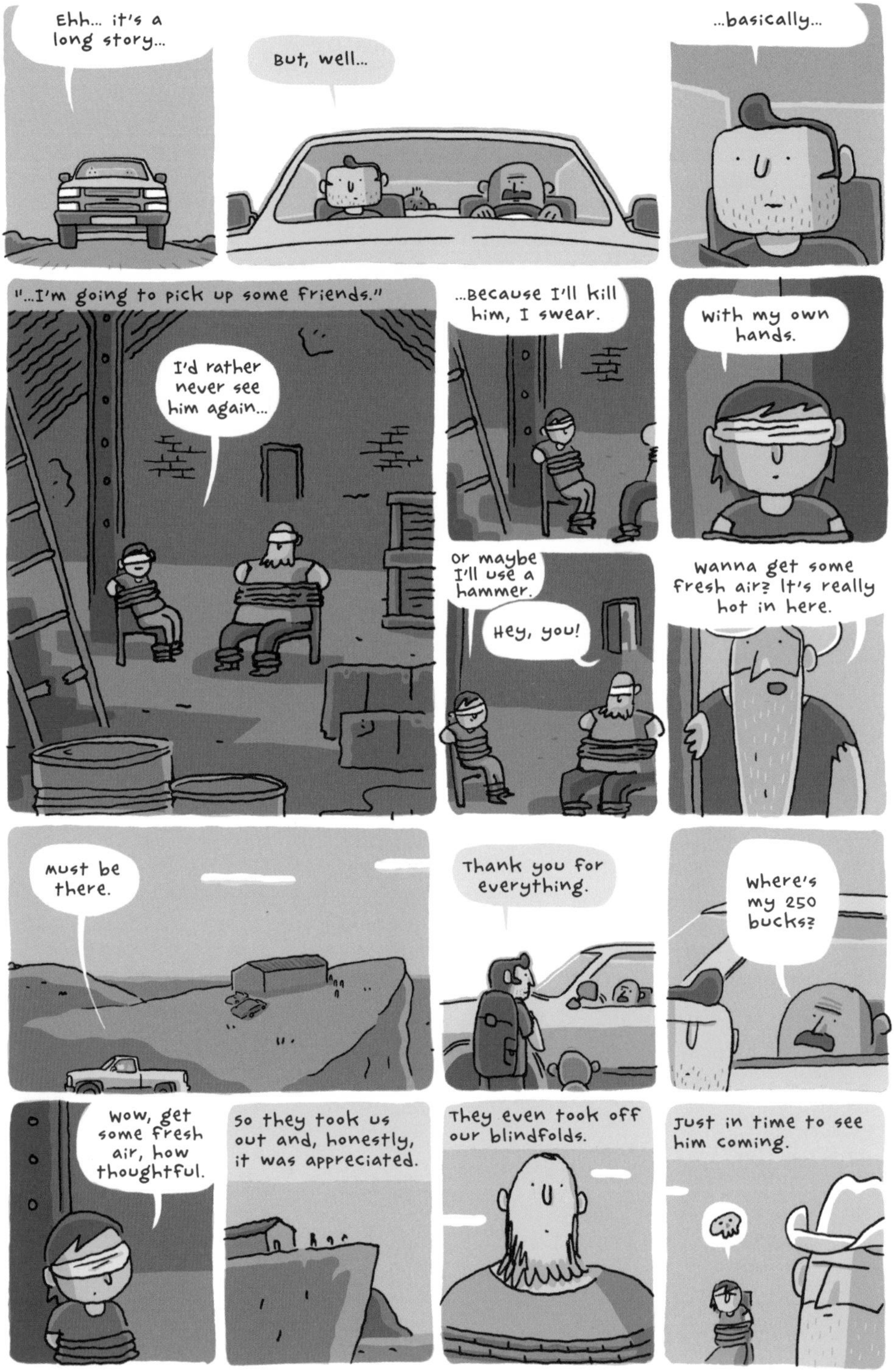
Ehh... it's a long story...
But, well...
...basically...
"...I'm going to pick up some friends."
I'd rather never see him again...
...Because I'll kill him, I swear.
With my own hands.
Or maybe I'll use a hammer.
Hey, you!
Wanna get some fresh air? It's really hot in here.
Must be there.
Thank you for everything.
Where's my 250 bucks?
Wow, get some fresh air, how thoughtful.
So they took us out and, honestly, it was appreciated.
They even took off our blindfolds.
Just in time to see him coming.

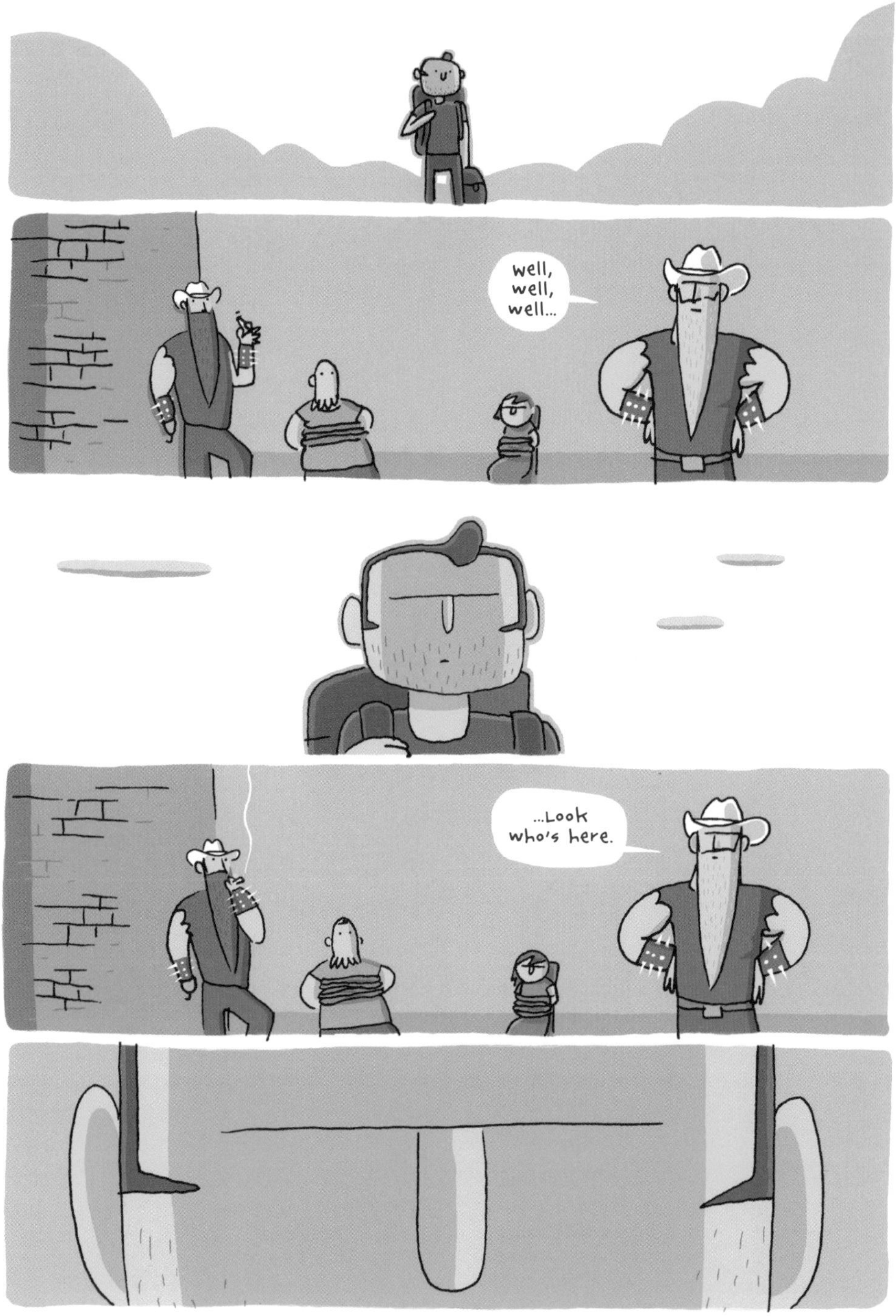
well, well, well...
...Look who's here.

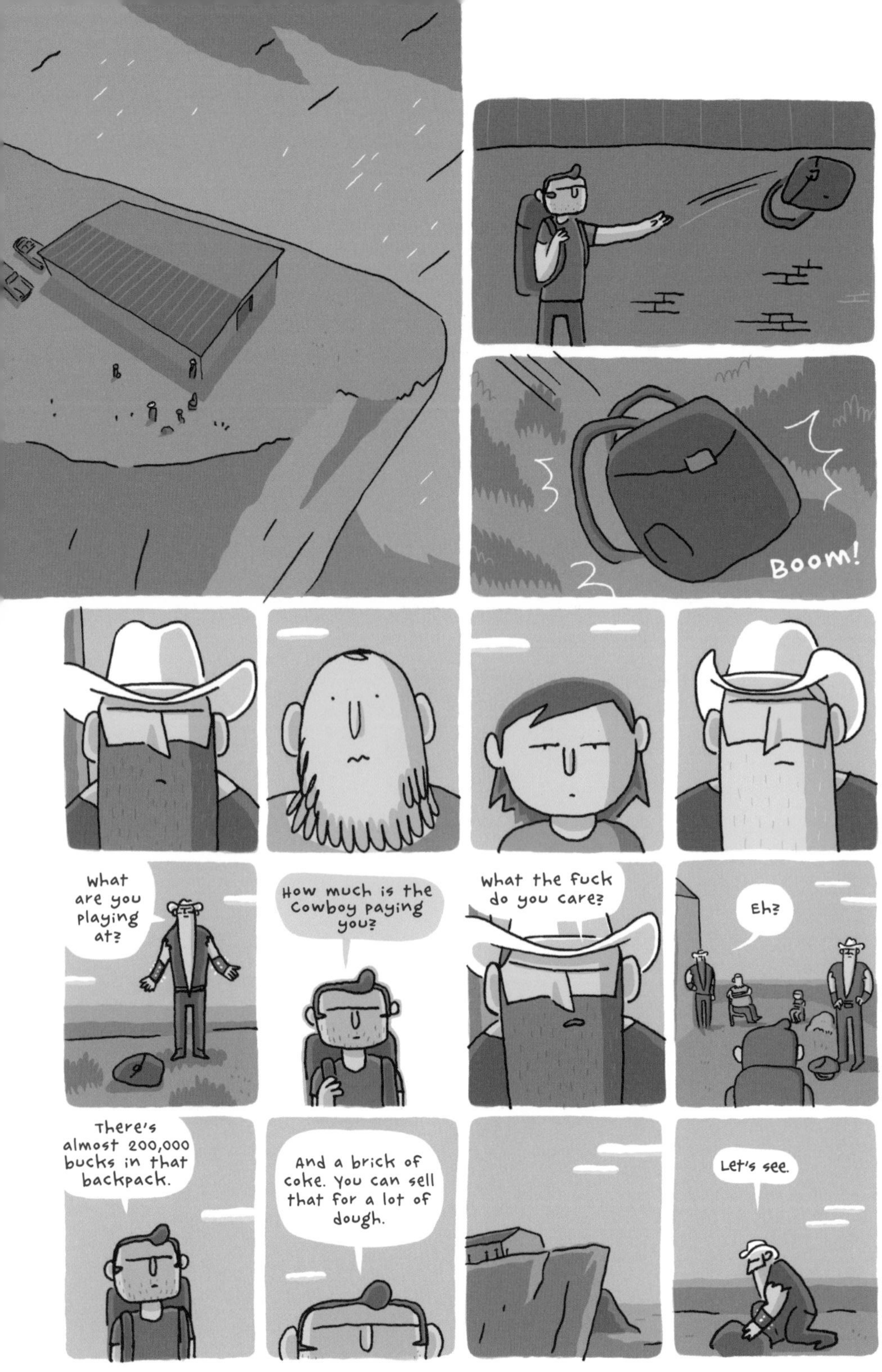
Boom!
What are you playing at?
How much is the cowboy paying you?
What the fuck do you care?
Eh?
There's almost 200,000 bucks in that backpack.
And a brick of coke. You can sell that for a lot of dough.
Let's see.

Be careful! Could be a trap.

Do I look like I know how to make a bomb?

He's right. This is full of money...

...and drugs.

What should we do?

There was total silence. The only sound was the waves crashing on the rocks.

The wind was blowing.

Until that moment Polly and I were not aware that...

...moho never delivered the backpack with the money.

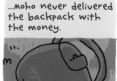

And there he was now, grim-faced...

...trying to buy our freedom.

And trying to avoid his legs being broken, of course.

It was something between heroic and pathetic.

...

Well?

Do you accept the exchange?

And then a noise startled everyone.

What the hell?

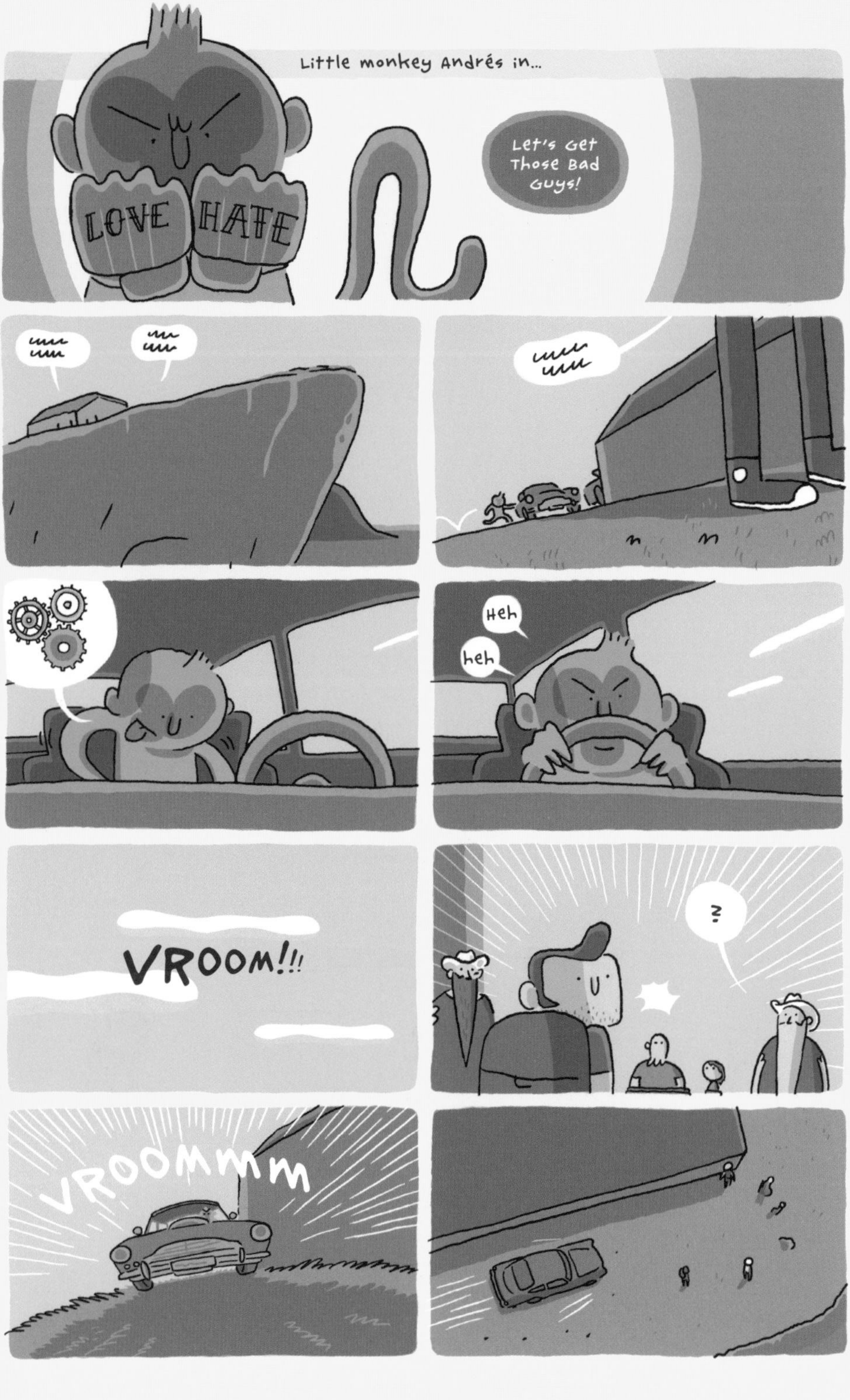
Little monkey Andrés in...
LOVE HATE
Let's Get Those Bad Guys!
Heh
heh
VROOM!!!
?
VROOMMMM

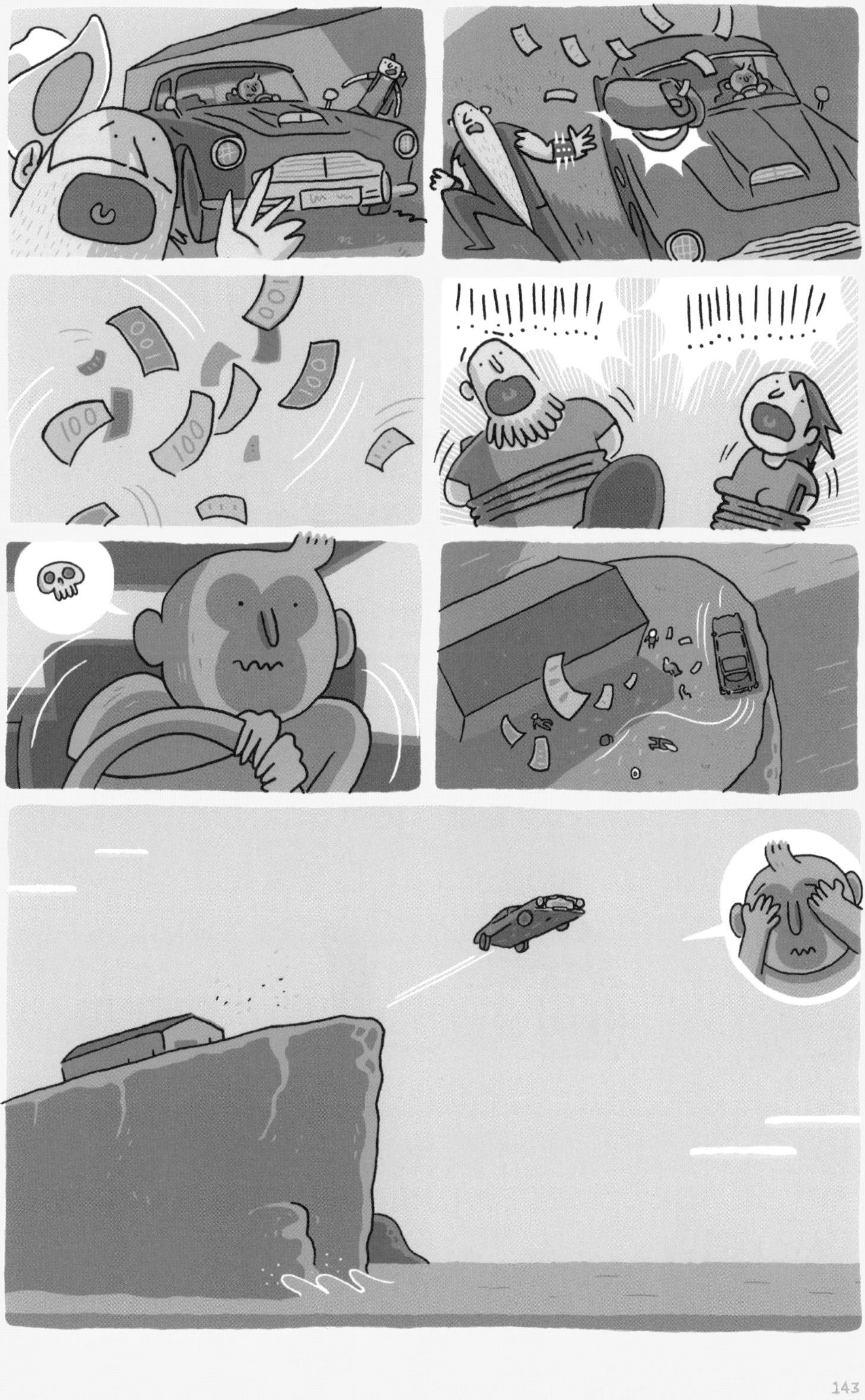

What the fuck was that?

The monkey...

Well, fuck the monkey!

He almost killed us all!

Tell me about it...

Andrés, buddy...

...what were you thinking?

The car, shit... The car was rented under my name...

...why couldn't he pick the other one...

Moho was in shock. Frozen.

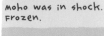

The ground was covered with bills.

Fortunately, the wind was blowing toward us, so very few fell into the sea.

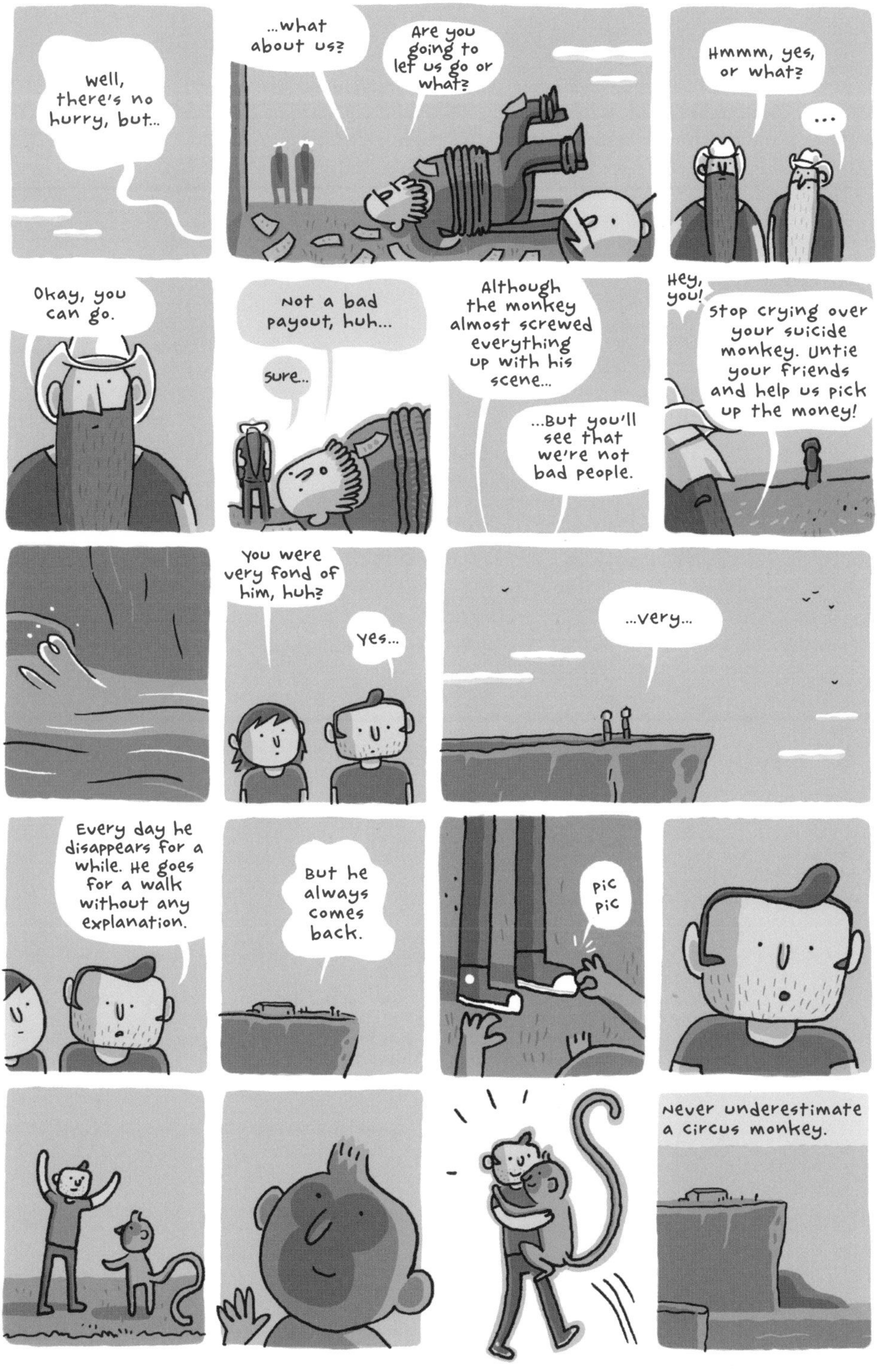
Well, there's no hurry, but...
...what about us?
Are you going to let us go or what?
Hmmm, yes, or what?
...
Okay, you can go.
Not a bad payout, huh...
Sure...
Although the monkey almost screwed everything up with his scene...
...But you'll see that we're not bad people.
Hey, you!
Stop crying over your suicide monkey. Untie your friends and help us pick up the money!
You were very fond of him, huh?
Yes...
...very...
Every day he disappears for a while. He goes for a walk without any explanation.
But he always comes back.
pic pic
Never underestimate a circus monkey.

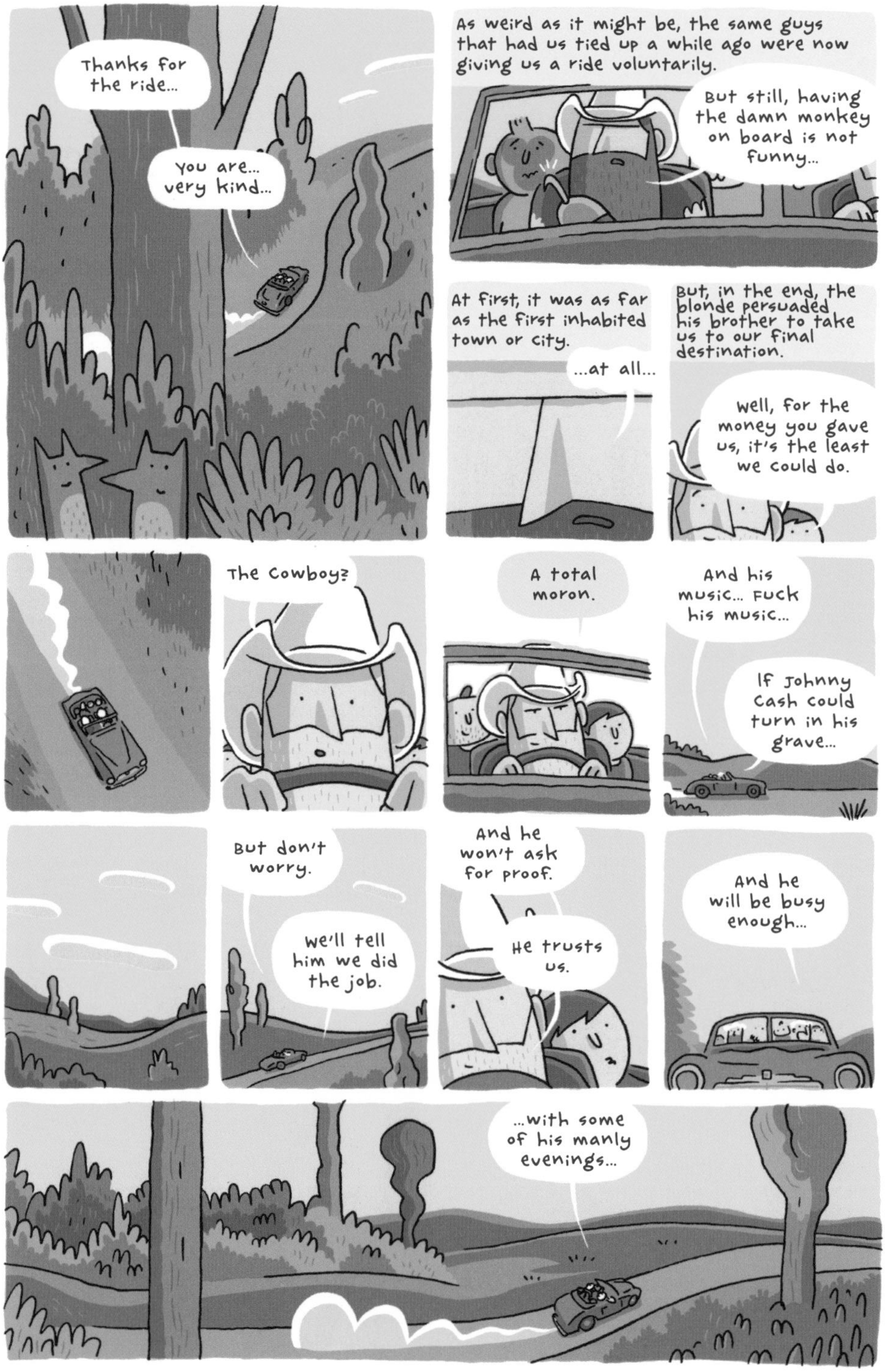

Thanks for the ride...
You are... very kind...
As weird as it might be, the same guys that had us tied up a while ago were now giving us a ride voluntarily.
But still, having the damn monkey on board is not funny...
At first, it was as far as the first inhabited town or city.
...at all...
But, in the end, the blonde persuaded his brother to take us to our final destination.
Well, for the money you gave us, it's the least we could do.
The cowboy?
A total moron.
And his music... Fuck his music...
If Johnny Cash could turn in his grave...
But don't worry.
We'll tell him we did the job.
And he won't ask for proof.
He trusts us.
And he will be busy enough...
...with some of his manly evenings...

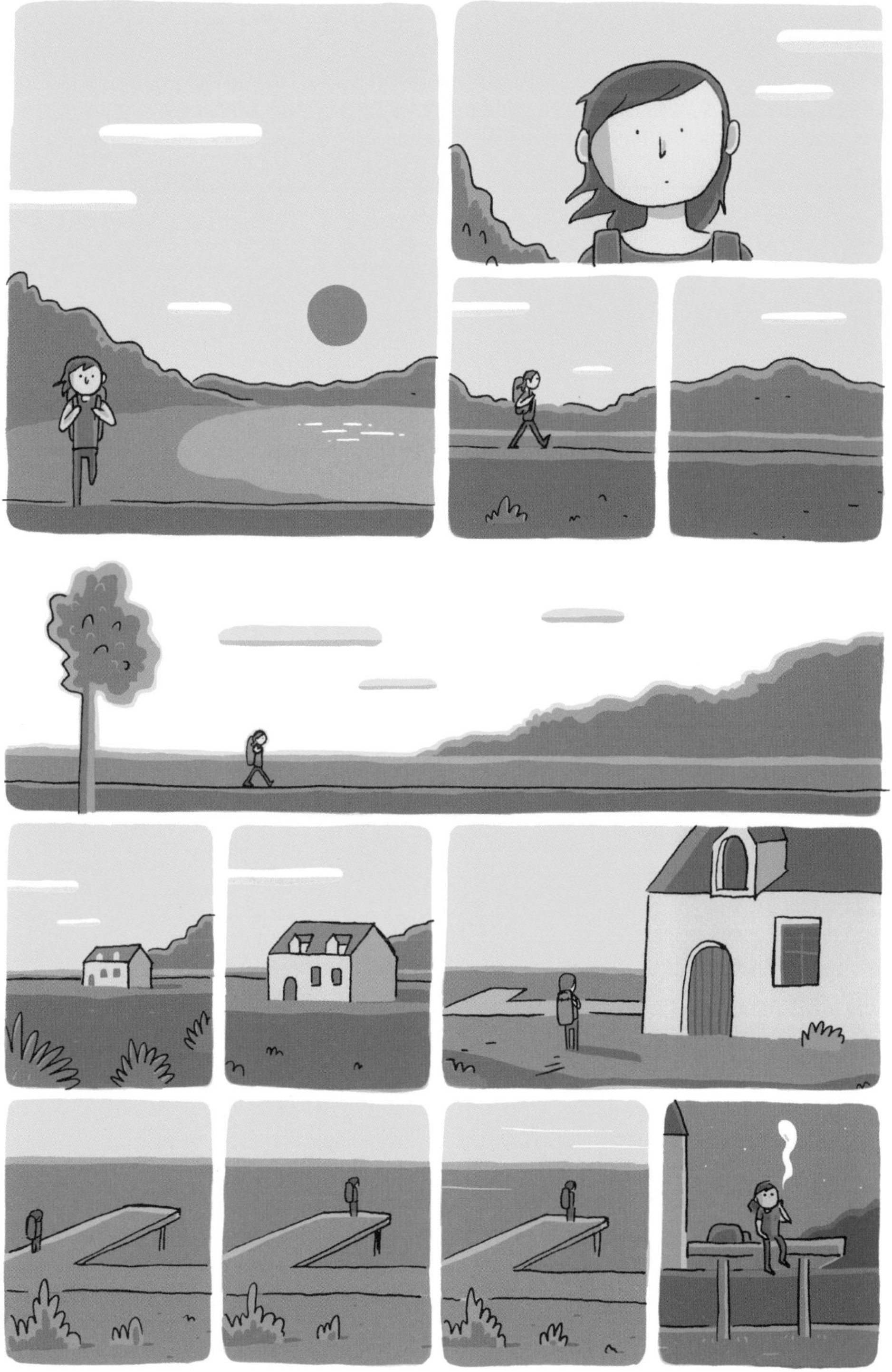

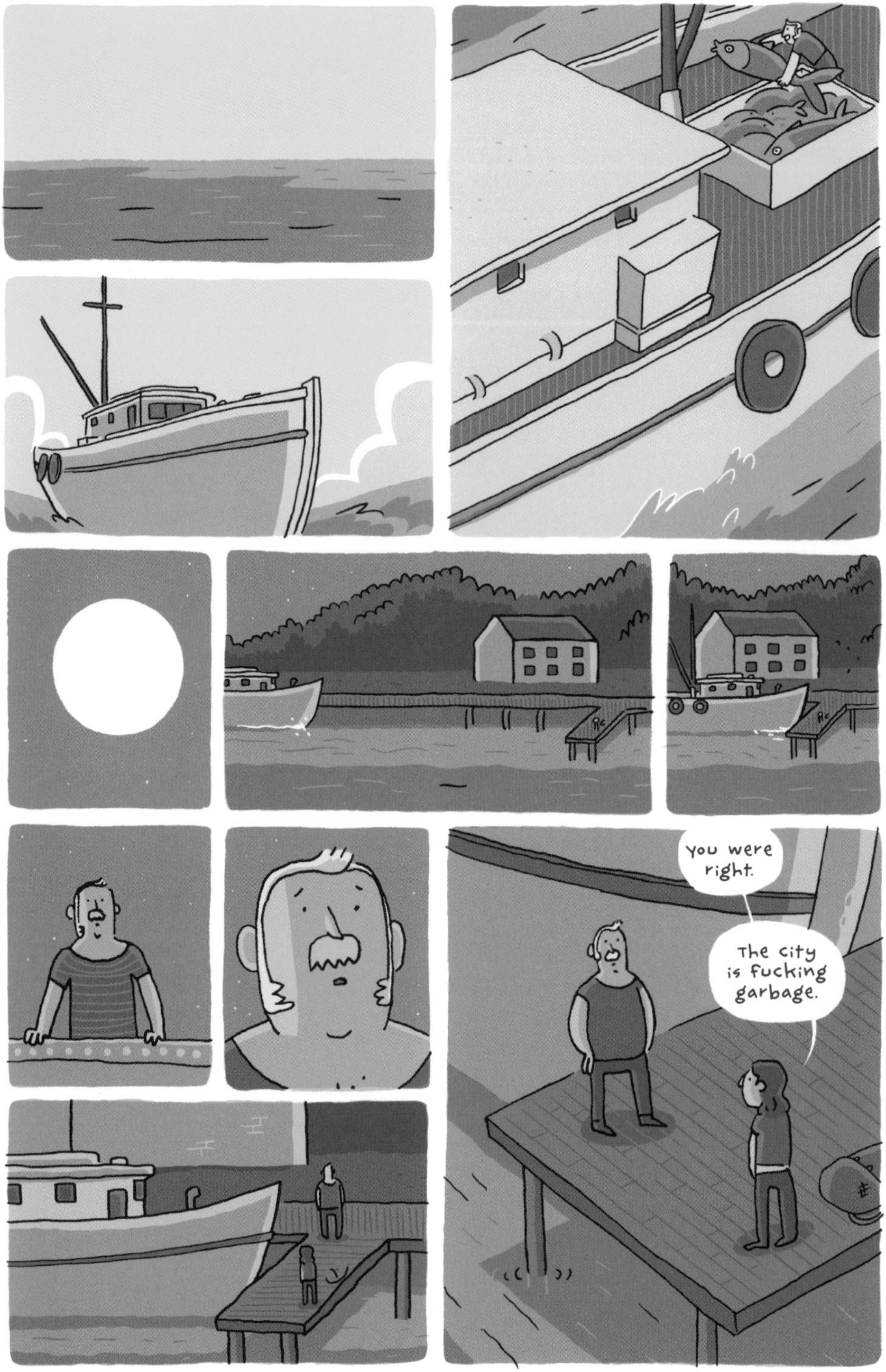
You were right.
The city is fucking garbage.

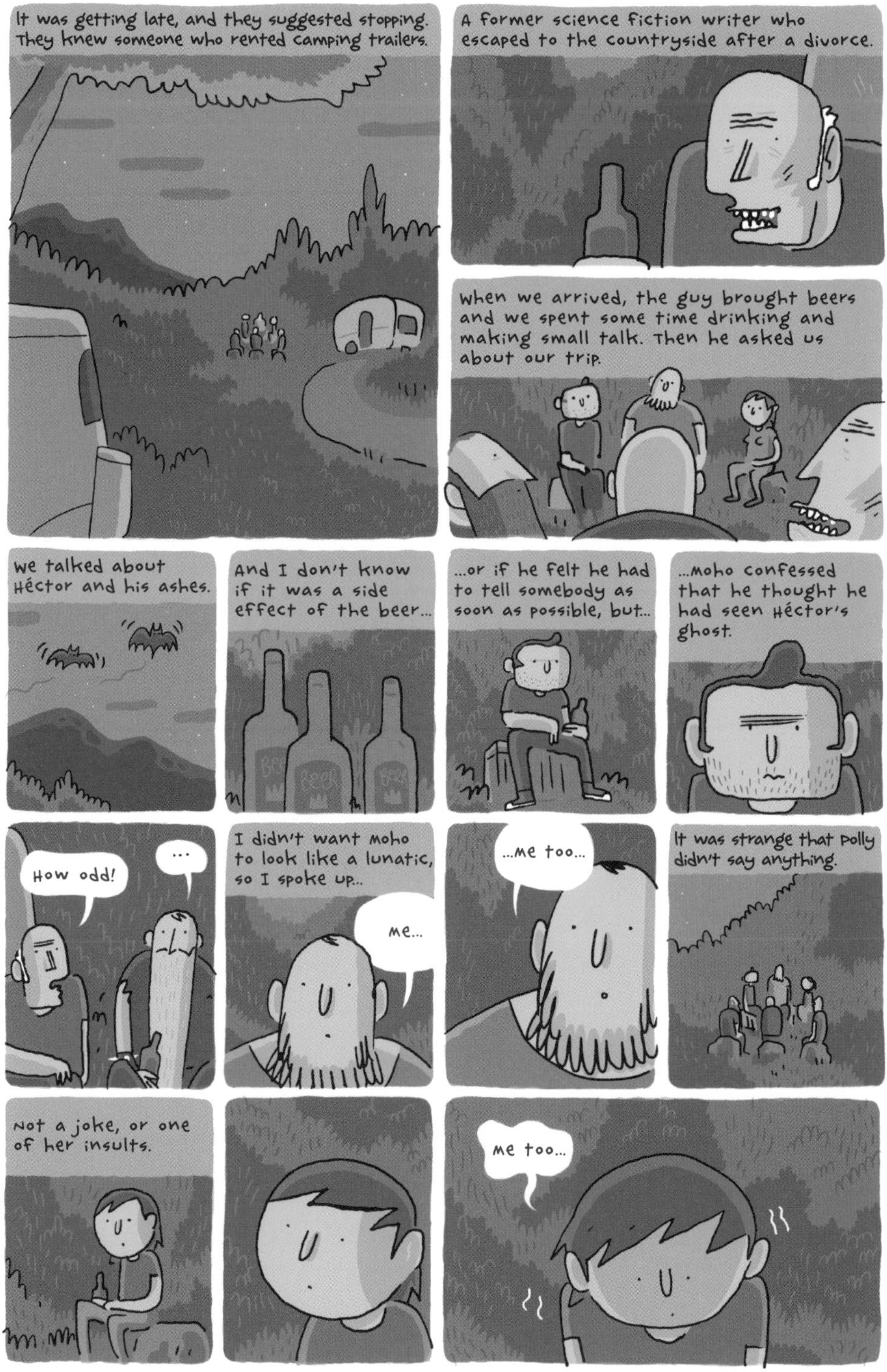
It was getting late, and they suggested stopping. They knew someone who rented camping trailers.
A former science fiction writer who escaped to the countryside after a divorce.
When we arrived, the guy brought beers and we spent some time drinking and making small talk. Then he asked us about our trip.
We talked about Héctor and his ashes.
And I don't know if it was a side effect of the beer...
...or if he felt he had to tell somebody as soon as possible, but...
...Moho confessed that he thought he had seen Héctor's ghost.
How odd!
...
I didn't want Moho to look like a lunatic, so I spoke up...
me...
...me too...
It was strange that Polly didn't say anything.
Not a joke, or one of her insults.
me too...

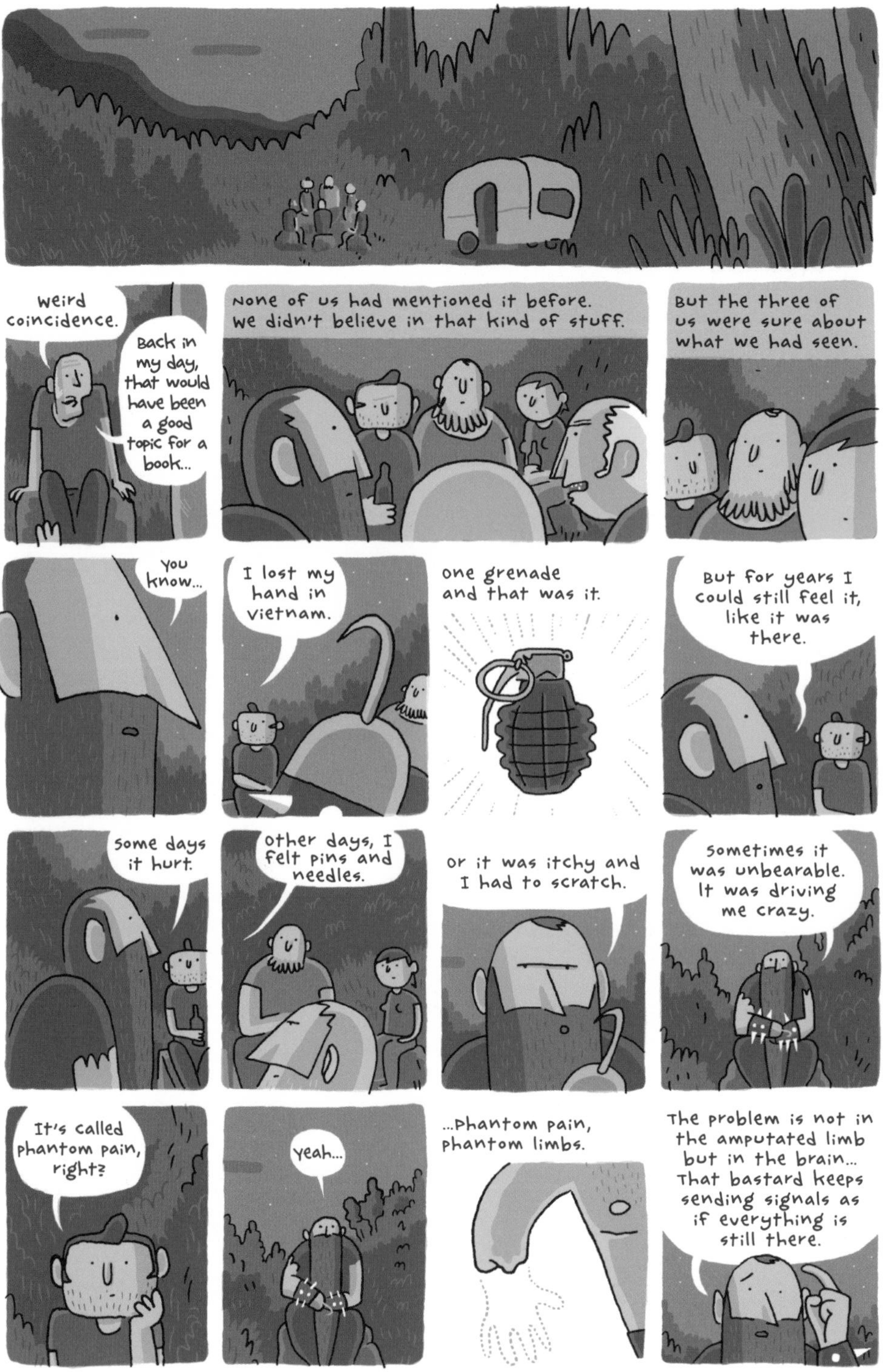
Weird coincidence.
Back in my day, that would have been a good topic for a book...
None of us had mentioned it before. We didn't believe in that kind of stuff.
But the three of us were sure about what we had seen.
You know...
I lost my hand in vietnam.
one grenade and that was it.
But for years I could still feel it, like it was there.
Some days it hurt.
other days, I felt pins and needles.
or it was itchy and I had to scratch.
Sometimes it was unbearable. It was driving me crazy.
It's called phantom pain, right?
Yeah...
...Phantom pain, phantom limbs.
The problem is not in the amputated limb but in the brain... That bastard keeps sending signals as if everything is still there.

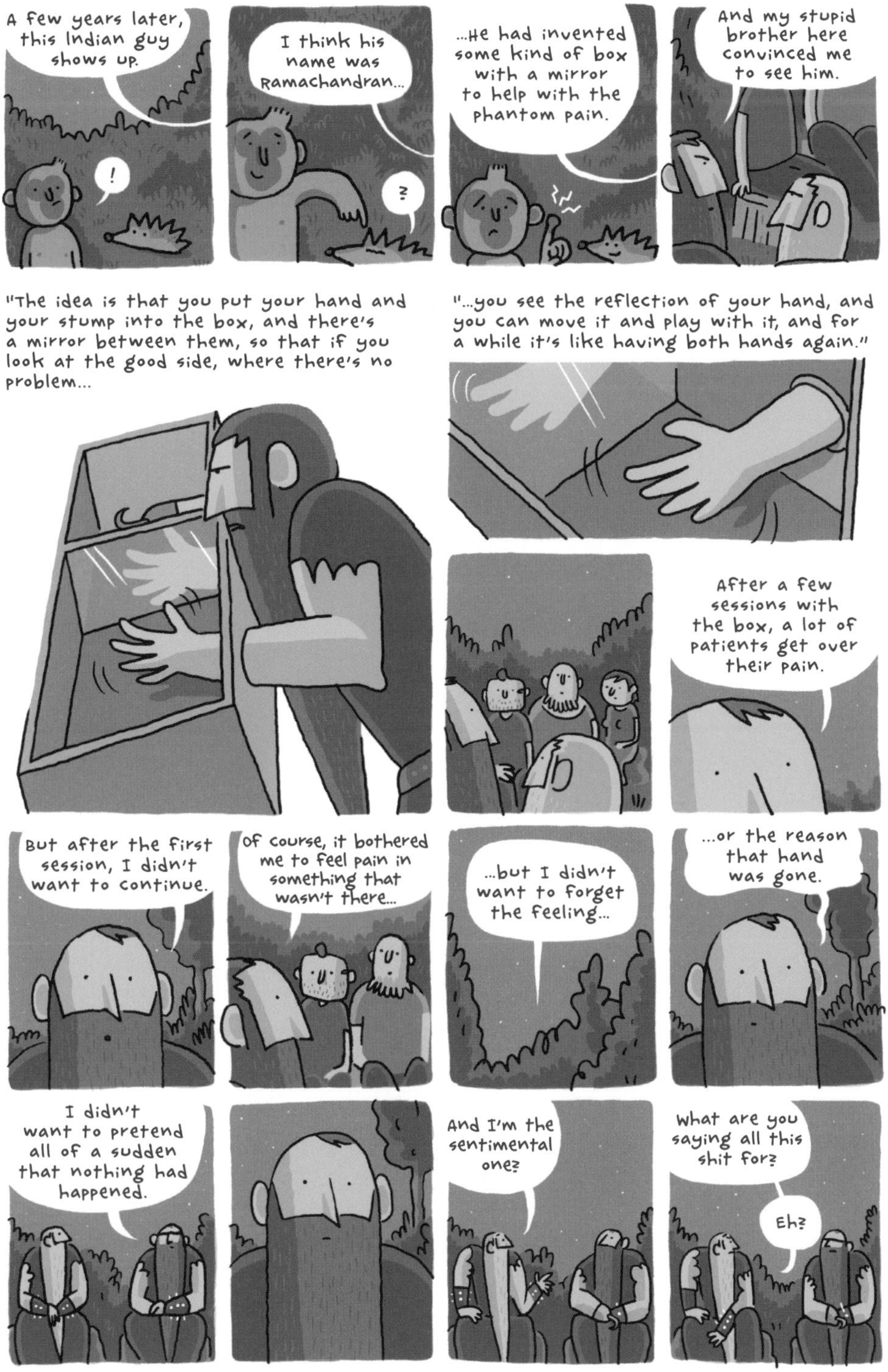
A few years later, this Indian guy shows up.
!
I think his name was Ramachandran...
?
...He had invented some kind of box with a mirror to help with the phantom pain.
And my stupid brother here convinced me to see him.
"The idea is that you put your hand and your stump into the box, and there's a mirror between them, so that if you look at the good side, where there's no problem...
"...you see the reflection of your hand, and you can move it and play with it, and for a while it's like having both hands again."
After a few sessions with the box, a lot of patients get over their pain.
But after the first session, I didn't want to continue.
Of course, it bothered me to feel pain in something that wasn't there...
...but I didn't want to forget the feeling...
...or the reason that hand was gone.
I didn't want to pretend all of a sudden that nothing had happened.
And I'm the sentimental one?
What are you saying all this shit for?
Eh?

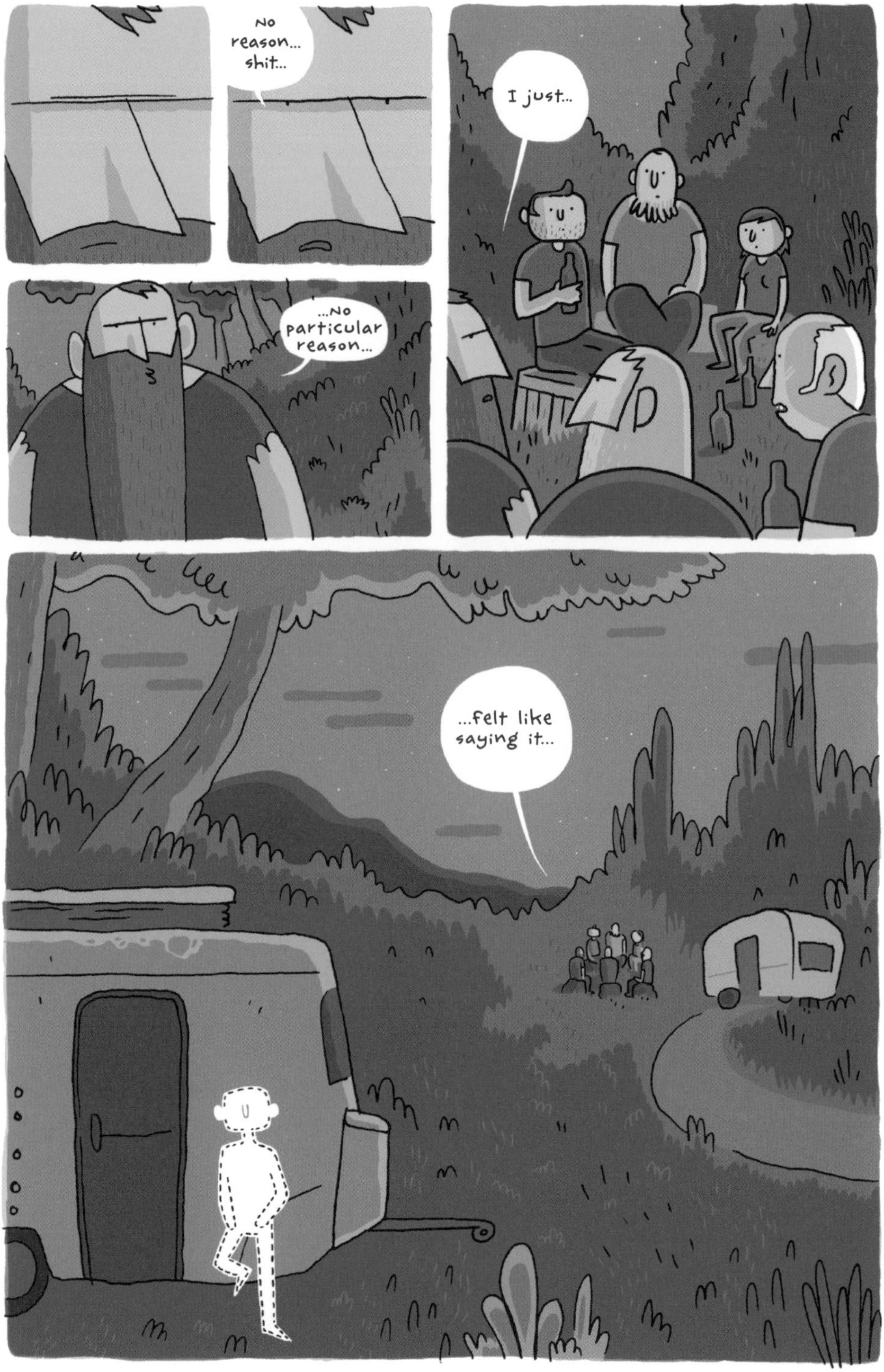
No reason... shit...
I just...
...No particular reason...
...felt like saying it...

DAY 6

(in which the pace
settles down)

Although cremation was accepted by Jews in the 19th century and part of the 20th due to lack of available space in cemeteries, nowadays it is frowned upon.

And there is no need to go back many years in order to understand why.

Ironically, history turned upside down and the cremator ended up cremated.

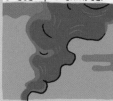

During the Nuremberg trials, several high-ranking officials from the Nazi Party and the SS were tried, executed, and cremated...

...and their ashes were scattered in secret places so that their graves would not become a pilgrimage site.

Although it is known that some of them were thrown into the Isar River...

...and others into the Baltic Sea.

In the late '60s, it was rumored that a pro-Nazi Austrian entrepreneur was using his fortune to try to recover the ashes of those executed.

On the other hand, Josef Mengele, hiding out in South America, was doing research on regenerating human bodies from small particles.

There is evidence that the Austrian entrepreneur met with Mengele in Argentina at least five times between 1968 and 1969.

Many fishermen and divers claim to have seen a strange diver in the waters of the Baltic Sea. All the descriptions matched.

155

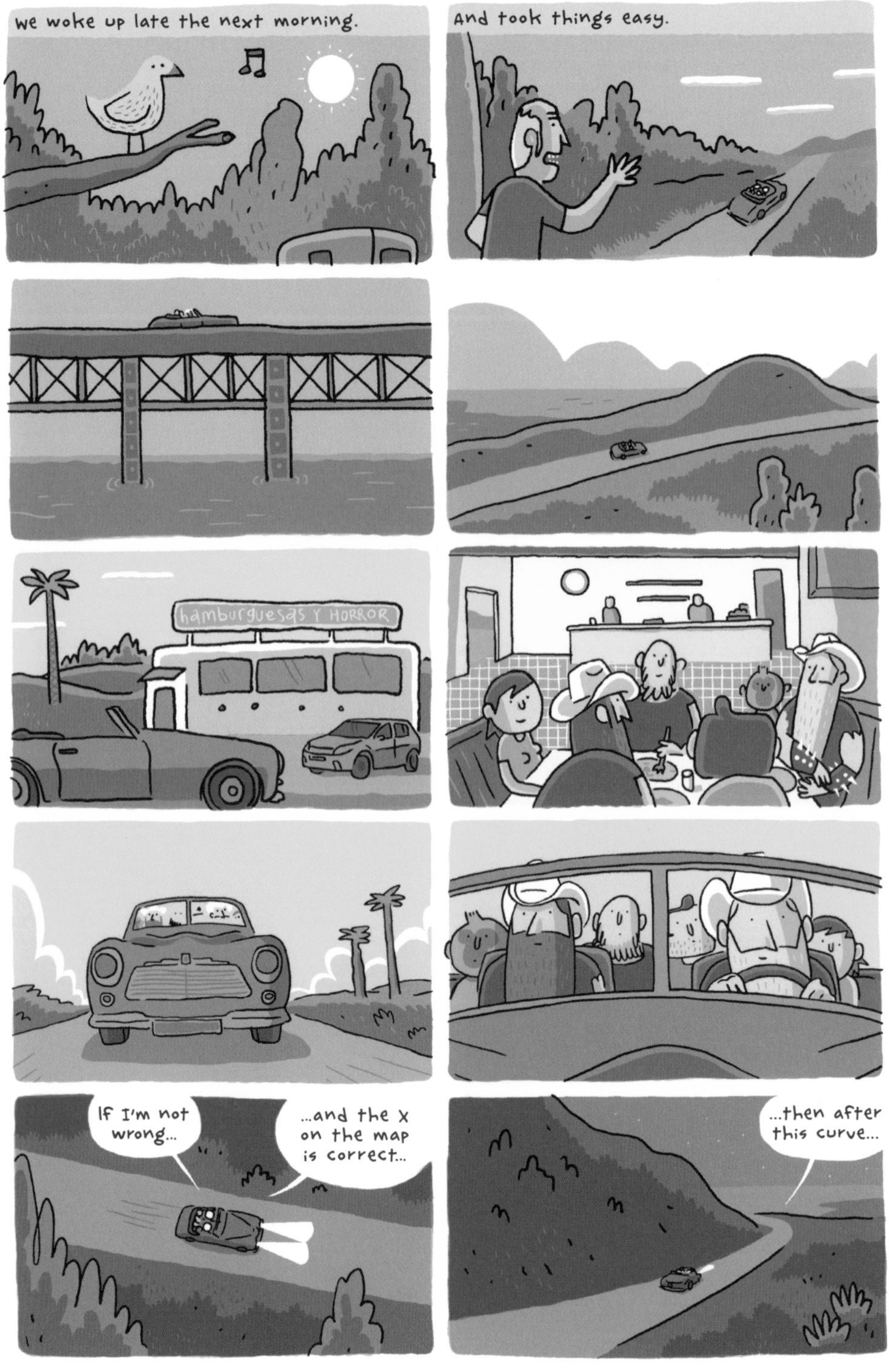
We woke up late the next morning.
And took things easy.
hamburguesas Y HORROR
If I'm not wrong...
...and the X on the map is correct...
...then after this curve...

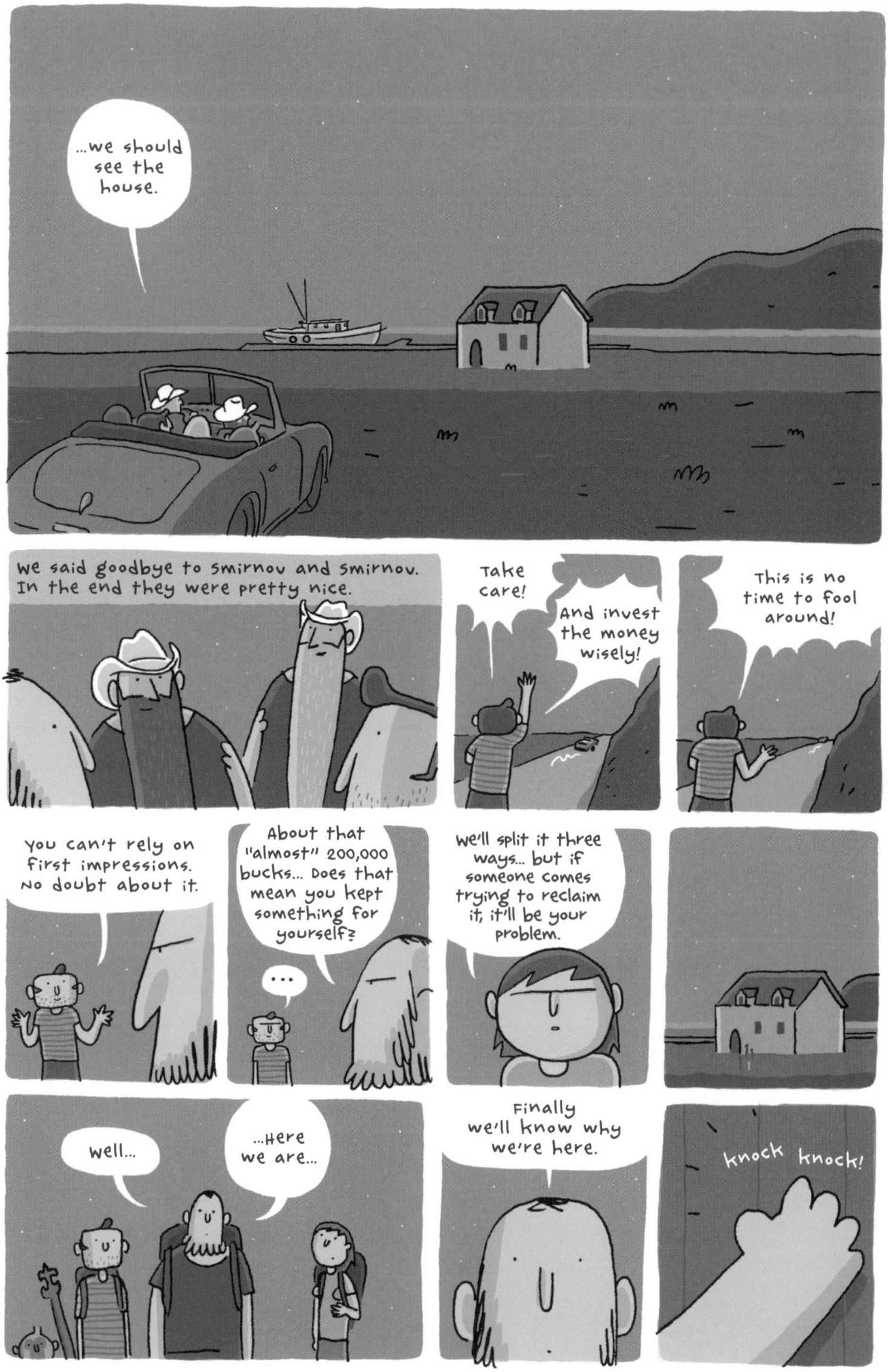
...we should see the house.
We said goodbye to Smirnov and Smirnov. In the end they were pretty nice.
Take care!
And invest the money wisely!
This is no time to fool around!
You can't rely on first impressions. No doubt about it.
About that "almost" 200,000 bucks... Does that mean you kept something for yourself?
...
We'll split it three ways... but if someone comes trying to reclaim it, it'll be your problem.
Well...
...Here we are...
Finally we'll know why we're here.
knock knock!

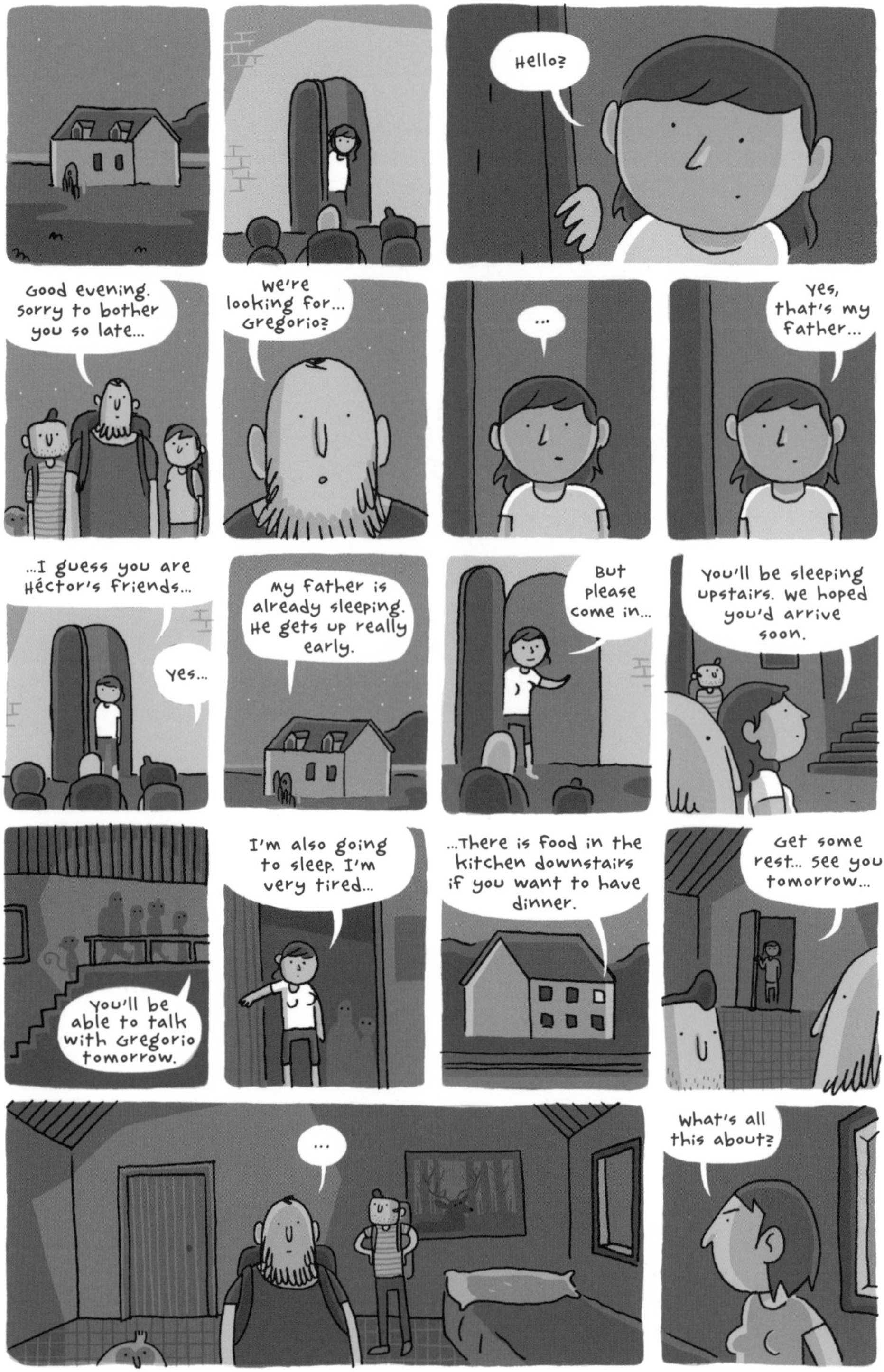
Hello?
Good evening. Sorry to bother you so late...
We're looking for... Gregorio?
...
Yes, that's my father...
...I guess you are Héctor's friends...
Yes...
My father is already sleeping. He gets up really early.
But please come in...
You'll be sleeping upstairs. We hoped you'd arrive soon.
You'll be able to talk with Gregorio tomorrow.
I'm also going to sleep. I'm very tired...
...There is food in the kitchen downstairs if you want to have dinner.
Get some rest... see you tomorrow...
...
What's all this about?

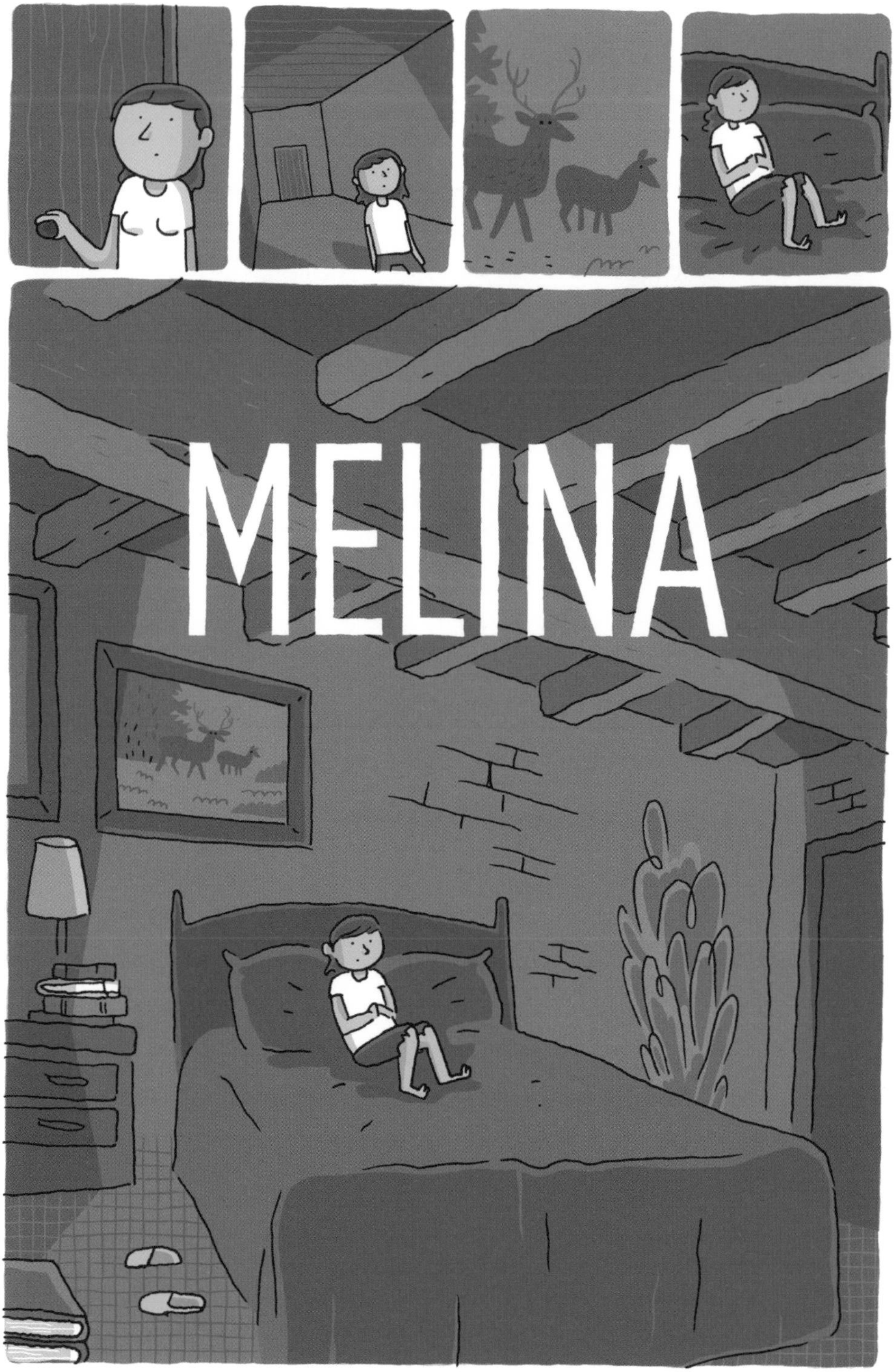
MELINA

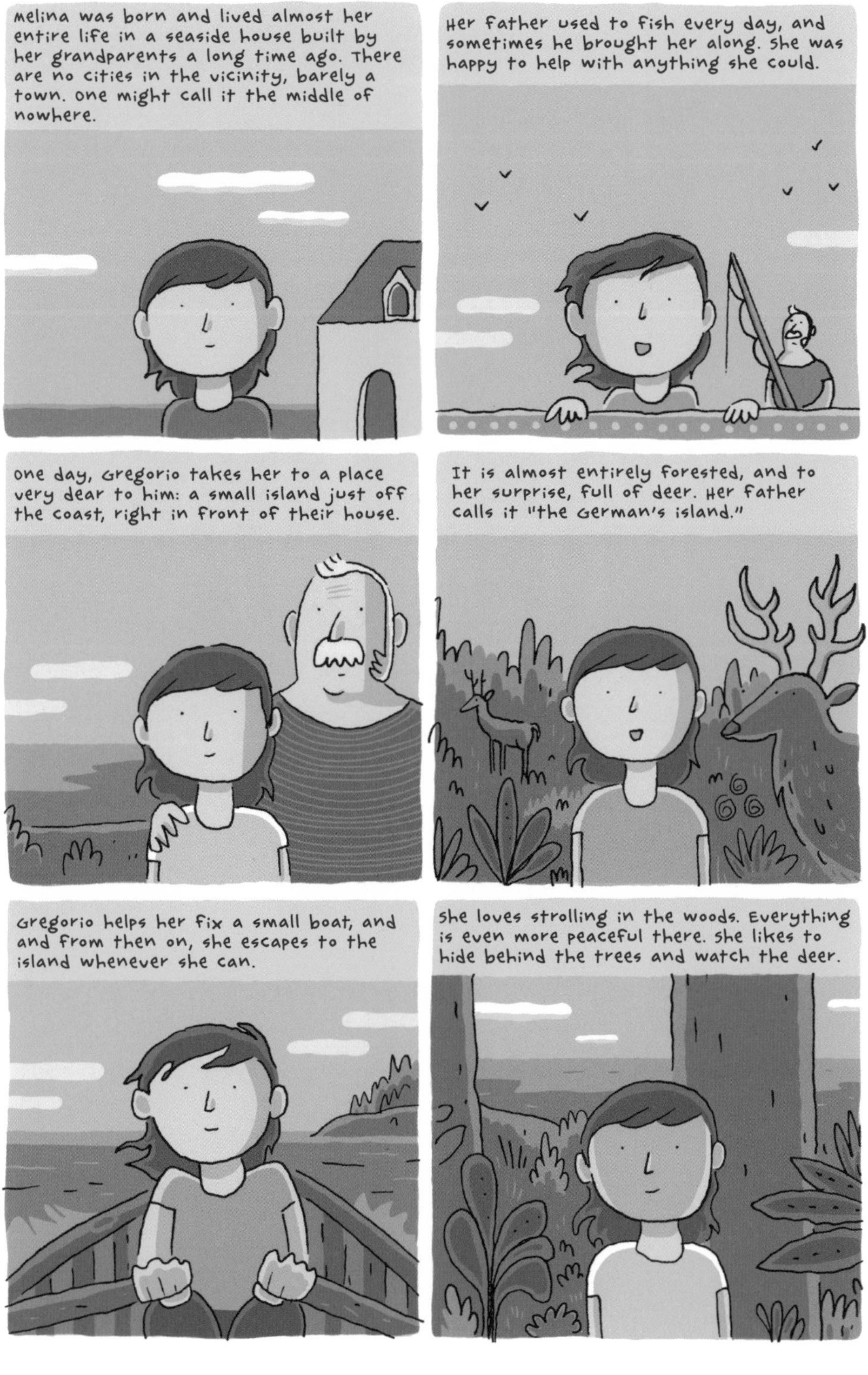
Melina was born and lived almost her entire life in a seaside house built by her grandparents a long time ago. There are no cities in the vicinity, barely a town. One might call it the middle of nowhere.
Her father used to fish every day, and sometimes he brought her along. She was happy to help with anything she could.
One day, Gregorio takes her to a place very dear to him: a small island just off the coast, right in front of their house.
It is almost entirely forested, and to her surprise, full of deer. Her father calls it "the German's island."
Gregorio helps her fix a small boat, and and from then on, she escapes to the island whenever she can.
She loves strolling in the woods. Everything is even more peaceful there. She likes to hide behind the trees and watch the deer.

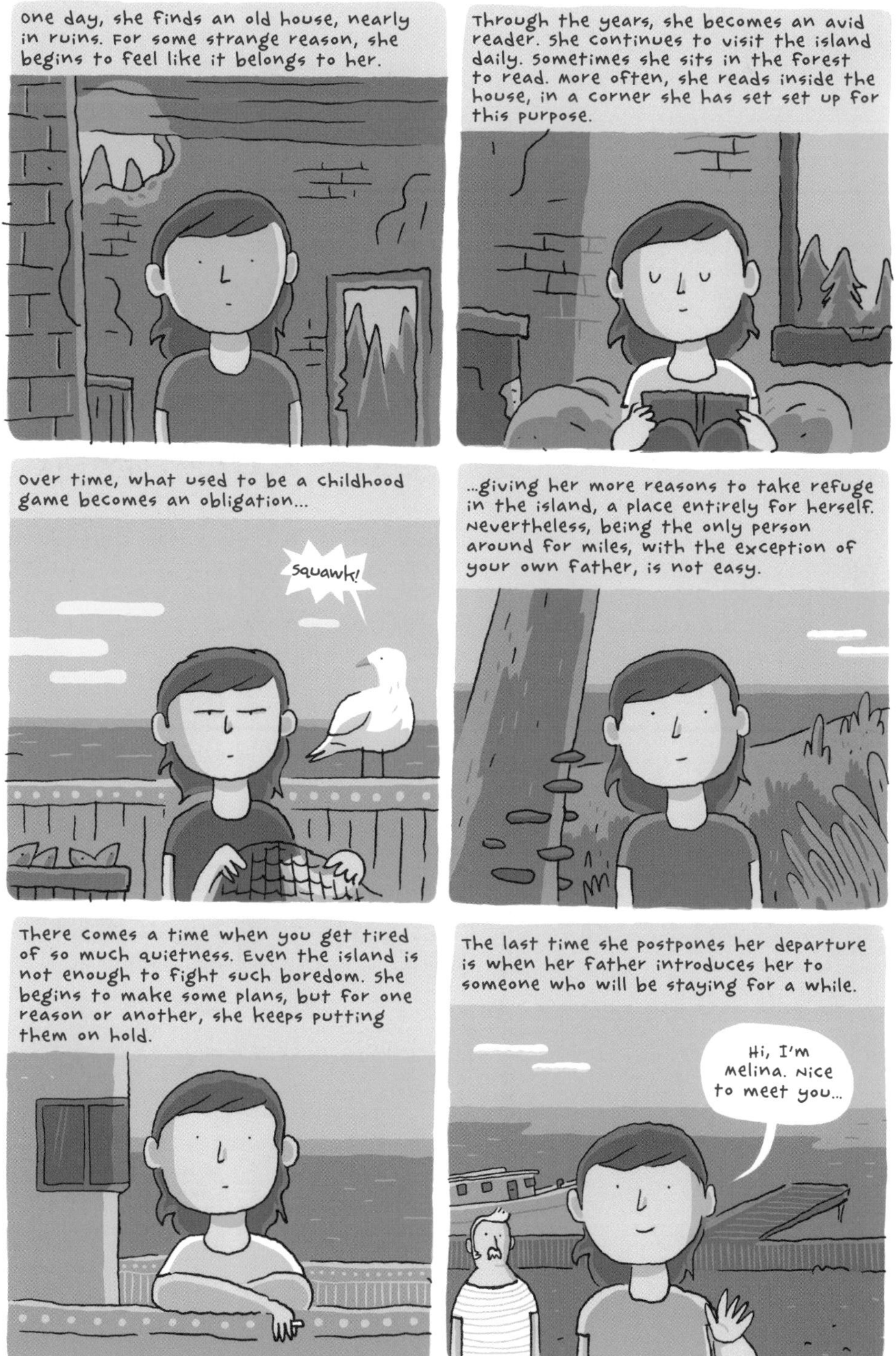
One day, she finds an old house, nearly in ruins. For some strange reason, she begins to feel like it belongs to her.
Through the years, she becomes an avid reader. She continues to visit the island daily. Sometimes she sits in the forest to read. More often, she reads inside the house, in a corner she has set set up for this purpose.
Over time, what used to be a childhood game becomes an obligation...
Squawk!
...giving her more reasons to take refuge in the island, a place entirely for herself. Nevertheless, being the only person around for miles, with the exception of your own father, is not easy.
There comes a time when you get tired of so much quietness. Even the island is not enough to fight such boredom. She begins to make some plans, but for one reason or another, she keeps putting them on hold.
The last time she postpones her departure is when her father introduces her to someone who will be staying for a while.
Hi, I'm Melina. Nice to meet you...

We went downstairs to eat something, but we didn't find any clues about Gregorio or his daughter (who hadn't even mentioned her name).

So we came back up.

At least this time we weren't locked up.

What are you reading?

I'm about to finish it.

I found it by accident in the library last week...

What a riot...

After what happened, I thought it would be...

...appropriate...

A Brief History of Cremation

● ● ● ● ● ● ● ● ●

Lázaro vitro

prologue by ziarat orlov

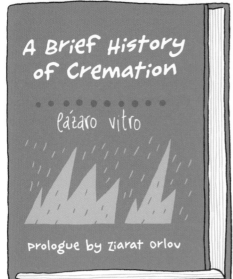

I see...

...And is it cool?

It has pretty interesting stories.

162

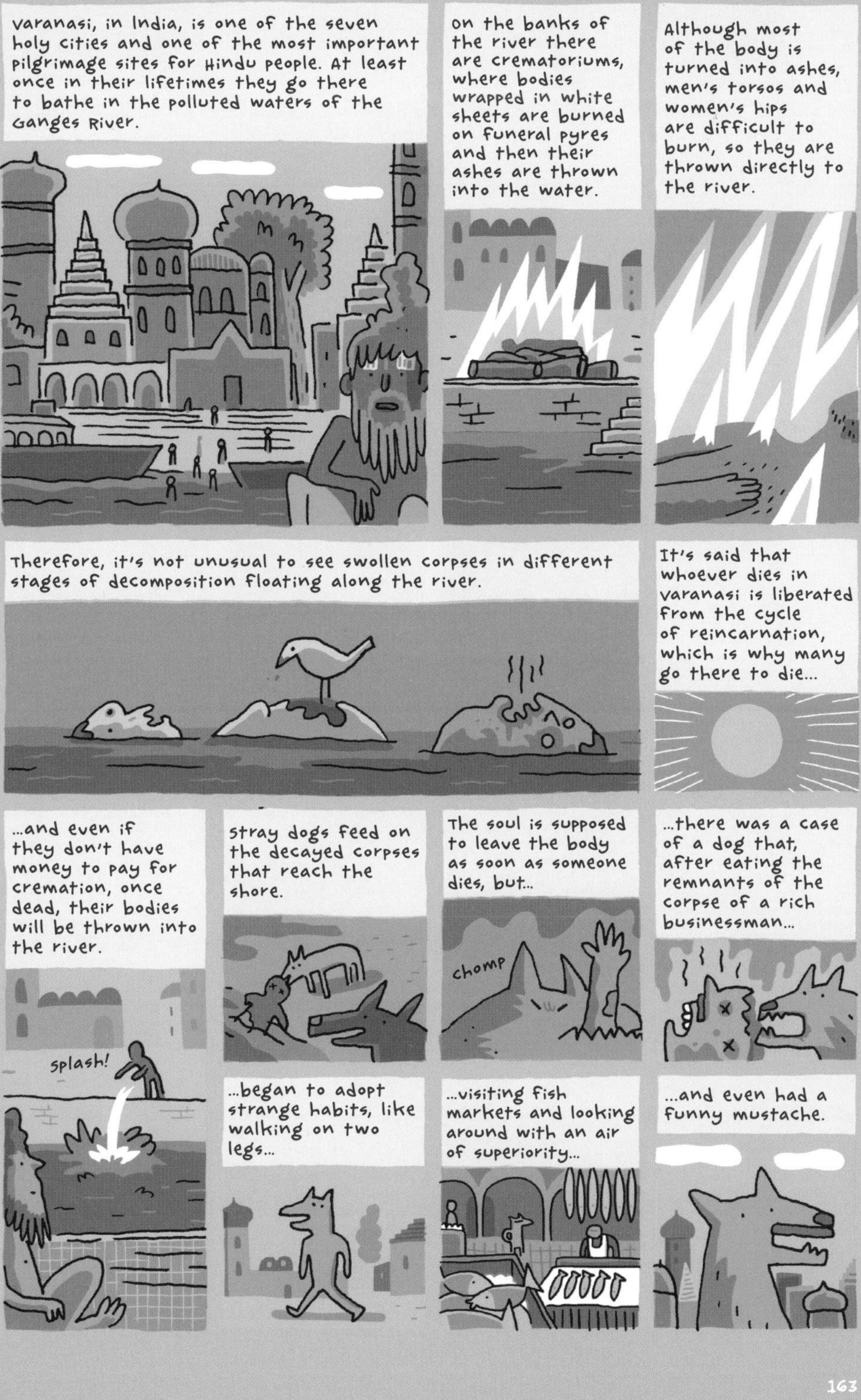
Varanasi, in India, is one of the seven holy cities and one of the most important pilgrimage sites for Hindu people. At least once in their lifetimes they go there to bathe in the polluted waters of the Ganges River.
On the banks of the river there are crematoriums, where bodies wrapped in white sheets are burned on funeral pyres and then their ashes are thrown into the water.
Although most of the body is turned into ashes, men's torsos and women's hips are difficult to burn, so they are thrown directly to the river.
Therefore, it's not unusual to see swollen corpses in different stages of decomposition floating along the river.
It's said that whoever dies in Varanasi is liberated from the cycle of reincarnation, which is why many go there to die...
...and even if they don't have money to pay for cremation, once dead, their bodies will be thrown into the river.
splash!
Stray dogs feed on the decayed corpses that reach the shore.
The soul is supposed to leave the body as soon as someone dies, but...
chomp
...there was a case of a dog that, after eating the remnants of the corpse of a rich businessman...
...began to adopt strange habits, like walking on two legs...
...visiting fish markets and looking around with an air of superiority...
...and even had a funny mustache.

Are they all like that one?

more or less.

It doesn't mention the creator of Star Trek?

He was one of the first whose ashes ended up floating in space.

Why are you looking at me like that?

Since when do you have a banjo?

Smirnov gave it to me just before saying goodbye.

I saw it in the car, told him I loved banjos, and he said that since he barely played it anymore, he would give it to me.

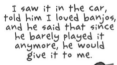

Nice, huh?

Oh... yeah...

...Great...

c'mon, move your ass! I want to get some sleep!

Wait... I can't find my banjo...

Heh, heh...

Heh, heh?

What'd you do with my banjo?

Eh? What'd you do with my banjo?

Me? Why do you think I have anything to do with it?

one of these days I'm gonna kill you, you bastard!

And throw your body in the middle of the desert for the coyotes to eat it!

164

DAY 7

(in which the story
almost ends)

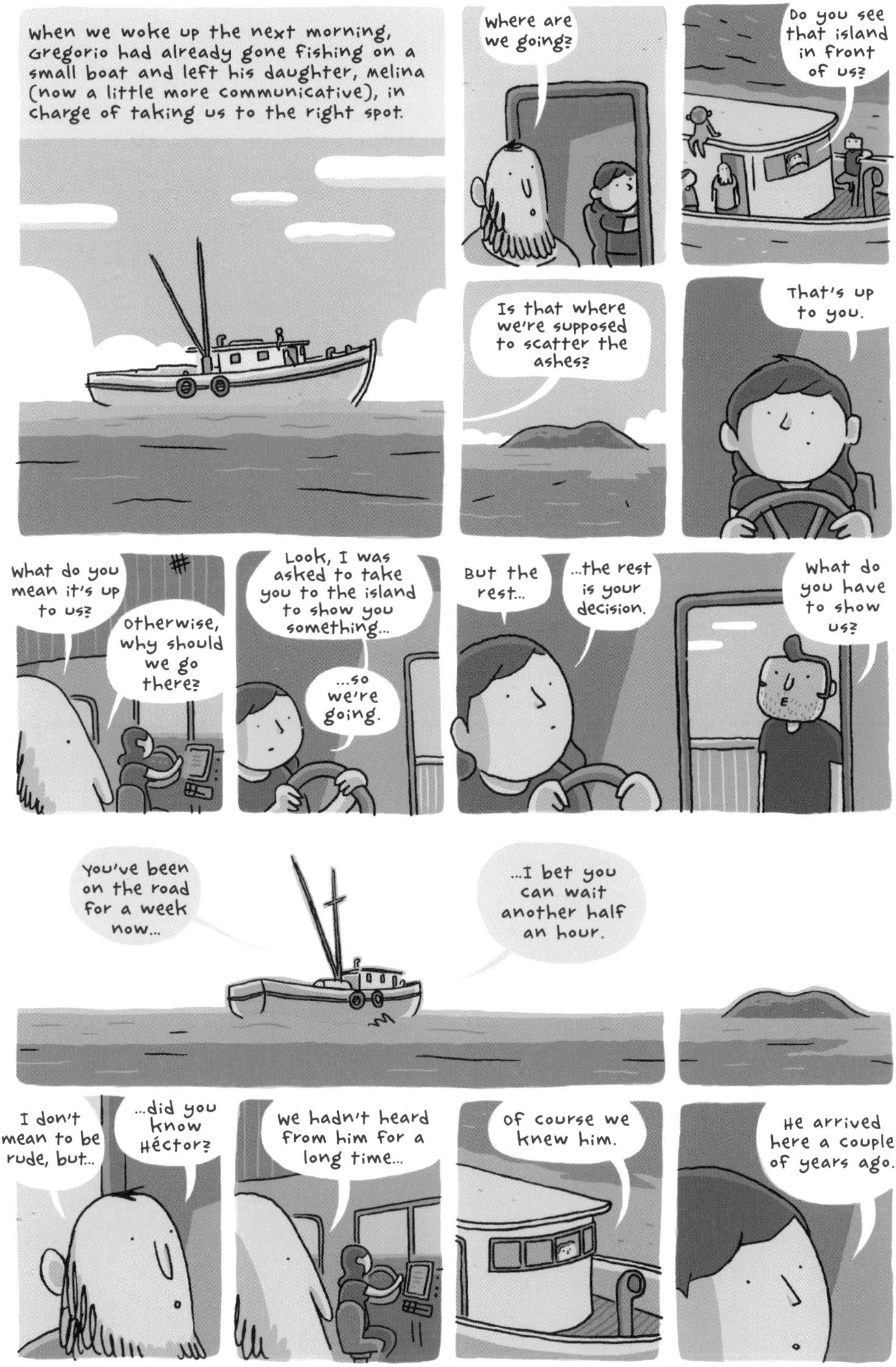
When we woke up the next morning, Gregorio had already gone fishing on a small boat and left his daughter, Melina (now a little more communicative), in charge of taking us to the right spot.
Where are we going?
Do you see that island in front of us?
Is that where we're supposed to scatter the ashes?
That's up to you.
What do you mean it's up to us?
Otherwise, why should we go there?
Look, I was asked to take you to the island to show you something...
...so we're going.
But the rest...
...the rest is your decision.
What do you have to show us?
You've been on the road for a week now...
...I bet you can wait another half an hour.
I don't mean to be rude, but...
...did you know Héctor?
We hadn't heard from him for a long time...
Of course we knew him.
He arrived here a couple of years ago.

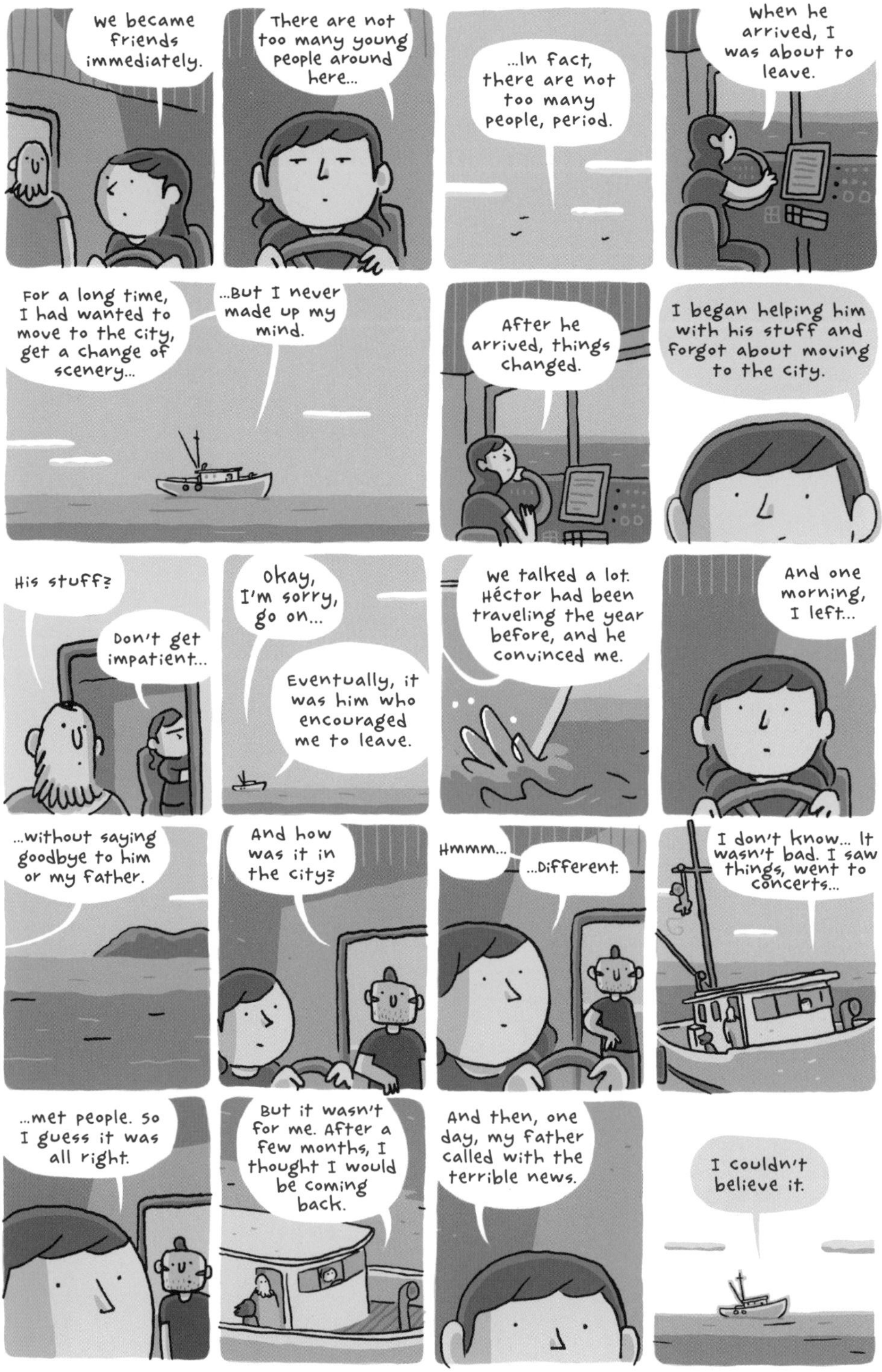
We became friends immediately.
There are not too many young people around here...
...In fact, there are not too many people, period.
When he arrived, I was about to leave.
For a long time, I had wanted to move to the city, get a change of scenery...
...But I never made up my mind.
After he arrived, things changed.
I began helping him with his stuff and forgot about moving to the city.
His stuff?
Don't get impatient...
Okay, I'm sorry, go on...
Eventually, it was him who encouraged me to leave.
We talked a lot. Héctor had been traveling the year before, and he convinced me.
And one morning, I left...
...without saying goodbye to him or my father.
And how was it in the city?
Hmmm...
...Different.
I don't know... It wasn't bad. I saw things, went to concerts...
...met people. So I guess it was all right.
But it wasn't for me. After a few months, I thought I would be coming back.
And then, one day, my father called with the terrible news.
I couldn't believe it.

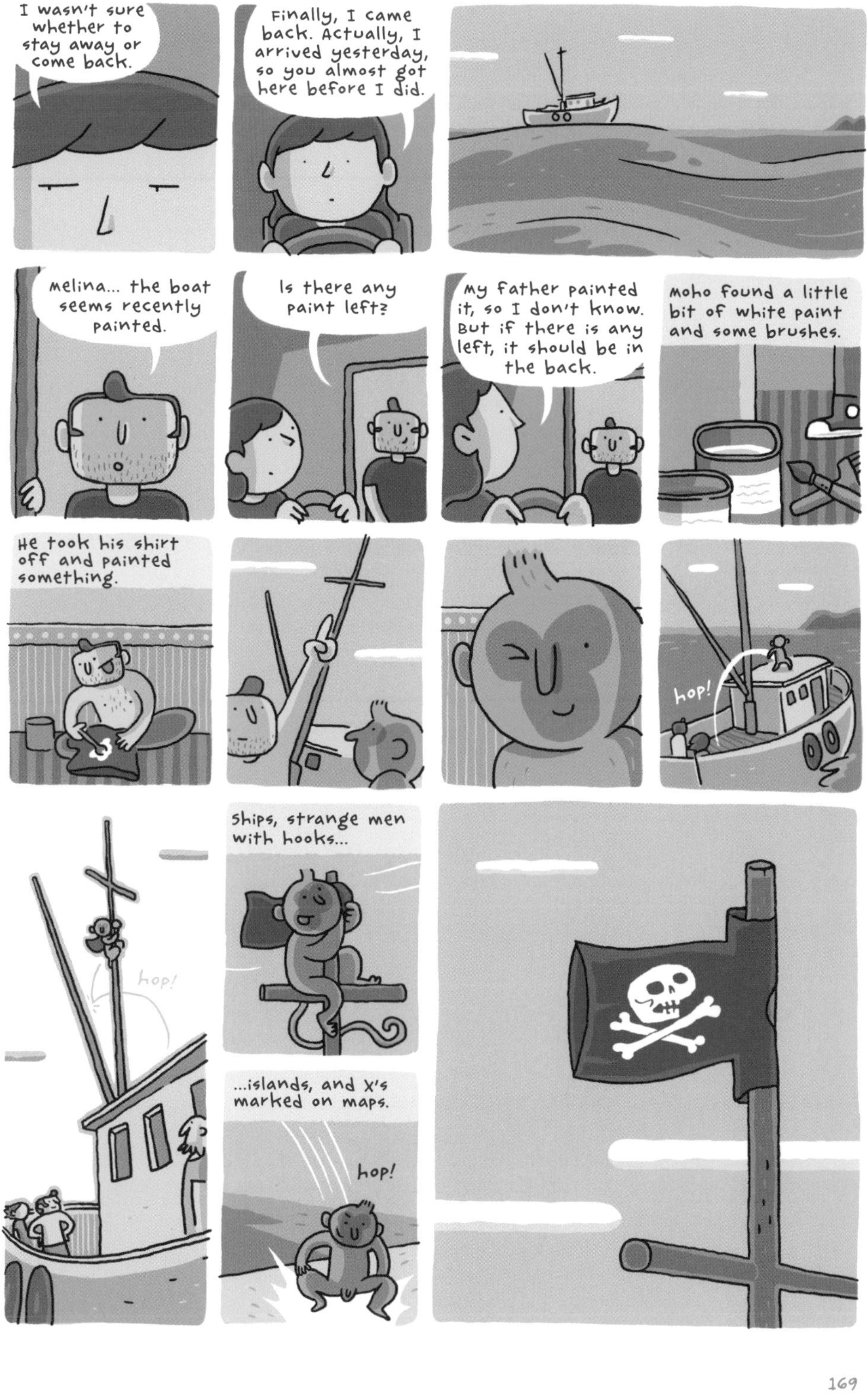

I wasn't sure whether to stay away or come back.
Finally, I came back. Actually, I arrived yesterday, so you almost got here before I did.
Melina... the boat seems recently painted.
Is there any paint left?
My father painted it, so I don't know. But if there is any left, it should be in the back.
Moho found a little bit of white paint and some brushes.
He took his shirt off and painted something.
hop!
hop!
Ships, strange men with hooks...
...islands, and X's marked on maps.
hop!

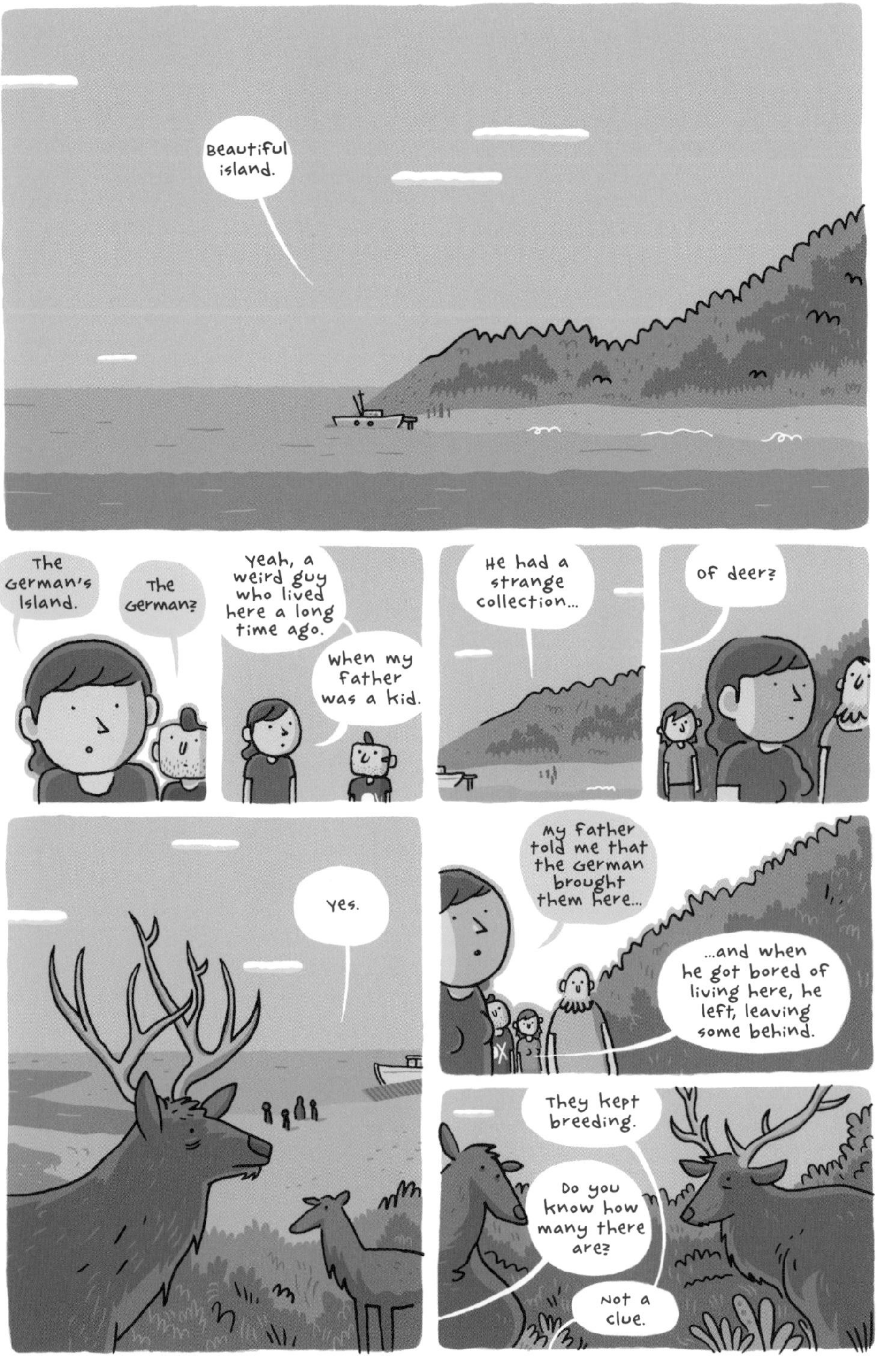
Beautiful island.
The German's Island.
The German?
Yeah, a weird guy who lived here a long time ago.
When my father was a kid.
He had a strange collection...
Of deer?
Yes.
My father told me that the German brought them here...
...and when he got bored of living here, he left, leaving some behind.
They kept breeding.
Do you know how many there are?
Not a clue.

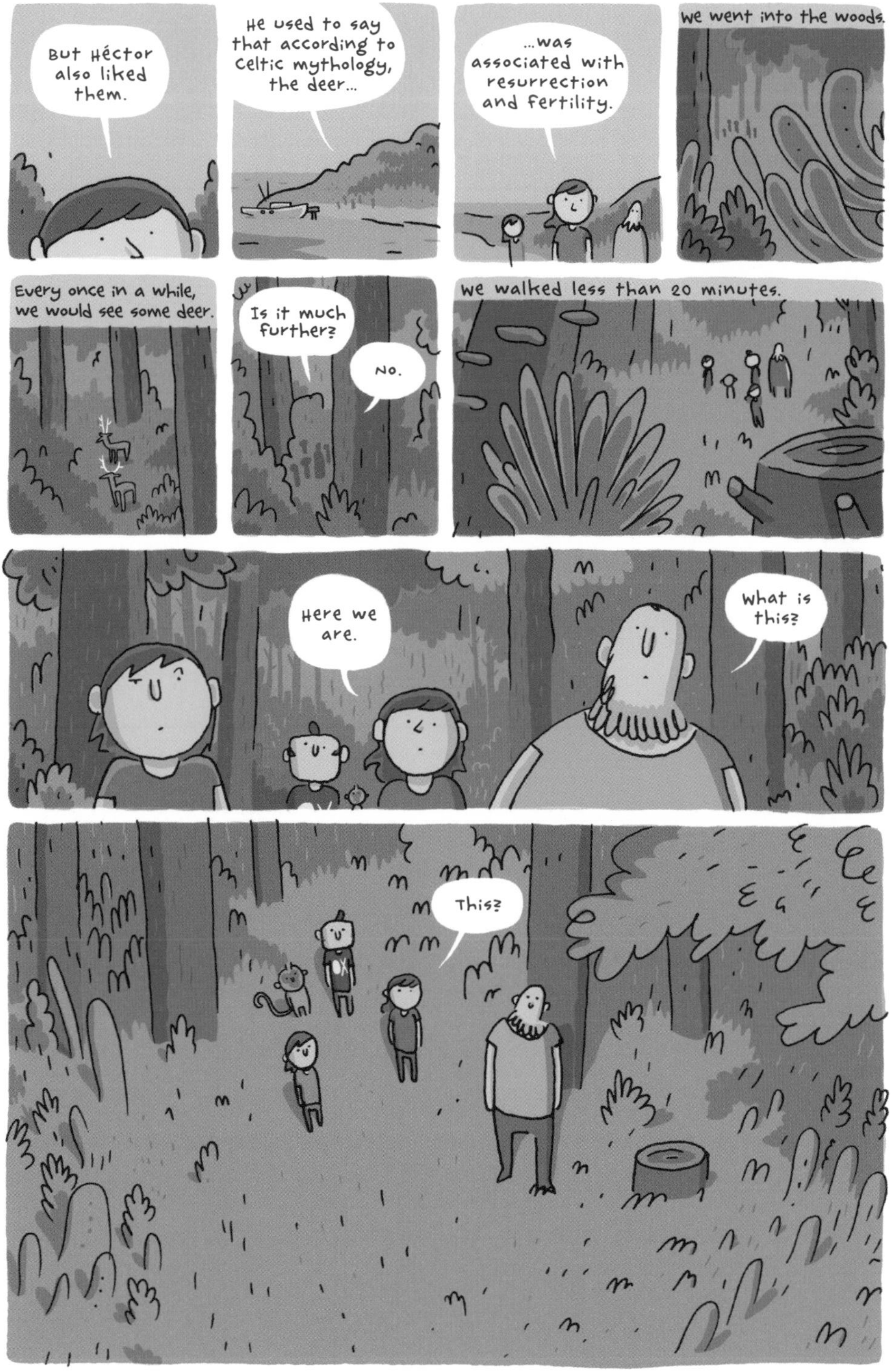
But Héctor also liked them.
He used to say that according to Celtic mythology, the deer...
...was associated with resurrection and fertility.
We went into the woods.
Every once in a while, we would see some deer.
Is it much further?
No.
We walked less than 20 minutes.
Here we are.
What is this?
This?

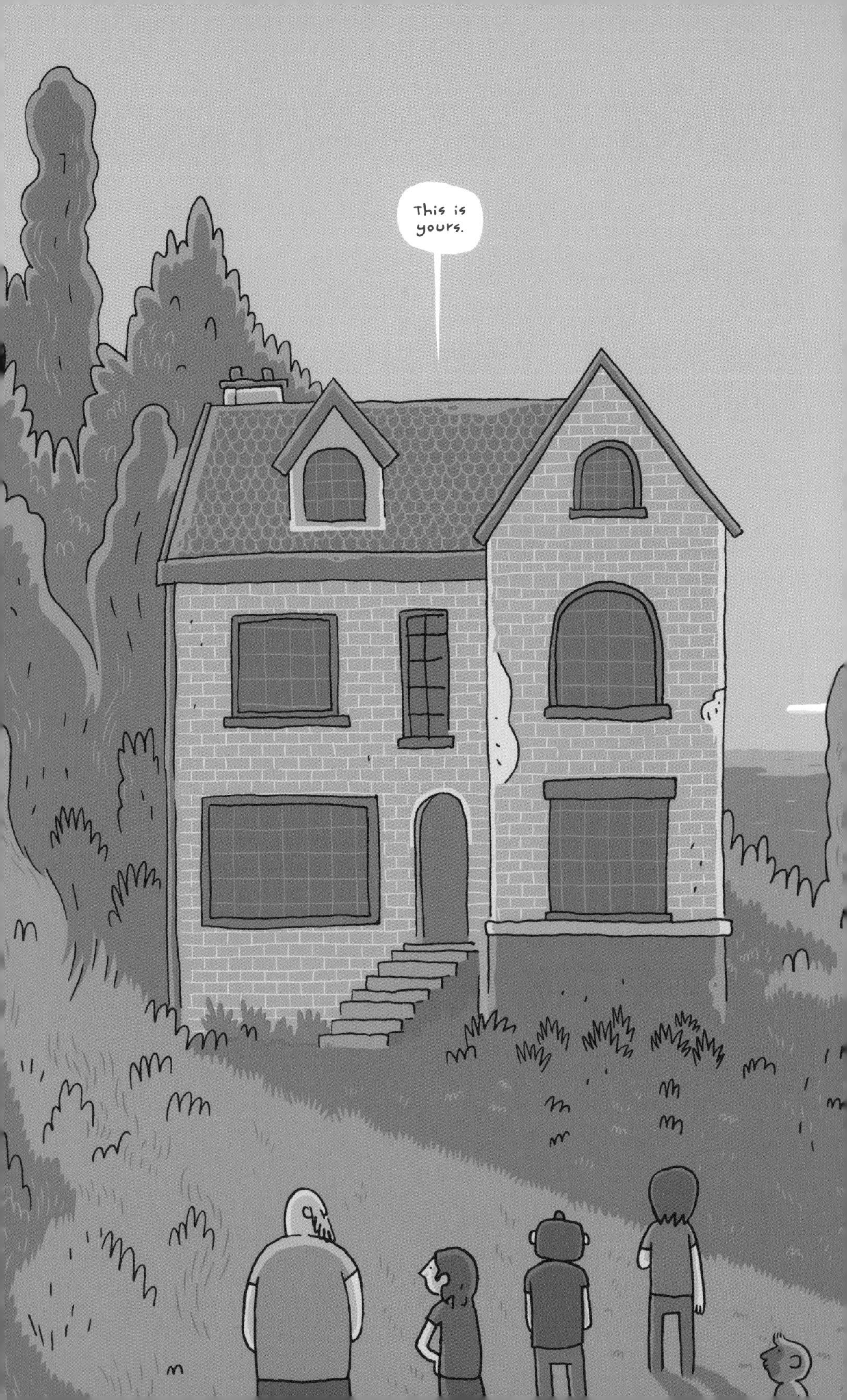
This is yours.

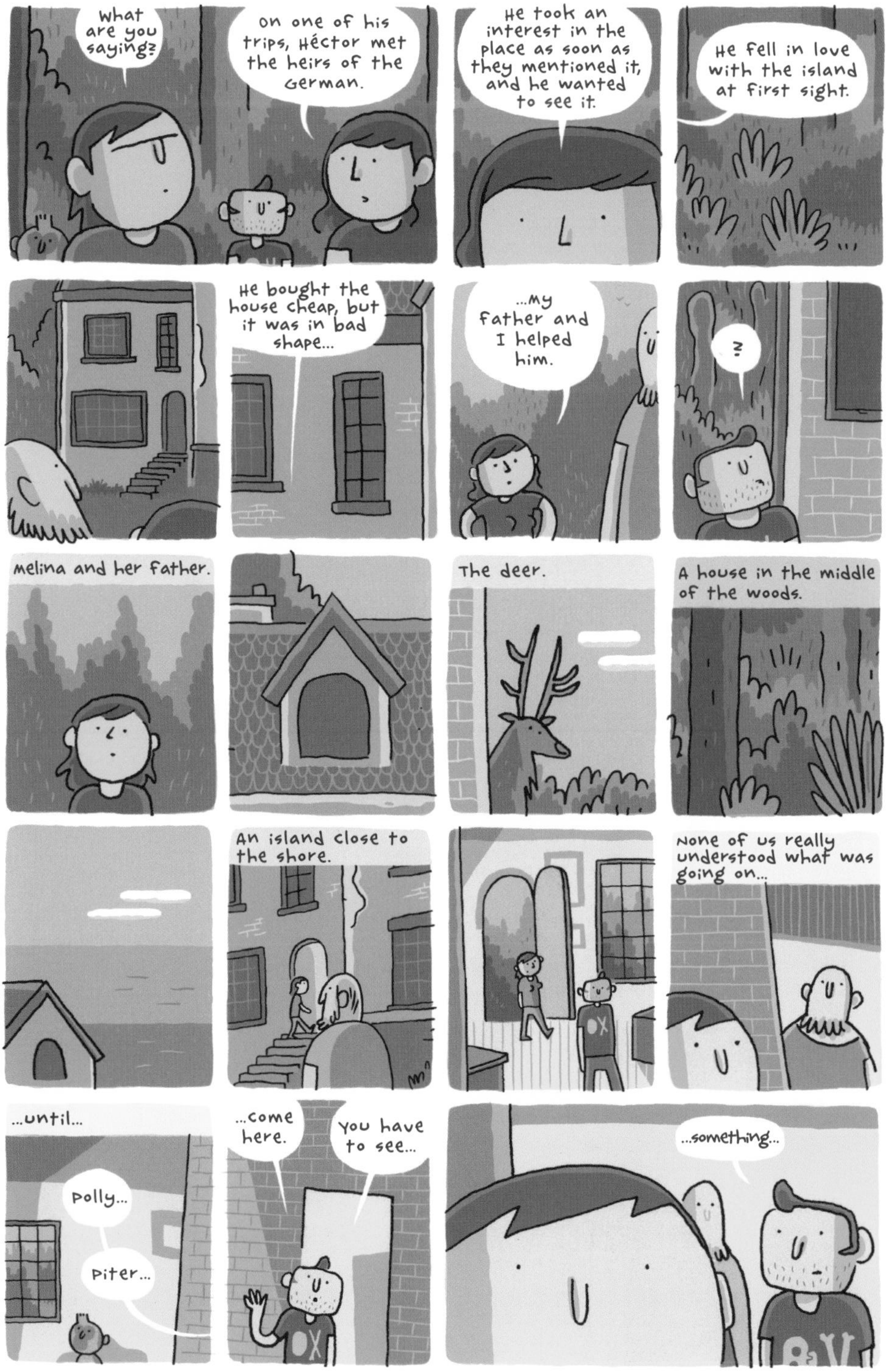
What are you saying?
On one of his trips, Héctor met the heirs of the German.
He took an interest in the place as soon as they mentioned it, and he wanted to see it.
He fell in love with the island at first sight.
He bought the house cheap, but it was in bad shape...
...my father and I helped him.
?
Melina and her father.
The deer.
A house in the middle of the woods.
An island close to the shore.
None of us really understood what was going on...
...until...
Polly...
Piter...
...come here.
You have to see...
...something...

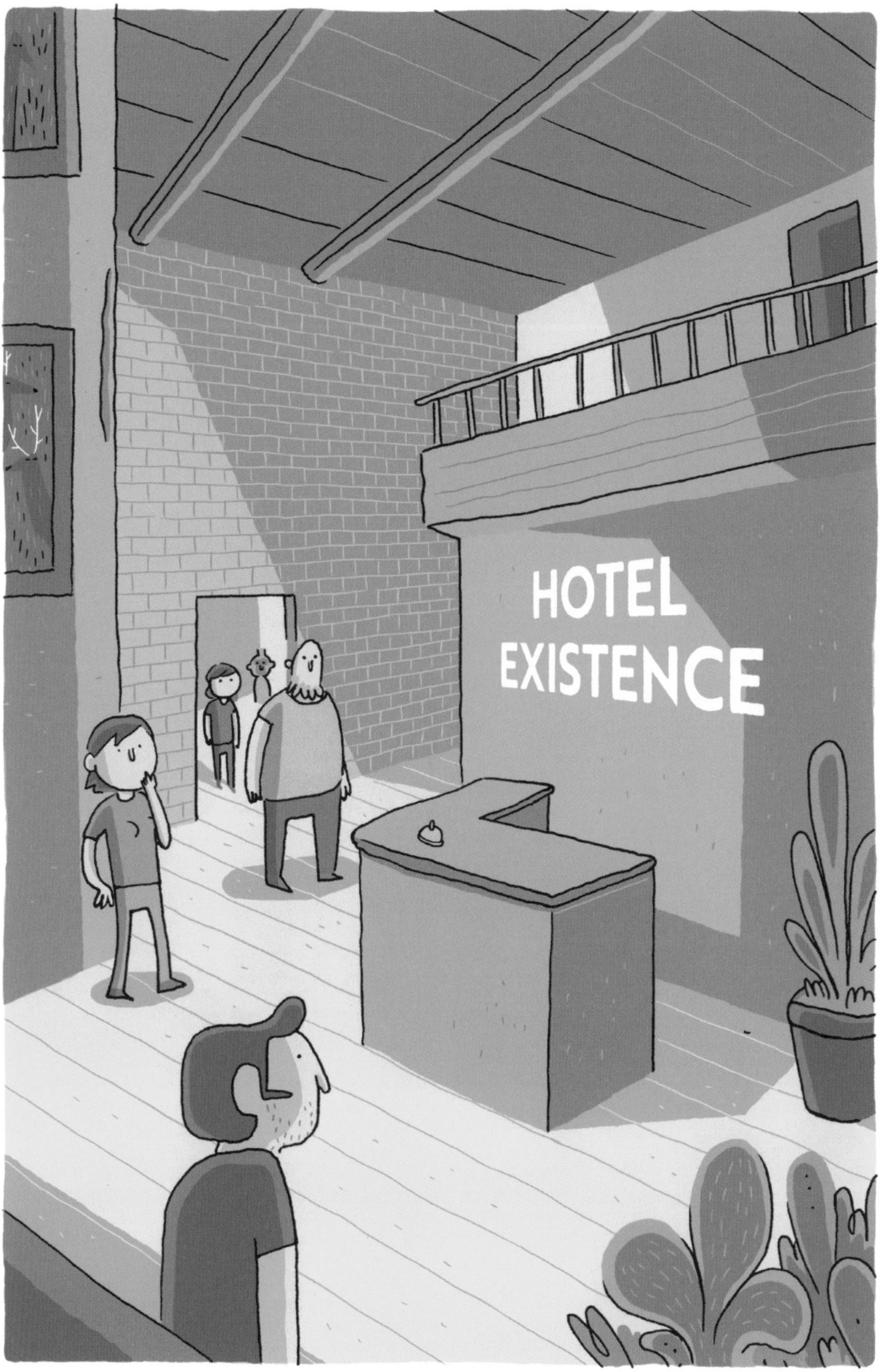
HOTEL
EXISTENCE

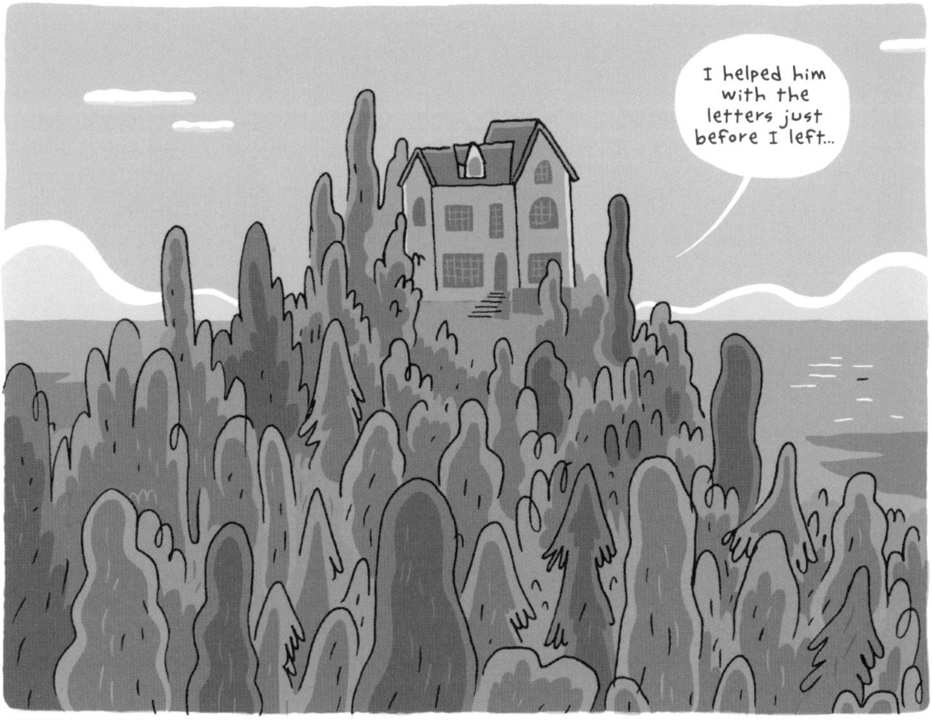
I helped him with the letters just before I left...

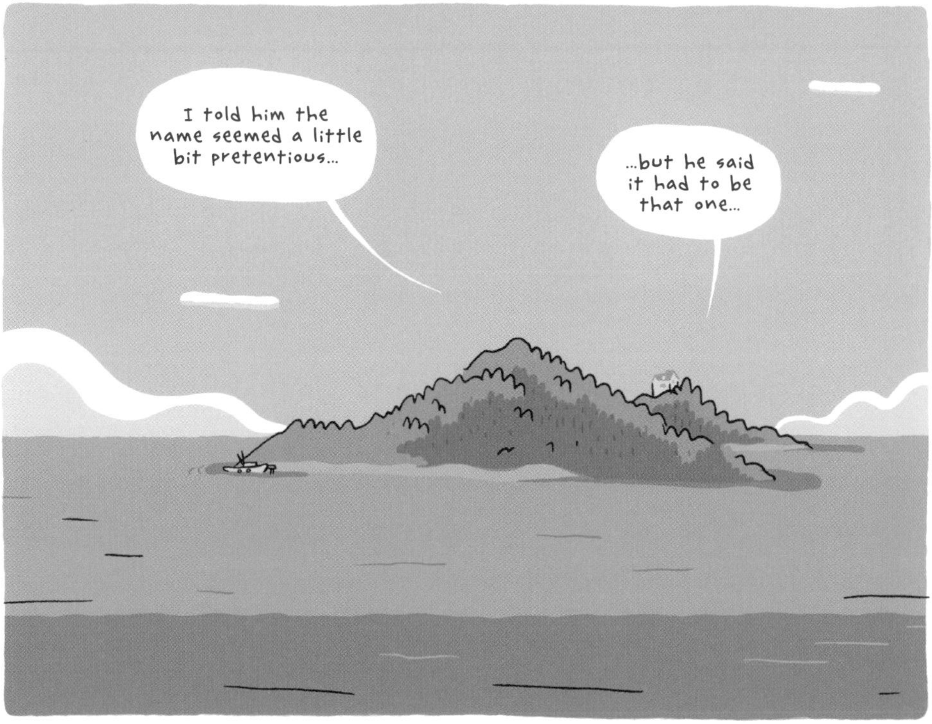
I told him the name seemed a little bit pretentious...
...but he said it had to be that one...

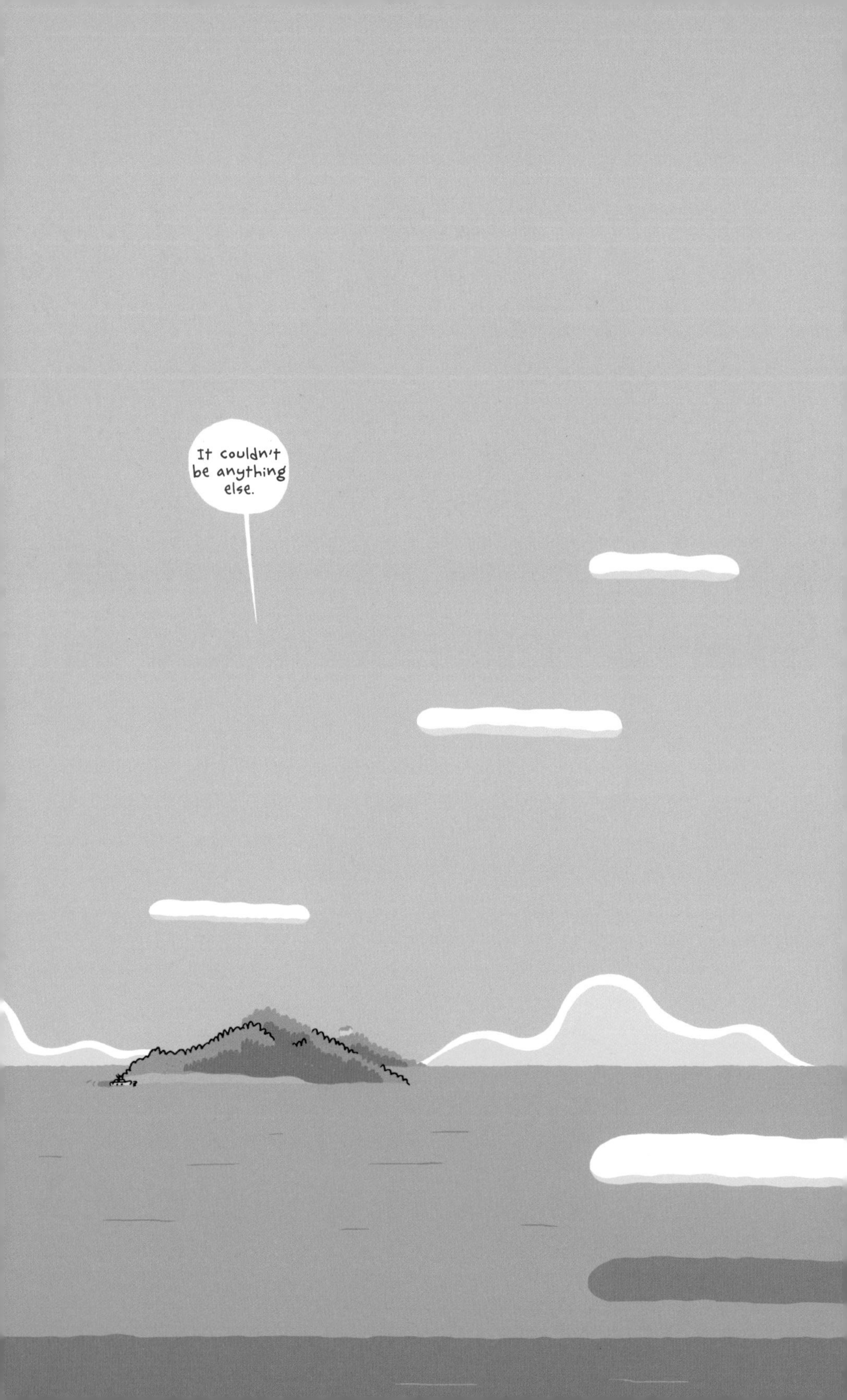
It couldn't be anything else.

Finishing this book has taken me almost a year and a half, and there are a lot of people to acknowledge. If I forget someone (very likely) I hope they can forgive me.

First of all, thanks to AlhóndigaBilbao for the grant and to all the judges who could see the potential of the simple project submitted, because without the grant, I don't know when or how Ashes would have seen the light of day.

To Pili, Brigitte, and the rest of the people at La Maison des Auteurs; to Martin and Emre, who shared the workshop with me for months; and also to Benoit, Julie, Rachel, Lucas, Giovanna, Lorenzo, Elric, Julien, Nathan, and the others... as well as Nofu and Irene.

Thanks to Zapico because, even if he consistently drove me crazy the whole time, he has been very excited about the project. A big hug for Manuela.

To all the people who visited me in Angoulême, who were quite a few: Guillermo, Alberto, Raúl, Adria, Cristina, Germán, and Alicia (who also helped me fill in colors on some pages when time was already pressing).

I can't forget my family: Dad, Mom, brothers, sisters-in-law, nephews, aunts, and uncles.

To my friends not mentioned before: Iván, Erica, Isaac, Víctor and his typographical advice, Jessica, Marta, Eva, León, Iñaki, and Leticia, who always included me in the email threads whenever they were planning to meet for drinks or concerts, since this comic deals with those subjects.

To Miguel Ángel, who in spite of taking a long time to download the files, was one of the few who read them through and corrected my spelling errors, and my other three proofreaders: Josep, Porto, and Diego. They read very quickly and made suggestions that I probably forgot.

To all the guys and gals of the "merienda de lobos" for their comments, to Pelegrin for the texts he sent me, and to Sergio for his offer of reviewing the dialogue, even though I didn't dare accept.

To all of you who patiently endured my complaining and moaning on Twitter, Facebook, and the blog for a year and a half, raising my spirits and cheering me on with an enthusiasm that often surpassed my own.

To the German publisher Die Lüge for kindly letting me use passages of the book A Brief History of Cremation and to its writer, Lázaro Vitro, who from the very first moment was glad to adapt some excerpts for the comic.

Special thanks to ISABEL, who experienced the creation of Ashes at first from a distance, then by Skype, and later on in her living room. She has reviewed texts, contributed ideas, helped to color some pages, and endured me until the last panel. For these reasons and many more, this book is dedicated to her. :)

Lastly, thanks to the whole team of Astiberri for their patience and audacity in publishing a comic that, for months, I was drawing without knowing if someone would be interested.

And, of course, thanks to the reader who has made it this far.

But it's not over yet. There is still more to come.

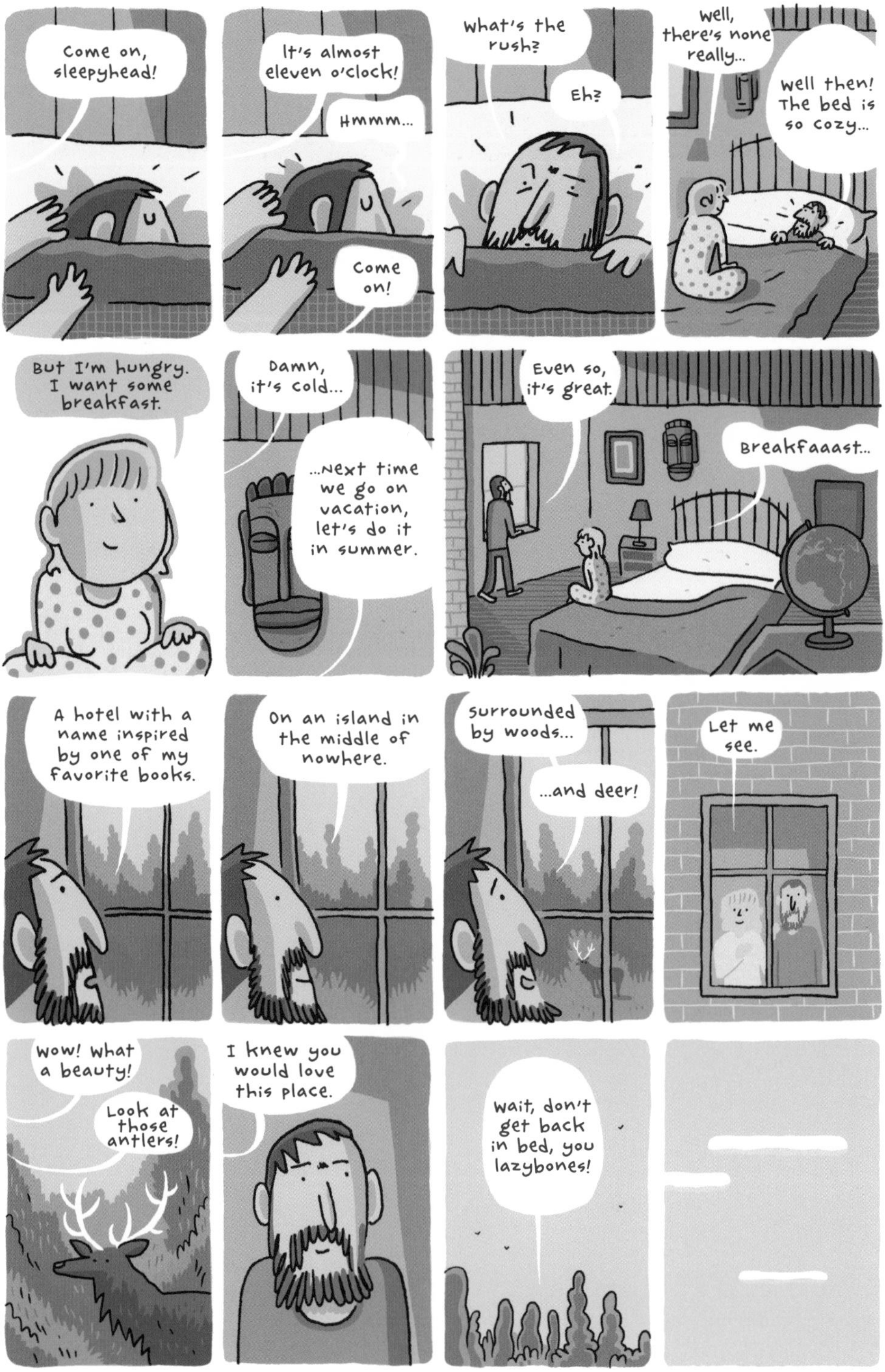
Come on, sleepyhead!
It's almost eleven o'clock!
Hmmm...
Come on!
What's the rush?
Eh?
Well, there's none really...
Well then! The bed is so cozy...
But I'm hungry. I want some breakfast.
Damn, it's cold...
...Next time we go on vacation, let's do it in summer.
Even so, it's great.
Breakfaaast...
A hotel with a name inspired by one of my favorite books.
On an island in the middle of nowhere.
Surrounded by woods...
...and deer!
Let me see.
Wow! What a beauty!
Look at those antlers!
I knew you would love this place.
Wait, don't get back in bed, you lazybones!

Let's see if one week relaxing here... ...gets you out of your "creative crisis."

Hey, don't joke. It's not funny.

Breakfaaast...

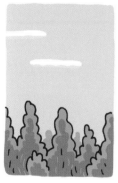

Hey!

They have, like, a million different coffees. I love it...

I read it on the website...

..."Enjoy our great selection of coffee from the five continents."

We can try any of them, right?

Last night the girl said they would be out this morning, that they had something to do.

And that we could take anything we want, to make ourselves at home.

It pays to be the first guests, heh heh.

Look.

They left a fire going in the living room.

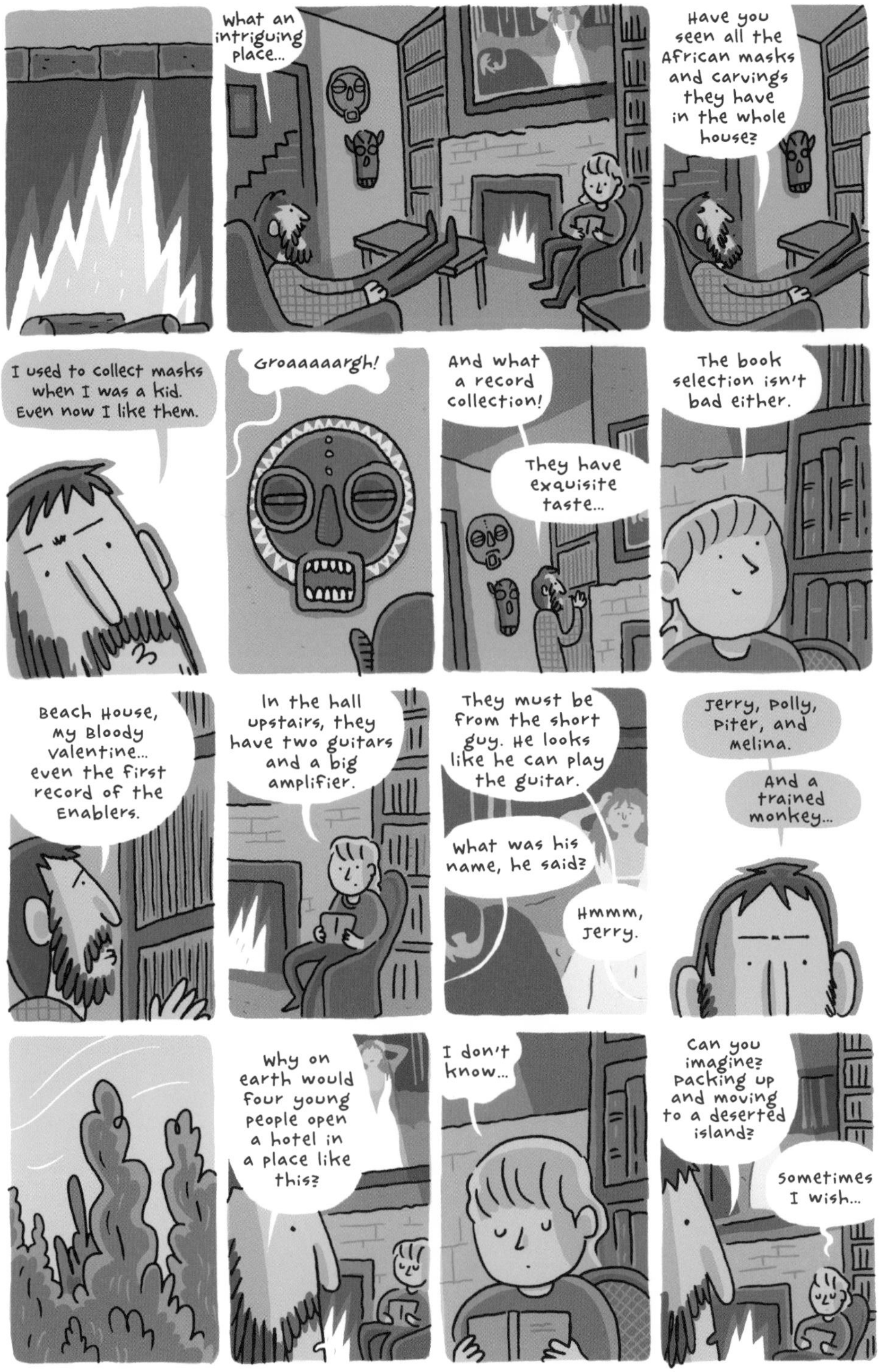

What an intriguing place...
Have you seen all the African masks and carvings they have in the whole house?
I used to collect masks when I was a kid. Even now I like them.
Groaaaaaargh!
And what a record collection!
They have exquisite taste...
The book selection isn't bad either.
Beach House, My Bloody Valentine... even the first record of the Enablers.
In the hall upstairs, they have two guitars and a big amplifier.
They must be from the short guy. He looks like he can play the guitar.
What was his name, he said?
Hmmm, Jerry.
Jerry, Polly, Piter, and Melina.
And a trained monkey...
Why on earth would four young people open a hotel in a place like this?
I don't know...
Can you imagine? Packing up and moving to a deserted island?
Sometimes I wish...

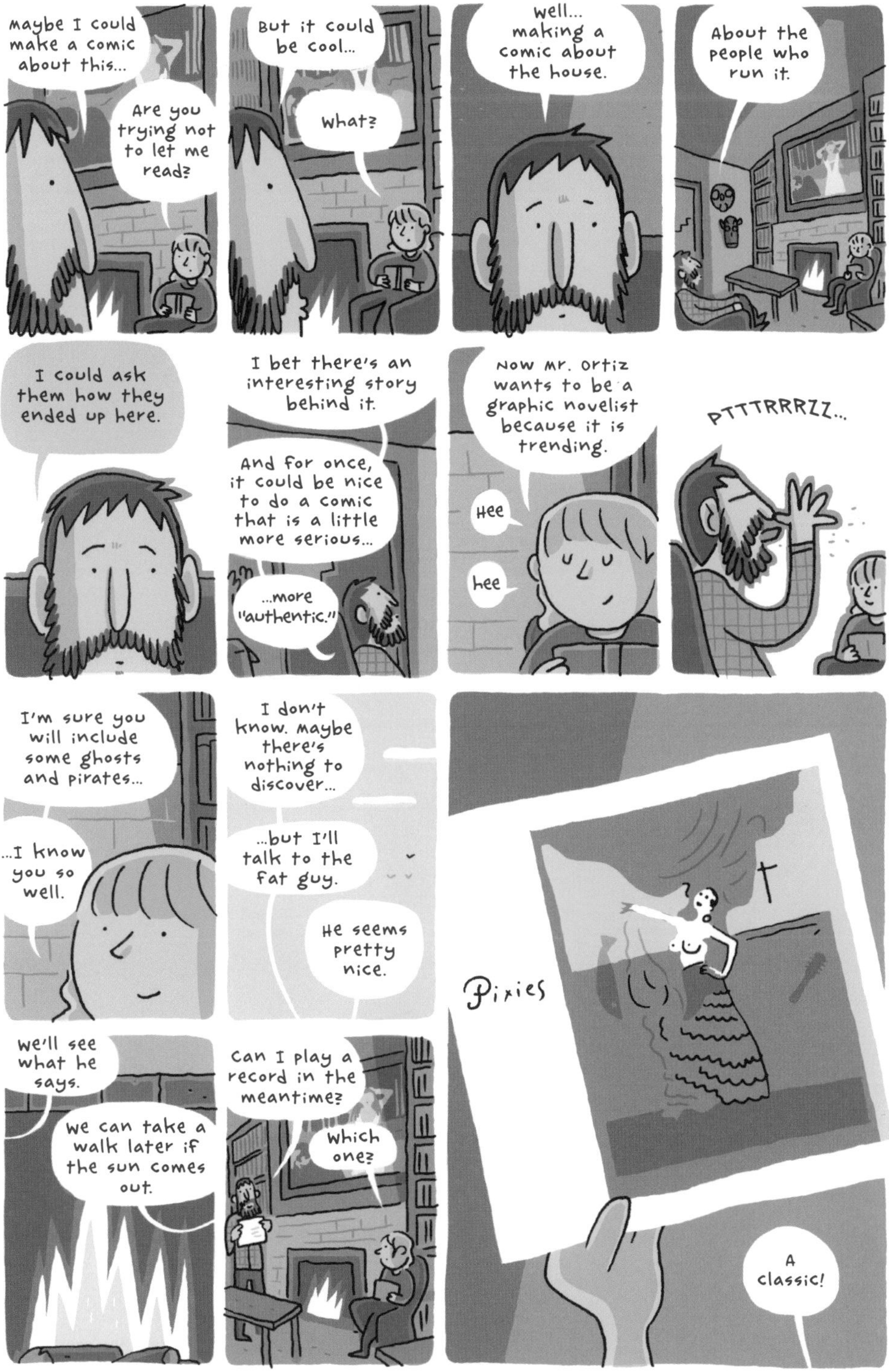
Maybe I could make a comic about this...
Are you trying not to let me read?
But it could be cool...
What?
Well... making a comic about the house.
About the people who run it.
I could ask them how they ended up here.
I bet there's an interesting story behind it.
And for once, it could be nice to do a comic that is a little more serious...
...more "authentic."
Now Mr. Ortiz wants to be a graphic novelist because it is trending.
Hee
hee
PTTTRRRZZ...
I'm sure you will include some ghosts and pirates...
...I know you so well.
I don't know. Maybe there's nothing to discover...
...but I'll talk to the fat guy.
He seems pretty nice.
We'll see what he says.
We can take a walk later if the sun comes out.
Can I play a record in the meantime?
Which one?
Pixies
A classic!

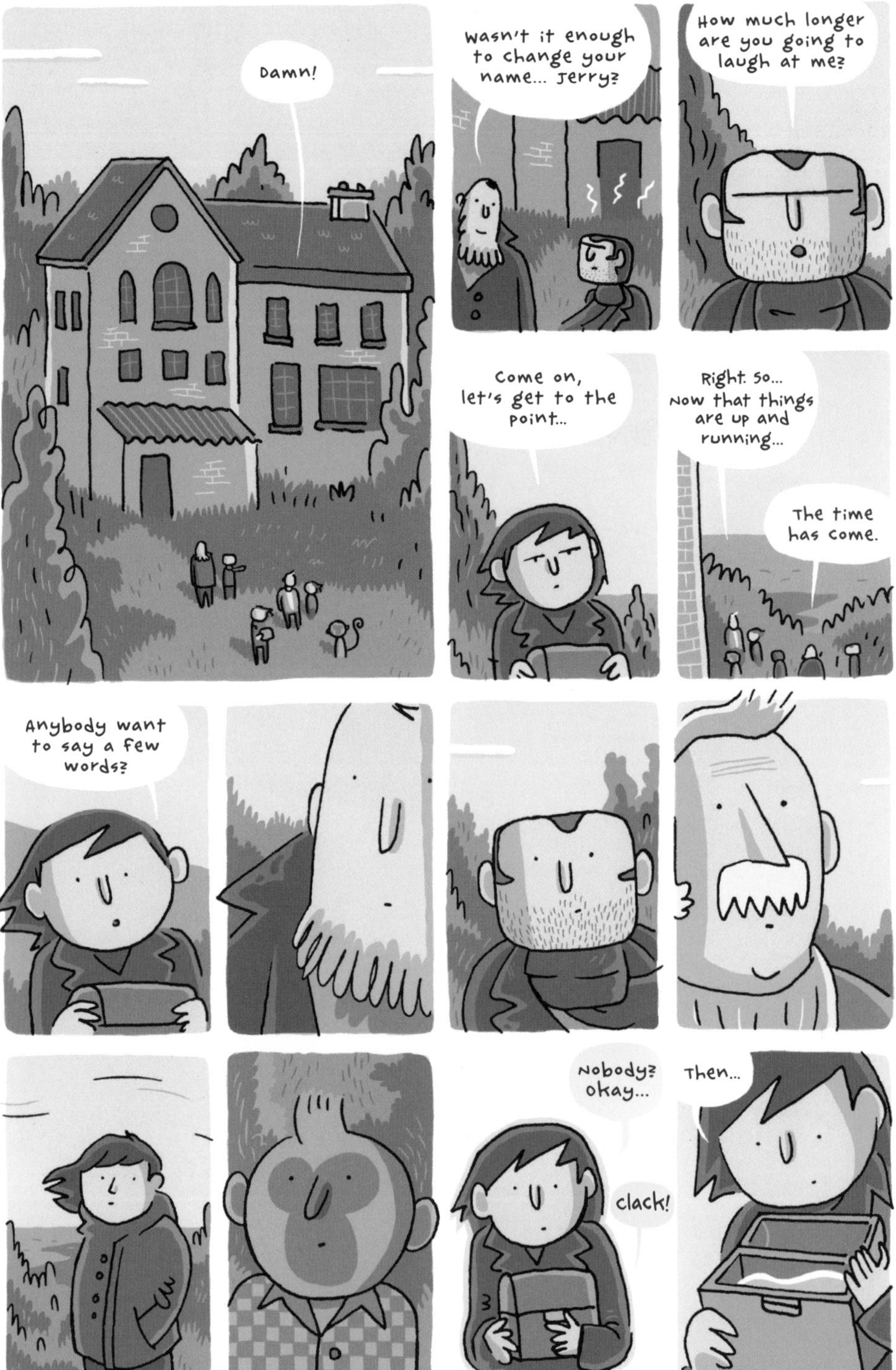
Damn!
Wasn't it enough to change your name... Jerry?
How much longer are you going to laugh at me?
Come on, let's get to the point...
Right. So... Now that things are up and running...
The time has come.
Anybody want to say a few words?
Nobody? Okay...
Clack!
Then...

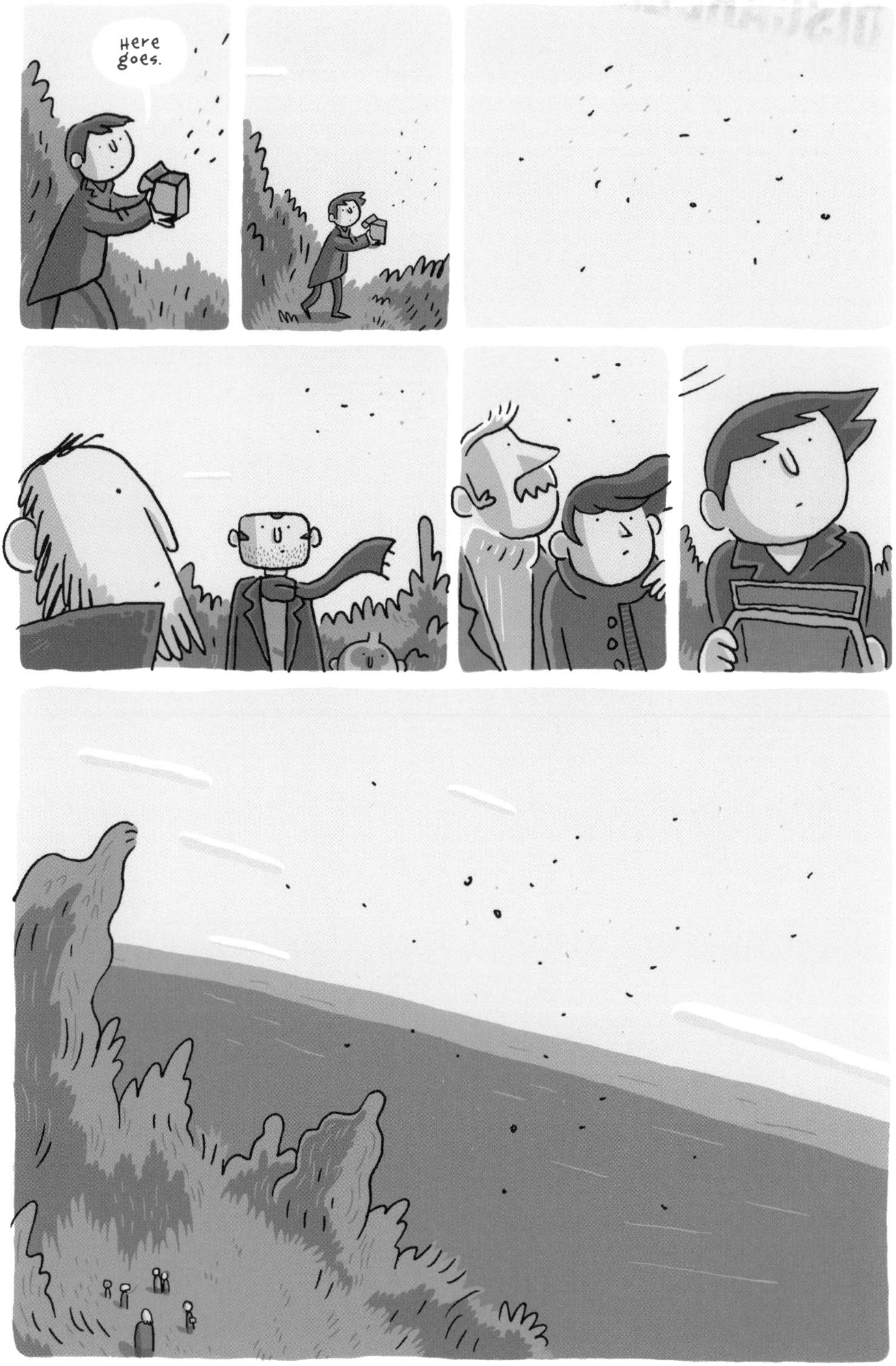
Here goes.

álvaro ortiz
2011/2012